Counting The Dead

Blake Detective Series, Volume 4

Jon Mason

Published by Jon Mason, 2023.

COUNTING THE DEAD

First edition. November 30, 2023.

ISBN: 978-1916757073

Written by Jon Mason.

Also by Jon Mason

Blake Detective Series
The Blooding of Brian Blake
Nemesis
Counting The Dead

Watch for more at www.jonmasonbooks.com.

Table of Contents

Dedicated to my mother who instilled in me a love of literature

Counting The Dead
Prologue

Wakefield. West Riding of Yorkshire.

Saturday, 18th September 1964. 10.30pm.

The stream of people leaving the Palais Ballroom increased as they made a dash for the car park, bus station or nearest pub. Get a couple more pints in before the towels went on. In Wakefield, on the edge of the Yorkshire coal field licensing hours were generously extended to 11pm. Amongst them an attractive couple, regulars over the past two months. The woman mid-twenties. A slim brunette, wearing a cream coloured dress with a red floral print. Cream coloured high-heeled shoes. Red coat and matching handbag. Her escort, fortyish. Nothing stopped him from participating to the full in the entertainment. Five eleven. Dark collar length hair. Expensive clothes. He enjoyed the company of attractive females. Vivienne had become his regular companion. He had seen to that.

In Vivienne's eyes there was little or no risk. As always the dance hall was crowded with revellers. Her car nearby in the car park. The initial frisson of dancing with strangers was long gone. Her friend with the Shakespearian name was charming, handsome and amusing. A perfect gentleman. A breath of fresh air. If she were honest with herself she looked forward to their meetings. A few dances. A chat. A coffee. Maybe a G&T. A break from the grind. From teaching. Duncan worked too hard and although they had discussed a second child, money was tight. Nevertheless, she made sure she had enough money and petrol for the Palais. Duncan had gone off sex, at least with her. She had even thought that he was paying too much attention to his sister. Or was she just looking under stones trying to find worms.

He stifled a shudder and looked down. They exchanged smiles. She really was beautiful. He was becoming too well known. People were beginning to ask too many questions. Ever since Betsy all those years ago ... The crystal clear image formed before his eyes. 'Hey twinnies!' Betsy shouted as she turned and ran up the meadow towards the moor, laughing. 'Gonna tell Dad ya made me do it.

'We didn't do anything,' he protested, although Betsy had been egging them on he couldn't get a hard-on, he never could.

'Ya mean ya couldn',' she retorted and laughed again. 'Fourteen and couldn' do it, you're weird. Weirdy, weirdy, weirdy, nah ni nah ni nah nee, Dad's gonna to kill ya,' she sang, and ran again.

She hadn't run twenty yards before he struck her between her shoulders knocking her to the ground. She lay there on the grass laughing up at the two boys, 'I'm gonna tell Dad ya did that as well. You'll be sorry, wait'n see.'

He dropped to his knees straddling her. As she attempted to get up he pushed her back and put his hands to her throat. 'We haven't done anything,' he said, almost pleading. 'You're making it up.'

'Who d'ya think my Dad's goin' ta believe then?' she said laughing at him and his brother, now standing silently to one side, watching. 'You and your weird brother or m...?' She stopped talking and swallowed hard as the grip tightened.

'You're hurtin, gerrof,' she gasped, grabbed his wrists trying in vain to prise them from her throat. He squeezed harder, a look of fear spreading across the girl's face as she struggled harder. For the first time in his fourteen years he felt his erection and knew he could.

Betsy, struggling to breathe, frantically attempted to claw his face and eyes. His left hand pressed against her windpipe took his entire weight as he let go with his right hand and pushed his trousers down to his knees and pulled her dress out of the way. Underneath she was naked. He forced her legs apart as she tried to wriggle out from beneath him and lowered his face down to hers, 'Who can't do it?' he hissed. Ignoring her frantic gasping and failing efforts to free herself he replaced his right hand and tightened his grip still further as he rammed himself inside of her and ejaculated; the feeling like nothing he had experienced before.

When he lifted himself up and opened his eyes his hands were still tight around her throat, Betsy Elstub lay still, unmoving, her lifeless eyes staring at him.

The image faded. He knew what must happen. This would be their last meeting. He would know within the next sixty seconds. Would Vivienne live, or, would she die?

One

Westleigh, West Riding of Yorkshire.

Saturday, 6th March, 1965.

Memories of the explosion at Buy Smart well and truly ameliorated by Claire's birth and the Palace investitures. It had been so close. A few inches closer to the shop window whilst I was talking with Mrs Carson and my name would have been added to the list of those killed. What I suffered was relatively minor. It had been Georgina Hoyle, the twenty eight year old accountant, two months pregnant, who stopped the large fragment of plate glass in her throat. As far as I was concerned it just lacerated my back, fastened my helmet on with several glass hatpins and used the rest of my left side as a dart board. Other than that I wasn't too bad. At least I was at home when Claire was born on Boxing Day; five days before Lucy's twenty second birthday. There were some compensations. That had been some Christmas celebration. I had a month off work sick when we were notified of the awards; Me with the George Cross, Lucy, Anne and Liz the British Empire Medal for Gallantry. We went to Buckingham Palace to be invested one month later during my attachment to the Prosecutions Office.

I loved being a police officer and today was my third day back at work. The first time that I'd walked passed the site *all* the memories came flooding back. The best? Coming out of the anaesthetic to find Lucy holding my hand. She'd been crying. But that smile. The same smile that I'd seen on the day she recovered consciousness, a week after the accident, never changed. It lit up my world like nothing else could. She turned my hand over placing it on her belly as the baby kicked. She squeezed my hand. We exchanged smiles. It brought a lump to my throat. I had been so near to missing all of this.

I looked at the devastation in front of me. What had been the busiest retail outlet in Westleigh was now a hole. The shop premises either side propped up by baulks of timber and scaffolding. Generally the memories weren't good. However, March was here, spring was on the horizon and this was England. It was cold with plenty of late snow and sleet showers driven on an easterly wind. As my gran used to say: *When the winds in the east it's no good for man nor beast.* Living at Outlane, overlooked by Pole Moor, she had plenty of experience.

I was early turn. Meal at ten. By eleven I had meandered along Northgate towards the civic gardens, currently being planted up. By late May it would be beautiful. As had happened on the previous two days several people came up to me and asked how I was going on and said that it was nice to see me back on duty. One or two commenting on my trip to London. It felt good to be appreciated. I'd just passed Blamires when I heard the distinctive double-clang of his door bell. A family jewellers, the present incumbent being Henry, great-grandson of the founder and a real gentleman, immaculately turned out and always a ready smile. 'Excuse me. ... Officer ... Pc Blake,' he called.

Several people turned as I greeted him. Today he looked worried and that wasn't like him at all. 'I'm sorry to trouble you, Pc Blake,' he began. 'Something's cropped up and I would like your assistance. Would you come into the shop, please?' Without waiting for an answer he hurried back followed by a puzzled yours truly.

Two

Henry Blamires closed and locked the door. Turned the sign to 'closed' and pulled the blind down. Curiouser and curiouser. 'This way if you please,' he hurried into his office.

It wasn't a large shop. Not a wasted inch of space. All the fixtures and fittings were highly polished mahogany or brass. The display cases gleamed. There was no plastic in this shop. The only modern things were the prices. His office likewise, not a thing out of place. What was unusual were the two young boys standing by his safe. Aged I thought twelve or thirteen. Both well muddied, torn jackets and jeans and, tearstained faces. Who they were I had no idea. Certainly not local lads but Mr Blamires trusted them enough to leave them unattended in the shop whilst he came to speak with me.

It was as warm in the office as it was in the shop. As for the tension, you could cut it with a knife. What was going on? 'Morning boys,' I smiled and hung my helmet and greatcoat on the stand. 'Now, Mr Blamires, what's the problem?'

Henry Blamires wasn't a fussy little man but today he was agitated. 'This is my grandson, Clive,' he said, indicating the boy on the left. He was the smaller of the two and the more dishevelled, wearing a torn green jacket and torn muddied jeans.

'Hello,' I said. 'I've got a younger brother called Clive, he's about your age, he's twelve.'

Clive nodded but said nothing.

'This,' Mr Blamires indicated the other boy. 'Is his friend, Michael.'

Michael was even more muddied than Clive. Wearing an almost new blue zip-up jacket, a large rip in the back of the right sleeve and muddied long grey-flannel trousers. 'Hello', I said. he nodded.

'They arrived just before you passed the shop, terrified out of their wits and in this state,' Mr Blamires gestured with his hand. 'The only thing either of them has said is that they didn't steal anything, but no explanation. The other funny thing is,' Mr Blamires continued. 'They both live in Hecton and go everywhere on their bicycles, but they've been running and no bicycles.'

There were three dining chairs outside in the corridor. Seconds later we were all sitting down, Mr Blamires in his Captain's chair. I leaned forwards resting my forearms on my knees trying to look even more friendly than I usually did. 'Whatever's happened,' I began. 'Whatever's frightened you, you're both quite safe. Now, who's going to start? How about you, Clive?'

I looked at him. He shook his head.

'We didn't steal anything,' said Michael. 'But he tried to run us over.'

'I believe you,' I said, 'But do you understand what telling the truth means?' I felt a bit rotten having to ask that particular question, but it had to be done.

They both looked at me in astonishment. 'Of course we do,' protested Clive, 'we're not making it up.'

'I want to be a policeman when I'm older,' said Michael. 'I'm not going to tell lies.'

I smiled at them both. 'That's all right,' I said, 'but I had to ask ... right, what didn't you steal?'

Clive and Michael glanced at each other. Clive put his hand in his pocket, took something out and held it out to me.

'Just put it on your grandad's desk, Clive,' I said.

I was puzzled but very interested in what Clive had produced: An oval plaque. A broken piece of chain with flattened and some distorted links at each end. It was Wainwright's bracelet. Now covered in mud and in a somewhat damaged state. It was the bracelet, a gift from his mother, the owner told me he never removed. What had happened to scare these two lads out of their wits and leave their bikes behind? Why was the bracelet parted from its owner and in this state? Was there a connection between the two? 'Look boys,' I said. 'You're quite safe. No-one is going to hurt you. Where did you find it? Who's first?'

They looked at each other again. Michael said. 'We were bird watching in ... is it Field Lane, Clive?'

Clive nodded. 'We go behind the old mill,' he said, now a little happier.

'But that's derelict, it's very dangerous,' protested Mr Blamires.

We don't go in, Grandad,' said Clive. 'Just round the back into the wood.'

Placated, Mr Blamires smiled.

I knew the spot well. The 'Old Mill' as it was known locally was a dilapidated former weaving-shed that should have been demolished years ago. The site was a magnet for the local kids. Used as a dumping ground for nicked cars, the odd bike, plus rubbish, tons of it.

'They get some good birds in that wood,' Michael said with enthusiasm. 'It's cold, we thought there might be a few late fieldfares or redwings, even a waxwing.'

Is that good?' I asked. I wasn't too familiar with our feathered friends.

'Good.' exclaimed Michael. 'There were a couple of waxwings last year, they're rare round here.'

Their enthusiasm made me smile. 'So, you were going bird watching and you had your bikes?'

They both nodded. 'Yes, we propped them up against a tree at the top, round the back,' said Clive.

'And your bikes are still at the mill?'

They nodded again.

'Was there anyone else at the mill?'

Michael shook his head. 'Nobody, just us.'

'Ok, tell me what happened.'

It took a few minutes to get the gist of their story. It's quite a large wood. They spent the next hour looking for their fieldfares, redwings and waxwings without a trace. Then decided to try somewhere else.

'There was a man by the stream,' said Michael. 'He was tubby and had dark wavy hair. Scruffy trousers. A white shirt with blue paint on his chest. An old Mac that flapped about and black wellies. He looked like a tramp.'

Clive joined in. 'He was the same height as grandad but not as old, but older than dad.'

Mr Blamires said he was 5'6" and his son thirty nine.

Wainwright was usually immaculate but the general description fitted.

'He didn't see us,' said Clive. 'He was building a bonfire. Dragging branches from the tip and piling them up.'

'Yeah, he was puffing and panting,' said Michael. 'We'd been watching for a couple of minutes when he stopped, put his hands on his knees and then stood up and arched his back.'

'Then he climbed back up the tip and disappeared,' said Clive. 'But we could see our bikes against the tree, and an old black car. We said we'd have a look at it later. Michael slipped in the mud and flicked that out,' he pointed at the bracelet. 'I picked it up and showed him.'

'The man came back,' interrupted Michael. 'He was carrying a spade and began to run down the tip.

'He swore at us,' said Clive with a cheeky grin.

'Was it very rude,' I asked and smiled.

'Hmm, not really,' he replied. Mr Blamires chuckled, 'It's what Dad says. He shouted, "Bugger off you little thieves," and lifted the spade above his head,' Clive mimicked the man's action and speech. "What ... ever ... you've just picked up ... is mine, hand it ... over." He was wheezing.'

'And he threatened you with a spade just because of this?' I said, indicating the bracelet.

They both nodded.

'We ran round him and up the tip.'

'I looked over my shoulder,' said Clive. 'He swung the spade at Michael and tore his jacket. It was frightening.'

'I thought he was going to kill us,' said Michael, wiping a few tears away with the back of his hand, 'but he couldn't catch us. 'He wasn't far behind when we got to the top. He was using the spade like a walking stick. We left the bikes and ran. Then we heard the engine start and the tyres squeal.'

The first house was fifty yards away. Michael pushed the gate open, grabbed Clive's coat and dragged him through. The black car, a Rover, swerved onto the footpath and slid to a stop.

Three

Jack Griffiths was between jobs. His twenty year stint as an Armourer in the Royal Navy had ended six months previously. The few jobs he'd tried lacked the structure and discipline he sought. On the coffee table application forms for the prison, police and fire services. Hearing the row outside he put his morning paper down. 'What's the matter, son,' he said as the breathless, muddied and tearstained Michael and Clive reached his door. The Rover's driver, face like fury, opened the gate. 'Now, what have you been up to?'

'Nothing, honest,' gasped Clive. 'We've just been bird watching in the wood. He started screaming at us and came after us with a spade.'

A worried looking Michael glanced over his shoulder. 'That's right,' he said. 'And he's just tried to run us over.'

Jack Griffiths glanced from the boys to the Rover and the angry but now smiling driver. He might have been dressed like a scruff but the car was a classic. 'Has he now,' Griffiths said. He cast his eyes over the pair again. These weren't local yobs. The only birds they were interested in wore knickers, or not, as the case may be. He pointed down the side of the house. 'At the end of the garden there's a gate, takes you onto the grammar school playing fields. Do you know your way home from there?'

'Yes, thanks,' said Clive casting a nervous eye towards the man, now just a few yards away. 'We can go to Grandad's.'

'Off you go then. I'll have a word with your friend.'

'Thanks Mister,' they said together and set off at a more sedate pace.

The driver, having got his breath back but lost his temper, let rip. 'Don't let them go you stupid fool,' he shouted at Griffiths trying to dodge round him. 'They're thieves.'

Jack Griffiths put his hand against the man's chest. 'Whoa, calm down, steady.'

'Never mind steady you bloody idiot,' he stormed grabbing Griffiths' wrist. 'They're thieves.'

One sharp right-handed jab to the abdomen put him on the floor gasping for breath. Jack Griffiths stood over him. 'Whilst you're getting your breath back,' he said, 'let me give you some advice. I don't give a damn who you are, don't you ever speak to me like that again. Keep off my property, in future pick on someone your own size. Understand?'

Rubbing his abdomen, he got to his feet. 'Why didn't you stop them? They're thieves.'

"What!? And let a bully like you get hold of them. They're children. If they *have* taken something report it to the police. If they want to know they can come and ask. Now, get out.'

He watched as the man walked slowly down the path. Got back in his car. U-turned and drove back to the lock-ups.

Josephine Griffiths walked up behind her husband and frowned. 'He looked a nasty beggar, Jack. Isn't he the councillor that owns the lock-ups?

'He's the one, Wainwright, I think his name is.'

I heard what you said. Do you know where the lads went?'

He smiled to himself. 'Aye, the little one told me. They're going to his grandad's.'

'Do you know his grandad?'

'Haven't a clue, love,' he said and smiled.

His wife chuckled as they walked back to the house. 'I'll put the kettle on. Coffee?'

Michael wasn't physically injured, just badly shaken. 'This man who let you through his garden, do you know his name?'

'No,' replied Michael. 'But it's the top house in Field Lane, the detached one.'

I knew the house and nodded. 'And after that you came straight here?'

'Yes,' said Clive.

I asked them both to stand whilst I made a quick examination. Michael was a very lucky lad. The back of his right sleeve had a muddied six or seven inch rip just below shoulder level. An inch closer and the blade would have struck him. Clive was muddy with a three inch tear in his jacket and a smaller one in the trousers. I smiled at the lads. 'Mr Blamires, I'll need statements from these two. Will you let their parents know, please?'

Four

I t was a five minute walk. Clive and Michael chattering ten to the dozen. The fear had gone. Everything was fine until we reached the police station. Parked in front was Wainwright's Rover. From the raised voices a lively conversation was ongoing inside.

Clive froze.

A frightened Michael pointed at Wainwright's Rover. 'That's the car. And his voice.'

The next few minutes would be very interesting. 'Nobody's going to hurt you, I promise. Stick close to me, you'll be fine.'

It was quite a sight. Sergeant McGill, wearing his familiar half-smile, was standing in his office doorway arms folded. Wainwright, now dressed in a suit and highly polished black shoes, had his back to me. From my point of view it was quite funny. Jim was on the receiving end of Wainwright's barrage. 'Don't you understand who *I am*? ... *I* want them found and arresting. They're thieves. You're supposed to be a policeman. Do what you're paid to do.'

'I'll repeat this again, Mr Wainwright,' said Jim. He glanced at me and raised his eyebrows. 'Can you describe them? Do you know their names? There are thousands of kids out there. We can't just go around arresting kids in the off chance they're the right ones.'

Wainwright's voice went up a few decibels. 'How on earth should I know?' He sounded as if he was going to lose it again. 'Just a couple of yobs. They stole something. I want it back. Try that idiot at the top of Field Lane, the old mill house. He let them go and assaulted *me*. He knows where they went.' Wainwright caught sight of the boys. He stopped and stared. 'It's them,' he shouted, pointing at Clive and Michael. I stepped in between them and Wainwright. 'Arrest them. Arrest them Blake. Arrest them.'

I put my hand on his chest as he stepped forwards. 'Calm down Mr Wainwright, just calm down. What's all this about?'

Wainwright took a deep breath and sighed. 'They're thieves, plain and simple. *I* want them arrested.' He sounded almost rational.

I took Mr Blamires' envelope from my greatcoat pocket and tipped Wainwright's bracelet into my hand. 'Is this what it's all about?' Wainwright's mother had commissioned the bracelet some thirty years earlier. Now the chain was at least an inch shorter with the end links distorted. It had been removed with some force.

Wainwright lunged for the bracelet. 'That's mine, give it back,' he snapped.

'How do you know?' I pulled it back out of reach. 'It's so muddy you can't tell what it is.'

'I know it is,' Wainwright persisted.

'Maybe you believe it is, Mr Wainwright,' I said. 'This chain is too short. and how did it get damaged? Yours was longer and you never took it off.'

'None of your business,' he snapped. He was becoming aggressive again. Up and down like a bride's nightie. 'Are you going to arrest these two before they run away again?'

There was some nervous fidgeting behind me. 'Talking about running away, Mr Wainwright,' I said. 'Why did you chase them?'

He looked at me as if I was stupid. 'Because they ran.'

'Is that why you tried to hit Michael with the spade you were carrying, damaging his jacket?' I glanced at Sergeant McGill and nodded. He stepped forward and examined the back of Michael's sleeve.

'Bloody rubbish. Total nonsense. I did no such thing.'

'Or try to run them over?'

'Ridiculous, why would I do that?'

I cautioned him and told him I was arresting him for causing criminal damage to Michael's jacket. 'You wouldn't dare,' he said and tried to push past me.

Five

There were thirty minutes missing. It was a four minute drive from the old mill to the nick. Max. The boys had run about a mile to Clive's grandfather's, told me their tale and we'd walked back to the nick arriving one minute after Wainwright. He'd washed and changed into his suit. If what had happened was so urgent, why the delay? Why the violent reaction? What else had he done?

There are more half-drunk cups of tea abandoned in police stations than enough. The fire brigade were attending the report of a fire behind the Old Mill, Field Lane. I don't like coincidences. Two minutes later the Sergeant and I were en route. The boys were in the office with a cuppa and a KitKat from our tuck box. Company for Jim.

Less than four minutes later. 'No rush, Sergeant,' Fireman Neville Adams called out as we hurried in the direction of the column of steam and smoke. 'Just rubbish, it's nothing.'

The boy's bikes were still leaning again the tree as we sluthered down the slope. 'It's only the kids lighting a bonfire, Sergeant,' Leading Fireman Croft looked confused. Why were *two* police officers attending a simple rubbish fire and in a hurry? 'We'll have it out in two ticks.'

With a generous dousing from the fire crew and a couple of shovels we cleared the site. Although the fire hadn't really got going there was enough heat in the ground to produce steam. The smell of petrol was strong. Although not obvious the water had caused some of the ground to sink. That was strange because the ground hadn't been disturbed for decades. Nevertheless there were a series of cut-lines. Linked together the shape was sinister. The thought ran through my mind: *had my dad ever had to do this? What thoughts and emotions did he have?*

We had a slow walk round. I tested the ground inside the lines with my boot. It was definitely softer than outside.

'Can we borrow those?' Sergeant McGill indicated the two shovels.

'Sure, Sergeant,' said Leading Fireman Croft. 'You think there's something buried?'

'Dunno,' he said. 'That's what I intend to find out.'

Under the watchful eye of Sergeant McGill and a silent audience of firemen *I* began to dig. Very carefully. The softer ground inside the cut line made it easy. Less than a minute later. 'Oh, Jesus Christ!' Mike Roberts, dripping hose in hand stared. Just visible the flared cuff of a wet and muddy long-sleeved blue dress. The upturned palm of an even muddier right hand. A hand with bright red nail varnish and torn and broken fingernails. Experience-hardened firemen used to death in many forms were visibly shaken and took a step backwards. No-one spoke. The post mortem aroma unmistakable.

Six

The fire crew wrapped up. Statements would be obtained in due course. A man came down the slope. From the look on his face there was no doubt he had seen what we had discovered. 'Excuse me, Sergeant, I'm Jack Griffiths, I live at the top house in Field Lane,' he said. 'Is this anything to do with those two youngsters who came to my house about three quarters of an hour ago?'

I wasn't sure how I felt. Yes, I'd seen several dead bodies and with the murders I witnessed at Pannal Ash, I suspect more than most. I'd even participated in post mortem examinations at university. They were carried out on people who had died naturally. Donating their bodies for medical research. All the relevant paperwork completed and countersigned by their families. This wasn't. Judging by the dress, skin, the broken and torn finger nails, it was a young woman who had died a violent death. Buried secretly at the foot of a rubbish dump with every effort made to prevent discovery. Somewhere there would be relatives: mother, father, brothers, sisters, husband, children. Somewhere, somebody was responsible. If it hadn't been for the chance discovery of a broken bracelet by two boys out bird watching, and a violent overreaction by Cuthbert Wainwright she may never have been discovered.

The fire-crew gone I was left on guard duty. Sergeant McGill walked Jack Griffiths back to his house. To make the necessary phone calls and to borrow a couple of garden spades and trowels so that we could complete the exhumation.

As the last of them disappeared over the brow of the tip I realised why my father had loved C.I.D. In that moment I knew what made him tick. That my choice of career had been the right choice, although it didn't stop me from feeling nauseous. Was that because of what was developing at my feet, or, because of the excitement? At least this time my life wasn't in danger. Could her name be Lucy, or even Claire? Time would tell. What I did know is that no matter how tragically this case would progress we could at least bring closure to her family. That was worth the effort. And, of course, there was Wainwright. ...

Seven

Within minutes a road traffic car arrived to act as the communications vehicle and keep the incident log. Seconds later Inspector Yates turned up with Jenny Ross, a brand new shiny probationer just five days out of Training School. The fact that she might be viewing the corpse of a murder victim on her third day at the sharp end would not have been mentioned. But anything and everything was possible. 'Hello, sir. Jenny,' I said. She had a nervous smile. 'Welcome to the club.' She was the daughter of a farmer from Kirkburton; what you might call a strapping lass.

'Have you ever seen a dead body before, Ross?' Said the Inspector.

Jenny had gone pale. 'My Gran when she died, but this is different.

Inspector Yates smiled. 'Indeed. Sudden deaths due to natural causes are common place. We are lucky that deaths of this nature aren't. How do you feel?'

'All right, I suppose, sir. I'll get used to it.'

'Perhaps,' he turned to me. 'Brian, how did you spot it?'

'When we cleared the site, sir. The dowsing from the fire brigade caused some of the ground to sink. Look,' I pointed to the cut lines. 'You can just make out what we saw. When I began to dig ...'

Jenny's only question was, 'When do you get her out?' Her job was to stop any rubberneckers, something well within her compass. She arrived at Westleigh with a reputation of being something of an arm wrestler. She returned to the car park. The rumour mill was in full flow and people were started to gather. She had to keep them back. Tell them nothing.

To add fuel to the imagination of the crowd Sergeant McGill rolled up with a couple of old garden spades and trowels. Under the joint supervision I began to extend the trench towards our victim's head. I'd reached the shoulder when the Sergeant began to dig at the victim's left side. I felt a bit like an archaeologist. In five minutes I'd reached the end of the cut. A further ten minutes of careful work, together we had exposed her face and head.

With the heart stopped the skin assumes a colour reminiscent of tallow but with a sheen like alabaster. Almost haunting in appearance. A dark haired young woman. The left side of her face severely bruised as was her throat. I know it's ridiculous but I felt better now that her mouth was uncovered. It wasn't going to make a blind bit of difference. It just made me feel better. Thankfully her skin was cold to the touch. The pathologist would give us an approximation of time of death in due course.

Eight

Over the next twenty minutes we were joined by Detective Constable Mark Smith and Carl Ramsbottom, formerly C.I.D. now back in uniform. He had just been awarded his Long Service and Good Conduct Medal, or as Carl called it – my reward for twenty two years of undetected crime. A strange sense of humour senior Pc's are wont to display. Chief Inspector Sampson from Hecton was next followed by a police fingerprint officer/photographer. The undertaker sat patiently in his hearse in the car park. DI Greening was on sick leave so ten minutes later DCI Valentine, senior divisional detective, accompanied by DS Cartwright and WDC 'Penny' Farthing. I'd worked with Mr Valentine and his team twice previously on the Marjorie Simmonds – Bill Vernon enquiry. It was good to see them again.

Valentine still felt guilty. He had been a DC when Douglas Blake, his sergeant, friend and mentor had been murdered. Yarney had plunged the knife into Douglas' chest before he could react. He had tackled Yarney to the ground. The two beat officers cuffed him. He cradled Douglas' head and watched the light fade from his friend's eyes. That night he cried. Now, looking across the grave at Douglas' son he wondered. He had already shown his mettle and was bound for higher things. However *he* had the authority. The duty to turn the tables. It was now his hand on the tiller.

Nine

For the third time in thirty five minutes I displayed the bracelet and told the tale. This time to the DCI, DS Cartwright, Penny, Chief Inspector Sampson and Inspector Yates. Our conversation was interrupted by Carl Ramsbottom. 'Excuse me, Mr Valentine, Brian,' he called, looking up from where he was carefully removing soil from round the victim's right hand. 'Is this what you're looking for?'

Barely visible. At the side of the victim's right-hand little finger nail. It was either one of the links from the chain or a remarkable likeness. DCI Valentine compared the link in the grave with the bracelet and laughed. 'You've got bloody good eyesight, well spotted. We'll let Forensic do the necessary. Can you get a shot of this in situ?' he asked the photographer. 'Well done. Keep your eyes peeled there may be more.' Carl Ramsbottom smiled and continued his search.

'Let's see the bastard crawl his way out of this,' the DCI said. 'No wonder he wanted his bracelet back.' Photograph taken the DCI took a small envelope from his pocket and slid the link inside, wrote BB 12.30hrs (side of right little finger nail), the date, initialled it and handed it to me. Then asked. 'Has anyone searched Wainwright's clothes? Pockets, linings etc?'

They hadn't. DC Smith left with instructions to log any evidence found and return as soon as practicable with Wainwright's keys. The DCI wanted to search the lock-up.

Seconds later there was a familiar voice. 'Good afternoon gentlemen and lady,' Dr O'Keefe, local GP and police surgeon, doctor's bag in hand, raincoat flapping in the breeze came gingerly down the slope and tipped his hat to Penny. 'I understand you've found me a client,' he said with a beaming smile. Standing at the edge of the grave he looked down at the girl. 'Poor child,' he said. 'I think we can safely say that she is no longer in the land of the living. Death certified at 12.35pm, Mr Valentine,' the DCI acknowledged. 'She's had no life and tasted death too soon ... any idea who she might be?' he said looking at me.

'Not as yet, Doctor,' I replied.

'Early days I suppose,' he said. 'Pc Blake, you're looking disgustingly healthy since the last time we met. How are you feeling?'

'Fine, Doctor, thank you for asking.' Dr O'Keefe had attended the scene of the explosion at Buy Smart. Until I almost collapsed right in front of him I hadn't realised I was injured. Stress induced analgesia according to the hospital doctor.

Doctor O'Keefe narrowed his eyes and smiled at me. Why did I feel nervous? 'I remember what you told me the first time we met,' he said. 'A little test I think. Any objections Mr Valentine?' There were none. There was however considerable interest. Everybody, including the photographer, crowded round as the doctor crouched beside his client and opened her right eye again. 'What are those?' he said, making no indication as to what he was referring.

I crouched and looked closely. I could see there were small clusters of tiny red dots, just like Julie Slater, the canteen worker murdered at Pannal Ash. 'Petechiae, Petechial haemorrhages?' I said.

The good doctor smiled. 'Very good. Which are caused by?'

Right, I thought, the sequence ... 'An increase in blood pressure in the blood vessels of the eye,' I replied, feeling more confident.

'Excellent,' he said, tilted his head slightly to the right and smiled again. 'Which in turn *is* caused by?'

I could feel the weight of expectation pressing down on my back. Doctor O'Keefe looked at me and raised a quizzical eyebrow. 'It *may* be indicative of manual strangulation,' I said, fairly certain I was correct.

'Textbook,' he declared as he stood up. I was on the end of some odd looks from Chief Inspector Sampson and the DCI. 'Well done.' He looked at the others, 'You will find petechial haemorrhages in cases other than strangulation. But that is not relevant here. I'm not going to second guess the pathologist's report, however, in this case you are probably correct. And, in my humble opinion as rigor is established death occurred sometime between nine pm last night and six am today. Once the pathologist has the temperature of the liver he will give you a more accurate time. I would also hazard a guess that the unfortunate young lady was not killed here. And, from the looks of it she put up quite a struggle. The injuries to her wrists and hands suggest to me that the assailant will have injuries anywhere within reach of her nails. Those are quite some talons she has. Have you any more questions?'

There were none.

'Then gentlemen, and lady,' he said smiling. 'I will bid you farewell.' With that he left.

Ten

Chief Inspector Sampson caught my eye. 'Fancy a transfer to Hecton, Blake?' he said to me, then looked at Calvin Yates.

'In due course, sir,' I replied. 'Perhaps.' Not that I could have done anything about it.

'I'll hold you to that,' he said. 'Calvin, keep me posted.'

'Certainly, sir,' he replied and winked at me.

The Chief Inspector and Inspector Yates followed in the doctor's footsteps.

'Right.' the DCI said. 'We now have an approximation of when the girl was killed.'

Penny motioned for me to stand by her at the side of the grave. 'You can learn a helluva lot from your observations, Brian. Tell me what you see.'

This was different. From my previous experiences at Pannal I had no input. At university our examination was purely anatomical. This wasn't. A young woman brutally beaten, probably strangled. I wasn't apprehensive. It was the opportunity no matter how tragic the circumstances to be involved with a team of experts at the start of a murder investigation. One question on my mind. Was this it? Back to beat duties?

Eleven

DCI Valentine stood at Penny's side. Watching. My father had made detective sergeant in eight years. Almost unheard of in his time, even now it was very fast. How would he have approached something like this? The only way to find out was to do what Penny had said. See, not overthink. I walked to the foot of the grave. By now the body was almost totally uncovered. I perused the grave and contents for a few seconds. The thought – what would *they* do running through my mind. 'She's bare footed,' I announced, although that was obvious. But wasn't that the point? By saying what you've seen you're registering that particular point and drawing everyone else's attention to it. Then, if you miss something there's a good chance that someone else will notice it. 'She's not apparently wearing any stockings, although they may be beneath her body, or inside her clothing ... There does not appear to be a handbag ... She has no apparent injuries to her lower legs . Wearing a mid-thigh, long-sleeved blue dress in good condition. Gold coloured buttons down the front, all fastened. The dress looks like an everyday dress, not one for a night out. The fabric is straight, not dishevelled.' I began to move slowly anti-clockwise, stopping when I reached a level with her left thigh, I crouched. 'Is it all right to touch anything?' I asked, looking up at Penny.

'What did you have in mind?'

'Dr O'Keefe mentioned marks to her wrists. So, possible defensive wounds, or signs of restraint.'

'As little as possible,' Penny replied.

The rigor made it impossible to move her arms so I had to crouch lower. 'No visible injuries to the palm of her left hand. Some bruising to her left wrist. Nail varnish badly chipped.' I continued my slow perambulation.

'There are some abrasions above and to the rear of her left ear. They look fresh.' I crouched a bit lower. 'It looks as though she's had some hair pulled out ... she has severe bruising to her left cheek. There is also left peri-orbital bruising. Her lips are swollen on the left side. Bleeding from the nose. Bruising and swelling to the throat. Both sides.' I was about to stand but crouched again and examined her throat. 'There are no ligature marks,' I looked up at Penny and the DCI. 'Manual strangulation?'

'Quite possibly,' the DCI replied. 'Well done.'

'Face to face? What ever happened she's taken quite a beating.'

'I would tend agree with that on both counts,' said the DCI. 'Although we'll have to wait for the PM to be certain of whether she was strangled and how.'

I set off once more, the DCI and Penny following my path to examine the head ... 'No signs of bruising to the right side of her head. Apart from the marks to the right side of the throat all the injuries appear to be left-sided. To me that suggests the assailant was right-handed.' The DCI agreed.

'I stopped opposite her right hip, crouched and took hold of her right wrist. 'She has a yellow metal ring on the middle finger of her right hand. Bruising and abrasions to her right palm and three broken and one torn finger nail ... Both pockets in the dress are empty.'

'Brian,' said Liz when I got back to my starting position. 'These are your observations. This is your picture. Once it's gone you can't reconstruct it as it is now. Can you make any deductions? It doesn't matter if you can't, but whatever you say is *your* supposition. It's all observation and interpretation.'

I took my time. 'Sir, there's a dichotomy. At first I thought she might have been simply dumped, but she hasn't. It's almost as if she's been laid out. Her body's straight. Arms by her sides. Clothes aren't dishevelled. Nevertheless, from her injuries she's died violently. However, whoever it was who buried her took some care though we're only a stone's throw from the houses in Field Lane and the lock-ups. Mind you, if it's Wainwright he would have an idea when it's likely to be quiet. It's almost as though there was more than one person involved.'

The DCI looked at me over the top of his glasses. 'Let's not overcomplicate matters, Blake. See what develops.'

I smiled and nodded. 'Yes, sir.'

Penny and the DCI smiled at each other, 'Anything else?'

Did she want me to say, 'no'. Or had I missed something? I looked again ...

'She's ...' Penny began to say.

'Buried,' I blurted out. 'She's been buried.' So obvious I overlooked it.

Penny grinned at me. 'Height and weight?'

'Five feet three, approximately eight stones.'

'Colour of eyes? Bearing in mind you've had a closer look than most.'

Bugger! That caught me off balance because I was concentrating on the haemorrhaging not the colour of the iris ... 'Brown,' I said, as confidently as I could.

Penny gave me an askance look, as if to say, I wonder. 'That'll do for now, Brian. Your examination was excellent. But saying what you see reinforces what you've seen in your mind. If anyone else is present as we are, we know what you've seen, or maybe you've overlooked something, or indeed you've seen something that someone else may have missed.'

A Dr Wheelwright arrived from the Forensic Lab at Harrogate. He and the DCI spent a few minutes together. The undertaker and his assistant joined us. There was nothing more for us to do at the scene. We'd walked about five yards when something struck me. 'The examination might have been all right but my memory isn't.'

'Why?' Penny asked. 'What have you forgotten?'

I conjured a picture of the girl's face in my mind. Penny and the DCI paying rapt attention. 'When I initially uncovered her face her eyes were closed. I'm sure I was told at Uni that in cases like this the victim's eyes would be open.'

'That's a good point,' commented the DCI. 'Although I'm not sure whether it applies in every case. However, it might fit in with your observation about her being laid out. Well remembered.'

Twelve

C all it a lucky day if you like, for me at least. At the back of my mind I'd hoped, but not expected, to be involved further. After all this was now a murder enquiry and not just some simple case of criminal damage. Mr Valentine had just told me that I was being seconded to his team for the duration of this investigation. Perhaps only for a week or so, but what could be better than working with these top detectives? He would notify Inspector Yates. That *would* screw up the Section duty rosters. My first task was to introduce him to Jack Griffiths. After that I would assist Penny with exhibits, or anything else that was required.

Wainwright had been transferred to Hecton still protesting his arrest and having to wear a boiler suit. His clothes had been bagged for forensic examination.

Hecton wasn't perfect but it had a dedicated cell area. Better interview facilities and a fully functioning canteen. In addition, a couple of large rooms that could serve as incident rooms. Almost anything was better than Westleigh.

Once again, I was sitting in the DCI's squad offices. 'All right everybody, settle down,' The DCI's voice silenced the verbal traffic. He painted a picture as to what we knew so far, the action taken and his proposed plan of action. The post mortem had been arranged for tomorrow morning.

Teleprinter and telex circulations to all in-Force divisions and those independent forces within the boundaries of the West Riding, plus surrounding forces, seeking identification of the victim. Four links of chain, which appeared similar to Wainwright's bracelet, had been recovered. Three by Carl Ramsbottom: One next to the victim's right little finger nail. The second lodged in a fold of her dress. The third from beneath her body. All photographed in situ. The fourth, found by DC Smith, snagged in the internal seam of the breast pocket of Wainwright's jacket. Wainwright's vehicle now en route to the Forensic Science Laboratory at Harrogate. Three search warrants obtained: Wainwright's house, where he lived with his wife; we had no idea if he had any children. His shop. Lastly, his lock-ups, to be executed tomorrow morning.

'Any questions before we go. Pc Blake should have been off at two.'

'Yes sir, I have,' it was Jenny Sendrove. The second female detective constable in the squad. 'Brian, what makes Wainwright tick? You seem to have gained his confidence over the last few months,' she smiled. There was a burst of laughter from the assembled, including me.

'Three prosecutions. Three final warnings re his driving. Three relatively hefty fines, sir,' He didn't like me one iota. 'Clean for twenty years. Five endorseable convictions in the past two. Now this arrest. She was what? Twentyish, without the beating nice looking. Wouldn't have thought he was her type.'

The general comments were in agreement. 'If he had enough money, he might have been,' said Penny.

'Give over, Penny,' Derek Myers chipped in. 'He's like a small whale. He'd have to be rolling in it.'

'Brian?' DS Cartwright joined in. 'I seem to remember you mentioned this chain the last time you were with us. His mother had it commissioned?'

'Hmm, About thirty years ago. His grandfather's Albert, fifteen carat rose gold. Blamires supplied the plaque; that's brass. His name and date of birth on one side and the sign of the fish on the other.'

'That's mid-thirties? Any specific reason that you know of?'

'Not that I'm aware of, sir.'

'You made it sound as if he fixated on it.'

'He gave me that impression, sir. He accused me of being covetous when he first saw me looking at it. I thought it was effeminate. He hammered the history: his grandfather's Albert. His mother's commission. It never left his wrist.'

'But no reason why she had it commissioned?'

'No, sir. He is deeply religious. The symbolism might suggest something but I don't know if Mr Jeavons might be able to shed some light on it.'

'Didn't stop him from trying to twist the system though, did it? I'm an Alderman. Know your place?'

'No, Derek, it didn't.'

'All right,' the DCI said. 'With luck it won't be long before we get the girl identified. Meantime we'll get the searches carried out. Then Blake, you can go home.'

Thirteen

Two of the search warrants were executed thirty minutes later. The two ladies who worked in Wainwright's shop were flabbergasted.

Mrs Wainwright could only be described as meek. Approximately fifty years old, five feet three and slim. She wore no make-up. Dressed very severely. To be honest, apart from the absence of headgear she reminded me of photographs I'd seen of the Amish.

'Mrs Wainwright, I'm Detective Sergeant Cartwright this is a warrant issued by Heckton Magistrates Court to search your premises.' He showed her the warrant

Confused, she glanced at the document. 'But my husband.'

'Mrs Wainwright, your husband is in custody and likely to be so for several days.'

Her reply was strange. 'The Lord moves in mysterious ways,' she said and smiled.

DS Cartwright said. 'This is a warrant to search your house. Please step back.'

Penny and I followed DS Cartwright into the house. It was a shock to the system. Everything about Wainwright spelled wealth, yet the living room – kitchen could have been Edwardian. A time warp. The furniture was old and shabby as were the carpets. An open fire with a creel – several items of clothing drying. In front of the fire a large table with four dining chairs. There was a Phillips radio on a sideboard but no television or fridge. Just basic store cupboards. A gas cooker that had seen better days. An old Parnell washing machine and a sink unit.

I grew up in houses with a multitude of books. Especially at Joe's where we had a large library. All Wainwright had was a large family bible on a small table adjacent to the fireplace.

However, we weren't here to criticise the furnishings.

'Mrs Wainwright,' said Penny. 'What is your first name, please?'

'Adele.'

'I'm Penny and this,' she indicated me, 'is Brian.'

'Hello,' I said.

Her reply was a thin smile. 'But what are you looking for?'

'Documentation relating to his business, Mrs Wainwright. We will give you a complete list of anything that we seize. Anything that is not required will be returned.'

There was nowhere to search down stairs.

'Does your husband have an office at home,' said Penny?'

'It's upstairs but he keeps it locked.'

'That's all right we have his keys. How many bedrooms are there?'

'Three. One is my husbands and another is mine and he has his office. I don't go into either of his.'

'Not even to clean?'

'No. I never go into his bedroom. I am not allowed into his office when he is not there. He doesn't like me interfering.'

'We will need to search all the rooms, Mrs Wainwright, including yours, but we won't make a mess. You can be present if you wish'

Searching the two bedrooms took a few minutes. Nothing was found. His office was a different matter. Compared to downstairs it was a palace. It was still in need of a coat of paint and new wallpaper. No carpet but a couple of substantial patterned rugs. A large mahogany desk with telephone and blotter. Behind the desk a dark red swivel chair. On the left side of the desk, furthest form the door, a safe. Two large well stocked bookcases. Mostly religious. Some historical concerning the Levant , in particular the Holy Land. And, a large collection of pornography. Some merely titillating, others definitely hard core and imported. Two wardrobes. One double-fronted. Both locked. Was he just security conscious or paranoid?

Between us we carried the items down stairs where Penny and I listed them in duplicate.

Penny handed Mrs Wainwright a copy. 'Do I keep this?'

'Yes, Mrs Wainwright. Anything of no evidential value will be returned.'

She nodded. 'Is there any money. He gives me money to buy food. He should give it to me today.'

'In his desk drawer,' said Penny, 'there is £79 in bank notes and, £11.14.6d in coins; also £1307:00 in bank notes in his safe, Mrs Wainwright. It is unlocked.' From the look on her face Adele Wainwright had difficulty in picturing what that amount of money might look like.

She was nervous. 'That is his money,' she said. 'He gives me what I can spend for food and he pays the bills. He will be angry if I take it.'

'It may be some time before he comes home,' said Penny. Adele Wainwright smiled again. 'Mrs Wainwright,' Penny continued. 'You have to eat and there will be bills to pay. If you keep a record of what you spend then he will understand.' She relaxed and nodded.

Adele Wainwright certainly related more to Penny than to either of us so she did most of the talking. Penny sat her down and explained again who we all were and gave our contact details. Then asked if she had any children. Apart from the archaic language, the sad tone of the reply surprised us all. Penny didn't bat an eyelid. 'You have to have lain with a man to have his children.' She sounded so calm it was unreal. How long had she and her husband been married? And still a virgin? Penny asked if she had any relatives we could contact for her. Before she could answer there was a rat-a-tat-tat at the door.

There were two women. One plumpish with a rosy complexion and a worn out perm. An open raincoat. Her pinafore clearly visible. The second, fifty or so, smartly dressed in blue: top coat, hat and shoes. 'Who are you?' she demanded of DS Cartwright.

'We're police officers,' he said and showed his warrant card. 'I'm Detective Sergeant Cartwright and, you are?'

'Elaine Carter, Adele's sister,' her tone business-like. 'And this is Nancy, she lives across the way. When she saw the activity she called me. Can we come in?'

The first thing she did was to ignore us and share a hug with her sister. She took a step back turned towards us observing each of us in turn. Her eyes narrowing slightly. 'Am I permitted to know what this is all about?'

I glanced at DS Cartwright, he nodded. 'Yes, Mrs Carter,' I said. 'I've arrested your brother-in-law for criminal damage. He's in custody.'

There was a look of astonishment. 'Two detectives and Pc Blake for a criminal damage. What has he done, tried to blow up the Houses of Parliament?'

Adele Wainwright responded with some vehemence. '*You* are Blake?' she said. 'You have made my husband very angry.' She lifted her left hand and stroked her cheek.

I'd never seen her before but Elaine Carter definitely knew me. She smiled. 'Yes, Mrs Wainwright, I am ...'

Elaine Carter turned to her sister. 'He's been hitting you again, hasn't he?'

It was a wan smile. 'He said that I provoked him ... but he was always sorry afterwards.'

Elaine Carter's eyes flashed. 'Provoked my foot,' she snapped. 'He's just mean and nasty; you should have left him years ago.'

'Please, do not speak like that, Elaine,' Adele Wainwright said. 'I made a promise before God. I cannot leave him. He is a good man but flawed and does not have a lot of money. We have to be careful.' It hadn't registered when Penny told her how much money we'd found in his office. For me that was almost two year's salary.

The items we selected were piled on the table. Financial ledgers and account books etc in one pile. Pornography stacked at the opposite end of the table – there was a lot. All other documents between. I was about to say something but a shake of the head from Penny made me bite my tongue. We looked on whilst Elaine Carter reached out and picked a bank book from the top of the pile. 'Adele, just listen to yourself. Look at this.' She turned to the last page and thrust it at her sister. 'Adele,' she said. 'Read it out loud. The last line.'

Adele Wainwright looked at the page and frowned. 'Go on Adele,' repeated her sister. 'Read out the last line.'

Adele Wainwright looked at the page again. 'But this cannot be right,' she looked puzzled. 'He told me that I should not worry about money. If we were frugal we would not have to leave the house.'

Elaine Carter looked exasperated. 'Adele. Read-out-the-last-line.'

She looked at the book and frowned. 'It says here that he has £187,783 in the bank,' she said as if it were impossible.

No-one had checked the book, that was for later. There was an exchange of looks between us and a rapid glance from Elaine Carter. 'He owns property all over the place,' she said before turning to speak to her sister. 'He's mean. He's nasty. Now he's in custody. You have to do something, Adele. He's violent. At least come and stay with me and Derek until we know what's happening. Please.'

Adele Wainwright looked lost. She nodded and looked at me. 'I can do this?' she said. 'Live with my sister without my husband's permission?'

'Yes, Mrs Wainwright,' said DS Cartwright. 'That's not a problem. As long as we have Mrs Carter's contact details. We will need to speak with you later.' He looked at me and nodded.

I recorded the details then asked Mrs Carter the question that was bugging me. 'We've never met, so could I ask how you know me?'

I was the recipient of a broad smile. 'I work for the Clerk to the Justices. When Cuthbert's name appeared on the documents I received from Inspector Felton with you shown as the OIC, I, how can I put it, took an interest.'

Fourteen

Sally Dunster, 20 years of age, five feet three inches tall, a brown eyed brunette, wearing a blue overall type dress with gold coloured buttons down the front, had been reported missing an hour earlier.

She lived with her parents, Kevin, forty two, a bus driver. Mother, Marlene, thirty nine, a cook. Brother, Craig, sixteen, an apprentice lathe operator. They lived in Brackshaw, a small village about six miles to the northeast. Sally had stayed with her friend, Sandra, in Gomersal the night before. She didn't work weekends so her parents had not been worried. She often stayed at Sandra's home. They became concerned when her employers, Greensmith & Wright – Warehousemen, where she worked as an invoice clerk, called. They had some urgent orders to dispatch. Her father was making the report when the teleprinter came through.

It had been real before. Now, she had a name: Sally Dunster. A young woman dead, distraught parents and younger brother. Thanks to two young boys we had recovered her body and Cuthbert Wainwright was in custody.

Fifteen

'What time do you call this?' A Claire-carrying Lucy demanded as I opened the door. No doubt I would hear it many times in the future. 'You were supposed to be off at two. We were going to go for a walk. You've even missed bath time,' she chided, lifting Claire up to me.

I put my arms round them holding them close. I breathed in her fragrance as well as that of a freshly bathed daughter. 'I love you Lucy Blake, never forget that.'

She looked up at me and frowned. 'I know you do. I love you too … what's the matter, Brian? What's happened?'

I smiled at her, took Claire in my arms and kissed her forehead. This was probably the first time that I began to really understand what my colleagues said about taking the job home. Don't! Home is protection from the job. Leave it outside the front door. Better still the front gate.

'Nothing for you to worry about, darling, but I'm working with Mr Valentine again. I'm on again at eight in the morning.' Thankfully Lucy didn't press the matter. She would find out soon enough.

Sixteen

It was on the BBC radio news bulletin at seven am: *Reports have been received that the body of a young woman was discovered yesterday, buried at the rear of property in Westleigh in the West Riding of Yorkshire. Police sources confirm that a local businessman, Cuthbert Wainwright, is in custody and helping the Police with their enquiries.'*

Of course Lucy heard the radio. 'Is this what you meant?'

I frowned and nodded. 'Yes, and it's right, but I can't say anything. To be honest I'm surprised anyone else did. The Boss isn't going to be pleased.'

He wasn't. I was twenty minutes early and beat the rain by three as I was whisked into an unhappy DCI's temporary office. 'Did you discuss this case with anyone after leaving here yesterday?'

I shook my head. 'No sir. Not even Lucy. No phone calls or callers. We put Claire to bed. Had our evening meal. Then I tackled the next question on the crime paper. We listened to The Navy Lark and had an early night.'

A press release had been scheduled for ten am. Now the cat was out of the bag. The gentlemen of the Press knew and their muddy footprints began to appear. Representations were made only to be informed that the police were only too ready to use the press when it suited them. And, in any case, the public had a right to know. The press were informed that was not the point. Any reporters interfering with potential witnesses or any aspect of the case would be dealt with by the courts. Not that any journalist would offer a cash inducement to say nothing to the police so the journalist could get a scoop. Who on earth would do that? An uneasy truce was agreed upon.

Who the police source was no-one knew. Or, if they did know said nothing. I couldn't believe it was one of the DCI's team. He spoke with the producer of the BBC news service who refused to divulge his source. However, they agreed that in future they would contact him if any further information came to light. Call me a cynic if you like but I had my doubts.

Seventeen

F irst task of the day. Contact all possible witnesses and warn them of possible approaches by reporters. We were too late. They had somehow gotten hold of Sally Dunster's details and already made an approach to her family. Another leak? It was a mess. The public did have the right to be aware of certain aspects, but that was not the decision of the Press. Having reporters trampling roughshod over the crime scene or other evidence could seriously interfere with the investigation. The Deputy Chief Constable, Rodney Gartside, who had overall responsibility for the day-to-day running of the Force, in particular the C.I.D., was unhappy. He wasn't a particularly tall man but compensated for his lack of stature in decibels.

DCI Valentine was in a meeting with Chief Superintendent Mithering at Headquarters. His second in command, DI Henderson set the days tasks.

'The word is out and there's nothing we can do about that. But, ensure that you keep everything buttoned up.

'DS Nicholson and DC Jackson. The lock-ups. The keys are on my desk. There's a beat officer waiting for you at Westleigh.

'WDC Sendrove and DC Smith. Interviews with the occupants in Field Lane.

'DS Cartwright, you and your team re-interview the Dunster family and neighbours. Ensure they haven't squirreled a reporter into the group.

'DC's Walker and Normington. Greensmith and Wrights followed by statements of the fire crew who attended the fire.

WDC Farthing, after the PM re-interview Adele Wainwright.

'And, there is now a uniformed officer outside the Wainwrights 24 hours a day until further notice.'

Nothing to do with Wainwright but I had to call in at the Magistrate's Court Office before attending the post mortem. Everything completed I walked out of the front doors of the Court easing my way through the crush of photographers and reporters. Thankfully, the rain had relented. I hadn't walked ten yards before ... 'Officer, could I have a word please?' Officer? I was in civvies. Did I have Police stamped across the back of my neck? I turned towards the voice. 'My name's Alistair McDonald,' he said in a noticeable Scots accent. 'I'm a reporter with the Argus. Was that this Wainwright character they've just rushed in through the back doors?'

This was news to me. 'Sorry, Mr McDonald,' I replied. 'I can't help you there, but officer?'

'You're Pc Blake,' he grinned. 'I remember you from the explosion at Westleigh. You've made a good recovery, I see.'

'I have thanks,' I replied and shook the offered hand. 'Sorry, I can't help you about Wainwright, I'm here on another matter. But, seeing as you're here as a result of this BBC broadcast I don't suppose you've any idea where it came from?'

As we'd been speaking three or four of his colleagues had wandered up and were earwigging. 'Not a clue!' he replied. I got the idea that they wouldn't have told me even if they did know. 'My editor used to work with that particular BBC editor on the Manchester Guardian. The only thing he managed to glean when they spoke was that it arrived by parachute.' Cryptic or what? Had it been an anonymous tip? A bolt from the blue? Or, someone the editor knew who had access to confidential information? That certainly did narrow the field. But who and why? A junior police officer would surely have gone to one of the local rags where they may have had a contact. Or, they could just have known this particular editor. There was no sense, just conjecture. Nevertheless it was an interesting comment which I passed on to the DCI when I arrived at the mortuary.

'And that's what he said, arrived by parachute, nothing else?'

'Yes sir, just that.'

'I see, did any of the other reporters say anything?'

'No sir. There were a few nods in agreement but no comments. They'd obviously been discussing it between themselves.'

'Have you mentioned this to anyone else?'

'No-one, sir.'

He thought for a moment. 'Of course it's probably just hot air … nevertheless keep it under your hat for now.' As things developed that was to become a mantra.

The autopsy was carried out by Professor Snodgrass. Sally Dunster was laid out on the slab and covered with a white sheet. Her clothes and property on a neighbouring table: One white brassiere. One blue dress. One yellow metal ring - from Sally Dunster's right hand. One clip-on earing (pearl) – found inside the dress. All were photographed. Placed in separate brown paper bags, sealed and referenced.

Eighteen

The Interview Room was windowless. Very warm. Ten feet by eight with an eight foot ceiling. The air foetid. An all-pervading aroma of stale sweat and cigarette smoke. Flaking beige paint. Names scratched on the old wooden table and walls. Polystyrene tiles on the ceiling. It had been set out as per the DCI's instructions. Just one chair on the far side of the table to let Wainwright know he was on his own. Opposite, were the DCI and DI Henderson. Behind the latter, yours truly. My being there might just provoke him into committing the odd indiscretion. Plus, I was making notes for my own benefit and, I had to stay schtum.

Wainwright was angry. He leant forward as the DCI sat. 'I have been in custody for twenty four hours, Chief Inspector. To treat me like a common criminal is unacceptable.'

The DCI put his briefcase on the floor. DI Henderson, a box-file on the table. 'I can assure you, Mr Wainwright,' he said making eye contact, 'that your arrest by Pc Blake was lawful. And, in the light of what we now know, reasonable.'

'That's your opinion,' snapped Wainwright.

Wainwright and the DCI locked eyes. 'Cuthbert Wainwright,' said the DCI. 'You are not obliged to say anything but whatever you say may be used in evidence. Do you understand?'

'Of course, Chief Inspector. I'm not stupid.'

The DCI made no comment. He took an envelope from the box-file and tipped the bracelet into his hand. 'Mr Wainwright, can you identify this?'

'Of course I can,' he snapped. His eyes fixed on the bracelet. 'It's mine and I want it back.'

'How do you know it's yours?' He emphasised every word.

'Because, Chief Inspector, my mother had it made for me over thirty years ago. If you want proof, my name and date of birth are on the front and the symbol of the Lord Jesus on the rear.'

DCI Valentine motioned me to pass the waste paper bin and proceeded to flake the dried mud into the bin and checked both sides. 'Yes, you're correct,' he said.

'Of course I am,' Wainwright replied with a smug smile. 'I told you, it's mine.'

'So you did, Mr Wainwright. But I was given to understand that you never took the bracelet from your wrist. Yet here it is and badly damaged. How did this happen?'

Wainwright took a deep breath and sighed. 'It was three days ago, Chief Inspector. I caught the bracelet on a bracket in my garage, it broke. Gold is a soft metal.'

'Your garage at home, or the lock-up in Field Lane?'

'Field Lane.'

'It must have been quite a jolt, Mr Wainwright, to do so much damage.'

'It was. I tripped and lost my balance. I caught the bracelet on the bracket where I keep my ladder,' he pulled up the sleeve of his boiler suit. There was a scratch and some shallow yellow bruising plainly visible on the inside of his wrist. 'Look you can see where the chain dug in.'

'Why hadn't you taken the bracelet to be repaired?'

'I had intended to take it to Blamires on the Saturday, but those two yobs had stolen it.'

'But that was yesterday, your shop premises are barely a hundred yards from Mr Blamires shop, why did you leave it so long?'

Wainwright shrugged. 'One of those things I suppose.'

'Then what did you do?' said the DCI. 'After you'd damaged the bracelet?'

'I put the bracelet and links that I could find in the breast pocket of my jacket; my dark grey suit, so I could have it repaired.'

The DCI pursed his lips. 'I see,' he said. 'The boys said they found it as a result of one of them slipping. It was buried in mud at the bottom of the slope behind your lock-up.'

'You mean they stole it,' Wainwright said. 'They're thieves, plain and simple.'

'Did you witness the boys finding your bracelet?'

'Yes.'

'If you saw them find the bracelet you know that they turned it up out of the mud when one of them slipped. Isn't that correct?'

'I just saw one of them with the bracelet in his hand.'

'Now you're saying that you didn't see them pick it up?'

'No. I suppose not. I'd realised that the bracelet and the links were missing from my pocket'

'When did you realise that they were missing?'

'Yesterday morning when I put my jacket on.'

'How did you know?'

'It's metallic,' he obviously thought it was a daft question. 'It rattled. Only this particular morning it didn't.'

'If you could hear the chain rattle when you put the jacket on, Mr Wainwright, why didn't you notice when you took the jacket off the night before?'

Wainwright shrugged. 'I don't know. I just didn't.'

'There was nothing on your mind? Something that might have distracted you?'

'Nothing that I can call to mind.'

'Very well. So what time did you realise the bracelet and links were missing?'

'About eight a.m.'

'But the boys came across you round about eleven thirty. Why the delay?'

'I had one or two things to do first. Business comes first, Chief Inspector.'

'Do you count getting changed into work clothes and piling up tree branches prior to setting a fire as business? More important?'

Wainwright shrugged his shoulders.

The DCI nodded. 'Just how many links were there, Mr Wainwright, just so we know.'

'Erm, five, six, I'm not sure. I picked up all I could find. Why?'

'Just for accuracy,' he replied. 'Mr Wainwright I think you're lying. I believe that you knew you had lost the links from your jacket during Friday night but weren't quite sure where. You started the fire to dry out the ground and hide any trace of what you had been doing. But when you saw the boys with your damaged bracelet in their hands you panicked and were desperate to retrieve it.'

Wainwright's eyes narrowed. 'No, it was daylight,' he insisted. 'There was no panic.'

'But, if you didn't know that the bracelet and links were missing until the morning how could you possibly know where they might be?'

Wainwright glared across the table but refused to answer.

The DCI smiled. 'You're lying, Mr Wainwright,' he said. 'The boys watched you for several minutes. You weren't searching for anything. Just shifting quite large branches and stacking them. They described you as dressed like a tramp. Scruffy. Paint on the shirt front. Old Mac and Wellington boots. If you put your jacket with the damaged bracelet and loose links in the breast pocket on first thing, when did you change your clothes?'

'When I got to my lock-up, I keep them there.'

The DCI nodded. 'You only appeared with your spade several minutes later. You were still not in a hurry until you saw the boys with what transpired to be your bracelet in their hands. These are not the actions of someone who is urgently seeking something which in their mind is valuable. As far as the area behind your lock-ups is concerned, I've been there, it's filthy. Near to the stream it's very muddy. How is it that the bracelet, which you state categorically was in the breast pocket of your jacket three days ago, was in the mud at the bottom of the slope?'

'I don't know

'When was the last time you went into this area wearing your suit?'

'Don't recall.'

'Mr Wainwright. In that case would you mind explaining how the bracelet managed to get from your suit to the bottom of the slope?

Wainwright's complexion froze. 'If I knew that I wouldn't have had to look for it,' he said a touch of insolence in his voice.

'So now you're claiming that you did know where it was.'

Wainwright sounded frustrated. 'I suspected that it was somewhere thereabouts. It was a possibility, Chief Inspector.'

'But you still had no idea how it got there?'

'No, I did not.'

The DI and the DCI exchange glances. 'So, why didn't you just tell the boys you'd lost something and ask for it back? They only picked it up because one of them slipped and flicked it out of the mud with his foot. They were simply curious.'

'They're thieves, they ran.'

'No, they ran because they're youngsters who saw a fully grown man charging at them waving a spade. That would be enough to make most people run. They're from good homes and they had been bird watching in the wood. They're not yobs.'

'As far as I'm concerned they were.'

'Can you explain why you keep a spade in your lock-up? Were you expecting to do some digging?'

'I've got all sorts of odds and sods there, one of them just happens to be a spade. It's handy for clearing rubbish.'

'Neither of the boys were doing any harm so why take a swing at them with the spade? You saw the damage you did to Michael's jacket. Had your swing connected with him, it could have killed him.'

There was a pregnant pause. Wainwright took a deep breath and sighed. His tone now apologetic. 'Yes, I'm sorry. It was a stupid thing to do. I didn't intend to cause any harm. I'll apologise to them both and their parents, and I will replace the jacket. I was overwrought.'

'You were so angry you didn't care what damage or injuries you caused, or to whom?'

'I didn't think. It was wrong of me. I'll apologise. I don't see what else I can do.'

'Mr Wainwright,' he continued. 'You probably aren't aware that every time the fire brigade are called out to an incident the police are informed. As you were being placed in the cell we received a call that the fire brigade were attending a fire at the rear of your premises in Field Lane.'

Wainwright sat back in his chair, a half-smile on his face. 'Is that relevant to the matter in hand, or is it something to do with the rubbish that I was burning?'

'It is. If this bracelet of yours is so important why, after your altercation with Mr Griffiths at the Mill House, did you not go straight to the police station?'

'I wanted to get changed, not to be seen in old clothes like that.'

'Personal vanity?'

'No, Chief Inspector, professionalism. I like my image to reflect my position in Westleigh.'

'You also doused your wood with petrol. Returned the can to the garage and washed yourself. It would have been more sensible to do that later after reporting the matter to the police, wouldn't it?'

'Perhaps, but I was there so I did it at the time. I washed my hands because my car has a leather steering wheel. Afterwards I changed into my suit. It's no big deal.'

'To me your behaviour is simply counter-intuitive.'

'Not to me.' He replied. 'When I arrived at the police station I was trying to make that dolt behind the counter understand what had happened when he,' he pointed at me, 'had the temerity to arrest me. That's disgraceful!'

The DCI smiled. 'Oh no, Mr Wainwright the fire was extinguished shortly after Pc Blake and Sergeant McGill arrived. There were obvious indications that someone had recently been digging in exactly the same spot as you had set your fire. Any recollections?'

Wainwright pursed his lips and shook his head. 'No, why should it?'

'You were carrying a spade, and it was very close to your lock-up.'

'Doesn't mean anything to me.'

'So why were you taking a spade to the site?'

'To look for my bracelet.'

'But how did you know where to look?'

'I assumed that was where I'd dropped it.'

'Of all the places, why there? ... I'll ask you again. Why would you be wearing a good suit at the bottom of a rubbish dump? What else might you be doing that in that area where you would be wearing a suit?'

'For goodness sake, Chief Inspector, this is going round in circles. You've asked these questions already.'

'And you still haven't given a satisfactory answer ... Very well. Sergeant McGill borrowed a couple of shovels from the fire brigade and under supervision Pc Blake began to dig. Would you care to hazard a guess what was found?'

Wainwright pursed his lips and shrugged his shoulders. 'A dead dog?'

Mr Valentine paused. I could see the tension in his jaw and his eyes narrow. Wainwright sat there in silence. Insolent. Challenging. 'No Mr Wainwright,' he continued. 'It was not a dead dog. It was a human hand ... would you care to comment?'

The nerves in Wainwright's jaw tightened as he gritted his teeth. 'It's nothing to do with me,' he replied and shook his head. 'I didn't kill her.'

Even from where I was sitting I could see the smile on the DCI's face. 'Her, Mr Wainwright?' he said. 'Nobody mentioned whether it was male or female. What made you say, her?'

It was strange watching Wainwright's face, his expression barely changed. Yet it was almost as if some of the tension had eased.

'Fifty-fifty chance,' he shrugged. 'I guessed.'

'I haven't confirmed the sex of the dead person. Why assume that you were correct. Unless you already knew?'

Wainwright shook his head. For the first time the bluster slipped. He was scared. 'No, I didn't know,' he said. 'It was just a guess.'

The DCI narrowed his eyes, the smile disappeared. 'No Mr Wainwright, as I am sure you are aware it was the body of a twenty year old woman. A young woman called Sally Dunster. Shortly after Sergeant McGill and Pc Blake found the body she was reported as missing from home. Well?'

Wainwright shook his head again. 'That's nothing to do with me,' he insisted. The shoulders sagged. The arrogance was gone. 'I did *not* kill her.'

The DCI leaned forwards resting his forearms on the table. 'Why don't I believe you?'

'I-I don't know,' said Wainwright. 'But I swear that I didn't.'

There was a pause of several seconds. 'It does help to explain, however,' the DCI continued, 'why, in spite of your claim that you wanted to find this bracelet of *immense* sentimental value, you returned to what we now know is a grave. You set fire to the brushwood and branches you had stacked using petrol to speed the effect. Your hope being that the heat would dry the ground to such an extent that the grave would be impossible to find. Sally Dunster might never have been found. That was your intention, was it not?'

Wainwright looked straight ahead and remained silent.

DI Henderson passed the DCI four small brown paper envelopes. 'Perhaps you would like to comment on these, Mr Wainwright.' He tipped the contents of the first envelope onto the table adjacent to the bracelet. 'This is a link which appears identical to those in the bracelet. The only difference being that it is now distorted. This was recovered from the breast pocket of your suit.'

Wainwright smiled. 'I told you that I had put them in there.'

The DCI smiled in return. ''So you did. But that does not answer the question with regard to what I am about to show you.' He tipped the contents of the next envelope onto the table next to the first link. 'This one is slightly muddied. It was found in the grave next to the little finger nail of Sally Dunster's right hand.'

DI Henderson took a large envelope from the box file removing a 10x8 black and white photograph, an arrow indicating the link, and slid it across to Wainwright. 'This is a photograph of the link on the table, in situ, Mr Wainwright,' he said.

Wainwright leaned forwards shook his head and shrugged. 'Planted by the police no doubt,' he said, looking at me. A gesture not missed by DCI Valentine.

'Unfortunately Mr Wainwright, at that precise moment Pc Blake was in conference with myself, Chief Inspector Sampson from

Hecton, and Inspector Yates some ten yards away; it was found by another officer.'

There was no reply.

'No matter. This third link, although out of shape and split, is nice and clean,' the DCI said placing it alongside the other two. 'It was recovered from a fold in Sally Dunster's dress.'

The DI slid a second photograph, one of the link in situ across the table.

Wainwright looked closely but made no comment.

And the last ...' he placed the fourth link on the table and looked Wainwright straight in the eye. 'This was recovered when the body of Sally Dunster was removed from the grave. It was beneath her.'

A third photograph was pushed across the table for Wainwright to examine.

Once again he made no comment.

Wainwright stared at the evidence on the table. 'Do you deny that these links appear identical?' asked the DCI. 'We will have them examined and tested in due course.'

He looked more at ease. Did he think the pressure was off? 'They appear similar,' was all Wainwright would say.

'In my opinion,' the DCI continued, 'You murdered Sally Dunster by manual strangulation. You dug the grave and buried her body at the bottom of the slope behind your lock-up during the hours of darkness. Completely oblivious to the fact that the broken bracelet and links of chain had fallen from your jacket pocket. It was only yesterday morning when you made the discovery that they were missing and realised where they might be. You fetched your spade in an attempt to recover them. When you saw those boys with, as you surmised, your bracelet in their hands you panicked.

Mr Wainwright, your explanation for want of a better word is simply bizarre.

Wainwright leaned forwards, forearms on the table his hands spread wide in supplication. 'Detective Chief Inspector. I have not killed anybody.'

'I don't believe you, Mr Wainwright. Where did you kill her?'

He closed his eyes and sighed. 'I did not.'

'Where was she murdered?'

'I have nothing to say,' He said and shook his head. *This was not supposed to happen.*

'But you do know, don't you, Mr Wainwright?'

'I have nothing to say.'

'Were you present when she was murdered?'

'Detective Chief Inspector, I was not.'

'If you did not kill Sally Dunster, who did?'

Wainwright's eyes flickered for a fraction of a second. 'I have nothing further to say.'

'Bearing in mind that we found the links of your chain in Sally Dunster's grave do you admit to burying her?'

'I have nothing further to say.'

'Mr Wainwright, this is your opportunity to explain. We have the body of a recently murdered young woman. A body buried in waste ground at the rear of your lock-up. In the grave are links from a bracelet owned by you and, that you claimed you had in your pocket along with the damaged bracelet. Two boys out bird watching come across your bracelet in the mud near to the grave. You set a fire on top of the grave in an attempt to conceal its location having attacked the boys with apparently the same spade used to dig the grave. Tests at the Forensic Science Laboratory will confirm that the mud on Michael's jacket and the spade are from the same source, the grave. And you refuse to give any explanation. ... Cuthbert Wainwright, I am arresting you on suspicion of the murder by strangulation of Sally Dunster. I will remind you that you are still under caution. Have you anything to say?'

Wainwright looked desolate. 'I haven't killed anybody, Chief Inspector.'

The DCI looked at Wainwright for a full ten seconds. Nodded to Mr Henderson and held his hand out for the file that the DI was holding. 'Mr Wainwright, earlier today a post mortem examination was carried out on the body of Sally Dunster, this is an extract from the findings of Professor Snodgrass, the pathologist. I will paraphrase it:

Sally Dunster was savagely beaten about the head and face and then strangled. The hyoid bone was fractured. She was also subjected to violent rape. Samples of semen were obtained and sent for analysis ...'

When Wainwright began to laugh I thought that the DCI was going to go over the table at him. I didn't think I'd ever seen anyone so angry. 'There is something that you find amusing about murder and rape, Mr Wainwright?'

'No, Detective Chief Inspector,' he said. He looked frightened as he stifled his laughter. 'Just the thought that I should be suspected of rape. That is impossible. I am not able. Bring your police doctor and I will submit to any examination. He will tell you. I have no testicles!'

It was a thought that came straight into the forefront of my mind from somewhere in the dark recesses. I'd attended a presentation in the university library entitled *Practises of the Early Christians,* given by a PhD student from my old school. Normally I wouldn't have entertained it but he promised it would be entertaining. It was, and now relevant. During the few moments that Wainwright was amusing himself and Mr Valentine and the DI were thinking, I scribbled **'Castrato?'** in my pocket book and handed it to DI Henderson. He glanced at it and handed it to Mr Valentine who did likewise and handed it back to me. 'Remind me later. Find the station sergeant and tell him to bring the detention sheet.'

'Just one last thing before the sergeant returns, Mr Wainwright,' the DCI said as I left the room. 'Please hold your hands out in front of you?'

Wainwright scowled but complied.

DCI Valentine took Wainwright's hands in turn and turned them over, pushed the sleeves of the boiler suit up to the elbows. Other than faint scratches there were no marks on his hands, face or neck.

Detention sheet endorsed authorising examination and taking of blood samples by the police surgeon Wainwright was back in his cell.

Nineteen

There was much wincing and crossing of male legs. Sergeant Cartwright spoke for them all. 'Brian, are you trying to tell us that this lunatic cut his own bollocks off, simply because of something that's written in the Bible?'

I smiled at their discomfort. 'If it's true, and he did, then yes. If I remember what Norman told us in the university library, it was written by St Paul. It was to take their minds from the carnal and concentrate on the sacred.' There was much ribald laughter as I continued. 'Yep. They would strip off at a festival. Take a sword and do the deed. Then run through the streets naked carrying their baubles held high. Lob them through a convenient house window and the occupants of the house would clothe them. It became so prevalent the Romans became worried. Those who committed it could be executed.'

'This friend of yours? Was this a student wind up?'

'No, Jenny, not at all. He was in his final year of a PhD in archaeology. His name was, Norman, Norman Castle.'

'An archaeologist called Norman Castle? Now we know you're taking the piss,' protested an incredulous Jacko.

'No, I'm not. It's perfectly genuine.'

That was an unusually prolonged light-hearted moment, and then it began again.

'Barmy bastards,' Jenny, with the female perspective.

'Well, at least he had the balls to do it,' Kevin Riley's offering triggering groans.

'Maybe so, but not for long,' quipped Penny.

'All right,' interrupted the DCI. 'Don't make a meal of it ... and, before this gets out of hand, John,' he said quelling the laughter. 'Find out where Wainwright was last Wednesday afternoon around 3pm. Begin with the staff at his shop in Westleigh. See if you can build up a picture of his routine. Following that the Town Clerk's Office. There's a diary in his property. Sign it out and see what that can tell us. When that's complete start with his business contacts, then the mayor and every single person at the town hall plus all councillors.'

DS Nicholson, DC Riley and DC Myers left the office.

'Thank you for sharing that illuminating moment of university life, Brian, fascinating.'

'Any time, sir,' I replied, returning the DCI's smile.

'Yeah,' said Jacko. 'You could write a book. An in depth study on the lives of East Midlands University undergraduates, call it, 'The Life of Brian.''

Before anything else disruptive could occur Sergeant Gledhill poked his head round the door. 'Sorry to interrupt, sir. Mrs Wainwright is at the counter asking for a DC Penny. She says that DC Penny and Pc Blake visited her home last evening. But to my knowledge we haven't a DC Penny. She is adamant.'

Penny stood up in the midst of the laughter. 'That'll be me, Sarge,' she said.

Sergeant Gledhill took one look and shook his head. 'Oh, bloody hell. Of course it is ... time I retired,' he shook his head again and chuckled to himself. 'She's got a black cash box. Will only hand it to you two.'

'Put her in an interview room please, Sergeant. Apologise and tell her they'll be along in a few minutes.'

Twenty

A dele Wainwright placed her cup back on the saucer as we entered. 'I'm pleased to see that the Sergeant is looking after you,' Penny said, indicating the tea as we sat.

'Thank you, yes,' she said and smiled. The change in her was marked. So much of the tension had gone. 'It was very kind.'

'Not at all,' Penny returned the smile.

Mrs Wainwright's brow furrowed. 'There is something that I do not understand,' she said. 'The Sergeant tells me that your name is not Penny, but Farthing.'

We both smiled. Penny explained. 'My Christian name is Elizabeth. I used to get called Liz. However, I met my husband David, David Farthing, whilst we were at school. We were always together and he began to call me Penny. The name stuck and I became known as Penny. It's been the same ever since.'

We sat in silence as Mrs Wainwright tried to reconcile the issue in her mind. We could hear her mumbling, 'Elizabeth Farthing, Liz Farthing but, why Penny Farthing? ...' And then the 'Penny' dropped. Her face broke into a broad smile. She began to laugh, softly. 'That is very funny, Penny Farthing.' She was laughing for a good two minutes, dabbing her eyes as the tears appeared. 'You have children?'

'Yes, I do. Christopher, he's nine and Carol is seven. Brian,' she smiled and indicated me, 'is a beginner. His daughter is ...?'

'Seven weeks,' I replied. 'We call her Claire.'

'You are both very lucky,' she looked and sounded sad. But if Wainwright had castrated himself there was no wonder.

'Now, Mrs Wainwright,' Penny said. 'You wanted to see us. How can we help?'

She took the box from her lap and placed it on the table. 'This is my husband's; he keeps a paper in it.'

'Could I ask where it was, Mrs Wainwright,' I said. 'We didn't notice it the other day.'

'On the top shelf in his wardrobe, behind his hats,' she said. 'When you left the house yesterday you did not lock the wardrobe door.'

I'd searched the wardrobe myself. Penny gave me a disapproving look and rolled her eyes. 'Sorry, I never noticed it.' *Come on Blake pull your finger out, I thought you wanted to be a detective!*

Penny lifted the box off the table. 'It's very light, Mrs Wainwright,' she said.

'I think it is only a single sheet of paper.'

'You've seen inside?' said Penny.

'Once,' Mrs Wainwright replied. 'I walked into his office. The box was open on his desk. He was putting a folded sheet of paper inside. I could see there was some writing on it. He was very angry.' She paused placing her hand on her cheek. 'He shouted at me.'

'He hit you because you interrupted him?' asked Penny.

'I had interrupted him before but he had never been this angry. I think it was only because I saw the paper but I couldn't read what was written on it. Then he locked the box and put it in his wardrobe.'

I'd searched the wardrobe. How on earth did I miss it?

I got a second reproving look from Penny. 'Never mind,' she said. 'We were only looking for paperwork yesterday.'

Ouch! That didn't make me feel any better, either.

'And you hadn't seen inside the box before, or since?'

'No, only on that occasion.'

'Was the key to the box on that key-ring he kept in his pocket?' I asked.

She nodded. 'Yes.'

I removed the sheet of paper. There was a column of twelve eight digit numbers written down the left-hand margin.

17081345
28760974
19102317
33551470
26931530
37013169
21303100
11720462
03531429
19910182
16401350
15433643

I showed it to Mrs Wainwright. 'Is this the same sheet that you saw?'

She looked at it briefly. Her face clouding over as if the sight of it brought back some unpleasant memories. 'Yes,' she said. 'That is his handwriting.'

'Do you know the significance of these numbers?'

She shook her head. 'Sorry, no.'

Having stared at the numbers for several seconds and receiving no revelations I put the paper back in the box.

Liz was staring at me. 'Something puzzling you, Brian?'

'Yes, there is. Mrs Wainwright, did you have many visitors at home?'

She laughed. 'Visitors? No. Cuthbert did not like people in the house. Sometimes Nancy would come across and have a cup of tea, but Elaine? Cuthbert did not like her being in the house at any time.'

'Because she stood up to him?'

She nodded. 'Yes, she is much stronger than I am, but I am his wife.'

'What about people from your church?' I asked. 'Or any of the ladies to see you. Trades people or people he did business with?'

'No one,' she shook her head. 'Anyone to do with business he meets elsewhere. Where that is I do not know. I used to meet the other ladies at the church, not at home.'

It seemed ridiculous that Wainwright should go to such lengths in hiding the box or use violence simply because his wife disturbed him. All that did was to draw his wife's attention to it.

'Mrs Wainwright,' I said. 'How long has he been like this?'

'Always,' she said. 'He has always been secretive.'

Nothing further forthcoming, Mrs Wainwright was on her way home.

Twenty-One

Mr Valentine broke the silence. 'Right, these numbers. Any ideas?' he said stemming the flow of intellectual sweat.

'They're not the correct format for dates.'

'No Peter, they're not,' the DCI agreed. 'None match details of any of the bank accounts in Wainwright's name that we know about.' He turned to us. 'Mrs Wainwright had no idea what was on the paper?'

'No sir,' Penny and I answered together.

DI Henderson ran his finger down the list. 'Map references have six digits so that rules that out.'

'OK, if no-one has any further suggestions the box and its contents can go in the property store. We're not wasting time on guessing games.' No-one had.

'Penny, did you get Mrs Wainwright's permission to search the house again?'

'Yes sir, carte blanche.'

'Excellent. Doctor O'Keefe has been delayed. So, Peter you Jenny and Blake, when you've finished your meal, search the Wainwright's house from top to bottom. Fine tooth comb. One room at a time. Everything, apart from taking the walls down and the floors up. We re-interview Wainwright this afternoon.'

2pm. Sergeant Cartwright smiled. 'Check the chimney, Brian.'

'Thanks, Serge,' I said and grinned removing my jacket, got on my knees and put my hand up the chimney. Apart from soot there was nothing.

We went through the house with a fine tooth comb. There was nothing new.

Blood sample and statement confirming Wainwright as bollock-free were handed over. A procedure carried out by either an amateur or a butcher. Cue more crossed legs and winces. Dr O'Keefe regaled us with his knowledge of the practice.

'Could he get an erection sufficient for penetration?' said DI Henderson.

'Theoretically? Yes. In ancient Rome all male slaves were castrated. Nevertheless, those who could perform sexually could be richly rewarded.'

There was a court warning for me in the mail run. Nothing novel about that. However, this was for the York Assize relating to the incident involving three police recruits that occurred at Pannal Ash early in my initial course. R v Marsden (Murder) and R v Widdowson (Accessory after the fact). The third officer, Smith, was, for some reason, not listed.

Twenty-Two

As instructed, I'd waited a full thirty seconds after Wainwright was brought to the interview room before I knocked and walked in holding the box in front of me. The idea being to see what response it might provoke. I sat on the chair behind the DI, put the box on my knees and said nothing. Wainwright's stare fixed on the box.

'Would you care to tell us about this box, Mr Wainwright? ... Mr Wainwright!?' He looked apprehensive.

'The box, Mr Wainwright?'

He looked across the table at the DCI. 'That's private, nothing to do with you,'

The DCI narrowed his eyes. 'Let me remind you,' he said. 'You are currently under arrest on suspicion of murder. Everything is to do with me. Now, this box. Why have you got a locked cash box, secreted in a locked wardrobe in a room which you keep locked and, to which only you have a key?'

'That's nothing to do with you.'

'When your wife interrupted you placing a folded sheet of paper in the box you lost your temper. What is so special about the contents of this box?'

'I've told you. That's nothing to do with you. It's private.'

'Your wife thinks it is, Mr Wainwright. She brought it to this police station this morning.'

'Much good may that do you,' he fired straight back. 'I'm her husband; she can't give evidence against me.'

'Really?' the DCI was laughing. 'Mr Wainwright, the law provides that no spouse *may be compelled* to give evidence against the other. However, they may volunteer.' he paused to allow the information to sink in. 'So you see, Mr Wainwright, if it were deemed necessary and your wife were at some time in the future called to give evidence against you, she could, *if she so desired.*'

Wainwright, his eyes narrowed, glared at us in turn. The tightness of his jaw muscles self-evident. 'But why did you mention your wife giving evidence against you? I never mentioned her giving evidence. All that I said was your wife had voluntarily delivered the box that you can see on Pc Blake's lap to the police station this morning. I'll ask you once more, Mr Wainwright. What is in the box?'

'No comment.'

Wainwright's eyes widened as I removed his keys from my pocket, unlocked the box and placed it on the table. They were transfixed as the DCI removed the sheet of paper, pushed the box out of the way and turned the sheet so that Wainwright could read the figures. 'Now, Mr Wainwright, what do these numbers represent?'

'I've told you,' he flared and leaned forwards. 'It's private. Mind your own business!'

That was that. Wainwright sat studying his knees, refusing to answer any further questions.

Twenty-Three

E nquiries were progressing at snail's pace. Wainwright had claimed that because he had no testicles, a statement now confirmed by Doctor O'Keefe, the semen recovered during the autopsy couldn't be his. Therefore he couldn't have raped Sally Dunster. However, the offence of rape is not about ejaculation but penetration. According to Doctor O'Keefe, Wainwright may be able to get an erection sufficient for penetration and could have taken part in both the rape and the murder. If, however, Wainwright could not produce ejaculate he could not have been acting alone.

Sally Dunster's parents had identified her body. The violence of the assault must have made those seconds even more harrowing. The inquest to establish Sally Dunster's identity had been fixed for tomorrow.

I'd typed out several copies of the numbers for the DCI. The box and contents consigned to the exhibits store. It was going to gather a lot of dust.

Twenty-Four

Sally Dunster's inquest was opened, identity established and adjourned *sine die*. The Coroner promising that her body would be released as soon as practicable. That did not sit well with her parents.

This was the hard slog. Concentrating on the criminal and any associates. Waiting to see what evidence may surface and where it would lead. Playing catch-up. We knew that Sally Dunster had told her friend, Sandra, she had a new boyfriend. Much older than she was. A smart dresser. Wore expensive aftershave. Drove a nice car. And was generous. Sandra had seen neither. Sally was a child of the 60s, free, fun loving and sexually liberated. She had ceased to frequent her old haunts in Westleigh and Hecton. New and exciting destinations beckoned, in particular a new club - The Glasshouse - in Leeds.

We had corroboration from her colleagues at Greensmith and Wrights. Malcolm Greensmith, Managing Director and General Manager, described her as a good worker when she could keep her mind on the job. But she was flighty. Never missed an opportunity to flirt with anything in trousers. Was this a case of a young woman out for a good time with a well-heeled male and falling foul of the wrong man, or something else?

A photograph had been obtained, copied, and circulated to every police station and police officer in the West Riding. All licensed premises to be visited. Information came in dribs and drabs. Yes, people recognised her photograph but couldn't recall who she was with. Just a handful had a vague idea of what he looked like. But, when interviewed and identikit likenesses prepared no two were near enough to give any confidence that the likeness was accurate. It did however create more interest with the public at large. The Press ran with the story. The BBC and Granada TV filmed a press conference held by the DCI and DI Henderson.

A security camera at the rear of The Glasshouse picked up a grainy image of the back view of a man accompanied by a young woman on the evening before Sally Dunster had been reported missing. It could have been her or a thousand others. As for the man? No-one at The Glasshouse had seen him since Sally Dunster had been murdered. However, two further pieces of information had been gleaned from The Glasshouse: firstly, that the man was clean shaven. That was all right as it went, but, two or three days without shaving could soon change that. Secondly, the car was possibly dark coloured. The image monochrome. Just shades of grey. One real stroke of luck though. The rear nearside light was caught on camera. We were looking for an F series Vauxhall Victor saloon – only one of the most popular cars on British roads. A new straw to clutch at. Probably sold in the West Riding, garages, car showrooms, repair and accessory shops and scrap yards were checked, Car parks in the centre of Leeds checked nightly but nothing positive. The trail was going cold.

A further week of the grind passed. Wainwright was interviewed twice more. It was more of the same. Wainwright's contacts from his personal diary and office at the Town Hall had been re-interviewed to no avail.

Twenty-Five

My weekend was pre-arranged. Saturday morning, a quick shop. Lunch at Salendine Nook. Followed this week by a run. Sunday afternoon Boston Spa.

It only seemed like five minutes and yet we'd been married for almost eleven months. Time was passing so fast it didn't seem fair. However, Claire made it all worthwhile. It was a bright sunny morning with a high cloud base and a light breeze when we arrived at Salendine Nook to be met Mum, Joe and Jen.

Frankie riding pillion to Vance had ridden to Tadcaster to meet Anne and Neil; they were going to York for the day. Clive visiting his friends. This was the first time I could remember that there was no martial arts practice on a Saturday afternoon. Joe had his Saturday morning class but the afternoons were fun sessions in the back garden; karate and or kendo. There were questions about the murder but nothing too intrusive. It was obvious it had been discussed. After all they had always taken a lively interest in what I'd done since I joined the police, why would they change now? They were nosey and wanted answers. They weren't the only ones.

Lucy and Jen had it all arranged in order that I could save my brain for the investigation. They were so thoughtful. Claire left in the loving clutches of Grandma Dorothy, she and Joe were going to parade her round the neighbours where she could demonstrate how she managed to roll over. The Health Visitor had been impressed and announced that Claire was too young to be able to do that. She would be going to university. *What on earth?*

Jen's planned route: a four mile run via Outlane, the old Roman signalling station at Slack, now beneath the golf club and car park, Horse Pond Lane, Scapegoat Hill and home. If I could keep up. Ha ha!

It was a steady jog up New Hey Road to Outlane. Left into Slack Lane and the golf club. The car-park was full. We stopped whilst Jen pointed out one or two things to Lucy. Apart from the cars in the car park and little stick figures in the distance it was all grass and a few flags. Half a dozen teenagers I recognised as being students from the College appeared from the front of the clubhouse, accompanied by a face I hadn't seen since university: Norman Castle, six feet three inches tall, sixteen stones in weight. He played his rugger like a battering ram and had a sense of humour to match.

'Hang on a mo,' I said, walked into the car park and slapped him on the back. 'Hello Norman. So you took up teaching after all.'

He spun on his heels. When he saw me his face split into the grin I'd seen so often. 'Bloody hell, Brian,' he said treating me to a bear hug. 'Where did you spring from?'

'Just out for a run...' I began. He saw the girls at the gate. ''What's this?' he grinned again, 'Brought your own harem?'

'A harem of one,' protested Lucy as she held up her left hand.

Jen shook her head. 'Not on your life.' she said with a laugh.

'Before you get into deep trouble, Norman. This is my wife Lucy, and Jennifer, one of my three sisters ... And this, ladies,' I said with my hand on Norman's shoulder, 'is an old rugby playing colleague from Uni, Dr. Castle, Norman Castle.'

'Ah yes,' he said, beaming a smile at them both. 'I seem to remember something about sisters. Good afternoon ladies, my apologies. But, there was no mention of a Lucy?'

Both Lucy and Jen were smiling at him. 'Oh, I only appeared on the scene fifteen months or so ago,' said Lucy.

'Really!?' he said, grinning in return as he gave my shoulders a friendly squeeze. 'And in case you're wondering, my name really is Norman Castle, and, I am an archaeologist. My parents must have known something.' He glanced at the students. 'Only these hirsute louts call me Doctor, or sir, unless they believe I'm out of earshot. They don't understand that I can hear a rat fart at fifty yards.' We all looked at the bunch of laughing students. Giving up their Saturdays to do practicals with someone like Norman must be a dream. 'In spite of your tender years, ladies, no formalities please, just call me Norman or Norm, should you so desire ... Smith, put the ... ...'

At that point I lost interest in the conversation. I was transfixed by what the aforementioned Smith was carrying. I don't know what it was called, but during my time at Uni I'd seen the archaeology students practice drawing using a very precisely constructed, spot-welded square mesh. Smith was carrying one. Except in my mind it was a huge ordnance survey map without features, just the grid of the map. Could it really be so simple?'

How long I stared I have no idea until I heard Lucy's voice. 'Brian! Brian, are you all right?'

I blinked and shook my head. 'Sorry, what?'

'You were talking to yourself, old man,' Norman said quietly. 'Away with the fairies.'

'Sorry Norman,' I pointed at the mesh. 'What do they call that?'

'It's a survey grid,' he explained. 'We use them so that we can position objects accurately. Is there a problem?'

'Sorry,' I iterated, looking at Lucy and Jennifer. 'No, it's fine, Norman. Look, you two keep going. I've got to get home. There's something I need to check.' Without further comment to the girls or saying goodbye to Norman I set off.

'Brian.' Jen shouted at my disappearing back. 'I've got the door key.'

Twenty-Six

They passed me with two hundred yards to go. Norman driving his old van, gear sticking out of the back. The girls in the front. His students would be waiting for the bus, or walking. I received a round of applause as I ran up the drive, followed by Mum with the pushchair and a Claire-carrying Joe. Chaos ensued. I apologised to Norman who was less than reluctantly press-ganged into staying for a coffee. Everyone else headed for the kitchen. I made a bee-line for the library.

'Something to do with his work?' Norman said as Mum put the kettle on.

'Probably,' Lucy sighed as she sat Claire on her knee and rubbed noses.

'To do with that body he found?'

'I don't know, Jen, honestly.'

'But he's not been like this before,' she persisted.

Jennifer, please stop playing games,' said Mum. That was that for then. Joe slid quietly out of the door.

I was on my knees ferreting around in the cupboard below the large bookcase opposite the fireplace. Joe knocked and walked in. 'Can I help?'

I sat back on my heels and relaxed. 'Please,' I said. 'I thought for a moment you were Jennifer wanting to help. Will you get me the maps, the long steel ruler, a pad and pencil and, can I borrow your lens?' During the War Joe had been in the photographic analysis section of the RAF. A few years ago he had found a lens of the same quality in a second hand shop at Aspley; this was monocular not the binocular type he'd used. Nevertheless, the quality and definition were superb. It had its own adjustable stand. I was going to need it.

'Anything else?' he asked and smiled.

I grinned in return. 'I've just got to nip upstairs. A coffee would be nice?'

Joe headed for the kettle. 'No Jennifer,' he said over his shoulder before anyone could speak. 'I don't know what he's doing or why. And I am not going to ask him. If he can tell us I'm sure he'll let us know.'

Jen slumped back on her chair. Norman smiled, 'Jennifer, don't you find not knowing is infuriating?'

Jen smiled at him and pulled a face. 'Typical.'

Lucy passed Claire back to Mum. 'Your daddy's busy even on his day off little lady,' she said, and kissed her forehead.

Twenty-Seven

We lived on the north-western edge of Huddersfield. The A640, the Huddersfield to Oldham road running past the end of the street. Surrounded by fields, farms and woods, a little further out, the moors. We'd spent hours up there with Joe learning to map read. Whilst I was not what I would call an expert I knew how to find a map reference. By the time Joe re-appeared with the coffee everything was ready. The right map. Edges weighted down with books. Joe's four inch lens positioned where I thought it should be. I hoped that I was wrong. An initial check suggested otherwise. My gut agreed. Joe's eyes swept the table. 'That's your police note book,' he said nodding to the far side of the table.

I nodded.

'Do you want me to leave?'

I shook my head. 'No, I need you to check my figures.'

'You're looking for a map reference of sorts?' he said and frowned.

I nodded again. 'Eight figures.'

'Eight?' he gasped. 'Hell, that's precise. And why you needed the big lens.'

'Precisely,' I replied, poker-faced.

Joe groaned. 'Ha. Very good,' he said. 'How do you want to play this?'

I pushed the pad across the table. I was glad he was here. It would be too easy to cock it up by myself. 'I'll give you the eastings and the northings for the square. You note them down but leave a suitable

gap for the third and fourth digit, then tag seven and eight on the
end. Then I want you to check my figures.'

He studied for a couple of seconds and nodded. 'Ok, when
you're ready.'

I looked through the lens. The map leapt towards my eyes. I
could never get used to this. I placed a small pencil dot where I
thought it should be and read off the easting, 'Easting 1 and 9.'
Eastings were the numbers across the top and bottom of the map.
Northings down the sides.

'1 and 9,' Joe confirmed.

I checked across to the right-hand edge of the map. 'Northings 2
and 3,'

'Northings 2 and 3.'

'Second eastings group,' I slid Joe's large ruler under the stand. It
was stainless steel, perfectly true and marked off in half-millimetres.
It was as precise an instrument as we had. '1 and 3.'

'1 and 3,' confirmed Joe.

'Second northings group,' I adjusted the ruler, '1 and 6.'

'1 and 6.'

I felt sick and cold. This was a test spot. Just a mile from home.
It was where Christine Jones' body had been discovered in 1949.
What the Hell was it doing on Wainwright's list? Had I screwed
up somewhere along the line? Or could Wainwright have been
involved? Were all the numbers linked? I stepped back from the table
and took the pad from Joe, then opened my pocket book. 'The actual
reference is 19 10 23 17.'

Joe looked at me closely. Then at the map and the notes I was
holding. 'You did this from memory?' he indicated the dot on the
map.

I just nodded.

He leant across the table and checked which map I'd been using, then studied the detail. 'This is to do with your father's death, isn't it?'

I took a deep breath and sighed. 'Honestly Joe? I don't know what to think. But if it's not it's one hell of a coincidence. But I could be wrong.' If, and I meant if I was correct, Wainwright had a list of twelve possible map references which may relate to a series of missing from homes, possibly murders, stretching back over fifteen years. In one way or another one of them may have involved my father. If I was right.

I remembered Joe from years ago. From the first time I saw him. We'd wandered into his karate class, all energy and fun and his three five year old daughters. Identical triplets. His wife had died of leukaemia three years earlier. He had the same light in his eyes then as he had now. But he wasn't just Joe. He'd helped me to deal with the grief and anger that followed my father's murder. Made Mum and me smile. He even had tears in his eyes the first time I called him, Dad. He wasn't just a loving step father he was now my friend. He had even been my Best Man when Lucy and I married. All that he could do now was to be there for me again and check my figures.

'You ok?' he said yanking me out of my reverie.

'Fine,' I replied. 'Just having a moment.'

'Private?'

'No, just thinking about the day we first met.'

He laughed and put his arm round my shoulders. 'There's a lot of water gone under a lot of bridges since then,' he said. 'We've both grown a lot. Are you going to call somebody?'

'I ought to,' I said, 'but I don't want to go off at half-cock and look a fool ... I want to check them all.'

Joe smiled again. 'Seeing you as you are now, Brian, your father would have been proud of you, really proud. Even more than we are.'

It was moments like this I would have loved to have swapped notes with my father. This wasn't possible. I had to make my own judgements. Stand or fall on my own. Nevertheless, it didn't stop me thinking. In one sense, everything I did was connected to my father's death. He died when I was eight. I suppose he was my hero. I could still picture the last birthday card he drew for me. Here was something that may connect to his death. A connection to his work as a copper. A direct link to him. I would be lying if I said I wasn't determined to find the truth behind these numbers. My father had made Detective Sergeant in eight years, unbelievable in those days. I needed to do this for him. The question was. Was I big enough to fill his boots?

Joe looked concerned. 'I don't know how to ask this, Brian, but you've said there's more than one number. The one we've just checked may be related to your father's death. Are they all related? ... To do with? ... You don't have to tell me, but ...'

'Sorry, Joe, I just don't know. It depends on what my boss says.'

We went through the same procedure with the first entry on the list – 1708 1345. I felt even more sick. 'If this is the right map,' I stood back from the table, 'This reference is in Greenhead Park.'

'Oh fuck!'

That made me laugh. 'I've never heard you swear like that before.'

I got an answering protest. 'I've never done anything like this before. How many numbers are there?'

I held my pocket book out.

He looked at me in disbelief. 'God Almighty,' he gasped. 'There are twelve!' He looked worse than I felt. 'This stays in this room.'

'Thanks.'

Next. Joe checked my measurements. Confirm or otherwise. We agreed.

The second entry – 2876 0974 was Cawthorne Park.

Number three we already knew.

Fourth – 3355 1470, Newmillerdam.

Fifth – 2693 1530, Midgely.

Sixth – 3701 3176, Temple Newsam House, Leeds

Seventh – 2130 3100, Park Wood, Tong.

Eight – 1172 0462, Yateholme.

Ninth – 0353 1429, Cupwith Hill, Nont Sarahs. That rattled Joe. The location was about four miles up the A640 towards Denshaw. We used to walk all over those moors. Go on picnics and swim in Cupwith Hill reservoir. It was where he taught us to read maps.

Tenth – 1991 0182, The Flouch, Penistone

Eleventh – 1640 1350, Farnley Bank, Farnley Tyas.

Twelfth – 1543 3643, Cold Hiendley, Wakefield.

It was a grim-faced Joe who put the pad back on the table and stood back. 'So that's it?'

'Just one more, Joe.' He looked puzzled until I opened OS Map 104 and placed the ruler to the west of Westleigh. 'Make a note of this will you. Eastings 1 and 7 ... ... northings 2 and 5 ... second eastings group 6 and 2 ... second northings group 4 and 3, Westleigh.'

'That's this Dunster girl?'

I nodded. 'Yep, if I'm right that would be the reference. But she's not on the list.'

Twenty-Eight

The phone began to ring. I looked at my watch. It had taken us near enough forty minutes.

'This is your weekend off, Blake,' there was the hint of a smile in the DCI's menacing tone. 'You'd better have a bloody good explanation why we're having this conversation.'

'Yes sir. I think I know what Wainwright's numbers refer to.'

'I'm listening.'

'I think that Mr Henderson may have been correct. They're ordnance survey map references.'

His chair creaked as he sat up. 'Eight digit map references?'

'Yes sir.'

'Just a minute ...' I heard the phone clatter on his desk. About a minute later he came back. 'In a square kilometre there are one million square metres. A six digit reference will give you an area one hundred metres square. That's ten thousand square metres. But the extra digits reduce that by ninety nine percent to just one hundred square metres, an area ten by ten.'

'That's correct, sir.'

'Have you taken this any further? Checked your hypothesis?'

'I have. All Wainwright's numbers are possible OS map locations on maps covering the southern half of the West Riding.'

'I see ... you realise where this may lead?'

'Yes sir.'

'Very well. Talk me through your thoughts.'

'It was after our first conversation when you told me about my father. I visited the farm where Christine Jones was murdered. The

84

old farmer and his wife both died some years ago. The farm is now owned by their son, Colin. He showed me where her body was found I....'

'Just a second,' he interrupted. 'Are you suggesting that Wainwright was involved with the death of Christine Jones?'

'If you have a copy of Wainwright's list to hand, sir, the spot where her body was found is the third reference on the list.'

If he hadn't been before, the DCI was now wide awake. 'Are you absolutely certain?'

'As I can be, sir. I have to admit it shook me rigid when I realised, and, assuming that I have the right map. Joe has a high powered lens, that's how I managed to check down to four figures.'

'Joe? He was with you?'

'Yes sir. He checked my figures.'

'If he's still there can I speak to him?'

I handed him the phone. 'Mr Valentine?'

Joe looked at me and smiled, 'Yes, I agree, he is ...'

'... RAF photographic interpretation and intelligence ... 1940 to 1946 ...'

'Brian made the initial search and called the references out; I noted them down. When each one was finished I checked his measurements ... to within point zero one.'

'Yes, of course,' he passed me the phone.

'Sir?'

'I accept that we have a basis to proceed further. But tell me, what gave you the idea?'

'Do you remember me mentioning an old university colleague, Norman Castle.'

'Yes, he was doing a PhD in archaeology, wasn't he?'

'He was. In fact we went to the same school. I bumped into him just over an hour ago. He's in our kitchen now drinking coffee ...' It didn't take long to explain my 'light bulb' moment.

'Like father like son,' he said. 'This is the kind of link that he made, quite often successfully. But you understand what this means?' That was the second time in as many minutes he had asked me that question.

'I understand, sir. Wainwright and at least one other have been very busy.'

'Correct, and in case it had crossed your mind you cannot have some time alone with him. Revenge is not a part of our modus operandi. Now, where's the first one on the list?'

'Greenhead Park, Huddersfield, sir.'

'Dear God!'

'However, Sally Dunster isn't on the list. I've checked.'

'Right. Please give my apologies to Lucy and the rest of your family. I'm recalling you to duty. I won't keep you any longer than is absolutely necessary, that I promise. A road traffic car will be with you within the next thirty minutes. ~And will put your overtime on your card.'

It wasn't too bad once I'd acceded to Jen's demand and confirmed that what I was doing was in some way connected to the death of Sally Dunster. I was sure that Joe, and Mum if necessary, could keep her diverted from the whole truth. Whether Joe would confide fully in Mum I had no idea. However, I trusted his judgement.

My transport arrived fifteen minutes later. I introduced Sergeant Canon to Norman Castle. Norman threw his head back and roared with laughter giving the impersonation that I knew him for, that of Fancy Smith, the actor Brian Blessed, star of the tv programme Z-Cars. There was no time to chat, we had to go.

Twenty-Nine

'Thought you were weekend off, Brian,' was the general comment that met me when I walked into the Hecton office. Almost everyone was present, but there was one face I didn't know – I soon would.

'So did I,' I replied. 'That'll teach me to open my big mouth.'

'Barmy bugger.' Derek Myers grinned.

Seconds later the DCI entered and put the black box on the table. DI Henderson joined us. 'Pleased you could make it, Blake,' the DCI said. 'A lot has happened in the last few hours. But before I tell you why Pc Blake is honouring us with his presence I'll bring you up to date ... This morning a phone call was received from Sandra, Sally Dunster's friend. She thought Sally's boyfriend's name was short. Began with the letter 'I', similar to Igor.'

'That narrows it down a bit, I suppose,' observed DS Cartwright.

'It does. Secondly, and this stays in this room, Forensic have reported that the semen sample taken from Sally Dunster indicates that the rapist is a secretor. You're *au fait* with that, Blake?'

'Yes sir.'

'No sir, I'm not.'

Yes, well I think I'll let Pc Blake explain it to DC Cavendish,' he nodded to me.

I looked round and identified DC Cavendish. The one I didn't know. 'From memory, approximately eighty percent of the population. A secretor puts their blood group into other body fluids: saliva, semen, mucus, etc, so you can get their blood group from non-blood fluids. Ok?'

'Cheers,' he replied, but he didn't look happy.

'Excuse me, sir.'

'Yes, Riley?'

'For the first time I understand. When I was on my C.I.D. course we had a presentation from Forensic. He just talked about stuff like antigens and antibodies. It was so far over my head I got a crick in my neck looking at it.'

Before the DCI could comment DC Cavendish put his size nines well and truly in it as his stage whisper carried across the room. 'He's a bloody sprog. I'm not going to be lectured to by a probationer.'

The room was deathly silent as the DCI fixed his eyes on DC Cavendish; his voice was so calm it was menacing. 'DC Cavendish?'

'Sir?'

'When I speak to you, you stand.'

The acutely embarrassed detective stood. 'Sir?'

'Pc Blake,' he began, 'like everyone else on my squad is hand-picked by me. There isn't a single person in this room, with one exception, that doesn't respect and trust him implicitly. I asked him to do a job and in thirty seconds he had explained a complicated matter to you and clarified the issue in the mind of another of my officers. That makes *him* a better detective. Pc Blake has a Batchelor of Science degree from East Midlands University because he has a brain, which he uses. Do you know what is in that black cash box on the table behind me?'

'No, sir.' DC Cavendish was not enjoying this.

The DCI looked to his right. 'DC Jackson?'

'It's a single sheet of paper, sir,' he replied, standing. 'Wainwright kept it in that box and always kept the key in his possession. It was brought in by his wife. On it is a series of twelve eight-digit numbers that maybe is connected in some way but he refuses to talk.' At this point he broke into a smile. 'However, judging from its presence here now, I suspect we might shortly know more about it and why Brian has suddenly re-appeared.'

A slight smile crossed the DCI's face. 'Patience, and it will be rewarded. Less than two hours ago, Pc Blake was *theoretically* enjoying his well-earned weekend off with his wife and infant daughter, visiting his parents. Whilst out for a run with his wife and sister he happened across a former student from East Midlands University. One that you know of, a certain Doctor Castle who is very knowledgeable with reference to religious castration.' A pause for the laughter and crossed legs. 'During their conversation he had what he describes as a flash of perspiration and realised just what those numbers might represent. Shortly afterwards spent almost threequarters of an hour of his own time, assisted by his stepfather, testing his hypothesis. There is a strong possibility that he may be correct. Hence everyone's appearance here. DC Cavendish, should you ever challenge any decision of mine or DI Henderson's in the future. Or disrespect any member of my team no matter how superior you consider yourself to be, then I guarantee that you will spend the rest of your service on uniform foot patrol, in Maltby. Do I make myself clear?'

'Abundantly, sir,' replied the ashen-faced detective. I wasn't surprised he was shocked – Maltby? No wonder. He turned to me, 'I apologise.' I nodded acceptance.

'Very well,' the DCI said as DC Cavendish sank into the pseudo-anonymity of his seat. 'I don't want to have to do that again.' He glanced round the room. There were no comments. 'Just waiting for two more. Oh, one more point, John,' he said to DS Nicholson. 'All being well, from today you will be working hand-in-glove with Pc Blake.' He raised his eyebrows and nodded.

Thirty

We all stood as the door swung open, Albert Weatherspoon, Assistant Chief Constable Crime entered, followed by divisional commander, Chief Superintendent Williams, Detective Chief Superintendent Mithering, Headquarters C.I.D., and Detective Superintendent Creighton, Southern Area C.I.D.

Mr Williams smiled as he walked passed. 'Good afternoon, Blake.'

'Good afternoon, sir.' He'd served with my father. I wondered how he would react to what I was about to explain.

It was obvious from DCS Mithering's expression that he would rather be somewhere else.

'Chief Inspector, will this take long?' Asked the ACC. 'Mr Mithering and I have been pulled away from other matters.' They had been invited to the Director's box to watch Leeds v Burnley.

The DCI looked at me. 'Ten to fifteen minutes, sir,' I replied, standing. 'Give or take.' It should take less but always better to err on the side of caution.

'Excellent,' the ACC declared. 'Are these seats for us?' He directed his question at the DCI, but without waiting for a reply picked up a chair and carried it to the back of the room, followed by the others. 'My eyes work better at long range these days,' he said as they sat down.

The DCI turned to me. 'Got your box of tricks, Blake?'

'Yes sir,' I said, pleased that I had been warned *two* senior officers would be attending. I put my box on the table and took everything out: maps, ruler, Joe's note pad and, last but by no means least, his lens.

'Thank you for coming gentlemen,' the DCI began. 'I appreciate that it was very short notice and has probably interfered with whatever you had planned for this afternoon. However, when Pc Blake called me just over an hour ago and told me what he's about to explain, I thought his idea had legs. When he told me how he had tested his hypothesis I was certain that it deserved further investigation. So I'll hand you over. Blake?'

As I stepped forward DS Creighton spoke, 'Excuse me. Pc Blake, is it?'

'Yes sir.'

'Detective Superintendent Creighton. I have to admit that this is the first time I've been lectured to by a probationer.'

That made me smile. 'More of a presentation, followed by a practical, sir.'

'Hmm,' he sounded doubtful. 'I was under the impression that the idea of Wainwright's list of numbers being OS map references had been ruled out simply because of the number of digits. Yet you've just put a stack of maps on the table along with what looks like a pretty useful lens.'

Before I could answer DCS Mithering jumped in. 'Give the lad a chance, Mike, otherwise we'll be here all day.'

DS Creighton smiled at me. 'Sorry.'

'Yes sir. You're correct and I believe the answer is possibly one of scale.' I switched the overhead projector on. Put a sheet of acetate on the platen and drew a freehand single square cell with the four lines intersecting at the corners. The vertical lines I numbered 22 and 23, from left to right. The horizontal lines 55 and 56 from bottom to top. This wasn't the simplest thing I'd ever done and called for a slow delivery.

'Sir, this is a representation of a single grid square that you would see on any OS map. Where the lower-left lines, 22 and 55 intersect, it could be referred to as point 2255 but in fact refers to the entire square ... to identify a single point or a smaller area within square 22 55 and, using a standard map reference you have to insert a third digit between the second 2 and the 5 and add a sixth. For example 220 550 ... the third and sixth digits breaking the sides of the square into tenths ... Therefore, the square into one hundred equal areas ... The point 220 550 would be the point where the lines intersected.' I passed a couple of OS maps out. 'The squares are of side 1 kilometre, an area of one million square metres. So, even by using a six point reference, which may be accurate, it is also the south-west, or bottom left corner of an area one 1/100 of the area of the square, or ten thousand square metres.'

I paused for a few seconds. DS Creighton chipped in. 'That's bloody good thinking, Blake,' he said, nodding. 'And by adding the extra digits you can reduce the area by, what?' He narrowed his eyes and rocked his head slowly from side to side, 'ninety nine percent, to one hundred square metres, or ten metres square. But not possible unless you can change the scale, because these squares,' he indicated the map in Mr Williams' hand, 'are too small. hence the appearance of your lens.'

'That was my line of thinking, sir.'

'I'm impressed. How did you think of it?'

'Earlier today I bumped into an archaeologist that I know. He runs a Saturday club for his senior students. They use a device like this,' – I drew the survey grid on a second acetate. 'It's a perfectly square mesh. When I saw it, it was a large scale OS map without the features. Just the grid. You get the idea from the cell I drew on the projector a few minutes ago.' I exchanged the acetate on the platen with my earlier effort.

It was suddenly deathly quiet.

DI Henderson joined in. 'Are you saying that these are eight digit map references?'

'What I'm suggesting, sir, is, it's a possibility. I've checked every number on Wainwright's list. Each one is a *possible* OS map-reference in the West Riding area south of Leeds and Bradford. But, I could be wrong.'

'Pc Blake,' ACC Weatherspoon chipped in. 'I'm not suggesting that you have made any mistakes, but has anyone confirmed your figures?'

The DCI held his hand up as I was about to answer. 'I can answer that, sir. Joe Mountain, Pc Blake's stepfather, worked with him in calculating and checking his figures. I spoke with Joe after Pc Blake contacted me. All the paraphernalia on the table is Joe's. He worked in RAF photographic interpretation and intelligence from 1940 to 1946.'

'I see,' the ACC nodded. 'You have these locations, Blake?'

'Yes sir. The first location is in Greenhead Park, Huddersfield.'

'Bloody Hell!' that was from Jacko and shocked looks all round.

'A public park?' Queried Mr Williams.

'Yes sir. Just below the larger of the two putting greens.'

'I know that park. Aren't there some rhododendrons there?'

'Yes sir. A large bank of rhododendrons that surround the offices of the park staff.'

Mr Williams nodded. 'Carry on.'

'The second is Cawthorne Park,' there were no comments. 'The third location is one that I know to be true. On the 1st of April 1949 a young prostitute called Christine Jones was murdered on this spot ...'

Detective Chief Superintendent Mithering leapt to his feet. 'STOP RIGHT THERE.' He thundered, his animosity taking everyone by surprise. 'This is a cockamamie idea. It's plain nonsense. This Dunster woman was buried. Jones wasn't. Dunster was strangled. Jones had her throat cut. The M.O.'s all wrong. Don't they teach you anything at Pannal these days? Criminals do not change their M.O. Your figures may be by chance the same as map references but this does not follow. It's a waste of time.' By the time he'd finished his face was flushed, he was breathless and perspiring. Not a good sign.

That woke everyone up. 'I appreciate that, sir. But Yarney was not working alone.'

'Oh really,' he replied, the sarcasm dripping from his lips. 'You were barely out of nappies. How do you know that?'

One thing that I'd learnt was that when people start playing the man and not the ball they're struggling. It needed to be answered. If he would let me. 'There are three reasons that come to mind, sir. I've read the file,' I'd read the file on numerous occasions. 'Yarney couldn't drive and yet he managed to get from Littletown to this police station liberally covered in Jones' blood without any public sighting. This is highly unlikely if he were on foot or using public transport or a taxi. Secondly, when he escaped from hospital twelve months later he had to have had transport. Enquiries at the time with local taxi firms and bus companies were negative. Had he been on foot he couldn't have reached Littletown by the time it was reported that he had taken a woman and her daughter hostage. Thirdly, and to my mind the most telling, if Wainwright is not somehow involved, why is that specific eight digit reference on his list?'

I could tell from his face that I'd made a friend for life. Although he had calmed down somewhat his face was still flushed. 'Well, I've heard enough.' Then Mr Williams introduced a welcome note of comedy into the mix.

He looked up at the angry DCS. 'Gilbert, stop waving your arms about you make the place look untidy. And please sit down before you have a heart attack.'

'Pah.' was the reply as the slightly embarrassed senior detective slumped back on his chair which immediately rocked onto its back legs. The occupant lucky that gravity didn't join in. 'Bloody Hell.' He said and laughed as he struggled to get his chair straight. He managed with a little help from Jenny Sendrove and Mr Williams. The tension dissipated. 'Thank you, Miss Sendrove,' he acknowledged and smiled.

'You're welcome, sir.'

It had just settled down when DS Creighton pitched in again. 'Blake, A couple of minutes ago you discussed with great in-depth knowledge a case the happened some time ago, 1st of April, 1949. Now I'm not saying you were wearing nappies,' he paused and waited for the laughter to cease. 'But you must have been, what, seven or eight years of age? Have I missed a trick somewhere along the line?'

Before I could answer DCI Valentine did. 'No sir, you're quite correct. Pc Blake was seven years of age. Yarney, the man who admitted to cutting Christine Jones' throat appeared at the front desk in this station. Put a blood stained craft knife on the public counter and asked speak to someone from C.I.D. That someone was Detective Sergeant Douglas Blake, Pc Blake's father. Subsequently, following lengthy psychiatric analysis, the Judge declared that he was unfit to plead. Apart from identifying the location where the murder had taken place, all Yarney would say during interviews was that he was, "Doing the Lord's work". He was subsequently sentenced to be detained at His Majesty's pleasure. Twelve months later he feigned injury. He was taken to hospital where he was left unsupervised on a visit to the toilet and escaped through a window. A short time later took a young woman, a Mrs Collins and her daughter hostage but stated he would allow the woman and her daughter to go free if he could surrender to DS Blake. DS Blake was fatally stabbed whilst securing their release. I was present. He was distracted by Mrs Collins saying something to him as they left the house. Yarney took advantage. He was transferred to a secure facility where he died nine years later. In my honest opinion he should have been topped. However, with all respect to you, sir,' he said to Mr Mithering. 'Pc Blake was correct in what he said about Yarney's travel arrangements. He couldn't drive. Whoever else was involved, and someone else must have been, they have either taken their secrets to the grave, or, kept their mouths shut and we haven't found them. I accept, as does Blake, that this presentation may be just an intellectual exercise. However, in the last fifteen years we have gotten absolutely nowhere, perhaps until today.'

Chris Wilson, the office clerk, knocked smartly at the door. 'There's an urgent call in the office, sir,' he said to the DCI. 'It's from forensic.'

'If you'll excuse me, sir,' he nodded to the ACC and left.

'That's quite a story, Blake,' DS Creighton said. 'It must have been tough. Tell me, when did you realise that the third reference was possibly from Wainwright's list.'

'Only after I had checked the relevant map and calculated the spot.'

'You copied it from the list?'

'No sir, from memory. I've been to the farm. The present farmer, the son of the farmer in 1949, showed me the spot where Christine Jones was murdered,' I took the pad from the table and handed it to him. 'The top line is where Joe wrote down the figures I called out. Beneath is where Joe wrote down the reference from Wainwright's list. I know that location by heart. Once I was half way through I knew it was the same.'

'Your memory's quite good, just a tenth or so out.'

I smiled and nodded, 'Yes sir.'

'I see you checked them all.'

'Yes sir. In case you're wondering, Sally Dunster for some reason is not on that list.' *Why was it missing*?

He smiled. 'Yes, I was, actually, thank you.'

The ACC held his hand out for the pad. 'May I, Mr Creighton?' After a quick glance at the list. 'Blake, I see all the locations are on this pad. Instead of you reading them out, we can read them. Now will you demonstrate how you did your calculations?'

The fact that Messrs Weatherspoon and Mithering were in a rush seemed to have slipped their minds. Once I'd demonstrated the process the team couldn't get near the table for senior officers. They were like children on Christmas Day. I wandered across to the DI. 'Sorry sir. I didn't anticipate this.'

'You haven't met enough senior officers,' he replied under his breath triggering smiles from those nearest.

'We'll be out of your hair shortly, Mr Henderson,' Mr Williams smiled.

'Yes sir,' he grimaced as Mr Valentine walked in and motioned the DI to join him with the others.

It wasn't a heated discussion, however, there was some excitement in the air. Thirty seconds later the DCI nodded and the group broke up. 'Find a seat,' he said to the room at large.

'After I'd spoken with Pc Blake earlier,' he began. 'I called forensic to check on some information I received some time ago just to make sure I'd remembered it correctly. The call that I've just taken confirms the original data and adds a little more to our knowledge. You remember our earlier chat with regard to secretors?' For some reason everybody did. 'The trigger for my enquiry was the mentioning by Pc Blake of Christine Jones,' he paused and looked at me.

I thought for a few seconds. 'Also a secretor, sir?'

'The same.'

'Same blood group? But if that's A positive, that will be huge.'

'Very close. AB positive.'

I whistled. 'That's not a common group.'

'According to forensic, three percent.'

'Christ,' exclaimed Jacko. 'What are the odds on there being two such men in these circumstances?'

It was so quiet you could have heard grass grow. People just sat and looked at each other. 'Somewhere between slim and zero. Which means,' the DCI paused as if he was trying to find the right words. 'That the three or more people who were involved in the rape and murder of Christine Jones some fifteen years ago, and led to the murder of Pc Blake's father are still acting in concert. And, involved in the death of Sally Dunster three days ago. I will stress,' he scanned us all. 'That information stays-in-this-room. The last thing we need is a panic!'

A sudden thought hit me like a thunderbolt. 'Sir?' I caught the DCI's attention.

'Yes, what is it?'

'Do you happen to know Magnus Yarney's blood group, because if ...'

'Chief Inspector!' The ACC snapped.

'Sir?' he said turning to the angry ACC.

'We all know that Pc Blake is very clever, but can we not lapse into flights of fancy. From the work he's done so far I'm sure you have enough to occupy your minds.'

Who's pissed on your cornflakes? I thought. That put a downer on the proceedings.

'I'll have a word with him, sir. And you want to know why I said three.'

'In a word, Yes.'

'Magnus Yarney, the man who cut Christine Jones throat died seven years ago in Broadmoor was not a secretor. '

'Well, what about Wainwright?'

There were smiles all round which seemed to displease the ACC. 'There's a small problem with Wainwright, sir. This has been confirmed by Doctor O'Keefe, the divisional police surgeon.

Wainwright has no testicles. Removed either by a butcher, or, an amateur. Hence the third man.'

Mr Williams already knew, however there was a shared look of intense pain on the faces of both DCS Mithering and DS Creighton, but no reaction from the ACC. 'Do we know when or why?' he asked.

'Not exactly, sir. According to the Doctor's report it was several decades ago.'

'And you have no idea as to who this third man might be?'

'No, sir. Magnus Yarney, other than claiming he was *doing the Lord's work,* refused to participate in the interviews.'

'What about Yarney's antecedents,' DS Creighton asked.

'Done by a local C.I.D. officer, sir, Keighley division. If my memory serves that element of the report stated that Yarney had no family and was a bit of a loner. There's a couple of statements on the original file which shed no light on the matter other than he came across as an odd-ball. There's a conflict somewhere. Reassessing the original Jones' file will be a part of this enquiry as to what, if anything, went wrong.'

'Quite,' the ACC replied. 'And what do you propose to be your plan of action?'

The DCI looked at me in a manner that gave me a strange feeling. 'In view of the revelation linking the murders of Dunster and Jones plus Pc Blake's connection, there's a strong argument that he is emotionally too close and should be removed from the enquiry.'

What!?

He put his hand up when he saw my reaction. 'Nevertheless, after the work that he's done, especially today, I can't think of anyone who deserves to be part of the team more than he does, even non-operational. He is, however, still a probationer and on Mr William's divisional strength, I will discuss it with him and submit a report to the Chief.'

'Well,' said Chief superintendent Williams, 'you have my support.' *Thank you, sir.* I nodded in acknowledgement.

'And mine,' said DS Creighton. 'Blake, when I heard that *you* were giving this presentation, I was, erm, concerned. But I found your presentation and demonstration of your techniques compelling. After Mr Valentine's news with regards to the blood group etc, we need to carry out a couple of investigations to ascertain the facts, one way or another.' Even DCS Mithering said I had a compelling explanation, even though he was not convinced that I was right. To be honest, neither was I.

ACC Weatherspoon didn't object but insisted that I be kept on a tight rein so as not to blot my copybook after a promising start to my career. Was this what the DCI had in mind when he said earlier that he wanted to see DS Nicholson and me later?

My ten minute presentation had lasted over thirty minutes and kick-off at Elland Road was in the next ten. On match days it was at least a thirty minute drive from here. Ah well.

'To get back to my original question, Mr Valentine.' The ACC still sounded terse. Perhaps he was missing his football. 'What action do you propose?'

'To use the first and the last numbers on Wainwright's list, sir. As Mr Creighton said, we need a couple to test Blake's theory. Once we know one way or the other we'll know what we're up against.

'When will you begin?'

'Monday, sir. Greenhead Park is very popular especially at weekends. Monday first thing will be much quieter. In addition it will give me the time to make the proper arrangements. After all these years an extra twenty four hours shouldn't make a great deal of difference.'

Thirty-One

Messrs Weatherspoon and Mithering left to try and catch the final whistle at Elland Road. Mr Williams to speak with the Chief Constable. I showed the team how I'd used Joe's lens. Detective Superintendent Creighton stayed to chat with the DCI and DI Henderson.

The DCI clapped his hands twice. 'All right everybody leave Joe's toys and sit down ... Assuming that Mr Barton agrees and Pc Blake is allowed to remain with us he will be handcuffed, metaphorically, to DS Nicholson. They will act as a two-man team when Blake is outside of the station. Can't let him loose on his own creating havoc and mayhem as he sees fit,' he held his hand up, the laughter subsided. 'When the need arises, Blake, you will work with WDC Farthing assisting with any exhibits.'

'Yes sir.' I couldn't have expected more.

'First things first. Special court. Mark, charge Wainwright with being an accessory after the fact. Have a word with Inspector Felton. I know it's Saturday but see if he can rustle up a special court this afternoon. That will do as a holding charge. And make an application for him to be remanded to police cells pending further enquiries. Next thing,' he said as the door closed behind the Inspector, 'DC Myers, first thing Monday contact the National Blood Transfusion Service, we need to know how many, if any, donors they have listed who are AB positive. And a nationwide list of those who are. '

'They have an office in Leeds, sir. I'll contact their supervisor, start there.'

'Fine. They may be reticent about divulging details. But worry about that if it happens.'

'Sir.'

'Right. Security. No pillow talk. No chatting over a jar, especially with other coppers. And, be damned careful over the air. Our channels are monitored by the press and others. We don't want your information appearing on the front page of the Post. Be careful. If Blake is right, sooner or later the shit will hit the fan with a vengeance. Refer any relevant enquiries to HQ Press Office. Give them something useful to do. Whatever happens we need to keep it under wraps for as long as possible ... Next point. If you haven't worked it out yet, assuming that Blake is correct, with that additional link between Dunster and Jones I believe that the balance of probabilities has swung markedly in favour. Monday, I hope, will provide an answer. We may be looking for another eleven bodies. From Wainwright's list there is one in each of: Huddersfield, Leeds, Bradford and Wakefield. The remainder are ours. We all know about inter–force rivalries, especially with talk of police amalgamations on the horizon. Any politics will be dealt with by myself and DI Henderson should that become necessary. Nevertheless, I expect you to be professional at all times. Any problems?

There were none.

'Your immediate job, John, is to work with Blake in re-calculating all the locations. Not only to reinforce Blake's earlier work but to ensure that should he not be available there is someone else who can take over.

Penny, get to know Elaine Carter. You know where she works. There's no love lost between her and Wainwright. Find out what she knows about Wainwright's business activities and the properties that she says he owns. Check with his solicitor. See if he will play ball. In addition, why is Adele Wainwright doing this? Pay-back time or what? Hand all the information over to DS Cartwright. We know next to nothing concerning Wainwright's early days. However, at the moment no-one is to go near Vernon Jeavons' house without my say-so. He can wait until we have more information.

Jenny, I want you and DC Cavendish to do the rounds of the Dunster's again. Also that friend of hers, Sandra. Thank her for the information re the boyfriend. See if she can dredge up any further information. When you've done that her former work colleagues and friends.'

'Yes sir,' she acknowledged.

DC Jackson, you're the senior DC. Whilst DS Nicholson is working with Blake, you will act up. In fact, it would be best if that were to be for the duration. Any problems?'

Jacko shook his head and smiled. 'Not from me, sir, there isn't. I can't speak for anyone else.'

The DCI returned his smile. 'Good ... Right I want to see all supervisory staff, new and old, and you Blake. The rest of you sign off and enjoy tomorrow. We begin at 0900 Monday. Off you go.'

As the last one left and the door closed Mr Valentine swivelled his chair round and sat facing us, his arms folded against the backrest. 'This is already a big job, come Monday it could be huge. In any case we will require an office manager. I've had a word with Chief Superintendent Williams and he's releasing Hazel for that task.'

'That's Hazel as in Hazel Granby, sir?' DS Cartwright asked tentatively.

'I thought you might like that,' he grinned at the expression on Peter Cartwright's face. Hazel was, to be polite, a martinet who cut her teeth as a doctor's receptionist but took a position with the police because she wanted a bigger challenge. What she didn't know about police regulations and expenses wasn't worth knowing. Woe betide ANY officer who couldn't add up. For goodness sake it was only a slip of the pencil. I've still got the bruises. Generally speaking they didn't make the same mistake twice. We had Hazel for the duration.

'A couple of points to close, both involving Pc Blake,' I don't know who looked more confused, me or the others. 'After the explosion at Westleigh, Blake, you're still in the eye of the press. That reporter from The Argus recognised you on the day of Dunster's post mortem. Once they realise what the investigation may become you will surface as a *person of interest*. That will attract attention. Secondly, we know that you're resilient. Apart from your adventures at Pannal and finding Sally Dunster's body you've dealt with sudden deaths and attended post mortems etc. But, and it's a big but, with the link to your father this is very close to home and no-one knows how this is going to affect you psychologically. I want you all to keep an eye on him. No need for the straight-jacket yet, just an eye.'

Apart from the DCI, DS Nicholson and myself were the last to leave. The DCI came across as we were setting the maps up. 'Right, what were you going to say?'

For a moment I wondered what he meant. 'Oh, yes, do you know Yarney's blood group, sir?'

'You've got me thinking now. I'm fairly certain it was type O, but I only asked about secretors. But you're thinking Yarney might be related in some way to either Wainwright or perhaps the rapist?'

'Yes sir. I was.'

'I agree, it's a fair point. But I have to agree with the ACC and it will have to wait. Put it in your book as with anything that springs to mind and make me or the DI aware at a convenient time. not when Mr Weatherspoon is around. And don't take his comments to heart.'

Thirty-Two

The DCI was still on the phone when., having re-checked everything twice DS Nicholson dropped me off at home. DI Henderson and Wainwright were still at court. Sneaking a few miles per hour it didn't take me long to reach Salendine Nook. What a surprise, Norman's van was still there. There was a reception committee and Mum threw her arms round my neck before I could close the door. She knew. By the look on everyone else's faces they thought they knew as well. Just what they thought they knew I wasn't sure.

'Brian, please be careful,' she whispered.

I wrapped my arms round her and kissed her on the cheek, 'It's all right, Mum,' I replied. 'Don't worry, *I'm* not in any danger, honestly.'

Claire made her presence known. Joe put his arm round Mum's shoulders. 'Come on, Dorothy, he'll be fine.'

Joe looked at me and nodded. I took charge of Miss Blake and got a kiss and that wonderful smile from Lucy. 'Is everything all right?' she asked, her eyes scanning my face for signs of stress. A knack she'd acquired from my first flight in an aeroplane.

'Everything's fine,' I said. What the reaction might be from Monday was anyone's guess.

Norman made his exit shortly afterwards. Jen came back with a broad smile after seeing him off. He'd asked her out for a drink the following Tuesday evening, down the road at the Spotted Cow.

Before we left, Joe and I had a quiet chat with Clive. Normally he could outtalk the yackety sax, and, for an eleven year old he was very perceptive. What he had gleaned from today had quietened him. Perhaps our chat had set his mind at rest.

As we were leaving Joe tugged my sleeve and raised a questioning eyebrow. 'Unless things have changed,' I said with my back to the others. 'We'll know by lunch-time Monday.' If there was anything it would be in the Stop Press of the Examiner. Mum always read the Examiner.

Sunday was Boston Spa day and Mum had been talking with Liz. It was, however, easier - no sisters. Liz asked the same question. 'By tomorrow lunch-time.'

We'd hardly closed the door when Claire began to protest at the telephone ringing. I had to be at Hecton by seven thirty in the morning.

Thirty-Three

Hecton was busy. Twice as many detectives as uniform. Half the team, including the DCI, heading for Huddersfield. DI Henderson had the remainder chasing up various lines of enquiry.

I was feeling apprehensive. Would I be known as the idiot who caused the destruction of a bed of rhododendrons that in a few weeks should be a riot of colour? Or, someone who had helped to bring closure to a family who had been grieving for over fifteen years? It was too late to worry about it now. Oh no it wasn't. I'd crossed the Rubicon. One positive thing, the Chief had agreed that I could remain on the team subject to tight restrictions. I would have the responsibility for pinpointing the locations to investigate. Should anything be found I would work with Penny. Our job, to log all exhibits and liaise with the Forensic Science Lab.

As you entered Greenhead Park by what was known as 'the top gates', in fact the wrought-iron gates had been removed in 1940 along with approximately two miles of iron railings to aid the war effort. In front of you on the right, the nine-hole putting green, beyond which are the tennis courts. On the left, the eighteen hole putting-green, beyond that a side road linking Park Drive with the main drive from the top gates, then the rhododendrons. It looked like a massive bed, fifteen feet high and dense. To some extent that was true. However, the rhododendrons surrounded the workmen's offices and workshops. I remember, not too many years ago, being chased out of there on more than one occasion. Today the sun was shining and I was staying. It was a beautiful park and like it or not the job had to be done.

Park Drive follows the park's north-eastern boundary. We parked on the town centre side of the side entrance adjacent to the lower end of the large putting green. There were fifteen present. Six from Hecton. The same from Huddersfield. Plus three park staff: Joe Briggs, Superintendent of Parks for Huddersfield. Rodney Lawrence, Greenhead Park supervisor. Duggie Dodds, spade wielder. Introductions and explanations made, an unbelieving Joe Briggs stood there open mouthed, 'Lawrence?'

Rodney Lawrence shook his head. 'Find that 'ard to believe, Mr Briggs, we'd 'ave noticed any disturbance int' topsoil,' he turned to the DCI. 'When did you say that it happened, sir?'

'Blake?'

'We believe sometime prior to 1st of April 1949, Mr Lawrence,' I replied. I hadn't felt as nervous as this since Lucy's first visit to the flat in Mirfield when she unzipped her motor cycle jacket, opening it wide and suggesting I pull the curtains.

'But, but, that's fifteen years ago,' he gasped. 'Maybe more. Where do we start to dig?'

'Between ten and twenty yards to your left,' I answered. That much I was certain of.

There were smirks from the Huddersfield Borough officers as the mighty 'We of the Riding', as we were uncomplimentarily known were about to get our comeuppance. 'Never heard so much crap,' DS Rhodes said. 'Who in their right bloody mind would bury a body next to a path in a public park?'

'Who in their right mind would have a need to bury a body, Sarge?' I said and took the tape measure and my compass from my pocket. 'Now, if you'll excuse me.'

As I walked passed him the Sergeant grabbed my arm. I looked at him. 'Why, you cheeky little sod. If you worked on my group I'd teach you some manners.'

'Leave him be, Sergeant. If there is a body here so much the good. If not, it's the Riding with egg on their faces.'

'Sir,' he replied and let go. 'You and me haven't finished this conversation.'

'I look forward to it, Sergeant.' *Nice bloke,* I thought.

Superintendent Edward 'Ted' Banks wasn't pleased at having to attend this *exhumation,* but the DI was off sick, so he stood at the DCI's side. DS Nicholson and I accompanied by Rodney Lawrence and Duggie Dodds, measured from the small drainage grate at the corner of the putting green, twenty five yards on a bearing of 135^0 - south east. I held the reel whilst Rodney Lawrence backed into the shrubbery and tripped over a branch. I wasn't daft. With a bit of a curse he stood up, 'Are you all right?' I called. Round about several grins appeared.

'Yes, thank you,' he grunted.

Slowly the distance on the tape increased. 'Okay Mr Lawrence,' I called. 'That's seventy five feet.' Tape and compass back in my pocket I went to have a look. Once inside the outer foliage it was remarkably open. The park staff referred to rhododendrons as shrubs. These were small trees and had been planted on a sloping bank. Fifteen feet tall, the lower branches over six inches thick in places trailing to ground level. Duggie Dodds was despatched to fetch a logging saw.

The C.I.D. officers coalesced into two groups with DCI Valentine and Detective Superintendent Banks standing apart.

'He's a bit young to be in C.I.D. Chief Inspector.'

'He's not in C.I.D., sir.' I heard the DCI say. 'He's on attachment, plus he's only got about eighteen months service.'

DS Nicholson and I grinned at each other as we heard a sharp almost explosive, 'What?' From Sergeant Rhodes.

We couldn't see anyone but we heard every word. 'Your fame is spreading, Brian.'

'Don't I know it, Sarge? Let's hope I'm right.'

'You convinced several senior officers, so, if this is a blank they're as much to blame as you.'

I didn't entirely buy that.

'Really?' The Detective Superintendent said. 'Then the deference that you afford him is justified?'

'I wouldn't go as far as to call it deference, but I do respect him as I do all my team, otherwise they wouldn't have been selected.'

'Quite,' Mr Banks mused. 'So, he's not C.I.D. He's a probationer and has your respect. That is a strong word to use from an officer of your rank about a probationer.'

He paused and studied the DCI's face looking for clues of which there was only a faint smile. 'In spite of his tender years he has been selected by you and given charge of taking these measurements where you suggest there may be a buried corpse. And, he was remarkably precise with that date, 1st of 'April, 1949. All that tends to lean towards the probability of that date in question is also when a murder occurred. How am I doing so far?'

'Pretty good, sir,' he acknowledged and smiled. As the Superintendent frowned several of the Huddersfield detectives had moved nearer in an attempt to earwig.

'You're giving nothing away, are you? Mind you, I wouldn't either. Sergeant Rhodes?'

'Sir?'

'Apart from the usual tomfoolery, what happened on or about the 1st of April, 1949?'

'Phew. Erm, long time ago, sir,' the sergeant replied and scratched his head.

Jeff Wheldon had joined the Huddersfield Borough police on his de-mob from the Army in 1946. He joined C.I.D. in 1950. 'Excuse me, sir?'

'Yes, what is it, Wheldon?'

'I couldn't help overhearing but I joined the Force in 1946. I seem to remember there was a police officer murdered about that time. I can't remember the exact date though, sorry.'

The Detective Superintendent thought for a moment, then nodded. 'Yes, Wheldon, you're quite correct.'

'I remember now,' DS Rhodes added. 'He was a DS in Leeds. Got himself stabbed making an arrest,' he paused and looked at the DCI. 'Didn't they call him Blake as well, sir?'

'He was actually a County man, Sergeant. But it was his father,' admitted the DCI. 'However, his father was killed almost a year to the day later, in March 1950.'

'The date that Pc Blake mentioned? An earlier murder connected to his father?' queried the Detective Superintendent.

'The arresting officer ...'

The area was marked out. I walked to the front of the shrubbery and interrupted their conversation. 'We're ready, sir.'

The uniformed officers fanned out to prevent early morning members of the public from getting too close. But that didn't prevent the natural protests from passers-by at the sight of the mass of Rhododendron branches lying on the drive. From the hard-packed nature of the ground there was no way that Duggie Dodds, or anyone else for that matter, could have expressed a reliable opinion as to whether someone had been digging fifteen years ago.

I explained where we were going to dig. The senior officers left. I took a new jar of Vicks from my pocket. There was in my mind a possibility that it would be required. Vicks Vapour Rub, handy for clearing the head. Also good for blocking the smell of decomposing corpses from turning you into a vomit machine. This one was at least fifteen years old and shouldn't be too bad. However, there was no point in taking unnecessary risks. I offered it round. Acceptance was split along force lines. For their sake I hoped I was wrong.

DS Nicholson and DS Rhodes plus the four of us, me, Kevin, Paul Calvert from Huddersfield and Duggie Dodds picked up our spades.

Mr Valentine followed Mr Banks and returned to their observation point. The latter folded his arms across his chest, settled on his left leg and gave Mr Valentine an accusatory stare. Mr Valentine laughed. 'You want to know why I have a probationer leading the excavation, don't you?'

Mr Banks said nothing, lowered his head and peered at Mr Valentine over his glasses.

'It's because only he knew where to dig.'

'No-one else?' said a shocked Superintendent. 'He's the only one?'

'Apart from those responsible for any burial in the first place, I suspect so. And my team following his presentation on Saturday, especially DS Nicholson, his minder.'

'This all stems from Wainwright?'

The DCI nodded. 'Yes, it does.

'Is this where I curb my curiosity?'

'For now, sir.'

Superintendent Banks chuckled to himself. 'I spoke with Mr Mithering on Saturday evening after Blake's presentation. Said Blake was too smart for his own good. Ruffled his feathers to some tune ... Oh, I've known Mr Mithering for years,' he continued in answer to Mr Valentine's puzzled look. 'He called me to let off steam, No, he didn't divulge anything, just said that the idea was cockamamie.'

'Yes he did,' laughed Valentine. 'But to be honest, Blake's theory was worth checking based on the results from his work alone. However we also have some forensic that supports his theory. The two together? It had to be done.'

Almost an hour later it wasn't looking good. Creating a ten metre square using the map reference as a centre, we cleared the ground to the depth of a spit. Two towards the centre, leaving only three rhododendrons in situ. We dug as close to the base of each plant as possible without them falling over. The mass of roots hadn't made our task any easier. Then, with the permission of Messrs Valentine and Banks a further two spade widths all round. That was now the full width of the bed. There was nothing. Not even a dead dog.

It was a sombre atmosphere as we began to leave the excavation. I wasn't sure how I felt. If I'd been right it would have fitted in perfectly with my theory that the numbers on Wainwright's sheet of paper were eight digit map references. Supporting the fact that the third set on the paper matched the location of Christine Jones' murder. It would have meant a huge amount of work. To somehow identify the remains. Give the relatives closure. Put the perpetrators behind bars. However, from this result I was wrong, although Mr Valentine had said we would excavate two further sites, just to make sure.

I scraped the mud from my boots across the top of the blade. Standing in the Park Drive entrance was Joe. I should have guessed he would make the effort. I waved to attract his attention. He acknowledged. I shook my head slowly and drew my forefinger across my throat.

Behind me there was a loud crack. A few seconds later DS Rhodes almost screamed. You could have heard it at Salendine Nook. 'Get these bloody things off me for Pete's sake.' In spite of the Vicks there was a faint but identifiable aroma that said it all.

Whether we had cut too close to the base of this particular rhododendron or the root system wasn't particularly robust, I don't know but DS Rhodes, who had ended up as tail-end-Charlie as we were leaving, slipped and made a reflex grab for the nearest thing. The rhododendron at the centre of the plot. The sudden jolt of his fifteen stone frame dragging it from the ground.

It was disrespectful. We shouldn't have laughed. But, in spite of the stench and the fact we were dealing with human remains I have to admit that the sight of DS Rhodes in that situation was funny. He vehemently disagreed. It was a sight that would remain with me for a long time. When Wainwright, or whoever it was, had buried the body it was very close to the base of the plant. Now, over fifteen years later, it was a tree. The mass of roots having invaded the skull conspiring to keep it intact. DS Rhodes was flat on his back his head almost touching the roots. Suspended inches above his face was a complete human skull. Roots like small snakes protruding through both eye sockets and between the mandible and maxilla. The entire skull nodding gently. For the first time in who knows how many years it was almost as if it was welcoming the sun. Vertebrae and a single clavicle were lying on his chest. I gave him a hand up and offered him the Vicks. 'Thanks,' he acknowledged and took a healthy dollop daubing it under his nose with one hand and brushed the loose soil from his head and coat with the other. 'Enough to give you the willies.' He said and shuddered. He didn't appear too badly scarred and any thought of continuing our conversation seemed to have slipped his mind. Nevertheless he shook my hand, 'No hard feelings?'

'About what, Sarge?'

'You'll do. Next time you're passing Peel Street, call in and we can go for a jar.' The offer tantamount to a peace treaty.

A couple of the Huddersfield lads got a bit sniffy when I refused to tell them how I'd worked it out. They'd live.

DS Nicholson's comment of, 'I was beginning to get a bit worried there, Brian,' matched my own.

It wasn't exactly party-time. However, any negativity had disappeared with the appearance of the skull. Mr Banks now took over supervision of the exhumation. It was his area and he had the men available. I wasn't required. Nevertheless, I stayed close and observed. The Huddersfield Borough police photographer arrived to take his photographs. A call went through to forensic. Expert supervision would be required to do the job properly. Having cleared so much topsoil and assisted by DS Rhodes' unintended acrobatics it didn't take too long to expose the remainder of the skeleton. Nevertheless, there was time enough for me to see that it was a female pelvis. I didn't need to see any more. Potentially thirteen bodies separated by over fifteen years. The first and the third on Wainwright's list were both female, as was Sally Dunster. What were the chances they all would be? The twelfth on the list would be this afternoon.

DI Henderson paid us a fleeting visit and had a quick chat with the DCI. He took a look in the grave and left, no doubt to inform DCS Mithering. There were enough Huddersfield Borough bobbies continuing the exercise, one more would be too many.

I brought Joe through the cordon. He had his own jar of Vicks. I introduced him to the DCI who thanked him for his assistance and asked after Mum. Pleasantries exchanged Joe left to pass the information on to Mum, and others.

The members of the public who were gathering both inside the park and in Park Drive were increasing rapidly. Shortly afterwards a hearse arrived parking at the bottom end of the putting green. Minutes later members of the Examiner staff arrived – it always amazed me how fast they could get there – they had to take their photos from distance.

Detective Superintendent Creighton arrived, threading his way through the crowd. 'You were right, Blake,' he said and smiled. 'Well done.'

After a bit of a confab and shaking of hands Messrs Creighton and Banks went to have a look at the remains. Two minutes later we were in the process of wrapping up when Mr Banks came over and buttonholed the DCI. 'You've been a bit tight-lipped about the scale of what you're dealing with. I know there's a conference tomorrow, Chief Inspector, but now we know the result of this morning's exercise can you tell me the scale of this operation?'

I can't think of anyone who would receive the news that we were looking for another eleven bodies by simply raising an eyebrow, but he did, 'And there is just this one in our area?'

'To the best of our knowledge, sir, yes.'

He nodded and turned to me. 'Blake.'

'Sir?'

He paused. A half smile playing on his lips. 'You had a trip to the palace, I understand. George Cross?'

I returned the smile. 'Yes sir.'

'Congratulations,' he held his hand out. 'I'm reliably informed that it concerned the security services?'

'Yes sir.'

'Beware of their alchemy, it could drive you mad. Now, every good detective deserves luck. Most of it they make themselves. You probably gathered that we were somewhat sceptical. However, you were right and we were wrong. I don't say that very often,' he said. 'Once you realised what the implications were it took a certain amount of courage to contact Chief Inspector Valentine. Even more to give that presentation to your ACC,' he laughed at my expression. 'I explained to Mr Valentine earlier, I've known Mr Mithering for a long time. I think he made it clear to you that he was not impressed.'

'Yes sir, he did,' I said and grimaced.

He smiled by return. 'Trust your hunch but back it with evidence and you won't go far wrong. Just bear in mind that no-one is right one hundred percent of the time. You've a bright future. However, you've just opened Pandora's Box and,' he paused and smiled. 'I wonder if you realise what's in store for you. Good luck.'

He shook my hand again and Mr Valentine's, before walking off to speak with the Coroner's Officer who had just arrived and was speaking with Kevin Riley.

'He's a good detective, Blake. Bear what he said in mind. And remember what I said on Saturday about the Press, once they get their collective teeth into this the shit will hit the fan with a vengeance ... I take it the skeleton is female.'

'Yes sir. Wide sciatic notch, certainly female.'

Thirty-Four

The clouds were low and looked loaded. So far, the rain was holding off. It took over an hour to reach Winterton, the home of the County Sailing Club, a place I'd never been to before. Sandwiches eaten and tea drunk en route. DS Nicholson had told me he thought the lake they used for sailing were ancient mine workings, which maybe so, but it was a beautiful place. Backing the car park were mature trees both deciduous and coniferous. Our destination about half a mile further. From the map, the woods were part of an estate. We were met by the local beat Inspector. Two uniformed officers. And, a face I hadn't seen for some time. Several cars in the car park, all bar two adjacent to the clubhouse. One of them a new beat car, black and white - nicknamed pandas.

'Oh God,' moaned DS Nicholson. 'It's Baines.'

'Problem?'

'An officious prick. One of the great I ams.'

'Ok,' I said. I'd met a few of those before.

DS Nicholson parked next to the panda. A florid-faced Inspector Baines stormed across the car park to greet us. 'What's all this about, Nicholson?' he demanded, spittle flying from his mouth. A man with an attitude problem. 'Why am I here? I'm short of men and, I've been ordered to supply two of what's left to assist you. Why?'

'Sorry, sir,' he replied. 'We're under orders from the ACC not to divulge anything.'

'Which ACC?'

'ACC Mr Weatherspoon, sir.'

Realising that he wasn't going to get an answer to his satisfaction he turned to me. His two uniformed officers and Dr Jack Hawkins, a forensic biologist, were waiting. 'Who are you?'

'Pc 547 Blake, sir,' I replied.

'I suppose you're covered by these orders as well?'

'Yes sir.'

'When were these orders supposedly given?'

Supposedly? 'Just after I'd finished giving a presentation to the ACC, Detective Chief Superintendent Mithering, Chief Superintendent Williams and Detective Superintendent Creighton on Saturday afternoon, sir.'

'You ...' Before the shock had time to clear from his face a convoy of four cars drove into the car park. The DCI, DI Henderson, DS Cartwright and Jacko alighted from the first. ACC Weatherspoon and Detective Chief Superintendent Mithering from the second. Penny, Jenny and Max from the third. Detective Superintendent Creighton from the last. The occupants slowly coalescing in the centre of the car park.

Inspector Baines just stood there looking from one senior officer to the next. 'Everything all right, Inspector Baines?' The DCI asked, wandering over.

'Yes, sir, er I ...'

'Good, then we won't detain you,' he said, his tone dismissive and turned to the two uniformed Pc's. 'You're the two local beat officers?'

'Yes, sir,' they answered together. The DCI turned away as someone called his name.

'What's it like underfoot?' I asked.

'Which way you going?'

I pointed at the hedge at the far end of the car park, 'About half a mile.'

'Lousy, you'll need your boots,' one of them replied indicating his own footwear.

Car boots were opened, spades and a pickaxe were extracted, overalls and wellies girded. Another car pulled into the car park. Three more detectives exited. This was getting to be a party. As I found out later a DI Bradshaw, DS Craig and DC Dodgson, all from Wakefield.

I took the few steps across the car park to the face that I knew well. All togged up and ready to go. 'Hi Jack,' we shook hands. Jack was one of the biologists from the Forensic Science Lab. He'd swabbed my hands and checked my clothing for blood spatter following the incident in the Valley Gardens, Harrogate, plus I'd been in his company on my day's attachment.

'Officer Blake,' he grinned broadly. 'How the hell are you?'

'Keeping busy,' I replied, glancing at the crowd behind me.

His forehead puckered. 'Yes, I heard you were involved in this little escapade. Connected to that body in Westleigh, and this morning's exercise?'

I nodded in agreement. He bit his lip and looked thoughtful. Then mentioned that since this morning they had secured an additional biologist from Nottingham to assist. I would imagine they knew how many bodies we were looking for.

Our conversation was cut short by the DCI. 'Blake, you can chat en route, lead the way.'

Thirty-Five

Jack and I, map in hand, turned left out of the car park. Doglegging to the right it was a half mile walk to Cold Hiendley Wood. It would be difficult to imagine a scene more different from this morning. A solid phalanx of conifers awaited us. Like the spears of some ancient giants guarding the secrets buried within. This was no Greenhead Park with its putting greens, children's playgrounds and tennis courts. Full of happy people having fun. More like the forest of Hansel and Gretel. Gloomy and full of foreboding. Threatening. Reminiscent of a Gothic horror story. If I was correct I hoped beyond hope that whoever was buried there hadn't been buried alive. I wasn't exactly wallowing in the slough of despond but it was a lonely place and with every step became more lonely. This was on my shoulders and mine alone. In spite of this morning's result, Superintendent Sheard's words were ringing in my ears.

Pc Jim Barton was correct. I'm glad I remembered to bring my boots. It was filthy, ankle deep in places. Half way to what I'd calculated was the grave site we circumnavigated a rudimentary gate. A metal barrier. A single pole hinged on the right from a vertical metal post and able to rotate across the track and rest on a Y-support. It was padlocked shut. If there was a body where the reference indicated and the gate had been locked at the time it had been carried a helluva long way.

The track was wide enough for a tractor. Ploughed, waterlogged fields either side. The land drier and rose slightly as we neared the trees and judging by the thickness of the tree trunks the wood was old. This location was twelfth on Wainwright's list. Assuming I was correct we shouldn't have too many large roots to contend with. The price we would have to pay were the gases released by decomposition.

At the edge of the wood I stopped. Detective Chief Superintendent Mithering walked to the front. 'Right, Blake, I understand from Mr Valentine that you and DS Nicholson have been through all your calculations.'

'Yes sir.'

He turned to his left. 'And they were in order, Sergeant?' There were a few smiles when he asked that.

'Fine sir,' DS Nicholson answered. 'I was never in the Boy Scouts so my knowledge of maps other than AA road maps is minimal.'

'Very well. Blake, can you show us the location of the grave on your map. Tell us how you calculated it, and, how do we get there?'

I opened the map and folded it so that the relevant section was exposed and held it against my chest. 'I hope you can all see,' I said. There were a few bodies who shuffled to one side. Mr Mithering made a better door than he did a window. 'Sir, I began with the assumption that the reference was correct,'

'Like it was this morning, Blake?' That was Superintendent Creighton; nice to have a bit of support. But I did notice the DCI smiling.

'Yes sir,' I replied. 'I was surprised how accurate it was.'

'Blake,' DS Creighton interrupted. 'Before you continue, You were surprised? Is that because you were so accurate in your calculations, or the manner in which the original figures were derived?'

'The latter, sir.'

The DCI understood and whispered something to DS Creighton. 'Nothing at all?'

'Nothing at all, sir,' was the reply.

'Sorry, go on.'

I'll bet the question was about Wainwright's map-reading apparatus, or lack of them. I reverted to the calculation. 'Using the lens and the ruler I calculated the position on the map.' I pointed to the red dot that I hoped was accurate for this particular search. 'Then it was a simple matter of measuring the angle between a line drawn connecting two known fixed points and the red dot. In this case from the point where we are now and a point that I measured a hundred and twenty feet along the tree-line in front of us.'

'Blake?' the ACC's tone was questioning. 'You talk about known fixed points. Yet,' he said with an expansive gesture, 'we can all see there are no fixed points. Are you playing games with us?'

There was a nervous shuffling amongst some of the group. 'Not at all, sir,' I replied, although I was puzzled by his challenge. 'Wainwright's number gave me the location where the body might be buried. Hence the red dot. So I simply created the fixed points by drawing a line on the map along the edge of the wood, as you can see here,' I pointed to the pencil line on the map. 'I took the first measurement from this point, where we are now at the edge of the path. The second point is forty yards from where we are standing, adjacent to the tree line. The angle from the tree line is ninety degrees.'

He still didn't look happy. 'So it's just guess work.' That wasn't a question; neither was the tone friendly.

'Not exactly, sir. The tree line is fixed. These trees have been here a long time. I already had the possible position of the grave. I just created the means to locate it.'

'Simple triangulation,' said DS Creighton. The ACC still didn't look convinced. Far from it.

'Yes, sir. It is.' This was a three-four-five right-angled triangle. The angles are: Ninety degrees, thirty seven degrees and fifty three degrees. 'I appreciate that the representation on the map is very small so I prepared this.' I took a folded piece of quarto sized paper from my pocket and opened it up. 'This is a larger representation of what is on the map. **X** is the spot on the map. That is thirty yards from the treeline – that's point **Y**. Where we are standing is point **Z**. The angles and ratios of the sides are the same as the map.' I passed it round.

Almost all seemed relaxed about it. I glanced at the DCI. He nodded. I took the long tape from my pocket, collared Jenny and DS Nicholson to help. Measured the forty yards along the tree line then a right-angle into the wood and measured the thirty yards. 'X' marked the spot. Now we were in the wood the outlook was much brighter, although the reason we were there hadn't changed. The weight of expectation? Where we were standing wasn't a clearing as such, just a slightly wider gap of about twenty yards between the trees

Jack Hawkins looked around at the assorted group. 'How close do you think you are?'

'Thanks. All things being equal and getting the measurements right, within ten metres.' All I got was an answering smile and a couple of nods.

'What's that in English money, Blake?' Mr Mithering grunted. A stranger to metric measurement.

Before I could answer DI Henderson did. 'Just short of eleven yards, sir.' There was a grunt of appreciation.

I'd brought my Vicks. This could be gross and I wasn't taking any chances. I wasn't too worried about those at the top of Wainwright's list, they were long gone as I'd experienced this morning. All that would be left would be bones perhaps with some skin fragments adhering. But this was last on the list. All that we knew was that it was prior to Sally Dunster. It could be truly nauseating. I applied the Vicks to both nostrils and saw Jack doing the same. I handed my Vicks to Jenny and suggested that she pass it round. No-one refused.

It was then that the two beat officers, whose job it would be to keep any random walkers away, realised why we were there.

A minute later a long-wheelbase Land Rover carrying a lead-lined coffin reversed to the barrier. The four occupants removed a heavy wheeled-barrow from the rear, placed the coffin onboard and trudged through the mud.

'Mr Weatherspoon, Mr Mithering,' Jack called stilling the conversation. 'Would it be possible to have a quick word with the troops?'

'Certainly,' replied the ACC, now sounding a little calmer. 'Go ahead, Doctor.'

All eyes were on Jack. 'I'm Doctor Hawkins, Jack Hawkins, no relation to the actor. I'm a biologist from the forensic science lab at Harrogate. Just a quick point for Sergeant Nicholson and Pc Blake,' he paused and smiled. 'In my honest opinion you two are about three yards from where you need to dig. As a quick estimate, which I probably shouldn't do, the body has been buried for somewhere from as recently as six months ago.' He furrowed his brow and nodded. 'More likely nine or more. Furthermore,' he added with deliberation, 'one of you is standing considerably nearer,' he paused and smiled as everyone looked around, especially those close by. 'And no Mr Weatherspoon,' he said looking at the ACC, 'I am not the murderer.'

'I'm very glad to hear that, Doctor,' he replied with a wry smile. 'But you concur with Blake that there is a body buried here?'

Jack smiled and nodded to the ACC. 'Yes, I do, although I have to say that I can't tell as yet whether the body is human or otherwise ... Has anybody here not attended a post mortem examination?'

No hands were raised.

'Good. With the greatest of respect I'll keep this simple. We don't know the date, but decomposition begins immediately following brain death. Enzymes are proteins that speed chemical reactions. They begin to digest our innards and the bacteria run amok. Two percent of your body is pure bacteria.' 'Yuk' was written large across several faces. 'The ensuing liquefaction and creation of gas has an odour which can only be described as incredibly disgusting and nauseating: Rotting flesh. Faeces. Rotten eggs. Rotten cabbage and a foul garlic-like odour.' *that was a shame I liked garlic.* 'After four to five weeks the liquid will have soaked into the ground but leaving the gases with their attendant odour waiting for us to let it out.' Jack smiled as he studied the reactions. He was laying it on with a trowel and with good reason. 'This is a natural reaction. Your ultimate destination, unless of course you intend to be cremated.' I think at that point most of those present had already made that decision. 'Tell me, what would happen if you poured undiluted liquid fertilizer onto your lawn?'

It was Jacko that answered. 'It's much too strong it would kill off the grass.'

'Correct. That is happening here. Now. The liquid that decomposition produces is a powerful natural fertilizer. A natural re-cycling. The liquid in this case was absorbed long ago. In the process killed off the overgrowth.'

Jack stood silently as seventeen pairs of eyes immediately began to search. 'Is that it, over there,' said Jenny, pointing. 'Where DC Jackson is standing?' There were two reactions. First of all Jacko leaping to one side with considerable alacrity. Secondly the ensuing laughter.

'In my professional opinion? Yes,' Jack replied. 'But it doesn't mean that every piece of land with dead vegetative matter has a body beneath it. At least I hope not. However, probably in the autumn of this year or next spring should your curiosity get the better of you and you return to this spot, you will find there has been a rapid re-growth, which will continue for some years.'

Doctor Gallagher, Wakefield divisional police surgeon arrived. Somewhat superfluous but death had to be certified.

Jack was correct. X did mark the spot. It took us an hour to completely expose the body. That was as much as we could do. Removal of the remains would be undertaken by Jack and the undertaker, under Jack's supervision. He would also take away as much of the soil as he deemed necessary, looking for insect residue and anything else that appeared relevant. It was not a job that I would like. There were no eyes and therefore no petechial haemorrhaging. It would be interesting to know whether or not the hyoid bone was fractured, a significant indication of strangulation. It was only a small bone and should drop somewhere close to the lower cervical vertebrae.

The odour was as described. *Vile.* Even with the Vicks it was bad, but it was manageable. No-one vomited. But it would put them off their food for a while.

The two uniformed officers were just visible some distance away, who could blame them. The rest of us stood round the grave. There was much to note but not a lot that we could do. The photographer, claiming to have been misdirected turned up late. Took his photographs and departed. I would have loved to drag Wainwright to this very spot and without the protection of Vicks make him breathe in the result of his work as we had had to. Perhaps reconsider his actions. Not much chance of that.

The body, or what was left of it, was female. That much was evident from the lack of penis and the skin of what had apparently been a full-breasted woman. She had been five feet three or four inches tall. Her hair, which was brown and permed, was visible. Discernible traces of bright red nail varnish on both finger and toe nails. A suspender belt around her pelvis still holding the remains of nylon stockings, other than that she was naked. There was sufficient skin remaining to cover much of the pelvis so I couldn't see the sciatic notch. A yellow metal ring on the third finger of her left hand. A wrist watch on her left wrist: ladies style, narrow yellow metal twisted bracelet, small oval face with Roman numerals. Her teeth, some of which had fallen out, could be used to reconstruct the jaw and were clearly visible, A dental identification might be obtained, but that was for Jack and his colleagues. Like this morning she was laid flat on her back arms by her side.

Jack revised his opinion; it was between six and nine months but would wait for confirmation before commenting further. One of the tests would be determined by the length of time that had elapsed between her death and burial; whether the flies and other insects that laid their eggs on dead animal matter had had their opportunity, although the science as I understood it wasn't fully developed. Whilst Jack continued his examination we searched the area one hundred yards round the grave. We found nothing.

I was collared by DI Bradshaw and his colleagues. They asked if I had any further information regarding this latest victim. Mr Valentine made sure he was at my shoulder, just in case ... In any event all I could tell them was that this was last on the list. Now they knew as much as we did. Jack's parting words as we left him, 'I'll be seeing you again over the next few days.' I had a feeling that he was right.

Thirty-Six

Back at the office nothing had changed. We had Wainwright remanded to police cells. Hazel Granby had arrived and taken up residence in the corner, hijacking one of the phones until the Post Office could attend and install an extra spur. She had also brought sheets of card and numbered them 1 to 13. Red dots were in the top right hand corner of those we had excavated, or in the case of No.3 i.e. Christine Jones, dealt with. At the moment that was Nos 1, 3, 12 and 13 with relevant dates in the bottom left. Personal details entered. There was a separate sheet of card to the left numbered 1 to 13 as an index. Four entries partially completed. Hazel was nothing if not efficient. I heard her footsteps before I heard her voice. 'Pc Blake,' she announced. I could hear the humour and I knew what was coming. 'I heard that you were here. Learned to add up yet?' She had such a way with words, and, she'd got Penny's attention.

Exasperated I replied. 'You're never going to let me forget that, are you?'

'She shook her head. 'Nope,' she smiled. 'By the way, I bumped into Lucy this lunchtime,' she'd met Lucy at the Christmas do last year. 'She was having a sandwich in The Coffee Shop with her mother. She asked that you telephone before you leave. And it's fish for tea, she's got some calamari?'

'Excellent. Calamari is very nice. It's squid,' I explained. Although the expression on both her face and Penny's said that neither were too sure. First eaten by me on our honeymoon on Capri.

Penny and I began to log the items recovered from the grave of No.12. Surprisingly enough there wasn't much of a bad smell. Penny dictated. I wrote. The ladies wrist watch had no hall marks or makers name, so it was: one ladies yellow metal wrist watch with yellow metal twisted strap, white face with Roman numerals. One gold wedding ring ... 'Just a sec, Brian, there's an inscription on the inside. Have you still got that lens?'

I had.

She looked up from the lens. '*VM forever DM,*' she said, 'and written in script. But which one is which?' She mused and paused for a few seconds. 'It's a bit odd though, I would have thought an inscription on a wedding ring would be just first names. Hopefully the *M* is a surname. Hmm, nevertheless it's worth a try. Brian, give M.O. a bell and ask them to check both sets of initials against the misper stripdex. If she's been reported in this region they should be able to tell us.'

All people reported as missing from home are circulated by teleprinter or telex. A copy sent to the regional criminal record office, known as M.O. – *modus operandi*. Details are entered on a strip of card and inserted in alphabetical and date order. Simple to enter, simple to check, but there were hundreds if not thousands.

I made the call and provided the information we had. It was a nerve racking wait. Ten minutes later they called back. I was almost shaking as I wrote down the details and turned to an expectant Penny. She was smiling. 'From the look on your face they've got a hit.'

I took a deep breath. 'Vivienne McKeen, born 23rd April 1938, reported missing 18th September 64. Full entry in Police Reports of the 10th October.'

Her face lit up. 'Brilliant, Brian. Absolutely brilliant. This is all down to you. Well done.'

Helen sat at her desk. She heard everything but said nothing, smiled and returned to what she'd been doing.

Inspector Meadowcroft was just leaving his office as I arrived. 'Excuse me, sir, where can I get hold of Police Reports for October last year?'

'Come in,' he said. The Inspectors at Hecton had their own set. It only took a couple of minutes to locate what I was looking for. Even less to explain why.

A black and white photograph. Vivienne McKeen was an attractive woman together with her husband and daughter. The text read: *Vivienne McKeen 25 years of age b. Sowerby Bridge 23.04.1938 5'3", proportionate build, brown permed shoulder length hair and brown eyes. Wearing red nail varnish on both finger and toe nails. Last seen Saturday 18.09.64. Wearing wedding ring with dedication VM forever DM inscribed on inner surface. Also wearing wrist watch, photo as above. Last seen dressed in cream coloured dress with floral print. Cream coloured high-heeled shoes. Red top coat and matching handbag containing blue purse with approximately £10 in cash, driving licence and usual accoutrements. School teacher. Lives with husband Duncan and four year old daughter in Sowerby Bridge. Attended friend's hen party at the Palais Ballroom, Wakefield, on above date. Motor car found on Palais car park; front offside side tyre wall punctured.*

Penny compared the photo with the watch. They were identical. Then she looked up. 'Brian, are you all right?' She sounded concerned.

I didn't know how I felt. Two potential sites investigated two sets of female human remains recovered. The enormity of what we were dealing with had hit. Emotions were spinning inside my head like a top. I needed to get some air. 'Just need to clear my head, Penny, I won't go far.'

I didn't. Within two minutes I was back in the Incident Room.

The DCI stood there smiling and shaking his head, the rest of the team standing, watching. 'I can understand you wanting to speak with Mr McKeen but that was a direct order from the Chief Constable. So the answer is, no. Besides, if we follow that logic to its bitter end you'd do everything and the rest of us would be redundant. But getting a hit so soon is a fantastic stroke of luck. Well done to both of you. This is another enquiry that we can get our teeth into.'

Another case of I didn't have to like it, but I had to accept it. 'Yes, sir,' I replied, resigned to the fact that it was 6pm and I would be going home. Then I heard Hazel's voice in the background.

'Pc Blake,' she said. I turned. She was holding the phone out to me. 'Your wife?' I must have looked puzzled. 'She asked you to call?' she said and smiled.

'Thanks Hazel,' Lucy was already on the line 'Hi, love. I'll be home in twenty minutes.'

Whilst I was getting my gear together the jobs were being handed out: DS Nicholson and Penny were en route to Sowerby Bridge to speak with the local coppers, and with a modicum of luck, Duncan McKeen. DS Cartwright to liaise with Wakefield, and Jacko wanted details of the best way to get statements from Joe, Norman, Jennifer, and Lucy. I suggested our lynch pin, Mum, and gave him the home number. Lucy, I would get her to call Hazel and arrange an appointment at Hecton. Everyone else back at 0800.

The DCI rang DI Bradshaw at Wakefield.

DI Henderson wandered over. 'You feeling better? You looked a bit out of sorts when we arrived,' he said it in a friendly way, but to me the tone of voice reflected what had been said earlier about the effect on me.

'I'm fine, sir, really. It was when I got confirmation from M.O. and the item in Police Reports that it hit. Yes, I knew the numbers, but this suddenly took it to a different level.'

'I understand,' he replied. 'We all do. But you're cutting your teeth on potentially one of the most comprehensive crime enquiries the County has ever seen. You're right in the middle. There'd be something wrong if you didn't feel overwhelmed by the enormity of it and that's without your personal link,' I nodded. I couldn't do much else. 'I'll be honest. No-one, and that includes Mr Valentine, has been involved in anything of this magnitude ... And before I forget there's a slight change of duty for you tomorrow afternoon, and, no,' he said noticing that I was about to speak. 'I'm not going to say what it is just yet. Tomorrow you'll have both DS Nicholson and DS Cartwright with you. You're to make sure that they can both do what you do to navigate to the scene. As soon as you are able you are to return here. Understood?'

By the time I'd arrived home DS Cartwright was en route to liaise with a DS Verity. DS Nicholson and Penny were en route to Sowerby Bridge to break the news to an unsuspecting widower. I'd done a few death warnings before. That was the worst possible job.

Calamari con pomodori. Squid with tomatoes poured over pasta. It was a simple dish perfect for simple people. As Lucy said, just like *me*. Claire, fed and bathed, was already in bed, no doubt tired out by Lucy's cooking lesson. She'd made some of her sponge drops and a tiramisu whilst giving directions, in Italian of course, to Claire in her highchair. Apart from the temperature, the house, flora, language and *Monte Solaro* we could have been back on Capri. A perfect distraction, almost as good as Lucy was. She was wearing her dressing gown, and a smile. I hadn't got round to the Chanel No5, yet. To make matters worse as I sat down to eat my tea she stood behind me and trailed her fingers up the sides of my neck. That nearly delayed tea, which in turn would have spoiled the calamari. Table cleared I scooped a shrieking Lucy up into my arms and carried her upstairs to the refrain: "That's your trouble, Brian, you've got a one-track mind". This time I did not trip over the bed-side mat. That was what you call an early night. The sponge drops and the tiramisu had to wait. It was a great way to relieve stress.

Thirty-Seven

1855. DS Nicholson and Penny following, DS Greatorix pulled up outside 27 South Parade Street, Bolton Brow, a mile from Sowerby Bridge police station. An inner terrace house so common in the West Riding. Neat and tidy. A single step to a sky-blue door. A slim and attractive woman in her late twenties answered. Music was playing in the background. DS Greatorix showed his warrant card. Introduced himself and the others, then asked to speak to Duncan McKeen. Her face dropped.

'Who is it, Norma?' a male voice responded to the conversation.

'It's the police, Duncan.'

With a fire half way up the fireback and five sitting down it was cramped. An apprehensive Duncan McKeen facing them. His sister Norma sitting by his side. Norma collected Geraldine, his daughter, immediately after breakfast and took her to the nursery. Collecting her later in the day before returning her home at six pm when Duncan returned from work. The little girl now upstairs in bed.

'Mr McKeen,' said DS Greatorix. 'These two officers are from the police incident room at Hecton. They would like to speak with you.'

Norma gripped her brother's arm, her knuckles white. 'I take it this is about Vivienne,' he said. 'From the looks on your faces it's not good news.'

'Mr McKeen, I'm Detective Sergeant Nicholson. This,' he indicated Penny, 'is Detective Constable Farthing. I'm sorry to have to inform you that as a result of information received, this afternoon we recovered female human remains which we believe may be those of your wife.' Norma began to sob uncontrollably. Her brother put his arm round her shoulders.

Duncan McKeen looked across at the DS. 'I'm sorry, I don't understand. You say that you believe it may be Vivienne, but the police have a photograph of Vivienne can't you just check her with that?'

Death warnings really were the worst part of the job, but as the cliché goes: it's a crap job but someone has to do it. The circumstances of this case didn't make the job any easier. 'We believe she'd been buried for over six months.' The DS explained, hoping that Duncan McKeen would understand.

He thought for a moment. Nodded. 'I see, but how did you find out who she was?

'We recovered these articles, Mr McKeen,' said Penny tipping the ring and the watch into her hand. 'Can you identify them, please?' She handed him the ring.

The overhead light shone on the inner surface. He nodded. 'There's an inscription on the inside,' he said. '*VM forever DM*. I had it inscribed.' He said, tears in his eyes as he placed the ring in Penny's outstretched hand. She handed him the watch. For the first time since they arrived, he smiled. 'I bought her this watch for her 21st,' he said. 'It wasn't expensive. I was a bit strapped, but it kept brilliant time. She wore it every day.' He handed it back to Penny.

'I'm sorry we have to take the ring and the watch back,' she said. 'Just as soon as we can they will be returned.'

He nodded.

'To answer your question as to how we knew who she was. We keep an index of all people reported missing. We checked the initials from the inscription against the index.'

'Thanks,' he said nodding. Norma was still sobbing.

'I'm sorry, Mr McKeen,' DS Nicholson said, 'but there are some personal questions that I have to ask about your marriage.'

'Yes, we had a good marriage,' his voice void of emotion he answered without any prompting. 'They asked me the last time. There were no personal problems and we were planning another child, a playmate for Geraldine. We had no outside interests. She was just going for a night out with a colleague from school on her hen night. That's all I want to say on the matter.'

'I understand from Sergeant Greatorix that you handed your wife's diaries and address books to them last September,' said DS Nicholson. 'Is there anything else that has come to mind in the interim? Any names, friends or colleagues, anybody you hadn't thought of before? Anyone she might have fallen out with?'

'Believe me, Sergeant, I've never stopped. I can't think of anybody who would wish her any harm.'

'I understand. Is there anything that you would like to ask us?'

Duncan McKeen looked at them his face expectant. 'When can I have her back?'

'Our forensic scientists are still examining her body and that may take a little while,' he explained. 'There will have to be an inquest to establish her identity which will be at Wakefield. That was where her body was discovered. I'm afraid that you will have to attend. The coroner will probably just ask you questions about the ring and the watch and then make the decision when her body will be released. I know that it sounds cold and uncaring but this is the way we ensure that we get it right.'

He nodded. Accepting without question. 'Can I visit where you found her? It seems only right that I should put some flowers on her grave.'

The DS and Penny glanced at each other. 'It's a rather beautiful spot,' said Penny, 'but at the moment it's very unpleasant. It might be better if you were to leave it for several weeks. It's also very isolated and if you don't know the area quite difficult to find. We'll give you our contact details. No doubt Sergeant Greatorix will be able to help.'

'Just contact the station, Mr McKeen, we'll sort something out. In the meantime you can contact an undertaker. Tell them to contact the Wakefield Coroner's Office. They will know what to do and liaise with you. Should you have any further questions don't hesitate to call the station.'

'You can contact us through Hecton Police Station,' said Penny handing him the contact numbers. 'Ask for Mrs Granby, she's our administrator. If there is any further news we will contact you.

She put the statement identifying the ring and wrist watch in her briefcase. 'Before we go is there anything else?'

He looked distraught. 'Yes,' he said. 'How the Hell do I tell Geraldine?'

Thirty-Eight

M iss Blake had no respect whatsoever for her parent's right to sleep and demanded attention. The trade-off was that she now smiled on demand. How can you resist that at 5.00am?

It was too early for the morning paper so I read yesterday evening's Examiner. The Stop Press caught my eye: *Human remains discovered in Greenhead Park, Marsh, police investigating.*

With a face of wide-eyed innocence and a stifled smile a Claire-carrying Lucy watched. 'Is this what last night's distraction therapy was about?' I pointed at the article.

'No, well, not exactly,' she replied, as her expression slipped. 'Any complaints?'

'Memorable.' I laughed and patted my knee. 'Are you ok?' I put my arms round her hips pulling her nearer.

'Of course,' she smiled. 'I was just testing your stamina.'

A tiny pair of hands reached out. One trying to get hold of my nose. The other in my mouth, accompanied by what could only be described as a cross between a gurgle and a chortle, was that a churgle or a gortle? I opened my eyes as wide as I could and made a popping sound with my lips and pretended to eat her hand. *There is nothing that I wouldn't do to protect you and your mother.*

'Good morning, ladies and gentlemen,' the DCI walked in followed by the DI. 'After yesterday's breakthrough by Penny and Pc Blake there is a change to today's order. And Hazel?' he said addressing our pet martinet. She looked up from her desk. 'We'll try and leave you alone today. However, the Press have gotten hold of the story and linked it to Wainwright's arrest and further detention. Should you receive extra attention just refer them to HQ Press Office. HQ switch board are aware and trying to filter the calls. How successful they will be remains to be seen.'

Hazel's smile was as determined as she was. 'I'll manage, Mr Valentine.'

'I'm sure you will,' he smiled. I think everyone in the room supported that comment. 'Penny, have you made any arrangements to meet with Mrs Wainwright, today?'

'No sir.'

'Ok. First thing, I want you to ring her sister's and should Mrs Wainwright be there advise her to stay in the house today unless it is urgent, and why. Then call the Court's office and speak with her sister, let her know the situation. You know what the Press is like when they smell blood. We don't need their muddy footprints cluttering up the place.'

Penny nodded and picked up the phone.

'To Wainwright's twelve we have added Sally Dunster,' the DCI said as he walked across to the list on the wall. 'So that's numbers one, three, twelve and thirteen, all female. However, other than gender we have no knowledge whatsoever about number one. Number three, Christine Jones, was a working prostitute, reputedly very attractive. Sally Dunster not a prostitute as far as we know. At least no convictions to her name. Described as flighty and an enthusiastic amateur. Would chat up anything in trousers. From her photograph a pretty girl. Vivienne McKeen, attractive, a twenty five year old brunette. According to her husband was a loyal and loving wife that didn't play away. He may be right. Peter,' he addressed DS Cartwright directly, 'when you get to Sowerby Bridge make contact with the locals. It was a DS Greatorix last night. I know him, he's a good detective. A word of advice, keep your hand on your wallet. The County Chief Super, also name of Cartwright, and the Sub-Divisional Super name of Villiers, if you didn't know are both ex-C.I.D. and nosey. Just be yourself. Halifax Borough have already been on the phone. Now, it's too soon to state categorically that all the victims will be female but it's looking that way. One final point, even if it was done when Vivienne McKeen was initially reported missing. Find out whose hen party she was supposed to be attending. Speak to the woman concerned in person. See what she can add.'

'Excuse me, sir?' It was Peter Normington.

'Yes?'

'Do we know that the first is female?'

The DCI nodded at me. 'It was a female pelvis, Pete,' I explained. 'The sciatic notch is much wider in females than males.'

'OK. But I don't know what that is.' There were a few others who didn't know.

'Well perhaps you'll find out later this morning,' the DCI followed up. 'A slight change from yesterday. You're with DS Nicholson and Pc Blake, who will be required back here not later than 1pm. So this afternoon will be down to you and DS Nicholson plus however many officers Bradford City send.'

'No pressure then, sir?'

'For officers on this squad,' he smiled, 'anything and everything is possible ... Next, Penny, when you've finished talking with Adele Wainwright and her sister I want you to go to M.O., DCI Shelton is aware. I want you to go through the misper index to see what entries there might be that fit what little we know. In particular the first two on Wainwright's list, i.e. female, and shall we say under thirty. The average age of the three that we have so far is twenty one. Age range eighteen to twenty five. I know it's not much of a sample but anything and everything will help.' She acknowledged.

'DC Myers, When did the Blood Transfusion Service intimate they would get back to you?'

'This morning, sir.'

'Ok. Should they have any male donors that fit the picture we need to know where they were on the night of the 5th, 6th March. Any without an alibi will have to be interviewed. Any in the West Riding let me have the details. Any outside the West Riding farm them out. We need facial Id. Make sure we know who we are talking to. Aged under fifty, the Blood transfusion service should have their dates of birth. They should be savvy enough but mention it anyway, not to mention the case or blood group link.'

'Yes sir, I'll be diplomatic.'

'DS Cartwright and DC Sendrove liaise with C.I.D. at Sowerby Bridge. They're not over blessed with C.I.D. officers. DC Cavendish and DC Smith, Sergeant Rhodes at Huddersfield. Mind their corns they're a mite touchy. No doubt they'll welcome another couple. And, if I haven't called your name out you're having a day out in Wakefield and District. The sub-division is Normanton where they have an Inspector Baines.' The name drawing a groan from DS Nicholson and the suggestion of a smile from the DCI. 'You can tell him that you're on enquiries with regards to sightings of Wainwright or his vehicle. About the body that we recovered yesterday. But not about how many more we are looking for, *or anything else*. Should you come across him and he try to pull rank, refer him to Mr Henderson, to me or Mr Creighton. In addition, details of Wainwright's vehicle were circulated last evening to all divisions and surrounding forces with a request for all officers to check their pocket books for offences and document productions. That car stands out. It's the type of motor vehicle that men in particular would notice.'

'Most men would notice it, sir,' offered Penny, just managing to keep a straight face. 'It's a surrogate penis. You can tell by the way they fondle the steering wheel.'

'Thank you for your observations WDC Farthing, I'm sure they'll bear it in mind.'

'No problem, sir,' she replied, and grinned as she was regaled with a series of pithy comments from the assembled male members.

Ten minutes later we were on our way. Because I had to be back by 1pm for this mysterious task I had permission to take my bike and claim mileage allowance. Every little helps.

Bullerthorpe Lane, rear entrance to Temple Newsam House was unexpectedly busy. The road almost blocked by stationary cars, both police and civilian plus a couple of cameramen and rubberneckers. That was a waste of time; they couldn't see anything from the road. We'd expected to be met by half a dozen Leeds City Officers but not this. Not only that it was pissing down. Thank heavens for Belstaff.

'You're too late, Sarge.' The uniformed Pc, who was trying to keep the traffic flowing, declared.

'Late for what?'

'We've got the body. A bloke walking his dog found the skull a couple of hours ago. It's all under control.'

'Nice of them to tell us,' retorted DS Nicholson. 'Still, it's part of an ongoing major enquiry that we're running, constable. Open the barrier, please. Then we can get out of the way.' But not out of the rain.

I wasn't going to be there in the afternoon so I left the navigating to the others. Apart from the pouring rain and the water dripping from the trees there were no problems.

Thirty-Nine

It was in the wrong place. Well, the skeleton was in *its* rightful place, it just wasn't our skeleton. Not that we knew what state ours would be in. The Leeds City DS and DI didn't seem too impressed when I told them that their skeleton, which was fully exposed, was male. 'And how do *you* know that?' demanded the DS. The question was a valid one, but his tone said smartarse.

I pointed out the relatively narrow sciatic notch. 'In females it's wider, to allow them to give birth more easily.'

The DS sneered. 'So, you're a Doctor as well?' Policemen do have a way with sarcasm.

'No.' interjected DS Nicholson in a tone that said he didn't like standing in the pouring rain. 'He's got a degree in physiology.' Near enough.

'You reckon there's another body in these woods,' said the DI.

'If I'm right, sir, ours is about forty to fifty yards nearer the house. I think yours has been here for a very long time.' In answer to a couple of quizzical looks I said, 'It doesn't smell enough.'

The DS frowned. 'I don't buy that, sir. Two bodies? If there is I'll bare my arse in Woolworths.'

'You're a brave man Sergeant,' the DI said. 'Ok gentlemen, let's see what you find.'

This was ridiculous. If anything it was raining even harder than before. It would have helped if the trees had been in leaf but the buds were barely swelling. We needed a tent. The sooner we got started the sooner we could finish. Not very charitable perhaps but it was how I felt. Maybe it was beginning to get to me. Maybe it was just the lousy weather. We were about five yards away from where I anticipated we should dig when Pete Normington pointed at the ground just in front of us. 'What the Hell is that? He said. Two yards away protruding slightly above the soil level was the left brow ridge and frontal bone of a human skull. I don't know who was the most shocked, us or DS Dixon.

'Oh bollocks!' He scowled and looked round at four smiling faces. 'Oh No,' he said, pointing at us in turn. 'You can get stuffed.'

Even the DI laughed. 'We have a problem, Sergeant.' he said. 'We have two bodies one of which is ours. Send Ridley down here to help these officers whilst I contact St Mark's House.

Pc Ridley arrived one minute later. Jack Hawkins and the hearse ten minutes after that, followed seconds later by a grumbling photographer – his case was heavy. To be fair we were over a quarter of a mile from the road, but, he could have driven. This grave was shallower than the others, the tree roots were in the way. Again the victim was female and requiring Vicks, although not as nauseating as Vivienne McKeen. Pc Ridley and Pete got a conducted tour from Jack. This lady was wearing the remains of a pale blue cotton blouse with embroidery visible on the collar, but nothing else. Nestling where the right trapezius muscle should have been was a pearl drop-earring. If it belonged to the lady in the grave she had pierced ears. Once again there was no handbag or shoes. Had this man a fetish?

The hearse departed, we carried out a full search of the grave and surroundings. There was nothing. We left Jack at the scene in the pouring rain as Pc Ridley went to re-join his colleagues. We said our farewells to DS Dixon and DI Hobson. The sun came out as I turned right for the office whilst DS Nicholson and DC Normington left for Park Wood, Tong, Bradford.

By the time I got back to the office, freshened up and put on a dry shirt the canteen was on the point of closing. I decided to have a hot meal instead of my sandwiches. What was it on Tuesdays? Oh yes, corned beef, a small mountain of chips, baked beans accompanied by a couple of slices of bread and butter. Rice pudding to follow. I was on the point of foregoing what looked like creosote, but Mary, the duty cook took pity on me and made a fresh pot of tea. As I sat down the DCI bounded in. He must be able to charm the birds from the trees. Mary re-opened the hatch and served him. That in itself was worthy of being mentioned in despatches. Over lunch I filled the DCI in as far as I could about Temple Newsam House, showing him the earring and mentioned my thought about a fetish. He was open-minded but said it might be useful. I explained the need for a tent or some other protection from the elements. He said that he'd get Hazel to make urgent arrangements. He told me what he thought I ought to know from the conference in the Oak Room. Mr Valentine gave me the impression that he was much more enlightened in relation to the junior ranks of the police than the run-of-the-mill senior officer.

Forty

1230. HQ had created a single map by cannibalising OS maps of the area covered by Wainwright's numbers. It had been delivered thirty minutes ago. The mysterious task alluded to by DI Henderson was to locate the map references and insert numbered flat-headed map pins. Now we knew where the points were it was a job that only took ten minutes. The DCI helped me to carry the map to the interview room. The door was locked when we left. The idea? Expose it to Wainwright during his next interview. I would love to have been there. Instead I had to go through to Wakefield, the Criminal Record Office and help Penny. She had more work than anticipated.

She wasn't wrong. The misper stripdex was around thirty pounds in weight and lived on the top of a filing cabinet. Head height, easier to check: a circular steel base, central column and cap. There were twenty plus metal leaves that rotated from the column, wider than the base. It enabled a quick examination of the fifty strips of card on each side of the leaves. Because of its' weight and difficulty in holding it - the leaves got in the way - moving it was a two-man job. However, the male cadet designated to move it to the nearest table decided not to seek assistance. Whether it was because he genuinely thought that he could or was just trying to impress Penny we may never know. He slid it from the top of the filing cabinet and dropped it, narrowly missing his right foot and making a substantial hole in the heavy duty floor covering and the floor boards beneath. Approximately half the strips, about eight hundred, were sprung from the leaves and scattered across the floor. They had been filed in alphabetical and date order. Now they could accurately be described as a heap. Penny had already checked about a quarter, and had a record of those which may be relevant. Now half of them were on the floor. We piled the strips on the nearest available table and began again. We were looking for females who had been reported as missing more than five months ago and aged thirty or less and, still outstanding. It only took a few seconds to physically check each strip and a few seconds more to write down the details of each one that was relevant. We elicited help from a couple of Pc's and a different cadet as a runner to dig out the relevant Police Report. Cadet Williams was busily writing a report as to how he managed to drop the damn thing. We ended up with a list of forty three, most of which were quite recent. They would be the first to be discarded.

It was seven o'clock when I arrived at *chez nous*. I closed the door to shut out the world. Well, that had been the plan. Fat chance. We had visitors: three aunts, two motor cyclists and an archaeologist. *We were not alone.*

Claire safely in the arms of an aunt I was met by an unencumbered Lucy with a passionate kiss, interrupted by of all people, Anne, poking her head round the door. 'Come on you two, you're married now and have a daughter, aren't you too old for that kind of frivolity?'

'I'll remember that when your children come along,' was Lucy's swift retort.

A quick swill, change of clothes and a bite to eat I joined the others in the lounge. It was the first time we had had eight to seat. We managed. We didn't have enough chairs so the seating arrangements were that the ladies perched on an appropriate lap. The highlight of the evening was Anne and Neil announcing the arrival of their first in seven months.

'So,' said Lucy,' pointing an accusatory finger at Anne and Neil. 'It's the end of kissing, is it?'

'Why,' said Neil who had missed the first exchange.

'Certainly not,' protested a grinning Anne.

The toast was in champagne courtesy of Liz, and orange.

An interesting debate was beginning to develop about the case and why I couldn't discuss it. Vance, Frankie's boyfriend and Captain of the Spartans made a reference to the fact that I might have signed the Official Secrets Act. Which I had. Plus he commented on what Lucy's cousin did for a living. There were a few lively comments but Norman was mystified until Lucy explained that her mother's cousin, her half-cousin, was the Chief Constable. Norman's response? A broad grin and, 'Good career move!'

Forty-One

It was hectic. The interview with Wainwright had been put back until this afternoon. The map with its easel returned to the office. Someone, nobody knew who, had knocked the damn thing onto the floor and dislodged several pins. Detective Chief Superintendent Mithering was en route for the press conference and was running late. I just had two pins to replace: numbers one and seven.

'What the blazes are *you* doing?' the voice surprised and angry. I was the only one in the office so they must have been talking at me. Inspector Hemmings, newly promoted and transferred from Keighley, yesterday. Highly polished shoes that could have doubled as shaving mirrors and creases in his trousers that could have served as the razor, 'Well? I'm waiting for an answer.'

I opened my hand showing him the pins. 'I'm just replacing these two pins, sir.' I explained.

He held his hand out. 'I'll take those until someone arrives who knows what they're doing.' I hesitated. He jutted his head forwards aggressively. I placed the pins on his outstretched hand. 'Whose rota are you on?' He demanded.

I was in the Incident Room and in civvies. I was surprised he asked the question. 'I'm not on any rota at this station, sir. I'm wor...'

He gave me a dirty look. 'I'll deal with you later,' he interrupted. 'In the meantime go and get me a coffee, white one sugar,' he gave me a two bob bit. 'I want the change.' *The cheeky bastard.*

I'd walked past him and put my hand out to open the door when it opened. The Chief Constable bowled in followed by DCS

Mithering and DCI Valentine. The Chief wasn't expected. However, being who he was I supposed he could do what he liked.

I snapped to attention. 'Good morning, sir.'

'Carry on,' he replied. I relaxed. 'Causing ripples again, Blake,' he smiled. 'Have you any idea just how much work you've caused?'

'I'm beginning to, sir.'

'I understand you described the moment as a flash of perspiration.'

'Something like that, sir. It was a shock when I realised it fitted certain facts and especially when it was correct.'

'And you're all right in yourself?'

'Fine, sir. Thank you.'

'And Lucy and, er, Claire?'

I got a couple of odd looks when the Chief asked that question. The DCI who knew, smiled. 'Wonderful, sir, couldn't be better.'

'Being married obviously suits you.'

'Indeed it does.'

'Excellent,' he replied and turned to my would be persecutor. 'Inspector Hemmings, settling in at Hecton?'

'Nicely, sir,' he said.

The Chief turned to the DCS and nodded. 'Sorry, taking your time.'

'We have a few minutes, sir,' he replied. 'Got those pins in yet, Blake?'

'Just two to do, sir.'

He started. 'Well, where were you going?' he said, his face clouding over.

'To fetch Inspector Hemmings a cup of coffee, sir.' *Bollocks! He could take care of himself.*

There was a strange angry expression bubbling to the surface as the DCS turned to Inspector Hemmings. 'Inspector?' The look was menacing and the tone he used no less. I'm glad that I wasn't to be on the receiving end.

A now uncertain Inspector Hemmings began to explain. 'Well, sir,' he began. The Chief took a political step to the rear. 'I found this officer, erm Pc Blake, playing with these two pins ...' he said and held his hand out.

Mr Mithering looking as if he were struggling to regain his power of speech. 'Oh, never mind, hand them back.'

'Not to me,' he said, as Inspector Hemmings tried to hand him the pins. 'To Pc Blake.'

I swapped his two shillings for the two pins and thanked him. Ten seconds later they were in place.

'And this is the map, Chief Inspector?' the Chief asked and moved across and stood in front of it.

'It is, sir,' he replied, stepping forwards.

DCS Mithering turned to Inspector Hemmings. 'You may stay and observe, or go for your coffee, Inspector. However, you will not speak of any of what you see or hear to anyone. Is that absolutely clear?'

'Yes, sir,' he looked confused.

Forty-Two

Burton Street, Birkby, Huddersfield, was typically working-class and Victorian. DS Cartwright and WDC Sendrove had followed DS Rhodes from the police station in Peel Street and were heading for the last known address of Isabel Bell. The only possible selection from the misper checks for number one on Wainwright's list. Either Isabel Bell's relatives still lived there or possibly the neighbours might be able to help. If this check proved to be negative ...?

'Here we are, Sarge, No. 37, and there's someone in the front garden.' Jenny Sendrove sighed as she exited the car. This was one bit of the job she hated. 'Take a deep breath,' she said to herself. The sun disappeared behind a vast wall of cloud as the first splodges appeared on the footpath.

Thirty year old Clarice Webster, Isabel Bell's younger sister trowel in hand, stood as the car drew to a halt. She put her right hand on the back of her hip, stretched and watched as they alighted. *Do all coppers look alike?* She thought.

'Excuse me, we're police officers ...'

'You don't say,' Clarice Webster smiled.

'I'm Detective Sergeant Rhodes from Huddersfield,' he returned the smile and showed his warrant card. 'These are my colleagues DS Cartwright and WDC Sendrove from Hecton. We're looking for the home of a Mr and Mrs Bell. This is the last address that we have on file.'

Clarice Webster felt her blood chill and her stomach knot. It might have been twenty years ago but she had dreaded this day. 'Yes,

153

this is my parent's house,' she said. 'Is this something to do with Isabel and the body you found in the park?'

DS Rhodes paused, summoning up as much sympathy as he could. 'Perhaps,' he said. 'Could we come in, please?'

Forty-Three

B efore I could start to explain the door opened. ACC
Weatherspoon arrived.

'Come in,' welcomed the Chief. 'I think we have a quorum.
Carry on, Blake.'

'Thank you, sir. You're obviously aware of Wainwright's list.'

'Yes, I have a copy. But there are only twelve numbers on the list.
There are thirteen on that index card on the wall.'

'That was my doing, sir,' the DCI offered. 'Sally Dunster is the
only one at the moment that we can prove has a direct connection
with Wainwright.'

'The others are purely through his list?'

'Yes sir. We will be relying on forensic and any items found in
the grave. It also relies to a considerable extent on the quality of any
missing from home reports completed at the time.'

The Chief turned to the Detective Chief Superintendent. 'That's
a good point. Mr Mithering, you're responsible for Force Standing
Orders with regard to missing persons?'

'I am, sir. I'll give it the once over, see if it needs amending. In
any case it won't do any harm to rattle a few cages.'

'Good. Carry on Blake.'

'Yes sir. The red spot in the top right corner indicates that there
has been an exhumation. The date is in the bottom left hand corner.
Once there has been an id then there is a tick next to the red spot.
Then photo and details filled in where possible. This was organised
by our office manager, Mrs Granby.'

Hazel sat in her corner looking slightly embarrassed. *Serves her right.*

'You have hidden talents, Mrs Granby,' said the Chief as she flushed.

'Thank you, sir,' she said and gave me a dirty look. Not for one moment could I understand why.

The Chief returned to studying the list. 'So, at the moment numbers one, three, six, seven, twelve and thirteen have been excavated, and three, twelve and thirteen positively identified, thirteen being Dunster?'

'That's correct, sir.'

'I see, and the numbers on these pins,' he indicated the map, 'correlate with the cards.'

DCS Mithering tapped his watch. 'Time sir.'

The Chief nodded. 'Blake, run through those we know something about. You can tell me the remainder in due course.'

'Yes sir,' I replied. 'This is the first,' I pointed to pin No.1. 'Greenhead Park, Huddersfield.'

'I remember that,' said the DCS. *He would.* 'Any identification yet?'

'Not confirmed, sir,' the DCI said. 'DS Cartwright and WDC Sendrove are en route to liaise with DS Rhodes from Huddersfield and hopefully speak with who we believe are the girl's parents. We need to confirm that the girl had a fractured right kneecap approximately three months before she disappeared.'

'That will confirm it?' queried the Chief.

'Yes sir. WDC Farthing and Pc Blake narrowed it to two possibles yesterday evening. However, this morning Dr Hawkins from forensic ruled out one of them because of age. The remains we recovered from Greenhead Park were of a teenage girl.'

'I see,' the Chief said and paused. 'So should this visit to Huddersfield prove to be fruitless it's back to the beginning.'

'Yes sir,' I replied. 'However, if that is the case the girl either wasn't reported missing in the first place or, there's a problem somewhere in the system.'

'Do you have details to hand?'

'Yes sir,' I handed him a list. 'This is what we know so far. If confirmed, number one is Isabel Bell, born Grange Moor, 10th July 1929, disappeared whilst walking home to Birkby from her friend's home in Deighton on the evening of the 29th March 1945. She *was* fifteen.'

'Christ! I remember her,' the DCS declared before the Chief could comment. 'We were drafted in from all over. Turned that end of Huddersfield upside down. Dragged both the canal and the river. Not so much as a sniff from anywhere.' It was heartfelt, but the use the word 'sniff' was, in the circumstances, perhaps not the most apposite.

The Chief simply nodded. 'And the next one is number three?'

'Yes sir. Christine Jones, she was the only one who wasn't buried. The third reference of Wainwright's list indicates where she was murdered and her body found. That was the 1st April 1949.'

'This was the one involving your father.'

I knew that Magnus Yarney would crop up throughout the investigation. Even though I was ready, the mention of the name still had an effect that I hadn't fully understood. 'Yes, sir. Magnus Yarney surrendered to him at this station shortly after he murdered Jones.'

The Chief turned to the DCI. 'You have interviewed Wainwright?'

'I have, sir. Just a brief preliminary interview. I will conduct the second at two this afternoon. At the moment we have so much information coming in I intend to leave any subsequent interviews until there is some clarity.'

The Chief nodded. 'Six and seven, Blake?'

'Six, in the grounds of Temple Newsam House, Leeds, yesterday morning, sir. Seven in Park Wood, Tong, Bradford in the afternoon. The last two, twelve and thirteen. Thirteen was Sally Dunster. She was the body recovered in Westleigh and added to Wainwright's list. Number twelve was Vivienne McKeen recovered from Cold Hiendley, south of Wakefield. She was identified by an inscription on the inside of her wedding ring, Her's and her husband's initials: VM and DM.'

'That was good police work, very well done.'

'Thank you, sir.'

'Chief Inspector, I should like to come and thank the whole team for their diligence so far, when is the best time?'

'Probably around six, sir.'

'Very well. Is there anything untoward concerning Vivienne McKeen, Chief Inspector?'

'We're still trying to sort that out, sir. The husband is adamant that they had a good marriage. However, enquiries from yesterday are tending to suggest that is not the case.'

The DCS smiled to himself. 'It's the old story, sir. No man likes to be thought of himself as a cuckold.'

'Indeed. So,' The Chief stood back and studied the board. 'We have thirteen victims,' he said to himself. 'Twelve from Wainwright's list and the Dunster woman. These are the ones that we know of and no suggestion there are any more. No doubt that will change with Press coverage. We know that there are two victims prior to the 1st April 1949, but nothing further as yet, although information from Huddersfield may arrive shortly. As things stand we know the identities of numbers three, twelve and thirteen, but with the exception of number three not where the crimes were committed ... Right. The gentlemen of the Press await. Thank you for your clarity, Blake and I'd like to see this lens of yours and how you calculated these locations.'

'Any time, sir,' I replied. 'Oh, before you go. Should any information come in during your press conference do you want me to leave it for Mr Valentine or bring it to you.'

He thought for a second. 'If it's positive i.e. confirmation of identification of number one, bring it to me.'

Before I could reply, they left the Incident Room. Mr Mithering's final words to Inspector Hemmings. 'And Inspector, not a single word to anyone.' He turned and followed the Chief.

Inspector Hemmings turned to the DCI. 'I'm just going upstairs for a coffee, sir. And yes, I know.'

The DCI and I carried the Board and easel to the interview room. He followed the Chief to the Press Conference. I locked the door and pocketed the key.

Forty-Four

The parade room was full. The Chief Constable and other senior officers seated behind two tables at one end, BBC and Granada TV crews, side-by-side at the rear and thirty plus seated reporters.

'Good morning gentlemen, My name is Ray Barton, Chief Constable. On my right is Assistant Chief Constable Weatherspoon. On my left Detective Chief Superintendent Mithering. On his left Detective Chief Inspector Valentine who heads this investigation, which I have to say is very fast moving. I shall make a short statement and then throw the floor open for your questions. However, I must advise you that not all your questions may be answered.' He scanned the reporters for a few seconds. 'On Saturday the 6th of March the body of a young woman, Sally Dunster, was recovered having been buried in waste land off Field Lane, Westleigh ...

0945. I received a call from a Detective Inspector Kenton of the York City Police. In answer to our telex regarding the remains recovered from the grounds of Temple Newsam House, a possible name had been found: Geraldine Vasey b. 02.03.1923, disappeared on 09.09.1953 in York. 5'4" in height with dark hair and brown eyes, slim build and wearing a grey skirt and top coat, blue cotton blouse with embroidered collar, nylon stockings, dark grey high-heeled shoes and pearl earrings. Police Reports Monday 12th October 1953 carried the circulation, including a photograph of the missing woman. He also mentioned a misper from Doncaster who had last been seen on York railway station on the 16th May 1963: Sandra Chase b. 06.05.1946 and, as far as he was aware, still outstanding. He gave me a date for Police Reports – 4th June 1963. I promised to call him back and to contact Doncaster.

It took less than five minutes. Inspector Hemmings was out of the station. The duty sergeant gave me the key to the filing room. There were two photographs, one of a vivacious looking woman wearing a blouse as described. Although the photograph was black and white the blouse we recovered was Wedgewood blue with an embroidered collar similar to the one recovered from Temple Newsam. The earrings looked similar to the one from the grave. The second photograph was of an earring. It was identical. The second Police Report regarding Sandra Chase. The photograph, a black and white snap taken on the prom at Blackpool. Born 6th May 1946. Description 5'4", slim build, dark hair, brown eyes, wearing grey skirt with black belt, green blouse, yellow metal bracelet on right wrist, small-faced wrist watch on left wrist,

I called Inspector Kenton back and told him that the photograph of the blouse that his misper was wearing appeared identical. I would pass the information on to DCI Valentine.

As I put the phone down it rang again. It was Jenny Sendrove. Isabel Bell had fallen from her pushbike four to five months before she disappeared and had fractured her kneecap. We now had the date when the sequence began. There was no screaming rush to get the information to the Chief so I took a few seconds to peruse the victims' list, such as it was.

'What are you thinking?'

I glanced at Hazel and smiled. 'DI Kenton from York gave me details of a young woman missing from Doncaster, last seen on York Railway station. Her date is sixteen months, give or take, before Vivienne McKeen.' I pointed at the cards. 'McKeen was No.12. If this other woman is on the list my guess is that it's No. 11, but obviously it's too soon ...'

The conversation ended as the phone rang. 'Incident room, Mrs Granby ... '

'... Just a second Sergeant, I'll put DC Blake on the line.'

I walked into the Parade Room just in time to hear: 'Chief Constable, if you are not short of detectives why do you have probationary constables leading your excavation team?'

The DCI motioned me outside. 'What have you got?' He asked, once we were in the corridor and the door closed.

'Isabel Bell fell off her bike four to five months before she disappeared and fractured her right kneecap, sir. That gives us a start date of the 29th March 1945.'

'Excellent, anything else.'

'Yes, sir. A couple of things. A phone call from a DI Kenton in York. They think they may have an identity for the remains recovered from Temple Newsam House. I have the details here.' I gave him my note.

'Police Reports?'

'The photograph of the ear-ring appears identical. I told him that you'd call him when you were free. I've put his contact details on your desk.'

He laughed. 'You're learning. And this other matter?'

'DI Kenton also mentioned a misper from Doncaster last seen on York railway station. I've put the relevant police report on your desk. Seconds later there was a call from a DS Rearden from Doncaster re the same girl, Sandra Chase, she was seventeen. The date she went missing is a couple of days over sixteen months prior to Vivienne McKeen. Too soon to make a judgement.'

He paused for a second. 'Where's the reference?'

'Farnley Bank, Farnley Tyas, sir.'

'Hell, York to Farnley Tyas, that's a stretch. When's it scheduled?'

'Tomorrow, sir.'

'Leave it for now.'

The last interchange I'd overheard was bugging me. 'What was that last question about, sir? Or shouldn't I ask?'

'No, it's fine. Just an awkward reporter,' he said and paused. 'How do you fancy a baptism of fire?'

'In there?' I grimaced. 'Yes, Ok. Can't be worse than Tadcaster.'

He laughed. 'OK, follow me. Wait by the door. If the Chief agrees come and stand by my shoulder. If he doesn't think it a good idea go back to the incident room.'

Forty-Five

Standing behind the DCI looking at the mass of reporters I wondered what I'd let myself in for. Me and my mouth.

'Gentlemen, this,' the Chief indicated me with his left hand, 'is Pc Blake, the officer that Mr Williams referred to a few minutes ago.'

I heard the sound of camera shutters and scratching of pencils. 'Any questions you consider relevant will first be put to me. Should I consider them suitable I will allow him to answer. So, if you would repeat the question. And no, he has not been briefed. He was bringing me further information with regard to *this* investigation ...

We now know that the first death occurred on the 29th of March 1945. Please go ahead with your question.'

This was not like Tadcaster where there were only seven or eight. More like a bear pit. It was like being at the receiving end of a firing squad but not knowing who was going to fire what. I couldn't see who was going to ask the question until a hand was raised. 'You're Pc Blake?' He was in his late thirties and wore wire-rimmed glasses, had receding sandy hair and a double-chin, he wore a brown suit and an uncertain expression.

'Yes, I am. But you have the advantage over me. Could I ask who you are?'

The shorthand writers sat up and began to write. I sensed movement from the DCI all along the line. 'Erm, David Williams, Sheffield Examiner. And, you're a probationary constable?'

I think the look I gave said to ask something that hadn't already been asked. But I answered anyway. 'Yes, I am.'

'Pc Blake, I have it on good authority that you were in charge of these exhumations.'

I paused, frowned and smiled. 'Mr Williams, I'm a probationary constable working with a team of highly experienced detectives on a murder enquiry. If your informant thinks that I was in charge of anything, you need a new informant.'

'So you deny it?'

'Of course I deny it,' I said and turned to the Chief. 'Sir, is there a problem with me outlining to these gentlemen just which supervisory officers were present at these exhumations?'

He glanced from side-to-side, no-one objected, and then back to me. 'No, Blake, that's fine.'

It only took a minute to explain, but he followed up with. 'Very well, I have to accept that. But it does not explain why, with all the experienced police officers in this force, and others, it was necessary to draft you in?'

'No, I'll take this,' Mr Valentine said as I was about to speak. He sounded cheesed off. 'Mr Williams, Pc Blake was not, as you put it, drafted in. He was already involved before me and my team were. Pc Blake was Wainwright's original arresting officer, and,' he held his hand up before Williams could interrupt, 'if you'll just let me finish. He had already arrested Wainwright for an offence of causing criminal damage. Separate from, but we now know linked to what followed. It was enquiries following Wainwright's arrest that led to the discovery of Sally Dunster's body. Then I and my team along with numerous other police officers and forensic scientists were brought in. The investigation that you now see is due entirely to a young police officer and his sergeant doing their job. Pc Blake remains working with us because he has a lot to offer and for his personal development as a police officer. Now, can we please have no more nonsense about Pc Blake's attachment to C.I.D.?'

'Excuse me,' said a fresh voice, 'Gavin Briggs, Vale of York Echo. Mr Barton, before my colleague has the opportunity to put another question, could I ask Pc Blake a personal question?'

The Chief looked at me. 'That's entirely up to you, Blake,' he said, a faint smile showing on his lips.

'Sir,' I acknowledged and turned to my interrogator. 'You can ask, Mr Briggs,' I said and smiled, 'However, I can't guarantee an answer.' A comment that attracted a few laughs and renewed concentration.

'Understood,' he replied. His brows tightened and he tilted his head a tad to his left. 'You went to university?'

'I did, East Midlands,' he raised his eyebrows inviting more. 'Exercise physiology.'

'Is that what we might call, sports science?'

'It is, most people forget the physiology bit.'

'Or can't spell it,' came an anonymous volunteer, triggering a round of laughter.

I smiled. 'Sports science is easier to remember,' I replied.

'Precisely,' he turned and scowled in the direction of his interrupter. 'What does the prospectus include? Erm, is that all right, Mr Barton?'

'I can give you a little longer.'

'Thank you, Pc Blake?'

I thought for a second. 'It concerns diet, exercise and its' intensity, genetic predisposition and studies the musculature and loading on the skeletal system, in particular the joints to ensure that exercise is safe. Also the oxygen-transport system, i.e. how efficiently the body distributes oxygen throughout the body. I paused for a second. 'However, if you're really serious in understanding exercise physiology I can recommend *Astrand's Textbook of Work Physiology*, it's an excellent book.' *It also had an exam question on every line!*

'I'm sure it is, but I think I'll give it a miss if it's all the same. So, it's a very wide scope?'

'It is.'

'Your skills are non-medical, non-diagnostic.'

'Non-diagnostic in a medical sense, certainly. However, if I find something that gives me cause for concern that thr individual goes to see a doctor, but that is all.'

'But you do know about petechial haemorrhages, don't you?' he said, a knowing smile on his face.

Where the Hell did he pull that from? It must have been someone who was present at Westleigh when Sally Dunster was found, or, our leak artist. It was too exotic to just nonchalantly pull out of thin air. Just play thick. 'That's not really my area of expertise, I'm afraid. About the only things I do remember is that they can be found anywhere in the epithelial tissue, that's the skin and includes the tissues that line the cavities that connect with it. Petechial haemorrhages are non-specific indicators. But you need a doctor to answer that fully, sorry.'

'But when you ...' He got no further.

'Mr Briggs,' The Chief interrupted. 'You stated that you wished to ask Pc Blake *a personal* question. He's told you that this is not an area in which he has in-depth knowledge. If you have no further questions?'

The Chief nodded to me. I was about to leave when another journalist stood up. 'Excuse me. Mr Barton, can I please clarify something that Pc Blake just said?'

The Chief glanced at me, then this other journalist. 'Go ahead.'

'Pc Blake. I was always under the impression that these patrechial haemorrhages were specific to strangulation which is at variance with what you said earlier.'

'There's no 'r',' I corrected, and smiled. 'It's petechial not patrechial. But think about what you've just said.'

'Thanks,' he said and stood there for a few seconds before looking embarrassed. 'Ah, I see. If they were specific to strangulation everyone who had them would have been strangled.'

I couldn't help smiling. 'Correct!' Three paces later.

'Mr Barton, can you confirm that this is the same Pc Blake who was invested with the George Cross recently?'

I stopped in the doorway. The Chief looked over his shoulder and motioned for me to leave. 'Yes, Mr Briggs it is. However all details of that case are subject to the restrictions imposed by the provisions of the Official Secrets Acts of 1911 and 1920.'

'Yes, I was aware. I just wanted to congratulate him.'

I heard the chorus of here heres. 'Thank you. I will pass your congratulations on the next time we meet.'

Five minutes later I was in the canteen with a cup of coffee.

Fifteen minutes later I was in Chief Inspector Sampson's office. The Chief in the Chief Inspector's chair, ACC, DCI and Chief Inspector Sampson stood to one side. The latter two were smiling. The Chief passed the congratulation of the Press on and pushed a minute sheet across the table towards me. 'Read this and acknowledge,' he said.

This was brilliant. I managed to write an acknowledgement and handed it back. 'This is not a transfer to C.I.D., Blake,' said the Chief, 'merely an acting post for the duration of this case. It *will* be entered on your personnel record. This report will go in your file. You will receive plain clothes allowance as a matter of course. At the completion you will revert to uniform.'

Talk about being lost for words. I settled for, 'Thank you, sir.' As it happens I was already in receipt of plain clothes allowance. However, instead of being shown as *duty elsewhere,* this decision by the Chief put my attachment to C.I.D. on an official footing. I could now use the title, detective constable, if only temporarily. Hazel already had.

1100. The DCI telephoned DI Kenton in York. DS Cartwright would go across to York for 7pm. He would take the remnants of the blouse and the ear ring for identification. Necessary, but traumatic for the widower. In the meantime DI Kenton was making arrangements to prepare them for the shock. Also to arrange for Mrs Vasey's dental records to be accessed. If confirmed it would make number six on the list, Geraldine Vasey. Her husband had apparently re-married. There were three children from his first marriage. Two boys now aged eighteen and sixteen and a thirteen year old daughter. Two stepsons, twelve and ten. A seven year old daughter with his second wife. I hoped they had a house like ours.

1110. A call from forensic. Our number one, Isabel Bell, had been strangled. Her hyoid bone had been fractured. The hyoid bone, a thin horseshoe shaped bone at the front of the neck, part of the anchorage of the tongue, in manual strangulation breaks. The halves had been recovered. Bearing in mind the mess when DS Rhodes slipped disturbing the remains we were incredibly lucky.

Forty-Six

1400. DCI Valentine and WDC Farthing entered the interview room. Wainwright already sitting at the table. An officer standing silently in front of the covered easel. The DCI nodded; the officer left the room. Wainwright's eyes drifted to his left.

'Mr Wainwright,' the DCI began. 'May I remind you that you are still under caution.'

'Yes, Chief Inspector,' he sighed. 'I understand.'

'We have something to show you,' he said and removed two sheets of paper from his briefcase, pushed one across the table. Penny took the other, stood at the side of the easel and removed the cover.

The DCI smiled. 'As you can see this is the list of numbers that your wife brought to the police station. Except, we have added a thirteenth.' Was the expression on Wainwright's face surprise, shock or fear? Or a combination of all three? It didn't matter. It had achieved what he wanted. It had provoked a response. 'Yes, Mr Wainwright we know your little secret. You thought those numbers were private. Your dirty little secret that would keep you safe. Now everyone, including your mother, will know. How do you think she will react once she finds out?' The look on Wainwright's face was fearful. 'You don't believe me? You should. It was all worked out by a young constable. It took him about an hour. In fact it's a constable that you know very well ... Pc Blake. He's an exceptionally bright young man. Because of what he has achieved you will be sentenced for all these thirteen murders.' He leaned across the table his face close to Wainwright's, pausing on every word. 'You are never going to see the outside of a prison again.'

'No. No, it isn't true,' he protested. 'I haven't killed anyone,'

'We shall see,' he said and stood a couple of feet from Penny. 'Come here.'

An apprehensive Wainwright stood and shuffled towards the map standing between the two officers. 'Mr Wainwright, are you familiar with Ordnance Survey maps?'

'A little,' he said.

'So you understand that this grid of fine lines that you see identified by the numbers around the edges of the map can be used to cross-reference locations on the map?'

'Yes.' This wasn't supposed to happen. *He* had promised. *He* had told him that the Lord had promised the locations could never be found. Yet, on the map in front of him the pins looked remarkably accurate in their placement. The DCI handed him the sheet of numbers from the table.

'Good. Now read out the first four numbers from the group at the bottom of the page,' he said.

Wainwright's delivery was halting. 'One ... seven...five...zero,' his eyes glued on the map he watched as Penny placed her finger on the pin marking Sally Dunster's grave and traced the grid line from the one-seven easting at the bottom of the map to the pin.

'And now the second four numbers.'

He swallowed hard. 'Two...five...three...eight.' Penny repeated the process tracing the line of the two-five northing from the right-hand edge of the map to the pin. 'That,' said the DCI, 'is where you buried Sally Dunster.'

In spite of his fright he shook his head. 'No, you could simply have worked that out from the location where you found the body. Then added it to the list in an attempt to frighten me, Chief Inspector.'

The DCI smiled. 'Come now, Mr Wainwright, that wouldn't be very clever would it? We need evidence that will stand up to the scrutiny of the Assize Court. Simply to concoct a map reference from the location of the grave and tag it onto your list of twelve numbers in the hope that we could scare you into an admission? No, our homework has been done. But thank you for confirming your knowledge of the map references. Up to midnight last night using this information we have recovered four sets of human remains. Three of which we have identified. These pins that you see in the map represent the locations at which you buried the bodies. This is why you are going to prison for the rest of your life.'

'I haven't killed anyone, Chief Inspector,' he pleaded. 'Why won't you believe me?'

'Read out the top group, Mr Wainwright,' he said.

Wainwright's voice was halting as he began to read: one...seven...zero...eight...one ...three...four...five.

'This is Greenhead Park, Huddersfield, Mr Wainwright,' said Penny, indicating pin No.1. 'Just below the larger of the two putting greens. The girl you buried there was called Isabel Bell. You did bury her didn't you, Mr Wainwright?'

'No!' he protested.

'In Sally Dunster's grave, she's the one you buried in Westleigh, you left several links from your bracelet. Have you forgotten what you left in this grave? Things that can now identify you.'

'I left nothing.'

Penny smiled to herself. Wainwright was not thinking straight. 'If you know you left nothing in the grave, then? ... I'll repeat the question, Mr Wainwright. Did you bury the girl who we now know to be Isabel Bell in Greenhead Park, Huddersfield?'

He simply nodded acknowledgement.

At last, progress. 'Was that a yes?' the DCI snapped.

'Yes,' he replied and nodded again.

'Isabel Bell was walking back to her parent's house in Birkby from her friend's home in Deighton.' The DCI thrust his face close to Wainwright's. 'She was just fifteen-years-old!'

Wainwright looked genuinely shocked. 'It was dark. I had no idea,' he protested.

Valentine took a tight hold of Wainwright's collar. He spoke slowly. 'No idea what?' He said keeping his face close to Wainwright's. 'That she was dead? ... That she was female? ... That she was fifteen? ... That she was naked? ... Was she pretty? ... Was she wearing make-up? ... Did she have that beautiful sheen on her skin like young girls have? ... Did you kiss her on the lips? ...On her breasts? ... Did you stroke her between her legs? ... Did you wish that you still had your testicles? ... Or were you simply revolted by the injuries caused by her strangulation? ... The eyes. It's always the eyes, isn't it? You must remember her eyes. Did you close her eyes like you did with Sally Dunster?'

There was no reaction from Wainwright.

He squirmed as the DCI tightened his grip. 'I'll bet you think about her every day ... Well? Answer me. If it wasn't you, who was it?'

'No. I cannot say.'

'Cannot or will not, Mr Wainwright? This is Cawthorne Park,' he said and dragged him back to the board and pointed to the second pin. 'As yet we haven't investigated this site. However, we will within the next three days. I wonder what we'll find there ... Where was Sally Dunster murdered?'

'I don't know.'

'Don't know or won't say?'

'I don't know, honestly.'

'Honestly?' the DCI said almost laughing. 'At what time was she killed?'

'I don't know.'

'Very well, at what time did you bury the girl?'

He looked back at him. 'About two am,' his voice almost a whisper.

Pointing to the pins in sequence the DCI directing Wainwright's face to each in turn. 'This is the fourth site at Midgely, just outside Wakefield. Not yet investigated.

'Site number five is Newmillerdam.'

'Site number six, the Temple Newsam House estate, believed to be Geraldine Vasey. She was a thirty year old mother of three children then aged three, five and six. Her husband was a schoolteacher. She disappeared on the 9th September, 1953.'

'Number seven. Remains recovered not yet identified.'

'Number eight. Yateholme reservoir at Holmfirth. Not yet investigated.'

'Number nine. The Flouch crossroads above Penistone. Not yet investigated.'

'Number ten. Cupwith Hill, on the moors above Huddersfield. Just past the Nont Sarah's Pub. Not yet investigated.'

'Number eleven. Farnley Tyas. Not yet investigated but it will be tomorrow. Tell me, where was this body from?'

He shrugged his shoulders. 'I don't know. I never knew.'

'Did you ask?'

'In the beginning, but he didn't like questions. I just dug the grave.'

The DCI shook his head. 'Number twelve. Cold Hiendley, south of Wakefield: Vivienne McKeen, 25 years of age, disappeared 18th April last year. She had been celebrating her friend's hen night in Wakefield. She and her husband lived in Sowerby Bridge. They had a four year old daughter ... Tell me, why did you remove all her clothes but leave her wedding ring and wrist watch on her body?'

He squirmed. 'I'm not a thief, Chief Inspector.'

'What did you do with her clothes and handbag?'

Wainwright stared at him for several seconds. 'Disposed of them,' he said flatly.

'That's not stealing?'

There was no answer. 'Very well. In that case why did you not remove her wedding ring, and wrist watch which had little or no value, other than sentimental?'

'I thought they were both gold.'

'In that case, why, with regard to Geraldine Vasey, the lady you buried in the grounds of Temple Newsam House. Why remove both her wedding and engagement rings but leave her wearing her blouse? Answer me that if you can.'

He refused to answer. 'Thou shalt not kill?' said the DCI. 'Thou shalt not steal? In truth Mr wainwright you're only a pseudo-Christian. You pick and choose which commandments you will adhere to as and when it suits you.' Valentine glanced at Penny and nodded.

'Lastly, but by no means least, Mr Wainwright,' said Penny, 'site number three. Slightly different this one, but you already knew that, didn't you?' she pointed to the pin. 'You didn't bury the body on this occasion. Why not? Why did you leave the body lying in the field?'

He looked at the floor and shook his head.

'Where did you first meet Magnus Yarney, Mr Wainwright?'

'This was not my doing,' he said and squirmed.

'Magnus Yarney walked into this police station and admitted to killing Christine Jones. The third set of numbers on your list is the very spot where she was murdered. Where we found her body. Were you present when Christine Jones was murdered?

He shook his head. 'No.'

'Why is that number on your list?'

He refused to answer.

'Yarney, Mr Wainwright,' the DCI said. 'Magnus Yarney, where and when did you first meet him?'

Looking at the floor he said nothing.

'Yarney,' the DCI persisted. 'Where did you first meet Magnus Yarney?'

Wainwright remained silently staring at the floor. 'Mr Wainwright, you could have stopped this fifteen year river of death at source,' Wainwright looked up in confusion. 'Yes, you.' he answered him. 'By not getting involved in the first place. By reporting what you knew to the police. We could have stopped this before it began. You chose not to act and as a result thirteen people,' he said, indicating the map with a sweep of his hand. 'So far all female. The youngest that we know of just fifteen years old, are dead. Numerous children deprived of a mother's love. How many children will not be born? Now, apart from yourself who was present when Magnus Yarney murdered Christine Jones? And how, and where, did you meet Yarney?

He dropped his gaze to the table and shook his head. 'I cannot.'

The DCI slammed his flat hand onto the table startling Wainwright. 'Where?'

As white as a sheet he shook his head rapidly from side to side. 'I cannot,' he whispered.

'Why not Mr Wainwright?' Penny asked in a quiet voice. 'We know that you are a God-fearing man. How do you think that will sit when you are judged? Why not help us to bring closure to the loved ones of those you buried? Do you not owe it to them for what you have put them through over all these years. For the lives that you have cut short? ... No matter what you have done, do you not think that it will stand well with God if you ease the suffering of the loved ones of those you buried?'

He looked at her in total confusion. Whatever thoughts were racing round his mind he was not getting any answers. 'You were present when Christine Jones was murdered, weren't you?'

He looked at her again and nodded. 'Yes,' he said, his voice bleak.

'How many others were there? After all these years it can't hurt to tell us.'

He flinched. 'Three,' he whispered in a low voice.

There was a rapid exchange of glances between Penny and the DCI. 'So there were five of you in all, including Christine Jones?' she asked.

He nodded. 'Yes.'

'Was it your car?'

'No.'

'Whose?'

He shook his head refusing to answer.

'Mr Wainwright, we know from the examination that was made at the time, that at least two men had sex with Jones, were you one of them?'

'No. Never,' he said in disgust.

'Why take that attitude, Mr Wainwright,' the DCI said. 'We seized a large quantity of pornographic material from your house. Much of it imported and illegal in this country.'

'You can burn it. I don't want it.'

'Very well. But this is a minor matter compared to the murders. You will be interviewed about that later.'

'Mr Wainwright, I'm a married woman with two children. I have been a police officer for over ten years. There is nothing that you can say that I haven't heard before. Did Magnus and these other two have sex with Jones?'

'Yes.'

'Will you tell us who either of them is?'

He shook his head. 'No, I cannot.'

She paused for a few seconds. 'Are both these men still alive?'

His eyes pleaded Stop. 'Yes,' He replied.

When did you last see the second man? Speak with him or receive any communication since you last saw him?'

'Many years ago. The night Jones was killed.'

That was fifteen years ago and he's still frightened. 'Not since?'

He shook his head. 'No.'

'Mr Wainwright,' she continued. 'The post mortem report on Jones stated that she had oral sex. There was semen in both her trachea and oesophagus. That's her windpipe and the tube that takes substances to the stomach, as well as her vagina. Who had sex with her orally?'

'Not Magnus.' He said.

'Both the others?' She asked.

'Yes.'

'What did she do to deserve such brutal inhuman treatment from four men, including you? Do you understand what you have done?'

'She was a whore,' he replied.

'Isabel Bell was fifteen years of age. Was she a whore as well?'

He stared back but refused to comment.

'Doesn't the bible say something about thou shalt not kill?'

He hung his head but made no comment.

'Mr Wainwright, were you present when all the victims were killed?'

'Only Jones,' he replied, and shuddered. 'It was terrible, so much blood.'

'And yet there were another ten after Jones, why?'

'You have no idea of his power. He will destroy me if I say.'

'You mean he will kill you?'

'He will strip my soul and I will go straight to Hell.' He was almost whimpering.

'I don't understand what you mean? Said Penny. 'Are you saying that this man has the same power as God? I've never read anything in the Bible that mentions this?'

Looking at the table he refused to answer.

'Mr Wainwright,' said the DCI. 'How do you know that he can strip your soul as you say? Have you seen him do it? In which case who was it? How did he do it? Or is it because he simply claims that he can do it and you believe him?

Again he refused to answer.

'Very well Mr Wainwright. If you weren't present at the scene of all the murders you must have made arrangements to meet so that you could collect the bodies.'

He nodded. 'He gave me a location where we would meet.'

'So you knew in advance? Please answer verbally.'

'Yes, I knew.'

'How far in advance were you made aware?'

He looked at the table and shook his head.

'Describe the vehicle he used.'

'I've only seen it during the night.'

'Well, was it light or dark?'

'Light.'

'What make was it?'

'I'm not sure. It was always dark.'

'Mr Wainwright. You drive a Classic car. You know your cars. What was the make?'

He paused and swallowed hard. 'Vauxhall.'

'Now, Mr Wainwright, turning to these map references? On this sheet,' said Penny, sliding it across the table, 'will you confirm that all the references are written in your hand.'

He nodded. 'Yes, my writing.'

Were you given the references, or did you calculate them yourself?'

He raised his eyes and shook his head. 'I cannot say.'

'Because you are afraid of him? And, what you think he can do?'

Again he refused to answer.

'Mr Wainwright,' said Penny. 'You're in a secure area in a police station. You are quite safe in here.'

Once again he refused to speak.

'Very well,' the DCI said. 'With the exception of Christine Jones you did bury all the bodies, didn't you?'

'Yes, but the Jones woman was not of my doing.'

'What was not of your doing?' He said and leaned across the table. 'You've already told us you were present when Jones was killed. Did you watch as Yarney slit her throat? Did you put your hand over her mouth to stop her screaming? Did you hold her head back to assist him? She wouldn't do that voluntarily. Were you surprised at just how much blood there was? There is a lot isn't there? '

'No,' he said shaking his head. 'That was not me, it was Iag...' He froze mid-word.

'What was that name?' the DCI demanded.

What little blood was left in Wainwright's face drained away. 'N-Nothing, I said nothing.'

'Of course you didn't, Mr Wainwright.' He turned his head. 'Did you hear what he said, Farthing?'

'Dunster's friend thought it was similar to Igor. It certainly began with the letter 'I', sir. Could possibly have been, Iago? Like Shakespeare's villain from Othello.'

'Yes it could,. ....Well, Mr Wainwright, Iago?'

Wainwright stood there a look of terror on his face. 'I have said too much already,' his voice a whisper. 'When he finds out he will destroy me.'

'Mr Wainwright, sit down please.' He leant on the table and took two shuffling steps to the side and sat on the chair. 'Let's get back to what you said. Magnus admitted to Detective Sergeant Blake that he had killed Christine Jones. As you are aware he died in prison. Are you now saying that it was this Iago that assisted him. You have nothing further to lose so you might as well tell us. Please answer, yes or no.'

He nodded slowly. 'Yes,' he confirmed. 'It was.'

'When you left Christine Jones dead in that field how many of you were in the car?'

Wainwright peered at them his expression bleak. 'Four,' he whispered.'

'Four? That would be? ...Mr Wainwright?'

'I was there, Magnus ...'

'And the other two? This Iago person and someone else?'

'Yes.'

'Whose car were you using?'

'Not mine.'

'Will you name this other man?'

Once again Wainwright shook his head and refused to answer.

Wainwright relaxed as the DCI asked the next question. 'Moving on to Magnus Yarney's escape. Were you aware that that it was to take place?'

'No, 'I read of it in the newspaper and heard it on the news.'

'Not from Iago or anyone else? Did you speak to Iago about it?'

'Several months later. He called me on the telephone.'

'What did he say?'

'He doesn't like being questioned. He ignored me,'

'Why did he call you, or is that a silly question?'

Wainwright flicked his eyes to the map.

'Number four, sir. Denby Dale,' Penny said. 'Not investigated, yet.'

'Thank you. Can you be more specific with the date?'

'October, I think. I don't keep a personal diary.'

'Yes, you do, Mr Wainwright,' the DCI fired back. 'We have your current one with your property. Would you care to reconsider your answer?'

'I didn't write the details in it.'

'I find that hard to believe, Mr Wainwright. You receive a phone call from this Iago. You have to remember times, dates, locations and an eight digit number for the location of the grave. That is a lot of information for you to remember accurately. Now, did he give you all the information and did you write the details down?'

Wainwright nodded. 'Yes, but I burned the papers after I copied the references.'

'That's very convenient. How did you contact him?'

'I didn't. I didn't have a telephone number or address.'

'Did he ever write to you?'

'No.'

'You said that when Iago telephoned he gave you a location. He also provided you with the map reference?' Wainwright's eyes flicked to the easel. 'Can you even read an ordnance survey map? Well, Mr Wainwright, can you?' Wainwright stared back defiantly. 'However, Mr Wainwright, a search of your shop, lock-up and house have revealed no maps, compasses or anything else that could be used to calculate these references. So?'

No response.

'You were just at his beck and call?'

Again no response.

'Why did you keep a list of the locations? This will lead to everyone concerned being arrested and going to prison. Was it the intention to put flowers on the graves? ... or,' he mused, 'for this Iago to visit the burial sites of his victims? Look down on his conquests? Well?'

A flicker of concern appeared on Wainwright's face.

'Where did you meet this Iago? How long ago?'

'I cannot say.'

'Are you related in any way to Magnus Yarney or to any of the others involved?'

'No,' he replied.

'Where did you all meet?'

'I cannot say.'

The DCI sat up and leaned across the table. 'Cannot say? Will not, you mean. You've admitted to burying Isabel Bell in March, 1945. Nobody would do that for a stranger. You are in this man's thrall. My belief is that you have known him for many years before that. As for your comment about them all being whores, I think not. He just hates women.'

'No. You are wrong. He respects women.'

'So why does he murder them in the most brutal manner? No, Mr Wainwright, thank you for the information. You can go back to your cell now. But one more thing before you go. You remember that it was Detective Sergeant Blake who was murdered by Magnus Yarney? Well, think about this. Pc Blake is his son. Your nemesis. He arrested you. It was he who broke your code. What next?'

Wainwright back in his cell Valentine sat with Penny in the Interview Room. 'Any observations?'

'You're right about him being terrified of this Iago, sir, it's etched in his eyes. And I agree, they have known each other for a long time, possibly since childhood. I'll instigate a search with the Police Reports editor re possible outstanding mispers roundabout October 1949. That might give us an edge with number four.'

'Good, do that. When we've finished take Jenny and visit Adele Wainwright. Get her talking about her childhood. Her life story down from thread to needle. Then the same with her sister, maybe even her husband, Derek. See if you can get hold of any photographs, family and otherwise. There's no pressure, if it takes a couple of days then so be it.'

'Yes, sir, will do.'

'In my mind there's a religious thread running through this but not as I originally thought ... Wainwright said with some conviction that all the women were whores. I think he believes it. However, from what he's just said that appears to be because this Iago has told him as such.'

'I agree, sir. If for nothing else that Isabel Bell was only fifteen at the time. I've never known of anyone on the game at that age. According to DS Rhodes all the family worked at Hopkinsons. The father in the foundry. Mother was a cook and Isabel an office junior. There's also the younger daughter. She was ten at the time. The mother took her to Birkby infants school on the way to work and collected her on the way home. Isabel attended the local youth club. No boyfriend, nothing special as far as they know.'

'Too many questions and precious few answers. From a female perspective what would entice a fifteen year old girl who's walking home from her friends through an area she knew well, a low crime area, albeit after dark to get into a car driven by a stranger?'

Penny glanced through the window in the interview room door and gathered her thoughts. 'One - she knew the driver. Two - thought she could trust the driver. Three - perhaps someone in uniform, police officer, vicar. Four - maybe even someone she recognised from Hopkinsons. But without knowing anything about this Iago it's only conjecture.'

'True. And this, stripping the soul? This is personal between him and this Iago. It appears to be the way he keeps him in line. Iago may even believe it himself. There must be something in their joint past that lead to this state of affairs.'

'I agree, sir. What's the link between the four of them? ... We know that these women are not all whores, so why tar them all with the same brush? Is it simply to justify his actions to the likes of Wainwright? And why only thirteen since 1945? If the plan was to rid the world of sin as Magnus Yarney originally claimed, we ought to be waist-deep in skeletons by now. Whatever the reason. Whatever goes through his mind is well planned.'

'Look, get cracking with what you've got. If anything further comes to light keep it to yourselves, Jenny as well. No mention of Iago or the fourth man, that stays between just you and me, at least for now. There's been too many leaks already. Understood?'

'Yes sir. And I'll see if I can get Adele Wainwright to say anything about his castration; surely she must know something. Was it purely as Brian suggested, to do with what it says in St Paul's gospel, or something else entirely. That might shed some light.'

'Let Hazel know. She can collate the information with the info regarding Wainwright's properties.'

Forty-Seven

He had a gnawing in his gut. He pushed the slide back: Do Not Disturb. Closed the door. Sitting at his desk and looking through the windows across the car park to the Admin Block he could see the typists in the pool. He spun his chair around picked up the telephone and dialled. It was answered at the third ring.

'They know about the list; Adele took it to the police'

'Do you know why?' The other replied, ignoring the urgency in his voice.

There was a sigh. 'As I understand it he hit her once too often.'

'Is that all?' he said in disbelief.

'You know what he's like. It was enough.'

'But they will not understand anything, we are still safe.'

'They know everything. They have all the locations.'

'Impossible!' Came the incredulous reply. 'Who has spoken? Was it you? Cuthbert?'

'No-one.' he stressed. '*He* wouldn't dare. Do you remember the detective that Magnus stabbed?'

'He died many years ago. It is of no consequence.'

'Yes it is. He had a son who is now a police officer. He is the one who arrested Cuthbert and is working with the C.I.D. It was he who worked out the code. It is time to stop. Now.'

'Are you trying to tell me the Lord is working against us through this Blake's son?'

'Highly unlikely, he is an atheist.'

'How do you know?'

'He admits as such, and does not take the oath in court.'

'And the courts believe him, even though he does not swear on the word of God?'

'Yes, they do. It is quite legal. You must stop.'

'I can look after myself. But you have the authority. Stop him.'

'I should have stopped *you* after Betsy Elstub.'

'Then you would never have got my mother into bed, would you? Don't think we didn't know?'

'I should have stopped you.'

'Well, you didn't. You knew from the beginning that the priest had lied and did nothing. Betsy's uncle? He could hardly stand. And now you're paying the price. You know what will happen if I get caught. Stop him.

'Blackmail!' he spat the word. 'That was Detective Inspector Brierley. Iago, get it into your head. There is only so much that I can do. If I interfere directly there will be trouble. This is not eastern Europe. My authority is not absolute.'

'You are a coward.'

'Neither of us foresaw this happening,' he protested. 'This is betrayal by Adele, not that she could tell anyone much. In case you've forgotten, Adele has a twenty four hour police guard. But I will take steps to terminate any possible links to us.'

'Just kill him!'

Weatherspoon put the phone done then re-dialled.

'Yes sir?'

Forty-Eight

The Russets, Bishopthorpe, six miles south of Clifford's Tower, York, was an impressive eight bedroomed, double-fronted detached house built in the 1920's with well-manicured wraparound gardens. The children dispatched to the playroom and the library. DS Cartwright and DS Dixon directed to the lounge.

'Peace reigns once more,' Jack Vasey exhaled and smiled. He motioned for them to sit in the armchairs facing the fireplace.

'It's a beautiful house that you have here, sir,' observed DS Cartwright.

'Thank you, but in reality it's Myrtle's. She inherited it when her first husband died about six months after Geraldine disappeared. I'm just here on sufferance,' he laughed. 'And, I suspect that comment will lead to questions from you, but can we leave those until the coffee arrives?'

'As you wish, sir. Firstly, just what have you been told regarding the discovery of your first wife's remains?'

'Only what we were told yesterday, plus the little that we have heard on the news and read in the newspapers. This news has really unsettled Anne. She was very young when Geraldine disappeared.'

'She thinks that her mother deserted her?'

'Yes she does. You have someone in custody, I believe?'

'Yes, we do, but we are still looking for others. I'm afraid that I can't tell you anymore because there isn't much more to tell, at the moment.'

'I understand, sergeant,' he said. 'You have some property recovered from the grave that you wish me to identify?'

'The first thing, sir,' DS Cartwright extracted a large manilla envelope from his briefcase. 'Can you identify this garment?' He drew a plastic bag containing the remnants of the blue cotton blouse from the envelope, laid it on top of the envelope and passed it across.

'Are you all right, sir,' asked DS Dixon, noticing Jack Vasey's sudden pallor.

He looked up with a bleak smile. 'Fine thanks,' he replied. 'It's just ... even after all these years it's come as a shock. With the news we received from you and seeing this blouse it's suddenly all the more true.' He handed the envelope back to DS Cartwright, rose and walked across to the window sill returning with a large colour photograph. 'We had this taken on our tenth wedding anniversary, Sergeant,' he passed the photograph across. 'She's wearing the same blouse. Yes, it is hers, you can see the embroidery on the collar,' he paused and returned the photograph to the window sill. 'There was something else. An earring?'

'Yes sir,' DS Cartwright removed a small envelope from his briefcase and tipped the contents into his right palm as Mrs Vasey entered with a hostess trolley.

'Oh, that's Geraldine's earring,' she said sadly. 'She loved those.'

'Yes, she did,' echoed her husband.

'Was that with her in ... ?'

'It was,'

'The discovery of Geraldine's remains came as a hell of a shock, but at least we know the truth. Are you in a position to tell us the cause of death?'

'Sorry, not at the moment. We're still waiting for the forensic scientists to complete their investigation.'

'Was she raped?'

'Again, sir, at the present time we're unable to confirm one way or another.'

'Thank you. There's only one question to ask. Are we suspect in some way?'

'No, sir, you are not in any way, either of you, suspects in the death of your wife.'

The feeling of relief was palpable.

'What happens next?'

'There will be an initial inquest next week; you'll be notified as soon as possible. That will be simply for the purposes of identification. The coroner in Leeds may release her remains for burial or cremation. Perhaps you might like to speak to your solicitor about this. Following that, notify an undertaker to arrange a proper internment. That might help your daughter. If you want the location where she was found we will let you know.'

'Thank you, but how did you know where to dig?'

'Good question. We have a very clever young policeman attached to the team. We had some information but didn't know where it fitted in, if at all. He called it a cross between a flash of perspiration and archaeology. And he was right.'

'We'd like to thank him. Would it be possible to meet?'

'At the moment I would say, no. If you would care to write to the chief constable at Wakefield, Mr R Barton, mark the envelope 'Personal', it will get there. A couple of final questions. Does the name Yarney mean anything to either of you? Secondly, would Geraldine have been likely to get into a car with a complete stranger?'

'I think, Sergeant, that the answer to both questions is, No.'

'So she would either have to have known the driver personally, or trust what she thought the driver represented, for example a policeman in uniform or, maybe, a man in holy orders?'

'Exactly. Is that what happened?'

'We don't know, sir. Just lines of enquiry.'

Statements obtained they were on the point of leaving when the children burst in demanding details.

'I don't envy them that job,' said DS Cartwright as they returned to their cars.

'Nor me. Is it rape and manual strangulation?'

'That's the pattern so far, one exception.'

'And it's twelve or thirteen victims?'

'Yep.'

Forty-Nine

The message was terse. 'Be at the Squad office in fifteen minutes.' Not Hecton. Expedite. No explanation.

Derek Myers let me in. Locked the door behind me and followed me into the DCI's office to join him, the DI and DS Nicholson. There were no smiles. He pointed to an empty chair. 'Tell me what you know about Norman Castle,' he said as I sat.

The atmosphere was brooding and unpleasant. This was not the time for me to ask questions. 'We first met at university.'

The DCI interrupted. 'I thought that you both went to the same school.'

'We did sir. But he left in the summer term as I joined in September.'

He nodded. 'I see. Go on.'

'I joined the rugby squad. He was the varsity captain. He wanted my personal details and when I said I'd been a student at The New College that was that. We weren't close, just university colleagues who loved rugby. Quite often we'd meet in the student's bar and chat.'

'Nothing further?'

'He's gregarious. Makes plenty of noise. He does a great impersonation of Brian Blessed. Likes company and beer. He did mention something unusual. Married at sixteen, divorced at eighteen. But I never enquired why. He is dating my sister, Jennifer, and produced his *decree absolute* and showed it to both her and Joe. He doesn't look anything like any of the identikits that have been produced. He occasionally grows a beard. I take it, sir, this is about the blood group. He's AB positive?'

Now there were smiles. 'He is, and he will have to be interviewed. You are not involved and will say nothing to anyone.'

'I understand, sir. I appreciate that it has to be done but I can't see it. Norman's too much in your face. Put him in a group of twenty strangers and six months later they'll all be able to give a good description. Our suspects appear to shun that kind of behaviour. When you interview him I'll bet he laughs.'

'Let's hope that he has something to laugh about. But there are only a half dozen in this region. Of course, it's entirely possible that our suspect isn't registered with the Blood Transfusion Service or may not even know his own blood group.'

I might have said that I was sure about Norman, but was I? Hopeful? Yes. But could I be absolutely sure? That possible betrayal began to gnaw at me. Jen was definitely smitten. After Tom there was no telling how it would affect her. There was nothing I could do but wait and wonder.

Twenty minutes later, DI Henderson and DC Myers were en route to The New College to interview Norman.

Fifty

The DCI motioned to the two empty chairs opposite his desk.
'John,' he handed DS Nicholson a hand-written note. 'This is the home address of Vernon Jeavons,' he said. 'I want you to pay him a visit. The Chief and the Force Medical Officer are aware and have no objections. Blake, I want you to go simply because of your relationships with both him and Wainwright. He will be intrigued. And, he will probably have questions. You can confirm anything that is in the public sphere, but nothing more.'

'If he asks, sir,' I said. 'Does that includes anything concerning the victims?'

'You may confirm the numbers but no details. If he starts to fish you know what to do, John. From the interview that Farthing and I carried out with Wainwright it appears that there is a definite religious thread running through this entire case. What I require from you two is a low key interview and statement with regard to his relationship with Wainwright. Any information about Wainwright, especially prior to Jeavons meeting him.'

Twenty five minutes later we were cruising along Turnton Grange Road, Westleigh. Lined by well-built detached and semi-detached houses and bungalows built in the late 1940s. We were looking for number 23.

It was a modest semi with bay window and dark blue front door. Neat moderately sized front garden. Rectangular lawn surrounded by a continuous flower bed about six feet wide crossed by a pathway of stepping stones leading to the house. In spite of the warm day he was wearing a dark coloured sweater as he manipulated an electric lawnmower up and down the lawn. He liked neat stripes. Looking up, the only reaction was a penetrating stare. Apart from the fact that I'd never seen him off-duty before it was a face I would never forget. He had aged considerably since our last meeting and there was a deep sadness in his eyes. How would he react?

I'd been out of training school for a couple of weeks when we'd had a blazing row over my reporting Wainwright, the upstanding church-attending pillar of society, for traffic offences. The fact that I'm an atheist and elected to affirm when giving evidence was, for him, the final straw and ordered me to take religious instruction. The culmination being I put my ticket in, albeit temporarily. He'd had a nervous breakdown and was retired on medical grounds. I was still here. This could be interesting.

'Good morning, Sergeant, Blake,' he said, and looked at me. 'I'd heard you were still in the job.'

'Good morning, sir,' we answered together.

'He's an acting DC for the duration of this case, sir.'

'Is he?' He sounded surprised. 'Well, you showed promise, Blake.' He said with a thin smile. 'I have been expecting you. This is where you ask me questions and I sign a statement. Then I ask you questions and you're not allowed to divulge anything.'

DS Nicholson chuckled. 'Sort of.'

His fleeting half-smile reflected in his eyes. 'Things haven't changed. You'd better come in out of public view.' He pressed the control lever on the lawnmower and walked it back to the house. Leaving it at the top of the lawn he crossed the stepping stones and faced me. 'I owe you an apology,' he looked sad. 'Things got a bit out of proportion. Since I've had a lot more time on my hands I've done a lot of thinking,' he held his hand out. 'No hard feelings?'

I saw the look of surprise on DS Nicholson's face. 'No sir,' I smiled and shook his hand. That was a weight off my mind. It could have been very awkward. 'Life's too short.' It was a turn up for the book.

He nodded, let go of my hand and opened the door ushering us inside. We were met by a lady with an immaculately permed coiffure and wearing navy blue slacks and a bright pink jumper that matched her smile. I took her to be his wife. She narrowed her eyes. 'You're Pc Blake,' she said. 'I was in town when the explosion happened. Are you fully recovered?'

'I am, Mrs Jeavons. Thank you for asking. Were you injured?'

'No, I was having my hair done round the corner, but it made everyone jump.'

'I know the feeling,' I think everyone smiled.

'I understand that you have a little girl,' she followed up.

'Yes. Claire. She was born on Boxing Day. She's even more beautiful than her mother.'

She laughed. 'Sorry, I'm taking up your time and getting looks from Vernon,' she said. 'Do you need the table or will you manage on your knee?'

'Knees are fine, Mrs Jeavons,' DS Nicholson said.

Vernon Jeavons took a step forward. 'We'll go in the lounge, Irene.'

'All right, I'll fetch the coffee in a few minutes.'

I turned to follow the others into the lounge, Mrs Jeavons put her hand on my arm. 'He won't admit it but he's very proud of what you've achieved,' her voice was very quiet. Then she left to make the coffee.

I took my seat on the sofa alongside DS Nicholson, Mr Jeavons in an easy chair beside the bay window. 'Whilst we're waiting for the coffee,' he said, looking at me. 'Can you salve my curiosity in regard to what I've heard about him attempting to hit a young lad with a spade. I find that unbelievable.'

I glanced at the DS, he nodded. 'Unfortunately true, sir,' I replied. 'Tore his jacket but fortunately didn't cause any physical injury.'

He just sat there in silence for about a minute. I don't think I've ever seen anyone look as sad as he did. Several times it seemed as though he was about to speak but thought better of it. 'It just goes to show,' he said at last. 'That you never really get to know anyone. I've known him since I came here in '57. Pillar of society. Regular churchgoer. It was Cuthbert who introduced me to his church ...' the words faded. He just sat there in silence until Mrs Jeavons arrived with a tea-trolley. She poured the coffee and placed something in Mr Jeavons hand which he promptly put in his mouth washing it down with coffee. 'Help yourselves to coffee and biscuits,' she said, smiled and left us to it.

DS Nicholson raised his cup. 'Away you go,' he said to me and smiled.

That was a surprise and a compliment. No doubt DS Nicholson would become involved should I miss anything. All we wanted was information. Information in regard to someone he thought he knew well. Someone he had held in the highest regard being involved in multiple murders. A chat, from which the statement we required would evolve.

'Mr Jeavons, you say you first met Cuthbert Wainwright on your transfer to Westleigh in 1957. What was your relationship with him?'

He glanced out of the window and smiled. He'd never been interviewed by a probationer before. 'Purely business. Where council and police business overlapped. Later on through the church; he introduced me. Never socially. In fact although I knew he was married he never told me she attended the same church.'

'Didn't you consider that to be a little strange?'

'Not at the time. Now? Well, yes, it was. But as I said, we had no social interaction.'

'I see. But what we are really interested in is his earlier life. Is there anything at all that you can tell us.'

'I thought you might.' He took some time to marshal his thoughts. 'The only thing that comes to mind was a conversation that took place one Thursday morning. That's when we held the Men's Group, an adult bible-study group. It was a passing reference to a Father Kender. I thought it odd because the title Father implied Catholicism. The church we attended was Anglican. I didn't follow it through. What was in his distant past was no concern of mine.'

'Did he say whereabouts this was?'

'No, just a passing reference.'

'Thanks. One last point, sir. Over the past year or so have you noticed any changes in Wainwright's demeanour.'

'I can't say that I have. Is there anything in particular?'

'Having checked his divisional record up to that time he only had the one minor driving conviction. That was much earlier in his driving career. But in the last eighteen months he has accumulated several more in quick succession and could have been disqualified on the last three occasions. It's as though something has been lying heavily on his mind.'

He thought for a few seconds. 'Nothing springs to mind.'

Statement completed and signed he held the door open for us. 'Just before you leave, are you at liberty to say when these murders began?'

It had been released during the Press Conference so. 'The first was March 1945, sir.'

He looked devastated. I thought he was going to break down. His wife stepped forwards and shepherded us out of the door. 'Thank you. I'll just see to him.' Without further comment she closed the door behind us.

It was a quiet walk back to the car. 'That apology was a bit of a turn-up, Brian,' DS Nicholson said as we drove away. 'He's not noted for that.'

'He was not. And that reaction as we left? What do you think, betrayal?'

'What, the relationship that he had with Wainwright?'

'With everybody. And don't forget it was Wainwright who introduced Jeavons to his church and all the while he's involved in murder.'

'True, and for the previous twelve years. That must have been as painful as a good kick in the nuts.'

'From the look on his face, you're right.'

Fifty-One

The DCI stood in the corridor and scanned the statement. 'And this comment relating to a Father Kender was the only thing he mentioned prior to 1957?'

'Yes sir.'

'He gave no location?'

'No sir.'

'Looks like you have some digging to do,' he said and handed me the statement, smiling as he did so. You could begin with St Agnes' Cathedral in Leeds. That's RC, it's as good a place as any.'

'St Agnes, sir? Ok, I'll do that.'

The DCI headed for the front door as I headed for the office telephone when Inspector Hemmings appeared from the Inspector's office. 'Mr Valentine, DC Blake, could I have a word?'

The DCI looked at the Inspector. He'd always known him as officious, but since his run-in with Mr Mithering he appeared to be making a bit of an effort. 'Yes, Inspector,' he said. 'What can we do for you?

'Sorry, sir, I couldn't help overhearing what you were discussing with DC Blake. There's a Father Kender at Braemont. At least there was when I left Keighley. Braemont's a farming community about six miles south of Keighley. He's been there donkey's years, could be the same one.'

'Thank you, Inspector,' he replied, looking puzzled. 'That's very useful. Your church was it?'

'No, sir,' he replied with a broad smile. 'They're Catholic. The missus and me are strictly Methodist.'

The DCI returned the smile. 'I thought I knew that area but I can't say the name Braemont rings any bells.'

The Inspector chuckled. 'I'm not surprised, sir. It's a real one-horse-community. There's no pub, no shop, although there's an old converted bus, a mobile shop does the rounds a couple of times a week. The telephone exchange is still manual. There's not many telephones in the village. You have to ring the operator, that's Mary, next to the rectory, to make a call.'

'Thank you once again,' he said as Inspector Hemmings retreated to the confines of his office. 'Blake, little job, find DS Nicholson and bring him to the chief inspector's office.'

The DCI closed the door and pointed to the two spare chairs and sat down. 'That reference made by ex-inspector Jeavons with regard to Wainwright mentioning a Father Kender. According to Inspector Hemmings he may be the same one who is currently at Braemont, south of Keighley. And the reason we are having the chat on the QT is that Braemont is where Magnus Yarney grew up.'

That was a stopper. Once again I felt my stomach twist itself into a knot and my heart rate increase by several beats.

'That puts a different complexion on Mr Jeavons' comment, sir,' DS Nicholson replied.

'Yes, it does, John. Blake, make that call to St Agnes. A general enquiry as to whether this Father Kender is at Braemont. If he is get the phone number. First thing tomorrow you and Blake are going to pay him a visit. Call him and fix up an appointment. Keep the interview low key. Meanwhile, I'll call HQ C.I.D. Admin and arrange for you, Blake, to extract the Christine Jones file from the cellar. Bring it back here. I want you to go through it from thread to needle. In particular all information concerning Yarney.'

I set off to collect the file whilst Hazel called Lucy and warned her that I might be late, although I hoped not. Forty five minutes

later I was safely ensconced in an interview room where I could work
without interference – I locked the door.

With Mr Valentine's permission I had previously copy-typed his
copy of what he referred to as the Christine Jones file. In fact it was
only the statements of evidence plus the prosecution summary. What
I had in front of me was, in addition to the copy file, every single
original sheet of paper: the statements in their original longhand;
that included my father's statement. I read that with a mixture of
excitement and trepidation. Apart from the Christmas and birthday
cards he'd sent to mum and me, which she'd kept, this was the only
example of his handwriting I had seen. It felt slightly odd to read it.
This was a time capsule. I'd joined the police because I wanted to
emulate him and now I could read everything he had written on this
case. Yes, it drew me nearer to Yarney, but more importantly much
closer to the man who was responsible for my being here. That was
far more important. I felt nearer to him now than I had ever done.

It was a matter of checking every individual sheet of paper. There
was a problem. The compressed file was several inches thick and
fixed by long star-binders so tight that it would have taken tin snips
to open it. Nothing was intended to be removed. But several
documents were missing, although it had taken some time to
establish that as a fact. There were no antecedents. No statement
from the police officer who had allegedly taken them and no copy.
That took long enough, but when I discovered they were missing I
stood the file on its' left-hand edge checking it again this time using
a bodkin to expose around the binder for each page, marking each
place as I did so. That took even longer. When I finished I went
hunting for the DCI.

He was in Chief Inspector Sampson's office. I told him what I'd
found. 'Are you absolutely certain?' He said, his expression a cross
between incredulity and anger.

'Yes sir. I originally checked manually and then used a bodkin to open the file. Both copies and originals have been ripped out in their entirety, with the exception of tiny traces of paper adhering to the shaft of the star binder, but they could be anything.'

'Can you show me?'

The typed copies were at the front behind the file summary. The original statements, all in longhand, behind. The miscellaneous documents behind the statements. Fortunately I'd put pieces of paper in the file to mark the relevant places. Five minutes later he was satisfied that I was correct. The documents were missing. Someone had removed all three documents from the file. 'Have you told anyone else of this?'

'No sir, just you.'

'Keep it that way,' he said, but I could see from his eyes that his mind was working overtime. 'Not even DS Nicholson, understand?'

'Perfectly, sir,' I replied. 'But why ...?' I looked at him in case he was about to shut me up.

There was a half-smile around his mouth and in his eyes as he said. 'There's just the two of us, carry on.'

I nodded in return. 'The papers that you asked me to find are not there. The traces of paper attached to the star binder may or may not be relevant. However, the fact that they are missing indicates they were important, but we can't say when they were removed. So where was the file kept?' I said, thinking aloud.

'In HQ C.I.D. cellar,' came the answer. 'Almost all files are kept at division, but major files are stored at Headquarters. The cellar is insecure.'

I nodded. 'So, why this file and why now? ...' There was an idea forming in my mind that I did not like. The more I thought the less I liked it. The DCI just stood there watching my expression but saying nothing. Eventually I decided to air my thoughts. 'Sir, at that first meeting where I explained my idea about Wainwright's list of numbers, Mr Creighton asked about Yarney's antecedents. You said that they had been obtained by someone from the local C.I.D. but you couldn't remember the name of the officer. However, your intention was to reassess the original file i.e. this one,' I put my hand on the file, 'as part of this enquiry.'

As I was speaking a smile began to appear on the DCI's face. 'Have you reached a conclusion?'

He might have been smiling but I wasn't. This scenario was not what I'd expected. 'Assuming that those individual pages have been removed very recently it would imply that someone in that room ...?'

'Not beyond the bounds of possibility,' he said and smiled. He'd already reached the same conclusion. 'It could however explain the leaks. So you say nothing to anyone. I'll brief you both tomorrow morning.'

The Chief was spot on time. He took about ten minutes to thank everyone for the results that we had achieved in a relatively short space of time. No matter what we heard. Saw on the television. Read in the media. The Metropolitan Police would not be brought in. We were at least as good. That pleased everyone and got a short round of applause. He gave us some information of his communication with the divisional commanders in this force and the chief constables from other forces involved, including the fact that their overtime budgets were being stretched – not necessarily a bad thing, at least for us; plus the positive effect on police morale. He also pointed out that with an enquiry of this type, i.e. murder, additional funding was available from the Home Office – a reply was awaited.

Then he asked about the lens. I was ready for him. Hazel's desk had been cleared and it only took a few seconds to set everything up. Using the eight digit number for Isabel Bell No. 17081345. I showed him how to break down the number using the first and third pairs to isolate the square. The second and forth pairs did the rest. He studied for a few seconds and quickly grasped what was involved. He tried a couple and stood back. 'Now I understand,' he began. 'So, whoever it was who put the list together had to have the same knowledge and skills as you, but in the belief that should we ever come into possession of the list we would be unable to work out its relevance, if indeed there was any relevance at all.'

'Whoever it was, sir, had to have had the idea in the first place. That was the clever bit.'

'Perhaps, but it was what you described as your flash of perspiration. The realisation that if you changed the scale of the map they might possibly be map references. Without which there would have been no investigation.'

'Yes sir,'

The Chief nodded slowly. 'Thank you, Blake. Well done.' He then turned to the rest of the team. 'Thank you all. I hope you can bring this to a speedy conclusion.' He shook hands with the DCI and left.

Fifty-Two

The Press scrum outside of Hecton nick was increasing on a daily basis. As always, they sought another comment, or photograph as DS Nicholson and I left for Braemont. Once again it was chucking it down.

As usual when I was being ferried about, we chatted. Today was no different. Sergeant Nicholson raised the subject of promotion and what I thought about supervision in general. The decisions that he and all the other supervisors in the squad took. How did I fancy my chances as I was being groomed for possible accelerated promotion via the Special Course? It was a daunting thought. Then he said something that really made me think. 'Mark my words Brian,' he said. 'You will get promoted providing you pass your exams. I don't know about Bramshill but I wouldn't rule it out. You will be making supervisory decisions in the not too distant future. It's a lot nearer than you think. No matter who the Chief is, Lucy's cousin or not ...'

I glanced at the grinning reflection in the rear view mirror. 'You knew?'

'Yup,' he said. 'The wife and I were chatting to the Chief and his wife at your wedding reception. He let it slip when I asked him if they were friends of the family. And no, I haven't told anyone else.'

'That's appreciated.'

'No problems,' he said. 'Just do *not* turn into a Baines!'

I promised I wouldn't. However, one of the things that I had noticed when it became known that I was being coached was that most, if not all, animosity emanated from a small number of Pc's.

Not from supervisors. Was it a question of, 'If I can't do it, why should you?'

It was a steady drive through Bradford, although the traffic in Forster Square was a nightmare. Nevertheless fifty minutes later we pulled up close to the gates of St Barnabus in Braemont and decamped.

It was a simple hamlet. There were plenty of spring flowering trees trying their best to drive winter away. As Inspector Hemmings had said: no shop, no pub, and, apart from the church, nothing. As for traffic? Even less.

Father Kender was stiffly built with a ruddy complexion and a remarkably good head of dark hair for a man of his age. He had a wary look in his piercing brown eyes. Nevertheless, it was a warm welcome.

I wasn't quite sure what it would be like. It was the first time that I had been in such an establishment, or spoke to anyone in holy orders since my father died. That had not been a success – I was eight. My father had just been murdered. The vicar told us in Sunday School that God would grant our prayers – he didn't. Dad stayed dead. I'd called the vicar a liar. Well, shouted at him.

However, the sitting room was pleasantly furnished, the chairs were leather, old and comfortable. Father Kender's the epitome of its occupant. I suppose it was to be expected but the only thing I found disconcerting was the mass of religious paintings and iconography littering the place. In particular a two feet tall bronze statuette of an angel with outstretched wings on a small table adjacent to the large bookcase.

Mrs Magee, Father Kender's housekeeper, brought in a tea tray, bid us help ourselves and left.

Satisfied that we were happy with our tea, Father Kender settled back into his Queen Anne Chesterfield, turned to face us and smiled. 'Now then, gentlemen, how can I help you?'

'Father,' said DS Nicholson. 'What can you tell us about Cuthbert Wainwright?'

Was the look on his face surprise, or was there an element of shock? 'You certainly know how to cast your net deep, Sergeant. That's a name that I hadn't heard for many years. Are we talking about the same man whose name I saw in the newspaper with regards to that young woman who was murdered?'

DS Nicholson smiled. 'We are, Father. Your name cropped up during our enquiries. According to St Agnes' there's only one Father Kender that they know of. What can you tell us about Wainwright?'

He took a deep breath, opened his eyes wide, and blew out. 'It must be, what? Forty – forty five years ago that I last saw him. Let-me-think.'

He was playing for time. Cuthbert Wainwright is not a particularly common name. If he saw it in the papers then it definitely registered with him. What was he going to tell us?

'The Wainwrights weren't Catholics,' he said at a speed that gave him thinking time. 'Cuthbert would be about, let me see … fifteen or so when he first attended St Barnabus.' He came with a friend. I don't think his father was too thrilled at the event, but *he* was welcome …'

DS Nicholson tapped his shoe against mine – at the first opportunity …. I leaned forward. 'Sorry for interrupting, Father,' I said. 'But this friend. It wouldn't happen to have been Magnus Yarney by any chance?'

The reaction was immediate. 'Magnus!' he gasped. This time he was genuinely shocked. 'But … well … er, no, not Magnus. The Yarney's were Catholic, and Magnus and Cuthbert attended at the same time. Offhand I honestly can't remember who it was. But, no, it wasn't Magnus.'

'That would be in the 1920s, Father?' I said.

'Erm, yes, I suppose it was, 1926 or 7.'

'You mentioned the Yarneys. Can you remember who exactly? Apart from Magnus.'

'Just his mother, Magda,' he said. 'His father was killed in the Great War. But I thought you wanted to speak about Cuthbert?'

'We do, Father,' replied DS Nicholson. 'We knew they knew each other. We just wanted corroboration of the information that we already had,' he said with a gesture to the priest. 'Who better than yourself.'

Father Kender nodded. His eyes told a different story. Already wary, he was now *en garde*.

'But can you clarify your dates, please?' I said. 'Cuthbert Wainwright is only in his mid-fifties now, if he didn't begin attending your church until he was about fifteen ...?'

He thought for a moment. 'Yes, of course ...' he said. 'You're correct. It's difficult to be precise after all this time. Cuthbert never converted and stopped attending services after nine months or thereabouts. So perhaps five years less, more than that I'm afraid I can't say.'

'Thank you. You say, they left the church, could you be more specific, please?'

He studied us gathering his thoughts. 'If you didn't live through the 1920s you can't begin to understand how difficult a time it was. This was a poor area to begin with and it didn't improve with the depression. Times were hard. Money was scarce. Poverty was a disease that affected all and sundry. Maybe partly because of that our congregation flourished. It's much improved today. In those days, which seem like centuries ago, the church was full. We had a very supportive and thriving congregation including a good number of young people. We had one young man who would have made an excellent priest. A powerful orator who really got his message across.

He became a sort of unofficial leader to his age group and several others who should have known better. Of course he couldn't preach to the congregation in church, and over time he upset a lot of people, including me. He fixated on one particular aspect of the gospel according to Mathew: chapter 5 verse 17. In it Jesus, when accused that he is trying to loosen the Law, says that he has not come to loosen the Law but to uphold it. Jesus is confirming that he is a Jew. They wanted to go back to the Law of Moses and the punishments laid down in the Old Testament.'

'Stoning?'

'Yes, Sergeant,' he said and laughed. 'Including stoning. In the end I had to exclude them from church premises. However, they found an ally in a local farmer, Robins at Cowgill Farm, who allowed them to use one of his barns.'

'Does this individual have a name?'

'Gregory, Sergeant. However as you might expect it was often shortened to 'Greg'.

'What happened to him?'

'He died. But Magnus and Cuthbert plus several others went with him.'

'Did the group include a young lady called Adele,' I asked. 'Sorry, I don't know her surname.'

Father Kender smiled to himself. 'Yes, I remember Adele. Adele Bagley, a very attractive young lady. One of those caught up in the fervour and totally besotted with Cuthbert, and he with her. The reason I smiled is that although Gregory was not ordained he claimed that he had God's gift to carry out His work, and that included performing the sacrament of marriage.'

'He married them?' I said. That was a surprise. In that case it's doubtful that the Wainwrights were married?

'He went through a form of marriage. However, it's not a ceremony that would be seen as legal in the eyes of the church, or the

State. Cuthbert also did something incredibly stupid, at least in my eyes.'

That caused me to smile. 'He castrated himself?'

'Oh, you know,' he didn't sound surprised.

'We do. He's quite proud of the fact that he did.'

Father Kender shook his head. 'Are they still together?' *He didn't say married.*

'They are, Father. Now, we know that Magnus is dead but can you tell us anything further about him?'

'Nothing that I didn't tell the other detective when Magnus was arrested all those years ago. In fact I remember making a statement with the details.' That was a shock, there was no statement made by Father Kender in the Jones file. Not even any sign that one had been removed.

'I'll check the file when we return to Hecton, Father,' I replied. 'In the meantime would you be willing to dredge your memory and tell us what you can remember?'

Nothing further was forthcoming. Statement obtained; we were getting ready to leave when DS Nicholson asked if any of the remaining members of the group lived in the vicinity. The answer? There weren't any. Well before Magnus was arrested the group began to disintegrate. After Farmer Robins died they were no longer welcomed at Cowgill Farm. Finally Gregory died. Even when pressed he refused to divulge this Gregory's surname. He said it would serve no purpose. How he knew that I have no idea. Perhaps it was divine inspiration.

We were leaving the lounge having thanked Father Kender for his assistance and hospitality, I tried to dodge Mrs Magee who was coming in to clear the dirty cups. We ended up doing a little dance in the doorway. Just one of those things, or so I thought, until she slipped something into my breast pocket. With profuse apologies and embarrassed smiles we disentangled, said our goodbyes at the door and got back into the car. The rain was now passed. The sun making valiant efforts to shine

Out of sight of the Rectory DS Nicholson stopped at the side of the road. 'What do you think?'

I chuckled. 'He's lying. He's only told us half a tale.'

DS Nicholson smiled. 'Agreed, but about what?'

'Firstly, there is no statement from Father Kender in the Jones' file. Of that I'm certain.'

'Well that's a good start, Brian. So, unlike the others it was either removed in its entirety or, it never saw the light of day. Anything else?'

'If he saw Wainwright's name in the paper linked to Dunster's death he would naturally make the link with Magnus Yarney. He wouldn't have been too surprised when I spoke with him and made the appointment, although we got a vigorous reaction when I dropped Yarney's name on his toes.'

'True,' he replied. 'That certainly had him rattled. One thing I found a bit strange was that he told us more about Wainwright and his marriage to Adele than about Yarney and his family; as for his reticence in providing this Gregory's surname.'

'Well, Sarge, we might have an extra clue,' I said and pulled the piece of paper donated by Mrs Magee from my pocket. 'I think Mrs Magee was waiting for us to leave and engineered that little waltz in the doorway. She slipped this into my pocket whilst we were dancing.'

His eyes lit up. 'The crafty devil, what's it say?'

'Mrs Angela Morton, 9 Carr Valley Road, Micklethwaite. I don't know where that is.'

'I do,' he turned the engine on and put the car in gear.

The door closed behind the two detectives; an angry Moira Magee rounded on Father Kender. ''Twas a wicked thing that you did Father, lying to the police like that.' she declared. 'If their enquiries take them to the right person they'll be back, then what? If you'd done the right thing by Betsy Elstub all those years ago none of this might have happened. You should've handed the twins over to the police at the time.'

His mind whirled. His memory as clear and sharp as it had ever been. *A parish priest at Braemont, five miles west of Keighley since July 1924. Similar in many ways to his own village outside of Claggan in County Galway on Ireland's Atlantic coast. Poverty was rife. Braemont was a poor community of farming people who followed the rhythms of the seasons eking out a living where they could. Different from Ireland in that the nearby town of Keighley was a relatively prosperous mill town not many miles from the City of Bradford.*

His next task that morning had been to visit Anne Clarkson. To his moral cost she was an attractive, vivacious and wealthy widow whose mill owner husband had been killed in a car crash shortly after his arrival in the village and, as he saw her, a temptress. When he made his confession to the Bishop he simply laughed: 'Ten Hail Mary's, Father, and learn the lesson!'

Now Anne was dying from cancer and not expected to survive the day, he felt he owed her something.

The twins, breathless and distressed, had burst on him as he wheeled his pedal cycle from the shed. Not regular attendees but they had kept out of trouble, until now? 'Now then boys,' he said. 'What's bothering you?'

'We found a dead body, Father,' Iago gasped. 'Betsy Elstub!'

Henry Elstub had been a farm labourer, his wife Felicity had died bringing their seventh, a still born infant into the world. Four of the six who had survived birth had died with the childhood diseases that attacked along with poverty. The will of God was it? Caroline, the eldest remaining child ran the house when she wasn't working on the farm, but sixteen years old Betsy was a wayward child, and, as the priest many rumours came his way.

The boys knelt at the altar rail. 'There's no-one here except for you, me and God,' he said looking each of them in the eye. 'Whatever you tell me I cannot repeat. If you lie to me I cannot help you, and, God will know. Now boys, I want the truth.'

So they told him.

'Betsy is now beyond my help,' he said calmly and paused for several seconds his mind churning. They're too young to hang but would anything be served by condemning these two to a life of penal servitude? 'Hopefully, the Almighty will take pity on the child,' he continued. 'As for you two, for your confession, I forgive you your sins and your penance is that you will attend Mass every Sunday.'

'For how long, Father?' said Magnus.

'Until I decide otherwise,' he replied with a grim smile. 'Now, I must contact the Police, they will want to talk to you. Betsy cannot be left up there, she deserves a Christian burial,' he smiled inwardly at the look of horror on the boy's faces. 'You will sit on those front pews and not move an inch,' he said sternly and wagged his finger at them. 'When the Police ask you questions you will tell them exactly what you told me about finding her body. Do you understand? Finding the body and nothing more, do not elaborate one little bit.'

He shook himself. 'I don't need you to tell me that, Moira,' he walked away whilst trying to control his emotions. 'But what is done is done.'

'I know that, Father. But when Cuthbert's name appeared in the papers you knew as well as I did who was responsible, and you did nothing. Nothing! How many bodies have they found so far? Six? Seven? May God have mercy on you.'

He spun round and glared at his housekeeper, the woman who had been his comforter since his visit to the Bishop some forty years earlier. He narrowed his eyes as he saw her anger fade. 'What have you done, Moira?' he demanded. 'For God's sake, what have you done?'

'Something that should have been done years ago, Father. You know he's insane. It's time!'

Fifty-Three

A burst water main in Keighley town centre extended the journey to Micklethwaite from twenty to forty-five minutes. 9 Carr Valley Road, a solid stone-built detached house facing south-west. Elevated, with a half dozen steps to neat and well tendered twin lawns surrounded by newly planted flower beds. Magnificent views across the valley to the moors. However, we weren't there to admire the scenery.

Mrs Morton reminded me of an older but much slimmer Mrs Brocklesby. Like her she was a magistrate, or at least a retired one. I'll bet she was. Beneath that pleasant smile there was something about her voice and look that said she wasn't to be trifled with.

'I take it like all police officers you drink tea?' she smiled and left us sitting in the lounge whilst she went to put the kettle on.

It didn't take long before we were all sitting with our refreshments. Nobody spoke. She took a sip of tea, placed her cup in its saucer on a side table and looked at us each in turn. 'So,' she said with a grim smile. 'It was Moira Magee who passed you my details?' Although her question was rhetorical, I agreed. 'Well, I think that it is fair to say that Moira Magee and I do not see eye to eye. For her to pass you my details following your meeting with Father Kender it must be something which she believes is of some considerable importance. And, which she believes I also consider important. The only matter that might be concerns the recent reports in the press concerning Cuthbert Wainwright and the recovery of a girl's body. Subsequently a series of other human remains.'

'That's correct Mrs Morton,' I replied. 'Plus a friend of his who lived in this area, Magnus Yarney.'

'Magnus?' she exclaimed. 'I know that he committed some terrible crimes but until the 30th of May 1936, he was a very pleasant boy. A dreamer who lived in a world of his own for much of the time, but basically harmless.'

That was a bolt from the blue and one that left me feeling nauseous. 'Are you ok, Brian?'

'Fine,' I replied. 'I just that I never thought that I'd hear him described in terms that made him sound human.'

Mrs Morton's eyes narrowed slightly. 'There is a problem?' she said. 'Surely you are far too young ever to have met him?'

'He is, Mrs Morton. After Magnus Yarney killed for the first time he surrendered to Brian's father, a detective sergeant, at Hecton police station.'

'I'm sorry, I wasn't aware. And the second time he killed?'

I nodded.

'I see. I'm very sorry. But I thought there was a rule in the police that with such a relationship as yours, Mr Blake, that you were not to be involved.'

That brought a smile to my face. 'There is, Mrs Morton,' I replied.

'Brian had already arrested Cuthbert Wainwright for an offence of causing criminal damage, which in turn led to the discovery of the first body,' DS Nicholson explained. 'We had further information but we didn't know if it had any real evidential value, or not. But it was some brilliant deduction by Brian that opened this case up and made it possible for us to recover further bodies. His reward was to remain as a member of the team. However, the price that he has to pay, because of who his father was, is that whenever we leave the station on enquiries he is shackled to me.'

'I understand,' she smiled. 'So you never met Magnus, and you don't know?'

'I've seen photographs of Magnus Yarney on the case file, Mrs Morton, but whatever it is that you think we don't know, we probably don't.'

She got to her feet. 'I'll be back shortly, please help yourselves to more tea.'

Cups refreshed but before we had chance to sit, she returned. Without any comment she handed us a photograph and sat down. An eight inches by ten, black and white of the inside of a large barn. Bales of hay were stacked in curved ranks to provide seating, like an amphitheatre. They were occupied by approximately twenty happy looking people, mostly appeared under thirty years of age. On the left there was an old cart, similar to the one in Constable's *The Hay Wain*. It contained two women, one of whom was sitting opposite us. My attention was drawn to a group of three males standing near the cart. The nearest, between the shafts, Father Kender. But it was the two young men standing next to Father Kender that caught and held my attention. Once again my stomach clenched. I felt my blood run cold. 'Twins?' I said, scarcely able to believe my eyes and looked at Mrs Morton. 'Magnus Yarney was a twin?'

'The younger,' she replied as a matter of fact. 'He's on the left, but they were like two peas from the same pod. The elder is Iago. Now he was a different kettle of fish altogether. He was arrogant, aggressive, very much the leader, and, if Moira or Father Kender had been anything like honest about the group they would have told you that Iago was a powerful speaker.'

'Father Kender implied that Magnus was an only child,' I replied.

She shook her head. 'Father Kender was always protective.'

There was nothing on the original file with regard to any close relatives. In view of what I had found regarding the missing documents this was relevant to our enquiry. However, there was no need to mention it even if Mrs Morton raised the matter.

'Father Kender mentioned a member of the group called, Gregory. He said Gregory was a powerful speaker.'

'Gregory?' she laughed. 'Gregory was Moira Magee's elder brother and with respect to Moira, a bit simple. Yes, there was a Gregory in the group but he was not a speaker, and, no, Mr Blake, the orator of the group was Iago, Magnus' twin brother.'

'You were a member of the group, Mrs Morton?'

'No, Sergeant. The photograph was taken at a picnic organised by the group. It transpired that they had begun to haemorrhage numbers, I believe because of the message they were attempting to propagate. I was invited by a friend of my daughter's, Adele. She's on the photograph next to Cuthbert Wainwright. They were hoping to recruit new members. But when Iago began to explain what they believed in people simply lost interest.' She got out of her chair and pointed out one or two people on the photograph. Cuthbert Wainwright and Adele Bagley seated to the left of the Robins, farmers at Cowgill Farm.

'And Father Kender,' I said, 'next to the cart.'

'Correct,' she replied. 'But he was ever-present.'

'He told us that he hadn't seen Magnus Yarney for forty years or more,' DS Nicholson said. 'He claimed they only became aware after Magnus Yarney murdered Christine Jones in 1949.'

'Really? It's true from what I heard that they were eventually refused permission to use St Barnabus, but he was always there or thereabouts. You might get a better picture of their relationship if you dig out the files, including the court papers for that case I mentioned on the 30th May 1936. It concerns the death of a local girl, Betsy Elstub. There was a great deal of publicity in the local and regional press. What followed was not one of the finest events in British police history.'

'And this Iago was the one that Father Kender referred to as Gregory?'

'So it appears.'

'Father Kender wouldn't say what Gregory's surname was. He believed it wasn't relevant because he was dead.'

Mrs Morton's smile was grim. 'Probably because if Moira heard the name being mentioned she would have reacted quite strongly; they were very close. As for dying? Gregory was killed in a farm accident some twelve years ago. The group dissipated after the death of Farmer Robins around the New Year following this photograph being taken. The new tenants of Cowgill farm refused the group access to the barn and to be honest I haven't thought about them for many years. For the most part, Magnus. However it was Cuthbert Wainwright's name appearing in the papers recently that refreshed my memory.'

I flipped the photograph over. There was a date written in the top left-hand corner: 23rd August, 1947. They'd already killed at least once by this date. 'This Gregory, Mrs Morton, is he in the photograph?'

'No, he isn't,' she replied. 'He was another who didn't like the message that Iago was trying to put across. And, by the way, Cuthbert married Adele, the young woman I told you about.'

'They're still together,' I said. I didn't see the need to mention Father Kender's comments re the legality of their marriage. 'You said that Adele was a friend of your daughter's, was she a member?'

'Brenda? Not really,' Mrs Morton said. 'She attended a couple of meetings because of her friendship with Adele, not because of the message. Brenda is in the photograph with me in the hay cart. She kept in touch with Adele for a while. They just drifted apart.'

There was a silence for a few seconds before DS Nicholson spoke again. 'We know that Magnus Yarney died. We have Wainwright in custody, but do you know the whereabouts of any other members of the group? Or perhaps your daughter may know?'

'Brenda married,' Mrs Morton said. 'She and her husband and two children emigrated to Australia over ten years ago. I'm due to call her tomorrow evening. I'll ask her and let you know. However, for my part, I can't think of anyone.'

'Do you know if Iago Yarney could drive, Mrs Morton?' I said.

'Yes he could,' she replied. 'I remember, he came before the bench on several occasions because of his aggressive driving. When a young man he was disqualified on at least one occasion. However, in spite of his nature he could be a very personable young man and at times charming.'

'Did he ever marry?'

'No, not to my knowledge he didn't.'

'Do you know if he had any girlfriends?'

'Sorry, no,' she replied. 'Friends, certainly, but I don't recall anyone specific. But it was a long time ago.'

I nodded and smiled. 'Do you know how the Yarney family made a living?'

She took a deep breath and exhaled, narrowing her eyes as she spoke. 'Jakob' - she pronounced the J as a Y – 'was an accountant. Magda, as was the norm, stayed at home. They were relatively prosperous without being ostentatious. Lived in a nice house in Laycock. There was a serious fire ten or fifteen years ago and it's since been demolished. There was a lot of bad feeling after Magnus murdered that girl. They all, including Iago, left the area. I believe they went to live somewhere near Skipton and because of what happened changed their name. Jakob and Magda were good people, a nice couple. They were destroyed by what Magnus did.'

'Do you know what they changed their name to,' I asked.

'I think Jakob became Jacob but sorry, I don't recall their adoptive surname.'

'Father Kender was of the opinion that Mr Yarney was killed during the Great War.'

'He most certainly was not,' she replied, sitting bolt upright in her chair. 'Jakob was my husband's accountant and very much alive. He died in 1953, twelve months after my husband. I seem to remember that Iago took over the business. In spite of everything he did well. Oh, and he changed his name to James.'

'It looks like we're going to have to pay Father Kender a return visit, Brian.'

I had to agree. 'Did they actually believe they could turn the clock back and introduce such barbaric punishments?'

'I don't know, Mr Blake,' she looked sad. 'My initial view was that they wanted a rigid legal and moral code enforced by the courts. When their group lost its numbers most people, myself included, thought it was finished and good riddance. It was only when Magnus murdered that young woman in 1949, that I, for one realised that one at least had decided to continue. I was amazed that it was Magnus.'

'Did you inform the local police of your fears?'

'Certainly, I understand that both Iago and Cuthbert Wainwright were interviewed but nothing came of it.'

'Just one further point, please, Mrs Morton, before I take your statement. Who was behind the camera?'

'I knew you were going to ask me that,' she smiled. 'I can tell you he was a policeman,' she laughed again at our joint looks of surprise, '... his family was Italian, they came to England after the First World War. His father was in partnership with a local printing company,' she smiled and nodded. 'If I keep talking it will come back to me ... Alberto,' she said at last. 'I remember him from my early days on the bench, they called him Albert. The family became naturalised British citizens well before the onset of the second world war, subsequently changing their surname by deed poll. But I can't remember what on earth their original surname was or what they changed it too ... it had been 'D', something or other ... No, it won't come,' she said after several seconds of ploughing her memory banks. 'I do recall that he had a younger sister who went back to Italy to get married, that would be fifteen, perhaps eighteen years ago.'

I was putting Mrs Morton's statement in the folder prior to leaving. She suddenly blurted out. 'It was Dem Eeteo,' she said with the emphasis on the 'Dem', 'that was the family name.'

'Can you remember how to spell it?' I said.

'Sorry, no, I can't.'

What Mrs Morton had said appeared to be wrong for an Italian name, not that I knew all that many. I jotted a few things in my pocket book. After a couple of attempts I tried – Di Meteo, and showed it to Mrs Morton. 'Could this possibly be it?' I said.

'Yes,' she nodded. 'It does look familiar. You speak Italian?'

I had to smile. 'My wife is fluent,' I said., 'She's trying to teach me.'

Mrs Morton opened the door for us. I asked her to clarify something. When she had first mentioned the 30th May 1936 it was, to my mind, specific and very quick. Was it because of her position as a magistrate and the severity of the case, or was there some other reason. The reason was unusual to say the least. Eight days earlier, on the 22nd, the German Zeppelin Hindenburg had deviated from its' normal route to America, flown low over Keighley and dropped flowers, with the request that they be placed on the grave of a German soldier, a former prisoner of war who was buried in Skipton churchyard. Although there had been a story circulating that there had been an alternative reason. The Germans had wanted to photograph Keighley's industrial base of textiles and engineering. It was different. A nine-day wonder.

'All right, what was that about?' DS Nicholson quizzed as we sped back towards Braemont in an attempt to beat the thunderstorm that was rapidly approaching from the moors north of the town.

'What?' I said and grinned. 'With Meteo?'

'Yup.'

'*Il meteo*,' is the weather forecast, Sarge,' I replied. 'More often than not, not that I know that much Italian, it's an adjective, such as *condizioni meteo,* weather conditions.'

We made eye contact via the rear-view mirror. 'Bloody Hell, Brian! Keep that one under your hat.'

It was still busy in Keighley town centre as we tried to negotiate our way through. Traffic slowed as a police car with bell sounding and blue light working overtime drew alongside. The front nearside passenger wound down his window. DS Nicholson did the same. The two cars drove side by side. The detective inspector shouted across. 'I thought your enquiries were at Braemont, sergeant.'

'They were, sir,' DS Nicholson answered. 'We left at eleven fifteen.'

'Then where did you go?'

'Mrs Morton's, 9 Carr Valley Road, Micklethwaite. What she told us led us to believe that Father Kender hadn't been exactly honest. We're on our way back.'

There was no humour in his smile. He shouted. 'I take it they were still alive when you left?' The look on the DI's face said everything.

A mutual glance in the rear view mirror was enough.

'You'd better follow us or you'll never get through this traffic.' He turned to the driver. 'Go.' The window closed, The police car turned left at the next junction and accelerated with us in close attendance. What was happening was anybody's guess. But the DI had said, "they".

Fifty-Four

It was busy for Braemont. There were two police cars and an ambulance outside the Rectory. A couple of nosey pedestrians standing opposite the Rectory gates braving the downpour. DS Nicholson followed DI Smith. I dodged next door to the cottage which housed the local telephone exchange. 'You must be Mary,' I said to the lady who answered the door. Mid-forties, trim with mousy hair, a little grey showing. She was dabbing her eyes with her handkerchief. I noticed that she was wearing a wedding ring. She blew her nose, and nodded. 'Inspector Hemmings asked to be remembered to you.'

'Did he?' she said and smiled. 'That was nice of him. Always calling in for a cup of tea, if he had five minutes.'

This was six miles from the Keighley town beat where he'd worked. What else was he calling in for? And he and his wife were "strictly Methodists" Tch, tch.

I introduced myself and showed my warrant card. 'My sergeant and me were here this morning, Mary. We left the Rectory at eleven fifteen. Were any calls made from the Rectory between then and now?'

'Yes,' she said and checked the time on her Call Pad. 'There was one call made by Father Kender,' as she spoke she began to weep again and wiped her eyes. 'That was at eleven twenty.'

'Who did he call, please?'

'Police Headquarters in Wakefield,' she replied.

Why on earth would he call Wakefield? And who in particular?
'Did he just ask for police headquarters at Wakefield, a particular person, or give you the number?'

'He gave me the number. He always did. And unlike some I don't eavesdrop the calls,' she said, pre-empting my next question.

'Did he call there often?'

'Not regularly,' she answered. 'Perhaps once a month, maybe a little longer.'

'How long did the call last, Mary?'

She glanced at her Call Pad. 'Very short, in total less than twenty seconds.'

'Just twenty seconds?' I confirmed. 'It sounds like the line was engaged.'

'Yes, I heard the call connect. Seconds later the call was terminated.'

'You've known Father Kender a long time, Mary. How did he sound?'

She paused for a few seconds. 'Agitated,' she said. 'Normally he takes time for a bit of a chat. Today he definitely wasn't in the mood.'

Something we said? But who did he call? 'Were there any incoming calls after that?'

'Yes, there was. About fifteen minutes afterwards. 'A man with a local accent. I don't know who it was, although I remembered the voice. I can't remember when the previous call was.'

'How long did the call last?'

She was apologetic. 'I can't say for certain. I'd popped out to put the kettle on, perhaps a minute or two.'

'Thank you. I know this is an imposition but could I make a call from here, please.'

'What number?'

'Hecton two-one-nine-seven. And the number of the Rectory?'

'Braemont two seven.'

Mary opened her desk drawer and took out a combined headset and mouth piece that was old enough to have been used by Marconi himself. 'Wakefield, no, sorry Hecton two-one-nine-seven, Janice, please,' she said ... 'Yes, it is, I've a policeman here with me at the moment.'

'Go ahead caller.'

I adjusted the headset as DS Cartwright's voice boomed in my left ear. 'Now then Brian, what do you know?'

'I'm speaking from the village exchange in Braemont, Sarge. Next door to the Rectory,' that was enough to tell him the line was insecure and exactly where we were.

'Understood.'

'A call was made from Braemont two seven, the Rectory in Braemont, at eleven twenty this morning. That was five minutes after we left. It lasted less than twenty seconds. The call was to Swallow Street and the caller was Father Kender, he's Irish. There was an incoming call put through to the Rectory some fifteen minutes later, but Mary doesn't know the origin.'

'Noted. Anything else.'

'Only that Magnus Yarney was an identical twin.'

'Christ. Any chance of a photograph?'

'Taken care of, but it's not a recent one.'

'Ok. One question. What are you doing back there?'

'Another line of enquiry, Sarge. We came across the local DI en route, a DI Smith. Apparently there's been at least one serious assault at the Rectory since we left. DS Nicholson is there and I'll be joining him shortly.'

'Anything else?'

'Not that I can think of.'

'Right, you get off, I'll sort these out.' He handed the phone to Hazel and re-wrote his notes. 'Give this to the Boss or DI

Henderson, Hazel, please. I'm off to Wakefield to do the enquiry I've ticked.'

The Rectory was a tip. Whoever had done this liked a mess. Mrs Magee would not have been pleased. Father Kender's body was in his lounge. Mrs Magee's in the kitchen. Everywhere was a mess. It must have made one helluva row.

'Where've you been?' Was the rather tetchy welcome I received from DI Smith in the hallway. He was five eleven, slim and lugubrious, shiny shoes but a careworn suit and raincoat. He had more nicotine on his fingers and his breath than on anyone else I had ever seen. Life was taking its' toll.

'Next door, sir,' I replied. 'Just to call the office and tell them we'd be late.'

There was a grunt of acceptance.

'By the way, sir. At twenty past eleven. Five minutes after we left this morning Father Kender made a phone call to Swallow Street,.'

DS Nicholson's eyes narrowed followed by a questioning smile.

'Know 'oo 'e called?'

'No, sir.'

'Ah well, can't 'ave everything. I'll check that later.'

'There was an incoming call to the Rectory about fifteen minutes later, but the lady in the exchange doesn't know where from.'

DI Smith nodded and smiled to himself lifting his lugubriosity. 'Ever seen a murder victim, son?'

'One or two, sir,' I replied, as DS Nicholson winked at me.

'Oh aye?' he didn't believe me. 'Come an' see the old papist. Beaten to death with one of 'is statuettes.'

Father Kender lay diagonally across the fireside rug his face towards the fire. As you got closer there were visible signs across the back of his head that something heavy had been used to administer a good beating. Two feet to the left, resting against the fender was a statuette of an angel with outspread wings, about two feet tall with blood and hair adhering to its square base. I'd noticed the statuette when we were there earlier. Considering the amount of punishment that he'd received there wasn't a lot of blood. 'Mind if I take a closer look, sir?' I asked.

'Fill yer boots, son. But I'm 'appy.'

I got down on my knees and had a look in his left eye. The light was on the dim side, too gloomy to see properly, but there was some petechial haemorrhaging visible. I sat back on my heels and turned to the others. 'There are indications that he's been strangled, sir.'

'Bollocks,' the DI was sceptical. DS Nicholson joined me.

'He's right, sir. There are.'

'Shit.' A grudging DI struggled to his feet and headed for the kitchen. Mrs Magee also had petechial haemorrhaging. In addition there were several marks to the back of her skull that closely resembled those on Father Kender's, but again, not enough blood.

A second detective and a uniformed officer joined us in the hall. Now there were five. 'Right, what 'ave we got?' queried DI Smith. 'Which one got it first?' There was silence.

'If it had been me, sir,' I volunteered. 'I'd have taken out Father Kender first and then Mrs Magee. Take care of the strong one first. '

'That makes sense,' DI Smith replied. 'Then beat 'em over the 'ead to make it look as if they'd been clubbed, followed by the mess. I'll buy that. Any observations?'

There were none.

It became a steady stream. The divisional police surgeon certified death but wouldn't be pinned down as to a precise time of death. Nevertheless he suggested within the preceding two hours. Couldn't disagree with that. The photographer. Chief Superintendent Bentley, the divisional commander and Detective Superintendent Wallace. Lastly the ambulance crew waiting for the victims.

Photographer departed, Detective Superintendent Wallace, a tall man with broad shoulders and a florid complexion turned to DI Smith. 'Right Inspector, what do you make of it so far?'

'Two murders made to look like robbery, sir.'

'Go on, Inspector.'

'I think Father Kender was strangled first, followed by 'is 'ousekeeper, Mrs Magee. The clubbing with the statuette followed and left on the fender. Then the perpetrators trashed the place.'

'And, what makes you think that?'

'Father Kender was a big bloke, sir, deal with him first. And 'e's got those little pateeky things in 'is eyes.' The DI glanced at me.

'Petechiae. Petechial haemorrhages, sir,' I replied.

'What 'e said, sir,' he replied flicking his head in my direction. 'And, there isn't a lot of blood from the 'ead wounds with either of 'em.'

'So you believe the victims were clubbed post-mortem?'

'Yes sir.'

'Let's have a look.'

It was only a cursory examination. A quick check of the eyes. There was no need to check if rigor mortis had set in or was in process. It wasn't.

'Have we got an eta for fingerprints?'

The DI looked at his watch. 'They were on their way thirty minutes ago, so anytime within the next fifteen.'

'Begin house-to-house. Has anyone spoken to the lady in the phone exchange to see if any calls were made.'

'I have sir,' I volunteered.

The Detective Superintendent spun round. 'Why?'

'I went to contact our office, sir, to let them know we'd be late. I took the opportunity to ask.'

'And?'

His eyebrows raised when I answered. 'Father Kender made a call to Swallow Street at eleven twenty. The call lasted less than twenty seconds.'

'Do we know who he contacted, or tried to contact?'

'No sir,' I replied. 'There was an incoming call about fifteen minutes later. She recognised the voice as one that had called before. A male with a local accent. She didn't know where the call had come from.'

'Who did you tell when you contacted your office? I take it you did tell someone,' he said with an expectant smile.

'DS Cartwright, sir,' I replied in kind.

'Peter Cartwright?' he said looking at DS Nicholson for confirmation.

'Yes sir.'

'No doubt that's in hand. Now, DS Nicholson I know of old.' he said turning to me. 'But you are a mystery.'

'Acting DC Blake, sir,' I replied.

'Ah. Mr Valentine's protégé, I should have known. Good afternoon.'

'Hello sir.' I replied.

'Congratulations on your trip to the palace, Blake. It was a good day?'

'Thank you. It was excellent, sir.'

He smiled and turned to DS Nicholson. "Now then Sergeant, this is a long way off your patch, what are you doing here?'

We showed him the photograph and note that Mrs Magee had pushed into my pocket and told him of our conversation with Mrs Morton.

'I was at the conference,' he began, 'when your DCI told us about this list and what it might mean. Little did I believe that we would be trawling over that old ground. However, it seems that we are. And, Father Kender would, were he not lying ten feet away be called upon to answer some serious questions. Now we have two murders very clumsily made to look like robbery. To me, that and this mess, smack of panic. I don't want to keep you anymore. If there's nothing further that you need you might as well go home. Will you ensure that you send me copies of the photograph and in the meantime I'll call Mr Valentine.'

Chief Superintendent Bentley, who had so far been content to observe exchanged a few words with Superintendent Wallace and came across to speak with us. 'You're DC Blake?' he said.

'Acting, sir.'

'If Mr Barton saw fit to appoint you as DC, acting or otherwise, Blake, on such an operation as this that is just splitting hairs. And you're the son of Douglas Blake?'

'I am, sir.'

'We were in C.I.D. together a long time ago. He was a good man,' he paused for a few seconds. 'After the award of the George Cross he would have been very proud of you as I am sure that your family are. Many congratulations.'

Before I could reply he switched his attention to DS Nicholson. 'And you're his minder?'

'I am, sir,' he replied and smiled. 'DC Blake isn't allowed out on his own because of that relationship.'

He nodded. 'And you're here because?'

'Initially, because Father Kender's name cropped up out of the blue in relation to what we believed to be an unrelated matter.'

'That would be Wainwright?'

'Yes sir. We had no idea what we were walking into.'

'I see. And Father Kender appears to have been less than honest,' he said and paused. 'Let me see that note and photograph again.'

He had a quick glance and handed them back. ' When you left I don't suppose that he would expect you to return. We will probably never know but this could hinge on any conversation that took place afterwards. You said the woman in the exchange next door said Father Kender sounded agitated.'

'Yes sir,' I said.

He bit his lip and nodded. 'Very well. This is not the time for an in depth chat; I'll let you get off.'

Well clear of Braemont DS Nicholson called the office from a roadside kiosk. Detective Superintendent Wallace had beaten us to it.

Fifty-Five

I handed the statements of Father Kender and Mrs Morton, plus photograph and notes to the DCI. DS Nicholson and I went for a belated lunch and a well-earned cuppa. We had a ten minute respite before the DCI joined us.

'No, don't get up, finish your tea,' we sat back down. 'I passed your little conundrum over the name to DS Roberts in Aliens and Immigration, it's an offshoot of Special Branch, inhabits a cubby-hole at Bishopgarth,' he said when he saw my puzzled look. 'The name wasn't Di Meteo, as you surmised, but, De Mateo.' He slid a piece of paper across the table. 'This is who they are now.'

I looked at the name and nearly choked on a mouthful of tea, as did DS Nicholson. The name wasn't a common one. However, we had one as ACC Crime – Weatherspoon. I don't believe anyone saw that coming. It left me with a sick feeling. My thoughts so outlandish it couldn't be right, could it? He hadn't mentioned anything at all about him knowing the Yarneys or Wainwright.

Ten minutes later we had the office to ourselves. Apart from me there were the DCI, DI and DS's Nicholson and Cartwright. The DCI stood stock still and frowned. He glanced at Mrs Morton's statement once again. 'Of course there may be a simple explanation ...' His voice tailed off. The look on his face more purposeful than angry. This enquiry had just been ratcheted up even more. 'In the light of this statement from Mrs Morton and the information I received from DS Roberts and DS Nicholson we need clarification. I will speak with Inspector Tansey from Personnel. John, I want you to put together a photo id folder. Twelve photos from studio of senior

234

officers, including ACC Weatherspoon – check the Home Office directives. They're in *my* office. There must be no mistakes. Then take Penny and Mrs Morton's photograph and interview Wainwright and his wife, if wife she is ... and try her sister as well, just in case. See if they remember this picnic. If so, can they identify the photographer. First thing tomorrow re-visit Mrs Morton, see if she can identify the photographer. Then the courts in Craven, including the Coroner's Court re the same case. See if Division can lay their hands on their original file. Blake, I want you to speak with a DS Griffiths in HQ C.I.D. Admin. Mention my name. Find the file Mrs Morton referred to re the death of that girl, Betsy Elstub, and read it. I want a précis. But first, Blake and I have a visit to make.'

Retired Detective Inspector Ivan Spencer, the officer in the case of both Christine Jones and my father's murders was seventy five if he was a day. For want of a better expression he looked knackered. 'If you'll take a bit of advice, son,' he said, 'Do your time an' retire, don't go to age limit. This job, no matter how good it is will suck everything out of you that you're prepared to give, then come back for more. Better still win the pools an' jack it in. Even better still, marry a blonde nympho that owns a brewery,' he added, a hesitant laugh triggering a coughing spasm.

I had to laugh. 'Well, sir, my wife is blonde, so is our daughter.'

'Well, that's a good start,' he said and chuckled. 'But you're the spit of your father. As good a copper from what I've heard.'

'Not yet.'

'Ah, experience will come. But you've got to have *the want*,' he said, 'like your father did. Without that no matter 'ow clever you are you'll just be a uniform carrier. Take my word for it there's plenty of those about,' he paused to catch his breath. 'Bloody cigs,' he said and put his right hand on his chest. 'They'll be the death of me.' His breathing once more under control he continued. Now then Graeme, what you want is in the boxes by the door. You might as well take 'em. They're no use to me now. When I've gone they'll just get binned, so help yourself ... I knew from the off that there were more'n Magnus Yarney involved. If this Wainwright is a part, then good on yer. Finish what we couldn't.'

We left shortly afterwards. It had been a real privilege meeting him, perhaps the contents of the three boxes might help. Nevertheless I wondered what he might say if we'd told him that Yarney had an identical twin and that we were investigating the actions of the now ACC Crime.

We dropped the boxes off at the squad office. It was more secure than the Incident Room. The fewer people with access to this potential source of information the better. Between us we checked the contents. There were full copies of every major crime that DI Spencer had dealt with during his thirty six years in service. The files we were looking for were at the bottom of the third box. Two files both with the same defendant – Magnus Yarney. Both for murder.

My search was of the earlier of the two files: Christine Jones - Murder.

Now I knew what to look for it was a simple task. Go through the file a page at a time checking only for the name of the officers making or taking the statements, or submitting the report.

And there they were. Statements bearing the name Detective Sergeant 811, Albert Weatherspoon, C.I.D. Keighley. A photostat of the antecedent form itself also bearing his signature. However there was no supervisory initials signifying that the form had been checked on submission.

Details of the form were minimal: Yarney was an only child who lived with his mother at 7 Hay Rick Lane, Laycock, Keighley. Had attended local schools leaving at the age of fourteen. Attended Technical School. Now worked as a clerk in the offices of Gartside & Smith, Spinners, Water Lane, Keighley.

The primary difference between these details and a similar form submitted again by Detective Sergeant Weatherspoon following my father's murder was the additional comment of Yarney's detention following the first trial.

There was no statement from Father Kender.

I had a little time to spare. I called DS Griffiths in HQ C.I.D. Admin. I told him that the DCI had asked me to call and why. Names open a lot of doors.

'How is he? Still causing havoc?'

'Sat in his office, Sarge, with the door open.'

'Fair enough,' he chuckled. 'Right, defendant's name?'

'Sorry, don't know. I can give you the victim's name, division and date.'

'That'll have to do. Shoot.'

'Name Betsy Elstub, that's E-L-S-T-U-B, Keighley division, and the date the 30th May 1936.'

'Bloody Hell!' The DCI obviously heard the response, lifted his head from what he was doing and smiled through the open door. 'You don't make it easy. When do you want it?'

'Tomorrow morning if that's all right? What time do you start?'

'I'm normally here for eight thirty. If we've still got it, it will be waiting for you.'

The news that the ACC Crime may have been involved was unexpected but the DCI had initiated actions to confirm or deny it. Tomorrow I should be able to make a start on the Elstub file.

A sigh of relief. Norman was in the clear. And yes he did laugh and even offered a blood sample if it would help the investigation. He had been attending an alumni event at East Midlands University on the evening of Friday 5th March. There were witnesses that he was drinking in the student's bar at 1am on the 6th. Since verified by at least a dozen fellow imbibers and a sober barman. There is no way that he could have been in the West Riding at the appropriate times.

Fifty-Six

I was early at Swallow Street the next morning. So was DS Griffiths.

R v Coch. Z
Murder & Rape.

'I was intrigued when I saw this file,' he said. 'I had a quick squint through it and it doesn't make for good reading. But I won't blunt your opinion by giving you mine. The upshot was that Coch committed suicide whilst on remand, which most people considered an *ipso facto* guilty plea. No further suspects therefore no trial. But you can make your own mind up. If nothing else you'll find it interesting.'

I signed for the file and left. Now I was intrigued. I let the DCI know I had arrived and brought him up to speed re the suicide and suggested that I pay a visit to the Coroner's office and the prison. He agreed. It was after 0900. I made the two calls. First to the Leeds Coroner's Office and asked if they still had the files from 1936. Silly question, of course they did, it had been a rape and murder investigation. I made arrangements to visit in one hour. Give them time to locate the file. The second call was to Armley prison to make arrangements to have sight of Coch's records during his detention.

The inquest file was small. It didn't take long to extract the relevant details, including details of Coch's prison medical record and copy them into my pocket book.

My reception at the prison wasn't what you would call frosty, however, there was an air of curiosity or was it suspicion. I was escorted to the Admin office where I was met by the Deputy

Governor, Graham Sidebottom, a sombre-looking man about my height and build but wearing a tired expression along with his suit. Coch's file was lying on a nearby desk.

'This is an unusual request, Mr Blake, enquiring into the death of a prisoner who was on remand here in 1936,' he said. His voice tailed off inviting an answer.

I didn't want to incur the wrath of the Deputy Chief or anyone else for that matter by divulging information that might just find its way onto the airwaves. The best answer? Say nothing. I settled on - 'I'm not at liberty to divulge any details, sir.'

He smiled as if that is what he expected to hear. 'I called the contact number that you left earlier and spoke with a Mrs Granby. She confirmed that you are attached to the Hecton incident room. And, unless I am mistaken, you are one of the detectives I saw on the News last night, visiting Braemont.'

I returned his smile. 'You're a good fisherman, sir. I can confirm I was there.' It seemed pointless to deny it. My face had been on the TV. Whoever took the photo of DS Nicholson and myself getting into the car was a mystery. I pointed to the file on the desk. 'If I might?'

'Of course,' he said indicating an adjacent desk.

It didn't read well: *Coch appeared malnourished however was reported to be eating well, but hungry after meals. Frequent drinking and urination. Breath smelled of acetone. Had difficulty in walking. Complains of dysesthesia. Some confusion. Cannot remember when he last saw a doctor. Does not wear glasses has trouble reading.*

Examination: Urine strip test: Glucose levels high. Charcot left foot (severe), mid-foot collapse. Loss of sensation in legs to mid-thigh. Diabetic ulcers, one on each foot – left infected. Chronic infected and untreated laceration to sole of left foot.

Chronic untreated diabetes mellitus, diabetic polyneuropathy, Charcot foot, diabetic ulcers and untreated laceration, left ulcer and laceration infected. This man should be in hospital - possible amputation?

I wasn't a doctor but I did understand that terms such as: *chronic untreated diabetes mellitus, diabetic polyneuropathy, diabetic ulcer (L), chronic infected and untreated laceration to sole of left foot, dysesthesia, charcot foot (L)* - Whatever the last two were, weren't good. Neither was the final comment – *difficulty in walking, possible amputation? This man should be in hospital!*

Zebadiah Coch, born C1890, died 9th June 1936. Had fashioned a ligature from his shirt, tied it round his neck and hanged himself from the bars of his cell. Verdict: Suicide whilst the balance of his mind was disturbed.

There were no photographs, either of the body at the prison or of the post mortem examination.

Evidence was given by prison officer Trevor Styles who had discovered Coch in his cell at 0630hrs. Checked for signs of life, which were absent. Coch's skin had been cold to the touch – Were they checked during the night? I would have thought that men who were on remand for rape and murder, especially when you consider that Betsy Elstub was his niece, would have been on a suicide watch. Or, was it just a sign of the times?

Mr Sidebottom was watching me. Did he think that I was going to try and pocket something, or, were they just being careful? 'There is a problem, officer?' He asked when he saw me sit back.

'Would it be possible to borrow this document, sir, and have it copied at our studio?'

'Yes, that isn't a problem,' he said, but the look on his face gave the impression that he wanted answers to the questions queuing up in his mind. They would have to wait.

Armed with my notes and the prison doctor's record I went straight back to Wakefield, and HQ Studio. They promised it for a.m. tomorrow. I wondered whose ear Mr Sidebottom was going to bend. He had certainly given that impression. Still, no point in worrying about things over which I had no control.

I managed to catch Dr O'Keefe at the start of his lunch-break. I asked him if he could help me out with a couple of medical terms. He found that amusing. 'Ok,' he said. 'Go ahead.'

'Dysesthesia?'

'You're talking diabetes aren't you?'

'Yes, Dr, I am.'

'Now,' he began. 'Dysesthesia means abnormal pain and is attributable to diabetic polyneuropathy. Diabetics lose feeling in their extremities,' Dr O'Keefe explained. 'The condition damages the long nerves. However, dysesthesia can manifest itself as a burning, stinging or quite severe stabbing pain, simply from the pressure of clothing or bed clothes. It can be very unpleasant ... What was the other thing?'

'Charcot foot.'

There was a silence for several seconds. 'This is connected with the case you're involved with?'

'Indirectly Dr., yes it is.'

'Ok ... Look, this is too complicated to discuss in a couple of minutes over the telephone. I can be free at ... 3pm. I'll come to Hecton between a quarter past and half past three. Is that all right?'

I put the phone back on the cradle and typed the prison doctor's notes from memory. Took refuge in an interview room and began to digest the tale of Zebadiah Coch: a forty-fiveish years old itinerant farm labourer. Only living relatives were a cousin by marriage, Henry Elstub and his two daughters, Caroline and Betsy. Had few friends but well known in the district. On his return from service in the Great War he found that his father had died. His mother and two younger brothers had been evicted from their small farm. Formerly tenant farmers had now gone to live with his mother's cousin, the Elstubs. Zebadiah Coch worked as a farm labourer taking any work that was available. His mother died four years later. His two brothers from diphtheria two years after that. *Life in those days was certainly brutal.* He drifted away from his cousin's tied-cottage and began sleeping in his employer's barns. He had two minor convictions for poaching. He was fined five shillings on each. There were two more for offences of simple larceny – theft of small amounts of food – no doubt to keep body and soul together. On the first offence of larceny he was fined ten shillings. The second, one day's detention in police cells. He became infirm, finding it more and more difficult to get about.

Arrested by detective constable Alberto De Mateo five hours after the body of his niece, Betsy Elstub, was found in the pastures above Braemont. He had been reported as being seen in the area by Father Kender immediately prior to the discovery of Betsy Elstub's body. There were verbatim statements from both Iago and Magnus Yarney who reported to Father Kender that they had found the body. No mention of seeing Coch, Elstub's uncle. Statements taken by De Mateo. There was no doubt that local feeling would be running high once reports of the rape and murder began to spread, but the statement taken by De Mateo and signed by Coch was derisory. Even I knew that. It was almost a question of:

'Did you rape and strangle Betsy Elstub?'

'Yes, I did.'

'All right, sign here!'

There were quick collars and quick collars. But this ... this was nonsense. I don't care who'd taken it.

I left my notes and the Coch file with the DCI whilst I went to grab a bite to eat.

1520. Dr O'Keefe paid us a visit. He took time to read my notes and then asked the DCI. 'Could I ask why this man was in custody?'

The DCI nodded. 'For the rape and manual strangulation of his sixteen year old niece.'

Dr O'Keefe looked troubled. 'Could I ask when?'

'The thirtieth of May, 1936, Doctor,' he replied with a wry smile,

Dr O'Keefe grimaced. 'That's a long time ago,' he said. 'However, I think not, Mr Valentine,' he said, then proceeded to give what I presumed to be a simplified explanation of the effects of chronic diabetes, including charcot foot and polyneuropathy.

The silence was palpable. The DCI broke the silence. 'Correct me if I'm wrong Dr, but every symptom mentioned by the prison doctor in this report,' he picked it up from the desk and handed it to Dr O'Keefe, 'is due entirely to untreated chronic diabetes?'

The Dr quickly scanned the notes. 'Absolutely, Chief Inspector, what we would now refer to as Type 1 diabetes. In 1936 it was just diabetes. There is no question in my mind whatsoever. However, there is one major effect of diabetes mellitus that the prison doctor did not mention in his report. It probably wouldn't have crossed his mind to enquire. This man would have been impotent, and been so for a long time.'

The DCI didn't comment he simply nodded and turned to me. 'Blake, do you know how far it was from the scene of the crime to where Coch was arrested?'

'Not exactly, sir. The farm where Coch was arrested, Burnthwaite Bridge Farm, is south of Silsden, so, in a direct line, at a guess five to six miles.'

'How long would it take a man in the condition that Coch found himself to walk that distance, Doctor?'

'If we're talking about the terrain in the general Keighley-Silsden area, he wouldn't. Apart from having no feeling in his legs having a charcot foot also affects the motor nerves so he would lose some control in the muscles that are used for walking. His balance would be adversely affected. He might have managed a much shorter distance on relatively level ground, but five or six miles over that terrain?' he pursed his lips and shook his head. 'Out of the question.

Neither, Chief Inspector, would he have been able to get to the scene. I take it the unfortunate victim was fit and healthy?'

'Sixteen and walked the moors, Doctor,' I added.

'I see.'

The DCI looked from me to the Dr. 'The notes made by Doctor Carmichaels with regard to hospital and amputation?'

'Essential to get him into hospital,' he declared in a tone that left no doubt that there was any reasonable alternative. 'Although there's no mention on this record there's a good chance that the wound on the left foot was gangrenous or heading that way. Remember that we're talking about the 1930s. The NHS didn't begin until 1948 and penicillin wasn't available at all until after 1942 when, for the most part, it was restricted to the military. Amputating this man's legs, certainly the left, and possibly both wouldn't be the end of the matter either. The underlying problem of the diabetes has to be dealt with. With a condition as severe as this, hospital is the only place. And, there are no guarantees that he would have survived operations of that magnitude.

There was a silence you could have cut with a knife.

'His sight problems, you say that was also as result of his diabetes?'

'Diabetic retinopathy it's called, and irreversible.'

'So,' the DCI mused, 'for a relatively young man, one used to an out-door life to suddenly find that he was likely to lose one or even both of his legs, plus his sight, that would be as good a spur to commit suicide as anything else I could think of. However, under the circumstances it appears to have been taken as a way of avoiding trial, and the noose had he been convicted i.e. the coward's way out. Once he'd actually killed himself there was no need to worry that a half-decent brief might get him off. Therefore no requirement to continue the enquiry – they already had their man.' He paused and looked at me. 'How was it written off?'

I looked at the offence report on the front of the crime file. 'Defendant committed suicide whilst on remand. NFA, sir, and signed by the chief superintendent, whose name is illegible.'

He nodded and stood up shaking hands with Dr O'Keefe. 'Doctor, many thanks for your time. I would also appreciate it if you would let me have a report in regard to what we have just been discussing.'

'I'll do better than that Chief Inspector; I'll go and see Professor Andrews at Leeds General. He's also the Professor of Endocrinology at the university, he will be interested.'

'Much obliged, and if you could stress the urgency it would be appreciated. Better still, if you could explain to him, then let me know and I can call him.'

'Certainly,' he replied. 'I'll bid you all a good-day.'

Fifty-Seven

The next day I accompanied DS Nicholson and Penny on the sojourn to Keighley. To re-visit Mrs Morton and Keighley DHQ seeking the original documentation for the Elstub murder. It was there, but we almost had to dig for it. After all whoever would need access to a twenty eight year old murder file? Talk about muck.

'Seeing as we're up here, Sarge. Do you think it would do any good to call in at the local rag? See what they've got that maybe didn't go into print?'

The Keighley Herald didn't have a dedicated archivist. What they did have was a very interested Editor. DS Nicholson explained what we would like. In the end the editor had a chat with Mr Valentine. They reached a deal. Agreeing to hold back on publication for ten days. We didn't want what we were doing to reach certain pairs of ears. After that they were as good as gold. We were introduced to staff-reporter, Oliver Randall, the son-in-law of the original journalist. Shortly afterwards to Mark Collins, his father-in-law. For us it was a gold mine. For them an exclusive.

Two days later I spent a full day in Aliens and Immigration with DS Roberts, which in turn lead to a transatlantic call to a Captain of Detectives, Marius Shaefer, in the Las Vegas police department. 'Anything for the Atlantic Alliance, detective,' he replied. They knew of Wainwright. He promised to telex the information we requested within three days. I'd been on the phone for almost half an hour. I'm pleased that I wasn't paying for that call.

The board was now complete. The last body to be recovered was No.10, identified as Anne Bellamy. Disappeared on the 4th

June,1959 from Kexborough, remains recovered 400 yards from The Flouch crossroads.

The last body to be identified was No.5, Sandra Thompson, disappeared 10th October, 1949, 5'6", fair hair, proportionate build. Midgely, recovered in Denby Dale.

Fifty-Eight

Deputy Chief Constable Rodney Gartside put the report back on his desk and looked up at DS Nicholson and myself, concern written in capital letters across his face.

For the time being he ignored the senior officers to his right concentrating on the young probationer in front of him. He'd done a remarkable job over the last week or so. The evidence he had gleaned would have been enough to hang anyone. He should be vying for a Chief Officer's post within the next dozen years. Not that he would tell him. That, he would have to determine for himself.

'Thank you, Sergeant, you may return to the Incident Room. Blake, you're au fait with what is required?'

'Yes, sir,' we replied simultaneously. It wasn't every day that you were about to be involved in the arrest of an Assistant Chief Constable.

'Very well. Wait outside, please.'

I closed the door behind us chopping off the conversation. 'Better not be caught making a noise outside the Chief's office. I'll see you back at Hecton.' I watched DS Nicholson until he turned right down the stairs. My mind wandered. There were two teams armed with search warrants: DS Cartwright's team en route to Oxenhope to search the home of James Sullivan, formerly Iago Yarney. DI Henderson's team en route to Silkstone and the home of Albert Weatherspoon, ACC Crime. I would love to have been in DS Cartwright's team. However I wasn't. I had to visit Swallow Street at the *request* of the Deputy Chief Constable. That was that.

The Deputy Chief glanced from DCI Valentine to DCS Mithering. 'There is nothing of the Elstub family?'

'No sir,' replied the DCI. 'It appears that they left the area at the end of the war. One report being that Caroline, the last surviving child, married a Canadian serviceman. As yet we can't confirm that. However, we have an ongoing enquiry through the Canadian High Commission. That will take some time.'

Gartside nodded. 'It's not ideal to do the interview first. In the circumstances I agree.

'Very well, use the meeting room at the end of the corridor. I've arranged for you to borrow the typist from the Admin office. A Mrs Watson, acts as the Chief Clerk's secretary, doubles up for the Chief's secretary when she's away, including discipline hearings. And, the odd spot of work for me, so she's up to the job. Also, she's married to a young copper. She knows how to keep her mouth shut.'

'Fair enough.'

'Another point Mr Valentine. Bearing in mind Blake's links in this case, are you happy with his involvement now?'

'I did have some concerns which I took to the Force Medical Officer, sir. He is of the opinion that this course of action will be beneficial for him. Help to bring things to a close.'

The DCC nodded. 'Very well. Is there anything else?'

DCS Mithering laughed. 'And to think when Blake gave that first presentation I told him his theory was cockamamie.'

'So I heard,' the DCC said and smiled. 'That's the trouble. When you pull the loose end of a piece of string sometimes the other end is fastened to the pin in a grenade.'

'Indeed sir. And this particular grenade is about to have its pin jerked out.'

'Quite.'

DCS Mithering opened the door jerking me out of my reverie. As directed I collected the large box of files and followed. The files laid out on the table I waited in the corridor. The DCI and DCS set off to surprise ACC Weatherspoon.

To add a little colour the Chief came back the other way. 'Everything all right, Blake?'

'Fine sir,' I replied'

'Good.' He didn't stop.

Chief out of the way I wandered into the meeting room. The window overlooking the carpark. The C.I.D. block opposite. Weatherspoon's back clearly visible as he sat at his desk. I didn't have long to wait. The ACC's office door opened. I'd been present at the planning and knew what was going to happen and wished I could hear the exchanges. Mithering and Valentine entered as Weatherspoon lifted his right hand to signal wait. He picked up the telephone in the other – that would be the Deputy Chief telling him to go with them for interview under caution. Seconds later Weatherspoon stood and left his office.

I caught sight of my reflection in the window. Smug smile or not I had earned the privilege. Weatherspoon had neither been arrested nor told the reason why he was being interviewed. His head must be spinning wondering what we had discovered during the last ten days. Tough bloody shit. We might never be able to prove that he was involved in my father's murder, but there was only one way that he was leaving his forthcoming interview.

I heard them climbing the stairs long before they came into view. One of the typists from Admin preceding them. We exchanged smiles. I looked at Mr Weatherspoon and wondered how he was feeling. I hope he was suffering. Unfortunately, I wasn't allowed to be present during the interview.

Mithering opened the door to the meeting room. Weatherspoon entered. Valentine stopped and turned to me. 'Blake, the Deputy wants to see you. Then go and get yourself a coffee. Be back in Reception in thirty minutes.'

I acknowledged and left.

Fifty-Nine

Valentine smiled at the typist, armed with three shorthand pads and at least half a dozen pencils. 'You're Mrs Watson?'

'Yes, sir.'

'Have you been briefed as to what is required of you?'

'Yes sir, but I've never done anything like this before.'

'But you have done discipline files?'

'Yes, sir.'

'Just think of it as a normal discipline file and you'll be fine. Some of the language may be a bit stronger than you're used to, and some of the things you have to record you may find distressing. Are you all right with that?'

'Yes, sir.' She nodded and wondered what she was going to hear.

Valentine ushered her into the room, followed and closed the door.

'Take a seat, sir,' Mithering indicated the chair opposite. He and Valentine sat.

'Sir,' said Valentine. 'This is Mrs Watson. As you can see she takes dictation. She will be recording the interview.' He looked at his watch. 'The time is now 10.17.'

Satisfied, Mrs Watson settled on her chair in the corner opened her pad and began to write.

Weatherspoon scanned the papers across the desk top wondering just what had gone wrong. What had he missed? 'What's all this about, Mr Mithering?' His tone merely questioning.

Mithering smiled. 'First things first, sir,' he replied. 'I have to tell you that you are not obliged to say anything unless you wish to do so but what you say may be put into writing ...'

His office door was open. I knocked twice. The Deputy Chief was on the telephone. He looked up and waved me in pointing to the chair in front of his desk. Call finished he sat forwards and picked up the file WAINWRIGHT from his desk. 'I agree with Mr Valentine's approbation. This is excellent work but do not make a habit of calling the Las Vegas police department. It's almost cheaper to get the plane.'

I had to smile. 'I won't, sir. I promise.'

He reciprocated. 'Good.' He sat back in his chair, clasped his hands across his stomach and smiled. 'Well Blake, in view of your links to this case how are you feeling?'

'Fine sir, thank you ...' I hesitated.

'You were going to say?'

'... I never dreamed when I saw the archaeological survey grid that Saturday afternoon that it would lead to this.'

'I'll bet you didn't. But you follow the evidence. It might be a dead end on occasions but at least that will rule out a possibility. This time, unfortunately for some, you were correct. Now then.' He sat up straight and removed an old OS map, hand lens and Wainwright's list from his right-hand desk drawer. 'Tell me about this light bulb moment. Show me how it works. It's a long time since I was in the Boy Scouts.'

It was difficult to think of the Deputy Chief in short trousers singing Ging Gang Gooly round a campfire. I set everything up. His memories returned in seconds. 'Ah, I'm with you. But your step-father's lens was larger and on a stand.'

'Yes sir. So much easier to manipulate everything with both hands free.'

'I agree.'

Back in my seat and his desk tidy, his next comment took me by surprise. 'Has it ever been suggested to you that the Freemasons might be an option? Further your career?'

There was a book in the library back home belonging to Joe's father which I'd read out of curiosity a few years ago. It stipulated that to be accepted into the Masons you had to believe in a higher power, which I did. However, I didn't think that Lucy was what they had in mind.

'I've read a bit about the Freemasons and I don't see how any police officer could possibly join. You can't serve two masters and the emphasis of the Masons appears, to my mind, about not only support but protection of the brotherhood. Besides, as an atheist I wouldn't fit in.'

He didn't press that point.

'Atheism. Do you think that might be a hinderance?'

'I had a similar conversation with Chief Superintendent Andrews at Pannal, sir. We're in the second half of the twentieth century. The country is becoming a more open secular society and, with time I hope that religious bigotry would have less influence. You have only consider Magnus and Iago Yarney and Father Kender to see the having strong religious convictions is no guarantee of good citizenship.' He didn't exactly glare at me but if you don't want to know the answer to the question you shouldn't ask.

I knew my moment of departure was fast approaching when he stood and walked round the desk, offered me his hand and said that no doubt our paths would cross often in the future.

Alone, Gartside snorted a laugh and thought about Blake's comments. 'Cheeky young bugger. Just what we need.' He sat and picked up the report once more. Signed by Valentine but typed by

Blake. In fact all the recent typing in the file had been done by
Blake. No chance of any leaks. He began to read the report again. It
wasn't good for Weatherspoon. In fact not too long ago it could have
seen the judge putting on the black cap. What did they call them in
Ireland, the cai-bais? They pronounced it kybosh. Apposite indeed.
This entire episode stemming from two young boys bird watching.
He read the last page again. Weatherspoon and Christine Jones had
history. Jones had been one of Weatherspoon's informants. There
were suggestions that the relationship was less than professional. In
fact, Inspector Charteris, the local uniform inspector had submitted
a report concerning what he described as a domestic disturbance
between the two. Jones had been a prostitute in Keighley. Prior to
being taken before the Magistrates had been given the two statutory
warnings for soliciting, both by Weatherspoon. The next paragraph
covered Weatherspoon's sickness record whilst acting as a detective
sergeant at Keighley. About the same time as Jones had appeared in
court Weatherspoon had been treated for syphilis. Gartside did not
like coincidences.

Sixty

'I understand,' Weatherspoon smiled. 'Now, what's all this about?' Mithering took the blue manilla folder from Valentine. Removed the single sheet of paper and put on his reading glasses.

'You were born on the 7th July 1906, christened Alberto, the youngest of three children of Luigi and Lucia De Mateo. The family moved to Keighley in the aftermath of the Great War. Your father was a printer?'

Weatherspoon smiled. 'He was. But you needn't have gone to all this trouble. If you wanted to know my history all you had to do was to ask.'

Mithering smiled in return. 'Thank you, but it's all in the records of Aliens and Immigration,' he continued. 'Your father applied for British citizenship when you wished to join the West Riding Police. Eventually changing the family name to Weatherspoon.

You joined the police on the 26th March 1925 and were transferred to C.I.D. on the 14th August 1930. You transferred to Pudsey on promotion to Sergeant in uniform on the 25th June 1936, returning to Keighley as a DS in February 1939. During the war years you worked for the security services. On demobilisation in 1947 you returned to the police taking up your previous post as detective sergeant at Keighley. In September 1950 you transferred on promotion to the rank of Inspector with the Bolton Borough Police. Two years later on promotion to Detective Chief Inspector in Sheffield City. November 1957 you transferred from Sheffield to Lincoln City on promotion to Superintendent, and August 1961 as

Chief Superintendent in the Hull City Police. In March 1964 you returned to the West Riding as Assistant Chief Constable Crime.' Mithering replaced the sheet in its folder and returned it to Valentine. 'That's quite a ladder you climbed after the war, sir,' Mithering said.

'Yes, it was, thank you,' he said, his voice terse. 'There were so many vacancies advertised weekly in the Police Review because they couldn't be filled internally. I'd passed both my promotion exams and thought, why not?'

'Why not indeed, sir,' said Valentine. 'What can you tell us about Christine Jones.'

Weatherspoon furrowed his brow. 'Number three of Wainwright's list?'

'The same.'

'Nothing, why?'

Valentine slid an open register across the desk, two pages marked. 'This is the prostitutes book from Keighley covering the period you were there. You have several entries including two for Jones. And this,' he slid a prosecution file, in the name of Jones, across the desk.'

Weatherspoon scrutinised them both. 'What you see,' he said. 'It's a long time ago I'd simply forgotten. You're not trying to make something out of this, surely?'

'Not at all, sir.' He said. 'Just clarifying the situation. But do you wish to comment on this. A sealed report opened by the Deputy. It will be sealed again in due course. It relates to a period of sick leave when you were treated for syphilis. Any connection to Jones?'

'Certainly not,' he said snorting a laugh. 'Not my finest moment I'll agree. A C.I.D. sports evening and too much alcohol. Didn't do my marriage much good at the time. No, just stupidity.'

'And this,' continued Valentine. He removed a Minute Sheet from his folder sliding it across the table to Weatherspoon. 'As you can see this is a report from Inspector Charteris. It relates to a domestic disturbance involving you and Christine Jones. Perhaps you would care to comment.'

Weatherspoon put the report on the table and frowned. 'The only thing that I can think of about this date was an argument over money, and no, I was not one of her clients. I had no need to use prostitutes. She was a minor informant. She thought that ten shillings wasn't enough for the information that she gave me. But to call it a domestic is a bit strong.'

'If you read the final minute, sir, Chief Superintendent Stringer thought otherwise: *Advised re bringing the police force into disrepute?*'

'Had Charteris been accurate I might have agreed. But Stringer and Charteris were strong churchmen and didn't believe that we should use prostitutes as informants at all. As far as I was concerned this was a personal attack on me, nothing more.'

'Very well.' Valentine nodded and reaching into the box of files by his side retrieved the Coch file, placing it on the table to his left in full view of the Assistant Chief Constable.

What the Hell! How did I miss that!?

Valentine saw the look on the ACC's face and smiled. 'You recognise it, sir?' he said indicating the file.

'How could I not?' Inside he was anything but calm. Valentine was good. Blake proving to be a nuisance. If they had done their homework properly this could be dangerous. 'That was my first arrest for murder, Zebadiah Coch. But that was, what? 1936? Near enough thirty years ago. What possible relevance could that file be to this enquiry?'

'Let me refresh your memory, sir,' Valentine smiled and opened the Coch file at his first marker. Weatherspoon, without further comment sat back and folded his arms across his chest. 'At Approximately half past ten on the morning of Saturday, 30th May 1936, you received a telephone call from Father Kender, the Roman

Catholic priest at Braemont, to the effect that two young boys had just run down from the moor and told him that they had found the body of a local girl, Betsy Elstub. You informed DI Brearley. With two uniform constables attended the scene. There were no other C.I.D. officers available at the time.

On your arrival at Braemont you were met by Father Kender and taken to where the two boys were sitting in the front pew of the church.' Valentine paused and fixed his gaze on Weatherspoon. 'Can you remember the boy's names, sir?'

Weatherspoon never flinched. 'Of course. Magnus and Iago Yarney, Chief Inspector. And if you're going to ask me why I haven't mentioned this before, it's because they are both dead. It's not relevant.'

There was a sharp intake of breath from Mithering as Valentine continued. 'Not relevant?' he said. Astounded.

'In my opinion, certainly not.'

'Why, sir, have you never mentioned that Yarney was a twin.'

'Not relevant.'

Valentine and Mithering exchanged glances. An answer such as just given by Weatherspoon was unbelievable. 'Two boys, who just happen to be identical twins, claim to have found the body of a young woman who, according to the doctor who attended at the scene had been raped and manually strangled within the preceding two hours. One of them, Magnus Yarney, goes on to rape and murder Christine Jones who we now know was number three on Wainwright's list. We also know that according to Wainwright, in addition to himself and Magnus Yarney there were two other men present and who participated in Jones' slaughter. Twelve months later he murdered his original arresting officer, Detective Sergeant Douglas Blake. You don't think that it was relevant and need not be mentioned?'

Weatherspoon pursed his lips and shrugged. 'Put like that I suppose you could make a case. However, they're both dead, so, no.'

'As the senior investigating officer I should have been made aware. We will return to that point later, sir.'

This was not good. 'As you wish, Chief Inspector.'

'Who attended the body?'

'I went with DI Brearley, Father Kender and a uniform Pc. The other uniformed officer stayed in the church with the boys.'

'And no photographs were taken of the body in situ because Father Kender had interfered with the deceased's clothing?'

'That's right. Apparently the girl's dress had been pulled up around her waist and she wasn't wearing any underwear. He didn't consider the fact that he was interfering in the investigation, to him it was simply a question of common decency.'

'Photographs could still have been taken of the girl's face and throat.'

'True,' he acceded. 'But Mr Brearley decided otherwise,'

Valentine nodded. 'You left the uniform Pc at the scene to ward off sightseers?'

'Indeed. By this time word had spread and the more ghoulish villagers were going to look at her.'

'At what point did Father Kender mention seeing Zebadiah Coch?'

'Whilst we were walking up to see the body. He mentioned having seen him hurrying across the fields above the Rectory, in the direction of Silsden.'

'He used the word 'hurrying' in his statement? When was this sighting?'

'Ten to fifteen minutes before the boys arrived.'

'I've been to the scene of the murder, or as near as I could. Those fields are quite steep. Off the footpath which runs from Cowgill farm at the bottom of the hill up to the moor it's rough underfoot. And you say the Father Kender saw Coch hurrying?'

'That's what he said. It's what I wrote in his statement.'

'It is indeed, sir. How did you find out where Coch was?'

'He was a local. I made enquiries and they pointed me in the direction of Burnthwaite Bridge Farm, which is where I found him.'

'As the crow flies this is a distance of approximately five miles.'

'So I understand.'

'Did you ask how long Coch had been working at Burnthwaite Bridge Farm?'

'No.' Weatherspoon said. 'I saw no reason why I would want to ask such a question.'

'Bearing in mind Coch had allegedly been seen six hundred yards from the scene of a murder some distance away, did you enquire at what time he had returned to Burnthwaite Bridge Farm?'

'Offhand? No. He had returned, that's all that matters.'

'I couldn't disagree more, sir,' said Valentine. 'Knowing when he returned could help to disprove or support an alibi.'

'Perhaps, but I didn't consider it necessary.'

How slapdash could you get? 'Moving on, the statements that you took from Magnus and Iago Yarney. They're verbatim. Did you take them whilst they were sitting together in the church?'

'Yes, it seemed the best way, why?'

'They were teenagers. Did you not consider returning to the police station and calling in their parents?'

'They were young men, besides the priest was present.'

Yes, I'll bet he was. 'They were fourteen. That is not the point as I'm sure you know, sir. The statements should have been taken separately. Each boy on his own. As they are, other than both stating they came across Betsy Elstub's body, they tell you nothing.'

'Chief Inspector, are you stating that I didn't know how to take a statement.'

'What I'm saying, sir, is that you had been in the police for eleven years. Five of those in C.I.D. This was an investigation into the rape and murder of a sixteen year old young woman. The statements taken from those two boys have minimal details. The footpath takes them through the yard of Cowgill Farm and onto the pasture. From that point you have a clear view to the spot where Betsy Elstub was murdered about six hundred yards away. From that point a clear view down to the Rectory, also along the edge of the valley. Nowhere do either of them mention having sight of Coch. Just of them going for a walk and coming across her body.'

'Obviously Coch had departed the scene.'

'Perhaps Coch wasn't there, was never there.'

'What are you inferring?'

'You know exactly what I'm inferring, sir, perhaps the priest lied.'

'Ridiculous. To what end?'

'You know exactly what I mean, sir,'

'You're suggesting the boys murdered Betsy Elstub?'

'I wouldn't rule it out. Children have murdered before, and, fourteen year old young men as you refer to them are more than capable of sexual intercourse.'

'Ridiculous. I was satisfied and so was Mr Brearley.'

'Are you saying that a fourteen year old male is incapable of sexual intercourse?'

'No, I am not. But why would they rape and murder the girl and then run and tell the priest?'

'Oh, I don't know. Confess to the priest and be protected by the seal of the confessional? Perhaps if you had interviewed them separately you might have found out. Variations in their story?'

'There was no reason. Father Kender had seen Coch hurrying from the scene.'

'Allegedly seen,' said Valentine and paused. 'So, you and Detective Inspector Brearley had made up your mind at this early stage that Coch was guilty; even though the evidence of Father Kender was at best circumstantial.'

'No, we had not,' said Weatherspoon. 'But it was a solid lead. It was good enough to talk to him.'

'If it were true I would agree. But I still believe Coch was nowhere near the scene at the time Betsy Elstub was murdered.'

'You're entitled to your opinion Chief Inspector. You weren't there and I was.'

'That is true, sir; and probably neither was Coch. Now, what happened when you arrived at Burnthwaite Bridge Farm.'

'Coch was sitting in the barn. He'd been drinking and was unsteady on his feet.'

'Drinking?'

'Yes, drinking alcohol. I don't know what. Probably some home-made brew but from memory his breath stunk.'

'What happened next?'

'I put it to him that he was responsible for the assault on his niece and that he had been seen in the area by Father Kender.'

'What was his reply?'

'He denied it of course. The farmer, his son and a couple of farmhands pitched in and said that he hadn't left the farm for a month. So I had to arrest Coch and get him out of there to quieten things down.'

'Did it ever cross your mind that Coch was telling the truth?'

'Father Kender saw him.'

'Father Kender *alleged* that he saw him. There is a difference. In any case, sir, Coch would only have been in the approximate vicinity, nothing more. You'd better read this,' Valentine took the photostat of Coch's medical examination from his folder and slid it across the table.

Completely impassive Weatherspoon read the report.

Valentine slid a further document across the table. 'This is a report that I requested from Professor Andrews, Professor of Endocrinology at Leeds University. His comments are based on the document that you have just read.'

For several minutes Weatherspoon read and re-read the report. At last he put it down on the table and looked across at the two officers, a worried look on his face. 'But why did he sign the statement admitting that he had raped and strangled his niece?'

'Because he was going blind. That's the diabetic retinopathy referred to in that report. He wouldn't be able to read what was put in front of him. Yet you signed as having taken Coch's statement admitting guilt.'

'Yes I did, Chief Inspector. I was ordered to.'

'Whose writing was it?'

'Mr Brearley's, I had to take a break and go to the toilet. When I came back it was done.'

The DCI furrowed his brow. 'Yet you have signed as to the fact that you took this statement.'

'It was put in front of me and I was ordered to sign it.'

'And you never queried it?'

Weatherspoon laughed. 'Believe me, you didn't query Mr Brearley, Chief Inspector.'

'You didn't even consider querying DI Brearley's actions?'

He almost laughed. 'Seriously?' He said. 'No-one who had ever met DI Brearley would have asked that question. No.'

'So it was a fait accompli? You just let it ride?'

'It was out of my hands.'

'You could have tried. Made some attempt. I agree with you that based on what you say Father Kender told you, you were fully justified in speaking to him. You might even justify the arrest. But a charge of murder based on a man who was going blind and, signing a statement admitting guilt when there is evidence from the farmer, his family and workforce that he had not left the farm for several weeks? Why didn't you make representations to your Chief Superintendent?'

'It was a long time ago, Chief Inspector, and I believe that I've already addressed that point.'

'I still find it hard to understand why you didn't take it upstairs?'
Weatherspoon made no reply.

Valentine paused and took a deep breath before continuing. 'Didn't Coch kick up a bit of a rumpus in Court the next morning?'

'He did. The prosecuting inspector pointed out to the Magistrates that, in addition to Father Kender's sighting, Coch had signed a confession. The Magistrates ordered that a not guilty plea be entered and remanded him.'

'Alleged sighting,' corrected Valentine. 'He was remanded to prison where he committed suicide.'

'Tell me, Chief Inspector. Why did he do that if he was innocent?'

'Read the last paragraph of the Professor's report again, sir, if you please.'

Weatherspoon glanced briefly at Professor Andrews report, placed it back on the table and looked quizzically at Valentine. 'I know what game you're playing Chief Inspector. But I can assure you that no matter what evidence you think you're bringing to the case the inquest would not be re-opened.'

'I couldn't agree more, sir. Whether Coch committed suicide because he was frightened of the noose or because of his parlous state of health the verdict would have been the same: that he took his own life whilst the balance of his mind was disturbed. But this is not about the inquest, is it? Father Kender's alleged sighting of Coch cannot put him at the scene of the crime.'

'Are you stating that the priest lied? To what end?'

'I've already said that. I believe that he did.' Valentine locked eyes with Weatherspoon. 'What a shame, now he's dead we can't ask him ... The statements that you took from both Magnus and Iago Yarney make no mention of Coch. The views when the Yarney twins crossed the bridge at Cowgill Farm looking towards the scene of the murder and from there down the valley are unimpaired. Bearing in mind Coch's difficulty in walking he must have been visible had he been there.'

'I do not accept that, Chief Inspector. It's only a difference in time. The time that Coch murdered the Elstub girl was simply earlier. He had more time. Quite simple.'

'Jim Mellor, the farmer at Burnthwaite Bridge Farm, his family and farm hands are adamant in their version of events. Because of his mobility problems Coch had not left the farm for over a month. A view supported by Professor Andrews reviewing the notes made by the prison doctor. The point raised by Professor Andrews that with Coch's chronic condition he would be incapable of getting an erection. That fact alone should be sufficient to bring your conclusions into question.

'As far as I am concerned, Chief Inspector, Coch was responsible for the rape and murder of Elstub. I have nothing further to say on the matter.

'That remains to be seen ... You mentioned earlier that both Magnus Yarney and his brother Iago were both dead. We know that Magnus Yarney died in prison, when did Iago Yarney die, and how?'

'I don't know.'

'But you know that he is dead?'

'Yes.'

'How?'

' Their mother, Magda, told me.'

'When did she tell you?'

'It's a long time ago, Chief Inspector, I don't remember.'

'Well, was it before or after the war?'

'I'm not sure, after I think.'

'Was it before or after the Coronation?'

'Definitely before the Coronation.'

Valentine looked across the table, nodded and smiled. 'Was it before or after you began a sexual relationship with Magda Yarney?'

Before Weatherspoon could recover from the shock of the revelation Mithering opened the blue manilla folder in front of him. 'This,' he slid a statement across the table. 'Is a statement made by Jeffrey Grey, owner of The Bryony Private Hotel in Harrogate, it's a very discreet establishment,' he paused and smiled at Weatherspoon. 'The hotel had been owned by his father. Jeffrey Grey took over after his father died in 1953. Because he has a deformed left foot he was deemed unfit for military service and worked there continuously throughout the war. He hadn't been working at The Bryony for long and remembers you quite distinctly. He thought the name De Mateo sounded *romantic,* even though we were eventually at war with Italy. Your first tryst with Magda Yarney was Wednesday 16th June 1939. Always Wednesday, 2pm until 4pm. Double room and a bottle of red wine. You were most *valued* customers,' he added, unable to keep the sarcasm from his voice and smiled. 'Mrs Yarney made the bookings in your name, Mrs De Mateo. This is a list of every booking she made.' He slid a typed schedule across the table. 'From June, 1939 until July, 1949 ...'

Weatherspoon scanned the sheet, re-placed it on the table.

Mithering looked across the table. 'Have you anything to say, sir?'

'No, it seems accurate enough,' he replied.

'You had an affair with the mother of Magnus Yarney for ten years and that's all you have to say?'

'I'm not denying it, Mr Mithering. But there's nothing to add. It was immoral, perhaps. Betrayal of my marriage vows, certainly. But please do not try and put too much emphasis on this, Magnus Yarney was not involved in Elstub's murder. That was Coch.'

'What about Iago Yarney.'

Weatherspoon sighed. 'It was Coch,' he said with some exasperation. 'The boys came across the body whilst out for a walk, nothing more.'

'So you say ... How did your relationship with Magda Yarney begin?'

'There was a break-in at the house, I attended.'

'As a Detective Sergeant?'

'Yes, there was a spate of sickness. We were short-handed. I logged the crime. She offered me a coffee. Thanked me for looking after her boys and commiserated over some bad press over Coch. A week or so later we bumped into each other in Keighley and had a coffee. One day she asked me back to the house when the boys were away from home with their father for the day. That was that. One question, if I may'

'How did we know?'

'Precisely.'

'From information that was gleaned following our last visit to interview Father Kender. We checked out the archives at the Keighley Herald. That in turn led us to Mark Collins. A reporter with the Keighley Herald.'

'Oh yes,' he said, nodding as he spoke. 'I remember him.'

'Yes, you would. He didn't think much of you as a police officer, did he?'

'Not at all,' he said and laughed. 'One of the hazards of the job.'

Valentine opened the folder in front of him, removed a statement, passing it across to Weatherspoon. 'The idea to call in at the offices of the Keighley Herald was DC Blake's. Once the staff at the Herald realised what enquiries were being made by DC Blake and the others, many doors opened. That statement is the result.'

'You mentioned the others, Chief Inspector, just who were they?'

'DS Nicholson and WDC Farthing. They were accompanied by Oliver Randall, a reporter with the Herald and Mark Collins' son-in-law; he arranged the interview.'

The look that Weatherspoon gifted Valentine less than complimentary.

'Mrs Watson,' Valentine turned to the short-hand writer. 'There is no need for you to write down the text of this statement, a copy will be attached to your type-written record.'

She nodded and placed her pad on her lap.

DCI Valentine began to read:

My name is Mark Collins and I live at the above address. Eight months ago I was diagnosed with terminal cancer and given between three and six months to live. I think my time is nearly up. It sounds gruesome but I make this statement in the settled and hopeless expectation of my imminent death.

I remember it as if it were yesterday. Saturday 30th of May, 1936. A beautiful day and the light on the hills was wonderful. A report came in that the body of a young girl had been found on the hill behind Braemont Rectory. I was the lucky one. In fact I was the only reporter available so I got the assignment, and the bike. There was no bus to Braemont and I had instructions to file the copy by 11.30am in time to make the first edition.

It was a six mile bike ride to Braemont and believe me, when I arrived, I was lathered. They were just bringing the poor lass, Betsy Elstub, through the Rectory gates, which is a bit odd because normally the dead go the other way. It's a one-way trip. Like all villages they have their jungle telegraph. There were plenty of opinions but it didn't take me long to get the story, just as long as you kept out of Detective Inspector Brearley's way. When he said jump you never asked why.

There was a big problem though, the police were talking about a farm labourer called Zebadiah Coch as being a suspect. In fact the priest, Patrick Kender, said that he'd seen him about ten minutes before two local lads, Magnus and Iago Yarney arrived at the Rectory claiming they'd found the body. People thought they were a couple of odd-balls. Magnus in a world of his own and Iago exactly the opposite. There were mutterings from the crowd that Coch hadn't been seen for weeks. I even managed to snatch a few minutes with the lass's father, Henry Elstub. Coch was his deceased wife's cousin. He told me that Coch was bad on his feet, could hardly walk and was staying at Burnthwaite Bridge Farm, Silsden. Henry Elstub's tale was as sad as most, his wife had died in childbirth with the baby stillborn. Now the sixth of his seven surviving children was dead, only Caroline was left. As if life wasn't hard enough.

There was a public phone box half way back to Keighley. The police and the hearse passed me long before I got there. I called it in. Old Josh, Mr Cradley, the editor thanked me and sent me to Burnthwaite Bridge Farm. That was a tow even though I was fit in those days. I arrived just as the police were literally dragging Mr Coch off to the lock-up. The place was in uproar. Jim Mellor, his lad, whose name escapes me, and a couple of his hands were swearing blind that Zeb hadn't left the farm for weeks because of his health and the police insisting that he had been seen near the scene of the murder. It was bedlam. That was the story I wrote and that was the story on the front page, under my by-line. That made my name. We got a helluva postbag. Again the following week when we followed up with the story of his suicide. Then that copper, De Mateo, or Weatherspoon, or whatever he calls himself now got a promotion to sergeant. There's no justice. Jim Mellor was so incensed he went to his solicitor, a Mr Bead at Inglis and Nightingale and swore an affidavit to the fact that Zeb hadn't left his farm for over a month. But with the suicide there was nothing we could do.

I kept digging away but eventually Mr Cradley said to let it lie, which I did.

A couple of years later, if I remember right it was Easter week, Tuesday I think. I was in town shopping about eleven when I saw Weatherspoon in the car park at the back of the Town Hall talking to Mrs Yarney, the mother of the boys that reported having found young Betsy Elstub. They were standing very close to each other. She handed him a small package, like a small carrier bag, which I knew came from Smedleys, that's a good shop, expensive. He took the package, they kissed, and went their separate ways. I knew they were both married so I went to the men's department in Smedleys and had a chat with the girl on the accessories counter. She was a cracking looking lass - I've got to say that, we got married a year later. It took a bit of persuading but eventually she told me that Mrs Yarney had bought a pair of gold cuff-links, they cost over a tenner; a fortune in those days.

A couple of weeks later I was covering a golf tournament over towards Ilkley, by now I'd got my own motor bike. I wasn't looking for them but I spotted them in the crowd and in the restaurant at the end. They didn't know me from Adam so I managed to get a table next to theirs, that cost me a bomb and out of my own pocket. I couldn't claim that on expenses. I couldn't hear a great deal except when I followed them to the car-park. I overheard them making arrangements to meet the following Wednesday, 'in the usual place'. I guessed right; it was behind the town hall. She collected him at one and I followed them, on my bike, to The Bryony. That's a small hotel in Harrogate. A quiet area and looked expensive. I gave them a half hour and wandered in just to chat with whoever was behind the desk. It was the owner. I told him that I was doing an article on the smaller Harrogate hotels. He told me the history of the hotel and of their, what he called, valued clientele. I asked him if he would divulge the details of who his guests might be, but he refused – they were a discreet establishment and valued their clientele's patronage. I put a couple of £1 notes in his pocket and pointed at the register. He turned his back whilst I took a quick look. I was only interested in Mrs Yarney and Weatherspoon. They were signed in the name of De Mateo, Mr & Mrs De Mateo. What a surprise. He did confide that this was the fourth time they had been to the hotel – a double room and a bottle of red wine, their 'appointments' as he put it, were always for two hours. What they got up to was nothing to do with him!

In August 1939 I took the story to Mr Cradley, but, apart from being an exposé of infidelity there were bigger fish to fry as we found out the following month when we declared war on Germany.

From '39 to '45 I was a war correspondent. The next time I heard the name Yarney was in April 1949 when Magnus Yarney cut that girls' throat. That raised a lot of questions in my mind and a lot of others as well.

Oliver Randall, my son-in-law, is present and I authorise him to allow the police access to all my files on the proviso that they are returned when the police have finished with them.

Mark Collins
Oliver Randall
Brian Blake DC 547

Weatherspoon laughed down his nose and passed the statement back across the table. 'A busy little bee.'

'He certainly was, sir,' replied Valentine. 'He died three days ago. The Herald is running with the story on the front page this week.'

'Chief Inspector, the dying declaration does not add anything to your enquiry and swearing an affidavit does not make the contents true.'

'I accept that, sir. However, if false it's perjury. And it is backing up the comments made by Henry Elstub, the prison doctor, and comments made by Professor Andrews.'

'Which in turn was made on the comments of the prison doctor. That in itself does not introduce any new evidence. I still accept the version given by Father Kender. Coch was there.'

'Even if that sighting were true,' responded Valentine, 'it cannot put Coch nearer to the murder scene than six hundred yards. 'He would have been in plain sight of the boys climbing the path. I would remind you that neither Magnus nor Iago Yarney made any mention of Coch in their statements taken *by you*. In fact you apparently made no mention of asking them at the time, surely they would have mentioned Coch had he been there?'

'After all this time I have no recollections of what I asked.'

'There is nothing in your statement either about asking them if Coch or anyone else was in sight.'

'I don't recall.'

'Furthermore, had Father Kender told you of his sighting of Coch before you attended the scene of the murder you would have known prior to speaking to the Yarney twins, and you apparently said nothing. Why is that?

'It's in Father Kender's statement.'

'True, but it is not in the boy's statements? That would have provided further evidence that Coch was at the scene, reinforcing your statement of what Father Kender had allegedly seen. Yet for some reason you didn't see fit. Why?'

'These were children,' he protested. 'They've just stumbled across the dead body of someone they knew. It was a pretty gruesome sight.'

'You described them as young men. And they should have been asked if they saw anyone else in the vicinity, shouldn't they? If they can give a statement about finding the body they can be asked if they saw anyone in the vicinity. They had excellent views from both the bottom of the hill and from the location of the murder.'

'Mr Brearley and I were satisfied with the action that we took.'

'An uncorroborated statement from Father Kender that could never be challenged once Coch had committed suicide, and now, Father Kender is dead ... it all leaves a nasty taste.'

'Not in my mouth Chief Inspector it doesn't. Coch was guilty.'

'That would have been for a court to decide, sir. There is still the evidence of Mark Collins when he spoke to Henry Elstub after the murder of his daughter, Jim Mellor and his son, who was also an eye-witness to the arrest. We obtained a statement from him three days ago.'

'I've already explained that, Chief Inspector. As far as Mr Brearley and I were concerned, the sighting of Coch by Father Kender hurrying away from the scene and his subsequent admission that he had murdered the girl carries far more evidential weight than the locals protesting as what they saw as one of their own being arrested.'

'Not if you consider that Betsy Elstub was also one of their own it doesn't. The evidence from the girl's father that Coch was bad on his feet. Jim Mellor, the farmer at Burnthwaite Bridge Farm, and the affidavit he swore immediately following the arrest, and, the notes made by the prison doctor, it doesn't. Oh, and a reminder from the prison doctor's notes. That the smell on Coch's breath was acetone, commonplace with sufferers of diabetes, it was not alcohol.'

'We shall never know, shall we, Chief Inspector?'

'I think, sir, all things considered, we know already,' Valentine reached down into the box at his feet and removed the top file: R v Yarney – Murder. 'This is the file concerning the death of Christine Jones, the third reference on Wainwright's list. Do you remember the first occasion that you were introduced to Blake's theory regarding Wainwright's list?'

'Certainly, it was most edifying.'

'Do you also recall Mr Creighton enquiring re Yarney's antecedents?'

'I have some vague recollection of it being mentioned, why?'

'My recollections were that the antecedents had been taken by a local C.I.D. officer, but I couldn't remember the officer's name. However, I did recollect the report stated that Magnus Yarney had no family and was a loner. It was my intention that should Wainwright's list prove to be genuine, as a part of the current enquiry I would re-investigate that element of the Jones case in regard to Magnus Yarney's antecedents.'

'And you want to know why I had the Jones file brought from the archive.'

'Amongst other things, sir, why did you?'

'Simple curiosity, Chief Inspector, nothing more. I wanted to refresh my memory.'

'But according to DS Griffiths, in HQ C.I.D. Admin you had the file for less than an hour, and, as you can see,' Valentine said. "This is a very big file.'

'I restricted my reading to the typed documents: summary and statements.' He replied.

'Nevertheless, you hardly had time to read all the typed documents. There are over forty statements. Those of the investigating officers are multi-paged, as are the interviews. The summary itself is forty eight pages in length.'

'I can speed-read,' he protested, 'There's nothing untoward.'

'Indeed. However. I had DC Blake collect the file and tasked him with finding the information regarding Yarney's antecedents. DC Blake has the makings of a very fine detective. He is very thorough. It wasn't too long before he came to me with a rather bizarre finding. Not only had the antecedents been removed from the file but so had the statement of the officer who took them.'

'Perhaps they had been lost.'

'No sir. They had been ripped out ... don't you think that it's rather strange that out of a file of this size just three sheets had been removed, and although in different parts of the file, all connected to you? The statement written by you concerning the taking of and submission of Yarney's antecedents, copy statement and the antecedents themselves.'

'The cellar is insecure. The obvious answer is that the documents to which you refer were removed in the cellar. The file was not signed out.'

'Then why, sir, why were only the documents that refer to you removed. You've been back in Force for less than two years. This file is very old. Can you answer that?'

Weatherspoon snapped upright on his chair. 'Are you accusing me of interfering with the file, Chief Inspector, because if you are ...'

Valentine looked at Weatherspoon. 'What, sir?'

'Nothing,' he replied and sank back into his chair. He was in deep trouble and he knew it. The ordure was rising towards his chin.

'As it happens, no sir, I'm not. But you must admit that it does tend to point the finger. The file has been signed out from the archive on just two occasions since it was originally filed. Once to you, the other by DC Blake on my behalf. Had it been you and knowing where they were stored in the cellar you would have just gone to the cellar and removed the entire file. Then no-one might have been any the wiser. The file had simply been lost.' Valentine sensed that Mithering, sitting on his right hand side was about to laugh out loud. 'However, all is not lost. Detective Inspector Spencer, he retired long ago, was the officer-in-charge in the Jones case; incidentally he was allowed to extend his service in order to complete the file in the case of the murder of DS Blake, DC Blake's father. He kept a complete duplicate of all the major crime files that fell within his remit and has very kindly donated them. In fact I have his copy of the Jones file here, and it is a complete duplicate not just extracts.'

Valentine opened the file at the last marker and turned it so that Weatherspoon could see. 'Will you please confirm that this is your signature, sir?'

Weatherspoon sat forwards, 'Yes, that's my signature.'

'And the statement refers to the submission of this document,' Valentine, opened the file at the first marker. 'And this is the antecedents form to which the statement I have just shown you refers?'

Weatherspoon glanced at the brief details on the form. 'Correct.'

Valentine closed the file. 'Considering the circumstances under which these antecedents were obtained, don't you consider it to be a little short on details?'

'Not really, Chief Inspector, It does cover all the salient points.'

'It has not been initialled by DI Spencer, as the OIC I would have thought he would have done so.'

'It was submitted, so I can only assume that it was an oversight on his part.'

Valentine nodded. Ivan Spencer was a stickler for detail, he read and initialled everything. Antecedents were an important aspect of any file that was going to court, especially the Assize. He hadn't seen this document. 'You dated this document on the 22nd April 1949. Can we take it from what you had stated previously that Iago Yarney was dead by this date? You've not mentioned him at all.'

'He was dead.'

'So you're inferring, what's the point?'

'Exactly.'

'You don't even mention a twin brother or siblings. The inference of what you have entered here is that Magnus Yarney was an only child and not a good mixer. If the defence had put forward that his mental state had been adversely affected by the death of his twin brother as a partial defence? The prosecution would have been caught with one leg up in the air.'

'He pleaded guilty.'

'No, he did not. He was declared unfit to plead. We don't know what he would have said had he been given the opportunity,' Valentine handed the file to Mithering. 'Sir?'

'I agree,' Mithering replied after a quick scan of the document. 'It should have been there. There should also have been a statement or other certification that Iago Yarney had died, that would have given us the cause and date of his death.'

Weatherspoon sneered. 'This is just playing around with history,' he said, but knowing where this interview was leading. 'You're just picking at what you see as faults in a thirty year old murder investigation, have you a point to make?'

Ignoring the question Mithering passed the photograph supplied by Mrs Morton across the table. 'What can you tell us about this photograph?'

'It's supposed to mean something to me?' said Weatherspoon giving the photograph a cursory glance.

'You took the photograph, so yes.'

'I did?' he queried and picked it up and turned it over.

Valentine watched Weatherspoon's face intently; there was the merest narrowing of his eyes. He knows. '23rd of August 1947, if that helps. Who do you know?'

'I have no recollection of this at all. What makes you think that I took it?'

'Please look at the photograph and tell us who you know.'

Weatherspoon slowly scanned the photograph. 'Well, the woman in the cart looks vaguely familiar. There's Father Kender and the Yarney twins, and in the bottom right-hand corner, I think … they were the Robbins, they were local farmers.' He put the photograph down.

Valentine smiled. 'No-one else?'

Weatherspoon glanced at the photograph and slowly shook his head. 'No, no-one else, why, should I?'

'They think so,' replied Valentine. 'The lady you thought was familiar was, during your time at Keighley, on the Bench.'

Weatherspoon looked at the photograph again and frowned. 'Mrs Morton?'

'Yes, it is. She loaned us the photograph, of which this is a copy.'

'She looked different on the Bench,' he said. 'You implied there was someone else, Chief Inspector.'

'Yes, the couple sitting adjacent to the Robbins are Cuthbert Wainwright and Adele Bagley, now of course, his wife. You never mentioned that you knew either of them. Yet they both claim to have met you several times. Under the circumstances I would have thought that you would have volunteered that information.'

'I didn't volunteer anything Chief Inspector simply because it's not true. I've never met them.'

'Never? Are you sure?'

'Absolutely.'

'Were you at the event shown on the photograph?'

'No, why would I be?'

'I don't know, why would you? You appear to have an affinity with Magnus and Iago Yarney.'

'That's absolute nonsense!' Weatherspoon snapped.

'Is it also nonsense that on the 13th of September 1956, whilst you were a Detective Chief Inspector with the Sheffield City Police, you flew with B.O.A.C. to Las Vegas in the United States of America in the company of one, Isabel Florea, who, incidentally paid for the flights by personal cheque?'

Weatherspoon's eyes tightened. 'And?'

Valentine smiled. 'Isabel Florea, born on the 10th April, 1901 in Bucharest, full name Magda Isabella Florea, met and subsequently married Jakob Yarney, an accountant. Following the Great War they moved to this country where, in 1922 she bore him twin boys, Iago and Magnus. After Magnus Yarney was charged with the murder of Christine Jones the Yarneys moved to Skipton where Jakob Yarney, by means of deed poll, changed his name to Jacob Sullivan, his wife's to Mary Isabel Sullivan and their older son, Iago, to James Sullivan. Ring any bells, sir?'

Weatherspoon made no reply, simply glaring at him across the table.

'I will grant you that the name Iago Yarney is dead but its previous owner certainly was not. Following the death of Jacob Sullivan in 1953, his son James took over the family business and by all accounts did very well, at least according to the tax returns he submitted he did.

In March of 1956 Mary Isabel Sullivan changed her name by deed poll to Isabel Florea and applied for a British passport.

In Las Vegas you stayed in a double room at the New Frontier Hotel where you and she married,' he smiled knowingly. 'That made you the stepfather of both Magnus Yarney and James Sullivan. Just how much did you know?'

'Very clever.'

'How much did you know?' He pressed.

Weatherspoon sat back and folded his arms tighter. 'No comment.'

'We know that in 1961 James Sullivan sold his accountancy business. In 1962 secretly married Mary Jane Caruthers, an elderly and very wealthy widow. They live in her home at Oxenhope. As we speak I have a team en route to search the premises and to arrest James Sullivan.'

'Good luck with that.'

'Meaning?'

'Simply, good luck.'

'A second team together with search warrant is en route to *your* home.'

All Valentine received in exchange was an uncomplimentary glare.

'The day of the first exhumations. Knowing that the morning's exhumation had been successful, why did you verbally attack DC

Blake, suggesting that he had made the whole thing up when he was explaining to everyone present how he had located the grave site?'

'He's a cocky little bastard.'

'He certainly knows his own worth, but cocky? I've not seen it. In any case, he'd proved by the morning's endeavours that he was correct and complying with Mr Mithering's request to demonstrate where No.12 on Wainwright's list was likely to be.'

There was no comment from across the table.

'Now, moving on to the day when Father Kender and Mrs Magee were murdered. Why did Father Kender ring Swallow Street and try to contact you minutes after DS Nicholson and DC Blake left the Rectory at Braemont?'

'I don't know, that's why I tried to call him back.'

'When you eventually made contact with Father Kender what did you discuss?'

'I don't remember.'

'According to the records kept by the lady who mans the Braemont exchange you spoke to each other approximately every four to six weeks, what did you discuss?'

'I don't remember.'

'Why did you never mention that you had regular conversations with Father Kender?'

'It wasn't important.'

'It wasn't important that someone closely identified with your step sons, who had a relationship with them going back at least to 1936. Someone who you had obviously known for many years has a conversation with you, one of many. Within two hours of two members of my team paying him a visit both Father Kender and his housekeeper are murdered, and you state that the call wasn't important.'

'No, it wasn't.'

'Five minutes after you made the call to Father Kender you made a further call, to whom? Was that call to Iago Yarney, James Sullivan?'

'I can't remember every telephone call I make.'

'I'm not asking that you remember every call, merely the one immediately preceding the murder of the last person you apparently called. Thankfully the HQ telephone operators keep records to be checked against forthcoming telephone accounts. How often did you speak with your step-son either in person or by telephone?'

'I have no idea, Chief Inspector.'

'Perhaps his mother will know,' Valentine replied. 'But somewhere in your telephone records, sir, there is a pattern. We are liaising with all the forces where you worked since the end of the war to obtain details of the phone numbers to which you had access and the calls you made. We will know the addresses at which you lived on your sojourn around the police forces of the North of England and cross-check that information with the telephone accounts. We know that the number of the Rectory at Braemont was Braemont two seven. It will take time but we will get that information.'

'No comment.'

'Once we had possession of Mrs Morton's photograph, further statements were obtained from those in the photograph who could be traced. I instructed DS Nicholson to construct a photo-ID folder of twelve senior police officers. The contents of that folder and the photograph loaned from Mrs Morton were then shown to everyone on the photograph who is still alive and in this country with the exception of James Sullivan. Without exception they identified you as the person who took that photograph.'

'No comment.'

'Interestingly enough, when DS Nicholson and WDC Farthing showed the folder to Cuthbert Wainwright ...' at the mention of Wainwright's name Weatherspoon took a sudden and noticeable interest. Valentine smiled at the reaction. '... I'll read you

Wainwright's statement, sir, and then you will understand. Mrs Watson, again there's no need for you to take down the text of the statement I will ensure that you have a copy ... The statement begins:

My name is Cuthbert Wainwright and I make this statement of my own free will. I am currently on remand at Hecton police station awaiting trial concerning the deaths of thirteen women from March 1945 to the present day. I have just been shown a photograph taken many years ago in the barn at Cowgill Farm, Braemont. At that time I was a member of an evangelical church group and we had invited people along to a group picnic to see if they were interested in joining us. The photograph was taken by a friend of Iago, Iago Yarney who led our little group. His name was Albert Weatherspoon, a policeman. After that I was shown a blue manilla folder containing photographs of twelve men, all wearing the uniform of senior police officers and asked if I recognised any of them. I recognised three. There was Mr Barton, the Chief Constable and Mr Gartside his deputy whom I had met previously at civic functions which I attended in my capacity as an alderman in Westleigh. The third was Albert Weatherspoon, the officer who had taken the photograph. He had also been involved in one of the murders ...'

Weatherspoon, his face contorted with rage, leapt to his feet as if he had been stung. 'What!?' Mrs Watson hurriedly began to write.

Valentine smiled and leaned back in his chair looking up at Weatherspoon, his anger and his fear. 'He seems to know you rather well, sir,' he said, indicating with his right hand that he should sit. 'Wainwright has admitted being present at the same time as yourself. Shall I continue?'

Weatherspoon slowly sank onto his chair. His knuckles white as he gripped the edge of the table. His breathing shallow and rapid. A genuine look of fear in his eyes. 'He wouldn't dare,' he said softly between gritted teeth.

'I heard that,' said Valentine, smiling. 'He wouldn't dare, you said. I take it you're talking about Wainwright? And what wouldn't he dare? Involve you in a murder? For you to say that you would have to know a person well to imply that he should be frightened if he spoke out of turn. Just what did you mean? Would you like to consider your earlier comment about never having met Wainwright or the lady who is now his wife?'

There was no comment from Weatherspoon. The DCI turned to his right and smiled. 'Are you all right, Mrs Watson,' he said.

'Yes, thank you, sir,' she replied. 'It made me jump.'

'Good, the bit I warned you about is coming up shortly. Just treat them as words, nothing more.'

'Just something for you to think about, Mr Weatherspoon. Wainwright was shown the folder containing the twelve photographs. Bearing in mind his background of being in public service and in business for well over twenty years, why would he single any one of them out and make that statement about involvement in a murder unless he had a reason? Wainwright's comment was voluntary. There was no inducement made for him to select any, or none, of the officers. He could just as well have accused any officer whose photograph was in the folder, or none at all. So why you?'

Again Weatherspoon made no comment His grip on the table tightened.

Valentine nodded to Mrs Watson. 'I'll continue reading:

It was the third murder. It was my job to bury the bodies, but this was the first time I had witnessed anyone being killed. There had been five in the car, Magnus and Iago, Albert Weatherspoon, me and a young prostitute called Christine Jones. Albert was driving, it was his car. He pulled off the road and into a field. I wasn't sure where it was. At the time everyone was happy including the woman, she thought she had four customers. We all got out of the car then Albert slapped her hard across the face and said that he had warned her in the past and that she was just a filthy whore. That she had given him VD. She protested and said to contact her doctor, she was clean. She began to cry as Iago hit her. Albert hit her again and knocked her to the ground then began to rip her clothes. He forced his handkerchief into her mouth to stop her screaming. They took turns at having sex with her. Albert was first, then Iago and lastly Magnus. Albert took the handkerchief out of her mouth when she was still on the floor. They then took turns at making her suck their penises, I found that disgusting. When they'd finished she began to sit up when Albert grabbed her hands pulling them away from her mouth. Iago grabbed her by the hair and yanked her head back. Magnus suddenly had a knife in his hand, it must have been in his coat pocket because he was naked from the waist down, they all were. It was one of those knives with a retractable blade. Iago had hold of Jones' hair and holding her head on the ground as Magnus reached across and cut the woman's throat. It was terrible. There was so much blood. I was sick. Iago told me that if I ever spoke about what had happened he would strip my soul and send me to Hell. They, Magnus, Iago and Albert, got dressed and we drove into Hecton. Just round the corner from the police station Albert stopped the car, Magnus got out and walked into the police station carrying the knife in his hand. I haven't seen Albert Weatherspoon since that date. That's all I want to say.

'The statement is signed Cuthbert Wainwright and witnessed by DS Nicholson and WDC Farthing.'

Weatherspoon sat facing forwards completely immobile. 'Have you anything to say, Mr Weatherspoon? Any comment about you knowing Christine Jones perhaps?

There was no reply.

'Stand up please.'

Mithering took the two paces necessary to walk round the table. He took hold of Weatherspoon's jacket and hoisted him from his chair.

'Albert Weatherspoon,' said Valentine. 'You are not obliged to say anything unless you wish to do so but whatever you say may be put into writing and given in evidence. I am arresting you on suspicion of the rape and murder of Christine Jones on the 1st April 1949. I am also arresting you that, on diverse dates, you did pervert the course of justice. Have you anything to say?

Weatherspoon made no reply.

Mithering let go of Weatherspoon's jacket. 'You go find Blake I'll look after him.' As Valentine left the room Weatherspoon sank back onto his chair. Mithering turned and smiled at the typist. 'Are you all right, Mrs Watson?' She nodded. 'For the sake of continuity we would like for you do all subsequent interviews. It keeps the job simple. Have you any problems with that.'

'No sir, that's all right. But he actually did that, what you've been talking about?'

'Oh yes.'

'But he's an ACC,' she replied.

'Yes, but not for much longer.'

Sixty-One

I'd been chatting to the staff in Admin when the DCI arrived and shooed me upstairs. I was met at the top of the stairs by both the Chief and Mr Gartside.

'Everything all right, Blake,' the Chief asked as I passed.

'Fine, sir,' I replied. I was sorely tempted to add - Two down one to go, but thought better of it. How did I really feel? From being present during the discussions over the last two days, I knew what the outcome of the interview would be. Now that it had happened it was cathartic, at least in part. The final piece would be the arrest of Iago Yarney – might as well use the name by which I'd always known the family until recently. I'm sure that it would have the same effect on those with longer memories than I. The net was nearly closed. It was only a matter of time.

Euphoric isn't the right word. That could wait until all three were in the bag but I did feel good. I took my cuffs from my pocket as I entered the interview room. Weatherspoon stood whilst I put the cuff round my right wrist and took hold of his left. 'You know, sir,' I said to the DCI. 'When I joined the force I was given the same collar number as my father, 547.'

He looked at me for a couple of seconds. All I did was smile. He glanced at the cuffs. 'So they did,' he said. 'Those were your father's cuffs?'

'Yes sir. Staff and cuffs. What do they say? What goes around comes around?' He laughed and put his hand on my shoulder.

Safely cuffed to my right wrist Mr Valentine and I led Weatherspoon like an automaton down the two flights of stairs, past the shocked staff who had heard that something was going on upstairs. Out of the back door to the waiting road traffic car. Twenty yards away in the C.I.D. block the doorway and every window was filled with shocked faces. Apart from the rain drumming on the roof of the traffic car there wasn't a sound.

We left the car park and collected an escort: a couple of Speed-Twins leading and a traffic car at the rear. Traffic was heavy for the time of day and the motor cyclists would be handy to get him into Hecton nick and out of sight.

The Speed-Twins leap-frogged to keep the road clear. It still took us twenty five minutes. There must have been half the sub-divisional strength waiting for us. Primarily to keep the Press at bay. It almost worked. There was no trouble. In Press terms, the world and his wife must have been alerted. We had to walk the last twenty yards. There was at least one TV crew. One face kept cropping up, Alistair McDonald from the Argus. He spotted me. 'Pc Blake,' he called. 'Have you anything you can tell us?' I could have ignored him but he wasn't a bad bloke. 'Sorry, you'll have to call the Press office.'

His face dropped. 'Thanks.'

Safely inside with the doors locked and two Pc's outside, just to keep everyone who shouldn't be in, out, much of the crowd dispersed. I divested myself of my prisoner. He was booked in. Arresting officer and officer in the case DCI Valentine. Me? The canteen beckoned. I had my sandwiches to dispose of and coffee to drink.

I was regaled from several quarters with requests for information as to whom I was cuffed. My answer became monotonous, 'Sorry, you'll have to ask either Mr Sampson or the DCI.'

Inspector Meadowcroft took a slightly different tack. He had this way of asking favours. I had almost finished my sandwiches when he arrived. He was on duty at two. 'Brian,' he said laconically and indicated the adjacent chair, 'May I.'

I smiled and nodded. 'Please do, sir.'

Comfortable, he half-turned towards me inclined his head and smiled. 'Are you able to deny that was the ACC Crime you've just brought in via the back door?' A euphemism at Hecton for the cell area.

I returned the smile. 'No sir, I am not able to deny it,' I said, winked.and gave him a quizzical look.

He reciprocated, laughed, stood up and left patting me on the shoulder as he passed. 'Brian, thank you for your clarity.'

'Any time, sir,' I called after him.

Two of Hecton's five cells were now semi-permanently occupied: Wainwright in cell number one - nearest the charge desk. Weatherspoon in number five. Wainwright was taken from his cell to cell five so that he could look through the hatch and see Weatherspoon sitting on the bench. Perhaps seeing him as a result of the statement that he had given would help him, although the look of hatred on Weatherspoon's face when he saw Wainwright can't have helped.

Sixty-Two

Seven Trees, Oxenhope, was an imposing early 17th century stone built manor house in two acres of gardens encompassed by an eight feet high stone wall, now exhibiting the advancing signs of dilapidation. The last known address for James Sullivan. A Morris Minor and Ford Cortina parked to the left of the door.

It was beginning to rain. One glance at the gathering clouds was enough.

The ambulance turned right in a tight arc, wheels biting into the gravel drawing to a halt close to the doorway. DS Cartwright left plenty of room. The ambulance crew exited and took a stretcher into the house. DS Cartwright, DC's Myers, Sendrove, and Cavendish waited, wondering who was ill.

They hadn't long to wait. On the stretcher a well-wrapped elderly and frail lady, eyes closed. A nurse and doctor with stethoscope round his neck, in close attendance. Behind them a smart middle-aged woman wearing a tabard. 'Can I help you?' she said to no-one in particular.

'Yes, I'm Detective Sergeant Cartwright. Is that lady Mrs Sullivan?'

'It is,' she replied. 'Why do you ask?'

Before he could answer. 'I'm Dr Ross. If you wanting to speak with Mrs Sullivan that's out of the question. She's had a stroke. I am taking her to the Keighley Victoria Hospital. I'm sure that Mrs Hogg will be able to assist you.'

'A slight stroke, doctor?'

It was a thin smile. 'At seventy nine years of age, Sergeant, there is no such thing. Now if you will excuse me.' Without waiting for a reply he followed the stretcher and nurse into the ambulance.

The blue light came on as the ambulance turned right out of the gate. Mrs Hogg watched until the ambulance disappeared behind the trees. 'Detective Sergeant?' She looked at the others, wondering. 'Obviously there is a problem. Could I ask what this is about?'

DS Cartwright withdrew the search warrant from his inside jacket pocket and handed it over. 'Mrs Hogg. This is a search warrant issued by Hecton Magistrates Court to search these premises.'

Mrs Hogg briefly scanned the warrant. 'Hecton, Sergeant?' she iterated. 'Isn't that ...'

'We are from the Hecton incident room, yes. These are my colleagues. Detective constables Myers, Sendrove and Cavendish.'

'That's disgusting. Surely you don't think that Mrs Sullivan has anything to do with that.'

The detective sergeant smiled. 'No, Mrs Hogg. We are here to look for evidence concerning her husband, James Sullivan.'

'But, I don't understand. He's a missionary in Malawi. He left the country last September.'

'Really?'

Mrs Hogg felt sick. 'He's not is he? In Malawi?'

'We believe not, Mrs Hogg.'

'Well, you'd better come in.' She handed the warrant back. 'Is it all right to telephone the solicitor?'

'Of course. My officers will commence the search immediately but nothing will be removed from the premises without your knowledge. And your room, Mrs Hogg. I'm afraid that will be searched as well by Constable Sendrove?'

She had been Housekeeper at Seven Trees for twenty years. Ten years before Mr Carruthers had passed away. Before the cancer took him. Until then it had been a happy home. Since then, the Mistress had retreated more and more into her grief. Even the appearance of the Reverend James Sullivan and their marriage hadn't drawn her fully back into her old ways. As the years passed she had spent more time in her bed. Her solace being that her fortune was being used to help the poor in Malawi. But now. She was pleased that Mrs Sullivan wasn't here to witness what was happening. 'My room is downstairs, overlooking the rear garden, Sergeant.'

'Once we complete upstairs, Mrs Hogg,' said Jenny, smiling. 'I promise I won't make a mess.'

Mrs Hogg spent several minutes speaking to George Mountford, the Carruthers family solicitor. She handed the telephone to DS Cartwright. 'He wants to talk to you, Sergeant.'

'Sergeant Cartwright.'

'Mountford. What's all this about, Sergeant. Mrs Hogg says that you're searching the house for evidence against James Sullivan. Looking to arrest him for rape and murder.'

'Yes, that's true, Mr Mountford. I was listening.'

'But the man's in Holy Orders. A missionary. He's in Malawi. I took him to the railway station myself last September.'

'Be that as it may. We have a court order to search the premises.'

'Very well. Please wait before you execute the warrant. I wish to oversee the proceedings.'

'We have already commenced the search. But nothing will be removed until you've verified it.'

Methodically. One room at a time. There was nothing to be found. Mrs Hogg did however inform them that the Master and Mrs Sullivan had never shared a bed the entire time they had been married.

Finally she took them back to 'the Master's' bedroom, opened the double wardrobe pointing to a hook on the rear wall and suggested they turn it clockwise. There was a faint click. A narrow panel pushed open revealing a flight of steps. At the bottom, an office.

Gregory Mountford, mid-fifties, looking every inch the solicitor, arrived thirty minutes later.

'Thank you, Mrs Hogg,' he said. His voice and facial expression indicating his concern. 'I will call Dr Ross later today.' He turned to DS Cartwright. 'May I see that warrant, please, Sergeant?' He read it twice and handed it back. 'There is no doubt this is the man you are looking for?'

'None whatsoever, sir,' he said. 'His birth name was Iago Yarney. His father changed their name by deed poll after the younger twin, Magnus, murdered a young woman in 1949.'

Gregory Mountford felt his stomach twist. 'To your knowledge, Sergeant, has Mr Sullivan ever taken holy orders?'

'To my knowledge, sir. No. Until the early sixties he was an accountant in Skipton. He took over the family business on the death of his father ... There is a problem, sir?' he asked when he saw the expression on the solicitor's face.

'Potentially. James Sullivan is not only the sole beneficiary of his wife's will, he also holds Power of Attorney.'

'That gives him a free hand?'

'It does. However, it was made clear that with the exception of a small stipend, the money from her estate had to be spent on the poor in Africa. I shall be busy.'

'Could I ask the value of the estate, sir?'

'Several millions of pounds, Sergeant.'

Mr Mountford left, satisfied with the promise that the list of documents seized would be forwarded as soon as practicable. Amongst them a passport which expired seven years ago. It would be interesting to see if Sullivan had applied for a duplicate in the interim.

There was a second telephone, in the office. It took a call to the exchange to ascertain the number - Oxenhope 67, not the house phone. That should be simple to spot on any telephone bill. Lastly, the cellar had its own entrance. Whoever had the key had unfettered access to the house without anyone else being any the wiser.

Sixty-Three

Thurlstone, on the outskirts of Penistone. A substantial stone-built detached house constructed towards the end of the 19th century for a Captain of Industry, its façade blackened by decades of pollution from neighbouring domestic chimneys.

Fully briefed of ACC Weatherspoon's involvement by DCI Valentine the four officers waited. The feeling of betrayal was raw. A rogue Chief Police Officer reflected on the entire police service. They were here to make amends. DI Henderson rang the doorbell.

Magda Weatherspoon was slim, about sixty years of age and smartly dressed. She looked at the four officers and frowned. 'How can I help you?'

DI Henderson produced his warrant card and the search warrant. 'Mrs Weatherspoon, we are police officers. I am Detective Inspector Henderson. This is a warrant to search your premises. Step back please.'

Never had she been so affronted and stood her ground. 'Do you know who my husband is?'

'Yes Mrs Weatherspoon, I am fully aware of who your husband is. I have to tell you that as we speak he is in custody for conspiring to pervert the course of justice. We also wish to speak to your son, Iago. Step back please.'

At the mention of her son's true name a combination of anger and fear surged through her brain. 'NO!' she screamed and swung the heavy door in an attempt to slam it shut. DI Henderson's left foot was quicker. The bruises would show in due course.

DI Henderson pushed the door open. 'Mrs Weatherspoon, this warrant will be executed. If you persist in interfering I will have you arrested. Do you understand?'

She glared at him, 'You can't do this. I will ring my solicitor.'

He turned to the team. 'Away you go.' DC's Jackson and Farthing upstairs. DC Riley downstairs. 'Please do Mrs Weatherspoon,' he said. Perhaps her solicitor could smooth the way.

All DI Henderson heard was, 'They can't do this. My husband is Assistant Chief Constable.' Followed seconds later by the phone being slammed onto the cradle. Mrs Weatherspoon ignored him and ran upstairs. DI Henderson followed.

Apart from endeavouring to prevent DC Farthing from searching the drawers and wardrobes all was going well until DC Riley shouted upstairs. 'Sir, you'd better come and see this.'

Mrs Weatherspoon barged past the detective inspector as he left the bedroom and ran downstairs screaming, 'You can't go in there.' She swung round the newel post and barged passed a surprised DC Riley into Weatherspoon's office. DI Henderson hot on her heels. On a table close to the window: maps, rulers and a large magnifying glass on a stand. Snatching a steel dagger-like letter-opener from the desk she swung to her right tearing DC Riley's sleeve. DC Riley applied an arm-lock followed by a pair of handcuffs. '*Ia-ți mâinile de pe mine, porc murdar*, (Get your hands off me, dirty pig) she screamed, but refused to translate.

Gervaise Benton, the Weatherspoon family solicitor for over ten years lowered the warrant, handing it back to the DI and worried. In the aftermath of the Second World War Albert Weatherspoon had carved a glittering path through the senior ranks of the police forces of the north of England. There was even some talk from the West Riding County Police Committee that when Roy Barton, the incumbent chief constable retired, Weatherspoon stood a good chance of taking over the post. But now? The question that he would like answered, but knew that he stood little chance of success at this juncture, was, around what did this perversion hinge? Would there be further substantive charges? If so, what? More to the point this was a conspiracy. Who else was involved?

He had a bad feeling. 'Detective Inspector could I ask where you are stationed?'

'Hecton incident room, sir,' he replied.

'Hecton?' DI Henderson nodded. A detective inspector plus three other detectives, probably from the same murder enquiry, would not have travelled twenty miles just to carry out a search that could have been done by local officers. This was far worse than he had imagined. 'This is a holding charge, isn't it, Inspector?' he said.

'You could see it like that, sir.'

'What do you intend to do with Mrs Weatherspoon?'

'Take her to Penistone and interview her there. She will be charged with assaulting a police officer, and causing damage to DC Riley's coat. She will be kept in custody and put before the court tomorrow morning.'

'Not bailed?'

'No sir. We are looking to speak to her son as a matter of some urgency.'

'I understand, and you believe she may try to warn him.'

'I can't comment, sir. But if you know where he might be it would be helpful if you tell me.'

'I don't know, Inspector,' he said. 'Her husband, he knows of this search?'

Henderson looked at his watch. 'ACC Weatherspoon was informed of this search within the last thirty minutes and will be arrested within the next thirty.'

There wasn't much he could say. Criminal work was not in his purview.

Cuffs removed, Magda Weatherspoon was escorted by WDC Farthing and DC Jackson to his car for transport to Penistone police station. A small group of interested neighbours standing at the side of the road. Gervaise Benton followed.

Forty minutes later DI Henderson and DC Riley placed three boxes of seized material in the DI's car and left, also en route to Penistone.

Sixty-Four

The step from catharsis to calamity is but small. It hit me straight between the eyes. I was whisked into the Chief Inspector's office. Apart from Chief Inspector Sampson and the DCI there was an unknown uniform inspector, my height, stocky build and receding hair accompanied by a tall, slim sergeant, thinning blond hair and blue eyes. His facial expression reminded me of one of the male children from the film of John Wyndham's book: The Midwich Cuckoos. The latter two from the Discipline and Complaints Department: Inspector Anderton and Sergeant Ruddlesden. As a result of undisclosed information, undisclosed to yours truly that is, I had been investigated for malfeasance in public office. What it was I hadn't a clue. Unless this was to turn into some Kafkaesque farce I hoped I would find out very shortly. All that I was certain of was I didn't know what the hell they were talking about. However, the possible options that might relate to me, as a probationer, were both serious but somewhat limited. Either, in my opinion, I was the source of the leaks, or bribery in any of its' various forms.

Chief Inspector Sampson gave me a strange look and made a political withdrawal.

The DCI sat in his chair as usual. Inspector Anderton and his sergeant at the side, leaving me standing in front of the desk.

'Are you in a position to proceed Inspector?'

'I believe that I have sufficient evidence to prove my case, Chief Inspector.'

'That wasn't what I asked. Pc Blake is a key member of my team and I need to know as a matter of urgency whether there has been any wrongdoing or not. You state that you have, in your opinion, sufficient evidence, so, are you in a position to proceed, now?'

Inspector Anderton looked at his watch. 'We're off duty in an hour, Chief Inspector. It was my intention to serve notices on Pc Blake, suspend him from duty, and arrange interviews for the same time next week.'

'That is not acceptable, Inspector. If your allegations are founded it may compromise this entire case. Should you require some other authority then make your telephone call. Failing that I will call Mr Gartside on your behalf.'

It took the two phone calls. With the exception of Notice of Suspension, the Inspector served the relevant notices on me. It was for accepting bribes and for breaches of the Official Secrets Act. I was reputed to be the person leaking information about the case. But bribery? It didn't make sense ... unless for some reason they had secured access to our bank account. We'd had some very generous wedding presents from Liz (£5000) and the Mirfield flat from Mum and Joe, where Lucy and I had lived prior to moving to our present abode. We were now renting it out. But who knew and who would turn that against me, and why? This could scupper any chance of me attending the Special Course. I took a second look at the Notice. 'This is ridiculous.'

Sergeant Ruddlesden was not amused. He glowered at me. 'Constable, you will speak when you are spoken to,' he said. In my mind this put him into the same category as Inspector Baines: An officious prick.

This was annoying, but before I had the chance to respond the DCI stepped in. 'Sergeant, Pc Blake is not a prisoner. This entire enquiry is as a result of the work carried out by Pc Blake. As a result we have reunited thirteen families with the remains of their murdered loved ones and have two persons in custody. You will treat him with due respect. Do I make myself clear?'

The sergeant insolently made no attempt to answer.

'Sergeant. I am not in the habit of repeating myself. Do you understand?'

After a weighty pause. 'I understand, Chief Inspector,' he replied, not quite through gritted teeth.

'Good, can we get on?'

If we were playing the rank game. 'Inspector, these are serious allegations, especially the one of bribery. Why have I not been arrested?' I could almost feel the DCI flinch when I said that. Sergeant Ruddlesden was less than pleased but said nothing.

Inspector Anderton made no reference to my speaking out of turn. He sat forward and smiled whilst he took a minute sheet out of his briefcase. I waited. 'It is the Chief Constable's policy, Pc Blake, that in such cases as this, unless it is absolutely essential that an officer should be taken into custody, there should be, how can I put it, a less painful means of dealing with it,' he said, then slid the minute sheet across the table. As I expected, I was being given the opportunity to resign. By signing this piece of paper I was accepting that I was guilty. Everything would be brushed under the carpet and any credibility that I might have as a witness at a future trial would be exactly nil. Who would want to do that?

I put the minute sheet on top of the discipline notices. 'Inspector, I am fully cognizant of the provisions of Force Standing Order 47, also of the contents of the Chief Constable's Policy Document 1796/64 upon which FSO 47 was based. I know what you're saying. This is my answer.' Professional or not I was getting angry. I picked the three sheets of paper up and slowly tore them in half. Inspector Anderton looked shocked and Sergeant Ruddlesden smiled.

'When handed the minute sheet Pc Blake made no reply,' he said to himself as he wrote in his pocket book

I spun round at the sergeant and let rip. Well and truly lost it. 'Don't you fucking dare Sergeant. You write exactly what happened and what I'm saying. I'm not being fitted up by you or anyone else.'

Even the DCI looked alarmed. 'Enough! Blake, calm down.'

I took a deep breath. 'Sorry, sir. I'm not quite sure who said what but someone has been in Lucy and my joint bank account. Only half a dozen people knew what I believe is behind this. I hope they had a warrant.'

'Inspector, is this true?'

'Yes, Chief Inspector,' he replied and took the court order from his briefcase handing it to the DCI. Who scrutinised it and handed it back.

'Care to join the dots for me, Blake?'

'Yes sir. This goes back to before Lucy and I were married. Joe rented the flat in Mirfield for me. You may remember that I lived there the first time I worked with you. When Lucy and I married he and Mum gave it to us as a wedding present. When Lucy became pregnant we were offered the house we now occupy. The flat we rent out. All the paper work has been submitted and there's a full set in my personnel file. Lucy's mother gave us a very generous wedding present, a cheque for £5000.'

It was too much for Sergeant Ruddlesden. 'You? A flat and £5000 for a wedding present, who do you think you're kidding ?'

That was too much for the DCI. 'Sergeant,' he said through gritted teeth. 'You are here to keep notes, not to comment. If you speak once more I will have you ejected from this police station. Do I make myself clear?'

'Yes sir,' he said quietly.

The DCI turned to Inspector Anderton. 'Is Pc Blake's hypothesis anywhere near correct?'

'Spot on, sir,' he replied. 'The large cheque and the regular income which would appear to be the rental he and his wife receives from the flat were put to us as bribery, and his breach of the Official Secrets Act

'A couple of phone calls will set the matter straight, sir.' The first call to Joe. The second to Liz. Both confirmed what I knew to be the truth. 'Who would want to destroy my credibility, sir.'

'I'm not able to identify the informant, sir.'

'Let me guess, Inspector,' I said, 'ACC Weatherspoon?'

The look on the Inspector's face spoke volumes.

'Brian, go and get yourself a cuppa. But you say nothing to anyone, clear?'

'Clear, sir.'

'Stay in the canteen ... Inspector, Sergeant, come with me.'

I'd been nursing a cup of tea for about five minutes when DS Nicholson came in and parked himself. 'You ok?'

'Fair.'

'We heard,' he said and grinned.

'From the Boss?'

'Nope, through the door. Your voice carries like Peter's does. It sounded interesting.'

'It was,' I laughed. Then I realised he hadn't gone for a cup of tea. 'This isn't a social visit is it?'

'Nope. I want a statement. And before you say anything I'm taking it. Mr Valentine painted a rough picture but I want the whole story from your own lips. Grab your tea. Let's go.'

Whilst I'd been in the canteen Mr Valentine had taken Inspector Anderton and Sergeant Ruddlesden to the cell area, pointed out ACC Weatherspoon's detention sheet and then had the gaoler open the cell door so they could see him. They left the station whilst he made a call to the Deputy Chief, who, apart from seeing a funny side for a few seconds was generally not amused. My temporary loss of control put down to the stress of the case. I could work with DS Nicholson, or make enquiries from the office but, I was not to be put into any confrontational situations. Nor was I to be interviewed about anything concerning the case without his express permission.

Sixty-Five

DS Nicholson and I had met DS Cartwright's team at the squad office just before three. There wasn't sufficient space at Hecton. There was a raised eyebrow as he walked through the door, answered by a nod from me. 'Great stuff, any problems?'

'None, Sarge. Tucked up safe and sound.'

'Any itches?' he said and grinned.

'Oh yes.' I returned his grin. 'Pity that I couldn't scratch 'em.' I got cracking with DS Cartwright sorting and logging the seized paperwork.

When the Thurlstone team returned no-one knew about what had happened back at the office. Not knowing wouldn't hurt anyone, so I kept quiet. Whilst the DI was speaking with the DCI at Hecton, Jenny joined me in logging the evidence whilst DS Cartwright was organising the mass of paper that had suddenly come into our possession. Max Cavendish and Derek Myers set to analysing the phone bills. Initially looking for Braemont 27, the number of the Rectory, and any patterns that emerged with the numbers dialled either side. A bit of a ball-ache but not everything is fun. Unfortunately, once Jenny and I had finished logging the property the 'simple task' of analysing the phone bills became mine alone. That made sense. I was indoors anyway and DS Nicholson was freed to continue enquiries elsewhere.

Shortly after 4pm the Post Office rang Hazel to give the address for the number dialled by Weatherspoon immediately following his return call to Father Kender. Barnoldswick 693. The address was 17 Pear Tree Garth, Barnoldswick. The addressee and account holder was James Sullivan. The DCI immediately passed the information on to Detective Superintendent Wallace at Keighley. Braemont was a mere six miles from Keighley. Keighley only seventeen miles from Barnoldswick.

Whilst we ploughed through the mountain of paperwork, Jacko and Jenny were making no progress at all with Mrs Weatherspoon. She was refusing to speak unless she could first speak with her husband. She would be there a long time. Eventually she was charged with causing damage and assaulting a police officer. She was kept in the cells to appear at Barnsley West Riding Magistrate's Court the following morning.

About the same time as that interview was terminated, DI Green at Barnoldswick had his application for a search warrant in relation to 17 Pear Tree Garth, Barnoldswick, granted. There was nobody at home. Enquiries with neighbours revealed that James Sullivan hadn't been seen for the last three days. No-one knew where he was or when he intended to return. We did manage to get a partial description of Sullivan: Five feet eleven inches tall, dark hair and sporting a beard – not much, but a start. A decision was taken not to force entry at that time. One bright spot however was that Sullivan drove a pale blue Vauxhall Victor saloon and not the dark coloured one that we suspected. Nobody knew the registered number. That was the make of car spotted on the security camera at the rear of The Glasshouse in the wake of the enquiries into the death of Sally Dunster. A potential step forwards. A DC Crabtree was despatched to the local garages seeking information. Wherever Sullivan was getting his car serviced, if indeed he was, it wasn't locally. So make and colour of the car were circulated in-Force by teleprinter, the driver believed to have a beard.

Sixty-Six

It was Sunday. After my travails of last week I was having an enforced and extended weekend off with dire threats from DCI Valentine what would happen if he heard from me before Tuesday.

On Friday evening we had two sets of parents visiting to find out what the fuss and palaver had been about earlier. Liz was horrified. Whether it was deliberate on the part of Weatherspoon's wife or not they had met a few times over the preceding three months for a coffee and chatted. What do ladies chat about? Their children. Amongst other things they had swapped details about weddings, grandchildren, presents etc. Somewhere Liz remembers talking about 'the cheque' and, Mum and Joe's gift of the flat and how we were renting it out. Whether the initial meeting between Liz and Magda Weatherspoon had been engineered wasn't certain, but if not it was a strange coincidence. However, it had been Weatherspoon who approached Discipline and Complaints with this fabrication that I was the leak artist. When an ACC comes with a tale like that, one that appears genuine, at least provides *prima facie* evidence, D&C were not going to question it. Liz wasn't to know the potential for harm she had so innocently caused.

Saturday we shopped early and paid the usual visit to Salendine Nook for another family get together: Liz, Gerald and Marianne plus Anne with growing bump and Neil – they travelled with Liz in the Bentley, Frankie and Vance, and Jen and Norman. Not that we needed an excuse. Even taking into account the events of the previous day it was a good time. There is great strength in families. I was able to feed the voracious enquiring minds of the girls. Not as

308

much as they would have liked, but you can't have everything. It was a beautiful day. Mum and I took the opportunity to go for a short walk by ourselves. In fact the route we took was the same as planned by Jen when we went for that fateful run the day that Norman came into her life. Thinking back we hadn't been for a walk on our own for a long time. At last, we were able to have a real in-depth chat about many things, much of the time returning to the subject of my biological Dad. It was good for both of us. Each arrest was good, but in turn it dredged up some pretty powerful and terrible memories, although not as sharp as I seemed to remember. Letting the light in did nothing to hinder the healing process. It's only when you can let things go that you realise just what the effect had been. The name Weatherspoon did upset her for a while. She remembered the name. They had met years earlier at a police social.

We always got Claire ready for bed before we left. The vibration of the car soon had her fast asleep. The trick? Get her from the car to the house and into her cot without her waking up. Tonight we were heading for Boston Spa.

Sunday was spent enjoying the fine weather, for the most part in the parkland that Liz called their back garden. By now she had gotten over her inadvertent faux pas and we were thankfully back to normal. The daffodils were at their best and the primroses and polyanthus not far behind. It would be glorious. Tommy, their ageing gardener, had done a great job as usual. Gerald and Marianne and their toddling daughter Olivia arrived about ten. It was another good day. We were going to York on the Monday so we stayed the night.

Sixty-Seven

Had we watched the news on the television the previous evening we would have seen the main story. Sullivan/Yarney, call him what you will. Two photographs. One clean shaven the other with full beard. Requests for sightings regarding the murders and a warning to contact the police immediately. Do not approach. The DCI had given a live interview to camera.

At breakfast time we caught the main details on the radio picking up a copy of the Yorkshire Post from the newsagents in Tadcaster as we headed for York. It was the headline story.

Several million people keeping their eyes open for him was an excellent idea. Just as long as no-one got too clever, there was no telling how he might react.

It was fine, warm and very sunny. We parked the car in Bishopthorpe Road, fifty yards on the York city centre side of the Terry's chocolate factory entrance. The smell of chocolate was everywhere, as were signs mounted on lamp-posts pointing to the City Centre and the Ecumenical Conference. We took the mandatory lungsful of chocolate-laced air. Showed Claire the lorries entering and leaving the site. Not that a three month old infant would care too much but she did like watching the movement. The steep footpath opposite the gates led to the southern bank of the Ouse. Turning left we followed the river upstream. Mid-morning found us strolling sedately through Rowntree Park with Claire propped up in her push-chair, her eyes everywhere. A garrulous charm of goldfinches flitted along the flower borders. As parks go Rowntree Park isn't huge, but it's ok; long and narrow pressed up against the River. Neat floral borders. Decent sized lake with its complement of ducks and a few geese. There were tennis courts, children's playground, well-trimmed grassy areas and mature trees. After the wet early spring nature had her head down and was charging, new shoots and leaves everywhere. The smell of spring. It was lovely. So quiet and tranquil. Waiting until we were a hundred yards passed the small elevated café, 'I fancy an ice-cream,' Lucy said and flashed me that smile.

I could take a hint. '99?'

'Go on then. Just a cone for Claire. We can put some ice-cream into it. Get one for yourself as well.'

'Why thank you Ma'am. Don't run away.'

There was a flight of steps to the left. Even at that time it was busy and the café was over half full. Probably accounting for the park appearing devoid of pedestrians. Having queued for several minutes I was now the proud owner of two 99's, plus a spare cone for Claire, trying to manipulate the door handle to get out of the café without tipping the ice cream onto the floor. My rescue came in the shape of a very pretty little girl. She can't have been older than five or six. 'Can I do that?' she said, and, without the slightest bit of trouble opened the door for me.

'Thank you, that's very kind,' I said and smiled, acknowledging her parents at a nearby table.

The little girl's mother smiled. 'Boy or girl?' she asked.

Boy or girl? And then I realised. 'Oh, the spare cone?' I grinned. 'Little girl, Claire, she's almost three months.'

'Wonderful, have a nice time.'

Free at last I turned left to descend the stair to find my way blocked by a breathless and quite elderly churchman. He was hanging onto the handrail with his left hand and supporting himself against the steps with the other. He was wearing a purple shirt with his dog-collar. 'Are you all right?' I asked.

He looked up at me, face flushed, sweat on his forehead. 'Not used to this,' he gasped, trying to catch his breath. 'Are you Brian?'

He looked of retirement age and not the sort that should have been running to this extent. I took the two steps down to where he was now managing to stand unaided. 'Yes, my name is Brian, what's the problem?'

He was struggling to speak. 'He looked like we do ... a cleric ... but he wasn't ... Your wife ...' he managed to gasp.

What the hell! 'Lucy? What about her? What's happened?' it was no good having half a conversation out here. 'Come on let's get you inside.'

With my left arm supporting him and dripping ice cream from the two ice-cream cones in my right hand I managed to get him into the café. There were plenty of willing hands to get him seated. I gave the two ice creams and the cone to the mother of the little girl and licked my hands clean. I'd heard enough of the story and asked to use the phone and for the lady behind the counter to get Bishop Ridgeway a cuppa. I put two shillings on the counter and dialled 999.

'Police emergency.'

'Detective Constable Blake from the Wainwright incident room at Hecton,' I rattled off. 'Who'm I speaking to?'

'Sergeant MacDonald.'

'Sarge, if you're not already aware there's been an abduction and double stabbing in Rowntree Park. I'm ringing from the café.'

This was York on a Monday morning. Incidents like this did not happen. 'Did you witness it?' Came the astounded reply.

'No, Sarge. There's an elderly Bishop, Bishop Ridgeway who did. He's in the café with me. He could do with medical assistance. The incident is near the lake. It's my wife and three month old daughter that's been abducted. The man responsible is James Sullivan AKA

Iago Yarney. Wanted for the murders. He's now clean shaven and dressed as a cleric.'

'Are you certain of his identity?'

'Apparently my wife recognised him from the photo in this morning's Post and challenged him.'

'Stay where you are. I'll get someone straight out.'

'Sorry, he's got my wife and daughter. Sullivan's clever. He won't have headed into the city centre. I'm going to search downstream. Will you give Hecton a ring?'

Sergeant Alan MacDonald stared at the dead handset for two seconds. 'Christ!' he ejaculated. He turned to Pc Turton, office clerk and radio operator. 'Mark, double stabbing and abduction of a child. Flash the pillars then get the ambulance to Rowntree Park, somewhere close to the lake and café and, something about an injured cleric in the café. Then ring North Yorks ... Jack!' he shouted as DC Jack Dufton walked past the open door. 'Double stabbing and abduction in Rowntree Park.'

'On a Monday morning?' He said, aghast. 'Bloody Hell, who called that in?'

'An off duty West Riding DC from the Wainwright team. His wife and daughter are the ones that have been abducted. The one we're looking for is Sullivan, confirmed he's now clean shaven, wearing a dog collar. Will you sort out your end, I'll ring Mr Patrickson.'

The sergeant reached across the console and flipped the talk key. 'Pc Jacques, over.'

'Sarge?'

'Where's the DI playing golf today?'

'Spofforth, but you just missed him. He's gone to pick up the Super.'

'Fine. Get yourself up to Rowntree Park. Find out what's happened. Serious incident between the lake and the café, ambulance attending. Double stabbing. We're looking for a clean shaven man in clerical garb. He's abducted a young woman and an infant.' Without waiting for an acknowledgement. 'Pc Longbottom, where are you?'

'Clifford's Tower, Sarge.'

'Likewise. But go to the café first. Report of an injured cleric. See how serious that is.'

Lucy was doing her best to slow down by feigning a twisted ankle. Leaving Rowntree Park she jarred her ankle easing Claire's pushchair over the car park kerb. She was also kicking herself. Waiting for her ice-cream she'd crouched at Claire's side pointing at the ducks and making quacking noises when she got into conversation with a group of clerics talking about the park, the weather and Claire. One of them turned and spoke to another cleric walking passed. Lucy recognised him from the photo on the front of today's Yorkshire Post, pulled it from her bag hanging from the handle of the push-chair. 'Look,' she said, thrusting the paper in front of the assembled clerics. 'That's him, Sullivan.'

Two of the younger clerics stepped forward. 'Excuse me,' he said. 'Can we have a quick word?'

Without a word Sullivan pulled a chef's knife from the waistband of his trousers, stabbed each of them in the abdomen and stepped back, the knife at chest level. 'Don't,' he said. 'Unless you want some.' He grabbed hold of Lucy by her arm and pulled hard. 'Come on, you're coming with me.' He backed away then turned and began to walk rapidly in the direction of York City centre. The two remaining clerics began to attend to their now collapsed colleagues, the elder said. 'What did she call her husband? Was it Brian?'

'It was, Your Grace,' he replied.

He struggled to his feet. 'I'll find him.'

Sullivan was a big man. Taller and heavier then Brian. The knife that he'd used to stab the two clerics was a very real chef's knife.

Very real indeed. He was nervous and threatening to use it again. Initially heading towards the city centre, but now, after ransacking her handbag and finding the car keys and her mother's business card he threatened her with the knife. 'Where's your car?' he'd said. They were now heading south towards where they'd parked. *At least this was wasting time.*

'Come on,' Sullivan snapped. 'Get a move on. I don't want to hurt you ... unless I have to.'

'I'm going as fast as I can,' Lucy protested. 'It's not easy. And my ankle's sore.'

'If you can't go any faster. I'll take the baby and leave you.'

She looked him in the face. He meant it. 'No, you won't,' she said, feeling a cold sweat break out on her forehead. 'You'll have to kill me first.'

'Don't tempt me. Move.'

Sixty-Eight

Superintendent Michael Patrickson picked up his golf bag and sighed as the phone began to ring. 'If that's for me, Mary, I've emigrated.'

'Of course you have, dear,' she smiled, removed her clip-on earring and picked up the phone, her husband waiting impatiently behind her. 'Mrs Patrickson ...' as she listened to Sergeant MacDonald her face fell. 'You'd better take this, Mike.' She said handing the phone to her less than pleased husband.

'Sergeant MacDonald, this had better be good. That first tee has my name on it ... Do we know how serious the injuries are?' *There would be no golf today!*

'No sir. We're just taking another call about it. But not firm details.'

'And this DC, it's his wife and daughter that's been abducted?'

'Apparently so, sir. DC Blake.'

'There is a DC Blake on that team,' he said. 'He's the young copper that decoded Wainwright's list. He's gone south?'

'Said it was more sensible. He wouldn't risk the city centre.'

'Quite possibly. That location is less than a quarter of a mile from where Geraldine Vasey disappeared in '53.'

Like all senior police officers in the region he was aware of Wainwright's list. However, unlike most he had been at the conference held at the West Riding Police Headquarters. Like most he wasn't sure that it was a good thing to have probationers working on multiple murder enquiries, such as the one currently running out of Hecton, even if he was the original arresting officer. However,

316

inspired or not it had been, with hindsight, a sound piece of judgement to include him on the team.

He had been a newly promoted sergeant in September 1953 when Geraldine Vasey had disappeared. Walking home after visiting her sister and new baby who lived just a half mile away from her home in South Bank Grove, she had disappeared without trace. The City had been turned upside down. Every house and commercial premises visited. Every person spoken to. Every allotment dug over. All schools and local government offices checked. The river dragged and the lake in Rowntree Park, two hundred yards from where Geraldine Vasey lived, drained. She had literally disappeared into thin air. Now her remains had been found almost twenty five miles away on the outskirts of Leeds. This stabbing and abduction in Rowntree Park, possibly by the same man, was the first solid lead in twelve years. All we had to do was locate the bastard.

'Before my time, sir.'

'He's certain it's Sullivan?'

'According to one of the clerics, Blake's wife recognised him from the photograph in this morning's Post.'

'Ok. C.I.D. aware?'

'Yes sir, Jack Dufton.'

'Fair enough. Who's beat cover?'

'Sergeant Neville. He took the first half time-off. He's got an enquiry to complete. But I've flashed the pillars.'

'Ok. Inspector?'

'Flake, sir. Working eleven seven.'

Simon Nigel Oliver Flake, known behind his back as SNOFLAKE, the first adult male in that family not to have taken holy orders, had strange ideas about punishment and the role of the police in society, especially where the church was concerned. 'Christ! ... You didn't hear that, Sergeant.'

'Sorry, sir, I'm a bit deaf in that ear.'

The superintendent chuckled. 'As soon as he comes in let him know, but tell him that I'm taking charge of the investigation, understood?'

'Perfectly, sir.'

'Hmm. Who's out on the bikes today?'

'Wilberforce.'

'Isn't his bike the one with the new radio, it has the VHF frequencies?'

'Yes, I believe it is.'

'Get him up to the factory and wait for this DC Blake. From Rowntree Park he should be there in less than fifteen minutes. In the meantime give Wakefield a call and pass what details we have. They'll probably ask for a telex, if so send one. I'll call DCI Valentine at Hecton.'

Sixty Nine

How much start they'd had I wasn't sure, but pure naked fear was pushing me. I daren't think about the possible consequences. Flat out I could do the four hundred in under a minute, but not in these shoes. From the café to the Terry's factory was over three quarters of a mile. I didn't have the time to admire the greenery or watch the ducks on the river. I'd had some strange looks from other pedestrians as I ran along the path, probably because I was carrying Claire's rattle in my left hand. It had been lying at the side of the path just past the end of the park railings where the footpath split. Diverged to the right. I wasn't sure whether it had just fallen out of the push-chair or Lucy had managed to drop it in the hope that I'd guessed which way they'd gone. I checked my watch. It was almost three minutes since I left the café and I could see where the path turned sharply to the right and climbed the hill. From there it was less than two hundred yards to the road. As yet there was no sign. At the bottom of the slope a small red diary on the grass. Lucy's name inside. It was a lung-bursting climb. I was fifty yards from the road when a middle-aged couple turned the corner towards me. I stopped, gasping for breath. I was absolutely lathered. 'Sorry,' I gasped. 'I'm a police officer and I'm looking for a young woman with blond hair with a baby in a push-chair.'

'We've just seen them,' the man said looking bemused at Claire's rattle. 'Not a minute ago crossing the road. But the woman was carrying the baby. The man she was with threw the push-chair over that fence,' he pointed to the fence on my left.

The bastard! Liz bought that.

319

He was just about to say something else when I set off.

'Isn't that wonderful,' the woman turned to her husband. 'A police officer chasing after that young woman to return her baby's rattle. I can't think of many who would do that.'

'I've told you before, Dear, our police are the best in the world.'

'Thanks,' I called over my shoulder. So close. Just another spurt. I glanced to the left as I reached the road. There was the push-chair looking slightly worse for wear.

A dark red Austin mini registered number B462VUR, Lucy at the wheel, Yarney, the knife clearly visible, in the front passenger seat and Claire in his arms drove sedately passed. 'Fuck!' I don't know which had the biggest impact, seeing Lucy smile when she saw the futile gesture of raising my left hand complete with rattle, or my feeling of utter frustration and helplessness. Not to mention the fear that our daughter was in the arms of a multiple murderer, for now beyond reach. I had no idea how I could rectify that particular problem. At least Lucy would know I wasn't too far behind. I got my breath back as I crossed the road and made a 999 call from the gateman's lodge. Passing on the details of where I was and the registered number of the car. Sergeant MacDonald told me there was a police bike en route. Now I was getting angry. So close and I couldn't do a bloody thing. No sooner had I got back to the gate than a York City police motor cyclist pulled up and kicked the gears into neutral. 'You DC Blake?' the rider lifted his visor.

I nodded, 'Brian Blake.'

'Pete Wilberforce.' The bike was a BSA SS80, maybe only a 250cc but this was the high performance model. Normally built for rider and pillion. This one was not. Yes, a seat for the rider but the remainder held the radio/battery pack. As usual chain to the left and exhaust to the right; but no rear footrests. Then I noticed the police radio. 'Is that a VHF set?'

'Yup,' he smiled. 'We've entered the twentieth century, fitted last week.'

'Have you got the West Riding?'

'Channel 5, why?' Then he spotted Claire's rattle. He looked puzzled.

'My daughter's.' I took the handset from the clip. 'Can I?'

'Help yourself.'

I turned to channel 5. There were no pips which indicated that there was no radio traffic. 'Wakefield from York City motor cycle, over.'

In Wakefield the Channel A operator, aware that information had been received from York pressed the talk key on his console. 'All cars stand by. York City motor cyclist, go ahead, over.'

'Observations requested for dark red Austin mini registered number: bravo four six two victor uniform romeo, last seen two minutes ago in Bishopthorpe Road, York, heading in the direction of the A64, driver female, Sullivan in front passenger seat with baby. Sullivan is armed. Over.'

'Received. Control to Whisky 131, location over.'

Mike Smales had just been turned out from the traffic office. 'Whisky 131, Tadcaster, over.'

'Received. Bilborough Top, observations for previously mentioned vehicle, if seen do not intercept, repeat, do not intercept. Discreet observations only. Understood, over.'

'All received.'

'Control to all cars A1, Tadcaster, Harrogate and Pontefract divisions. Observations re last vehicle. If seen do not ...'

'What's all this about?' Pc Peter Wilberforce enjoyed the freedom he got from being on mobile patrol. The incident that had begun less that fifteen minutes ago in Rowntree Park was something he would like to get involved with. Perhaps this was the chance. 'All I know is there's been a couple of stabbings in Rowntree Park.'

'The car's mine. The passenger is James Sullivan, and he's holding my daughter. My wife's driving. Sullivan is the man we're looking for, for the Wainwright murders.'

'Bloody Hell.' he said. *When opportunity knocks never look a gift horse in the mouth* ... 'I'll squeeze up, get on.'

Dangerous or not, and this was, I wasn't going to be asked twice. It took a couple of seconds to tuck my trousers into my socks, getting them caught in the chain was a recipe for disaster. Claire's rattle went into my belt. It was a tight squeeze but with my backside against the radio pack I wasn't going to slide off the back end. I'd have to make sure I kept my feet out of the way of the chain and the exhaust. Depending on how far we had to go I was going to get cold and tired. There was just enough room. He could control the bike. A couple of things I was acutely aware of was that I didn't have a crash helmet, goggles or any other protective gear. I crouched behind Pete and sought to see with my left eye over his shoulder. It would have been safer with footrests, then I wouldn't slide from side to side and destabilize the bike. It must have been hard enough for Pete as it was. Staying on board kept my mind occupied. Two things I remembered about Bishopthorpe Road: in places it was narrow and wasn't exactly straight. Swinging bends some bordering on being blind. Blue light flashing and what passed for an electronic siren he didn't hang about. Just had to make sure that I didn't kiss the hedges.

We were two and a half miles from the A64 with time to make up. Less than two minutes later – Bishopthorpe. Pete eased right back for the right turn into Church Road. Fifty yards ahead the mini had hit, or been hit by a van, Johnston's Bakers. I almost fell off the bike and raced to the car. Pete right behind me. Both front doors wide open, no occupants and thankfully no blood. I noticed that the choke was fully open. Lucy had deliberately flooded the engine. The gear lever in fourth. Good Girl. A quick glance at the front was enough to see that the damage was slight. The van driver wasn't happy. 'Look at my bloody van,' he wailed, waving his arms at the damage. 'Stupid bitch. Women drivers shouldn't be allowed anywhere near a sodding road.'

I wasn't going to get into an argument over the merits of women drivers. He wasn't hurt and Lucy and Claire were missing.

'Did you see where they went?' I said.

'Don't sodding care. Look at my van,' he wailed again and looked at Pete. 'What are you going to do about it?'

Before I could speak Pete took over; I was having difficulty in remaining calm. 'Mr Johnston, there was a man carrying a baby and a woman in the mini. Where did they go?'

'They ran off that way,' he said waving his arm the way we'd come.

'We didn't pass them,' I said. 'Does that track lead to the church we passed?'

'It does.' Pete switched his radio back to the local channel. '190 over.'

'Go ahead.'

'Sarge, the mini has crashed in Church Lane, Bishopthorpe, slight damage no apparent injuries. Occupants believed to have made off on foot into the church grounds. Can we have obs in Sim Balk Lane, and this side of Warren Pond? Back-up. And an ambulance just in case. Oh, and someone to take details of this RTA. We're just going to check the church out.'

'Received. Don't do anything stupid.'

It was a hundred yards to the church. Twenty yards from the door the vicar, according to the notice board at the roadside the Reverend Martin Pomphrey, appeared in the porch and leant on the open door, his left hand supporting his right arm. A large bloody patch on the sleeve, blood dripping freely. Looking at him he was mid-thirties, my height, perhaps a stone heavier - more rounded in the middle, dark hair cut into his neck and greying round the temples. Claire crying in the background. I was torn. Rushing in would do no good. I had to think.

The reverend sitting on a nearby bench I took his pulse. It was weak and rapid. He was in shock. 'Are you all right, Reverend,' asked Pete.

'There's a man in there.'

'Yes, we know,' I interjected. 'He isn't a vicar. And, as you've discovered he's got a very sharp knife. You're the third cleric he's stabbed in the last half hour.'

He looked sick. 'Three?' he said. He didn't believe me.

'That's correct. And how are my wife and daughter?'

'Yours? They're by the communion rail.'

'At the front?'

'She's sitting on the chancel steps. He's standing, holding your daughter in his left arm.'

We helped him off with his jacket. It was a deep two inch cut across the brachioradialis and the wrist extensors of his right arm. I had a clean handkerchief clamped across the cut whilst Pete removed his tie and secured it as tight as possible. Within seconds the blood was seeping through. My tie became a collar and cuff support still supported by his left hand.

'Reverend, can I borrow your shirt front, collar and jacket, please.'

'But.'

'I'm a police officer from Hecton. The man inside is the man we're looking for. All I need to do is to get close to him. Dressed as you are should make it easier.'

Grudgingly he agreed. I don't think he had any real objections; he just didn't want to see anyone else get hurt. Neither did I, especially Lucy and Claire. Sullivan? That was possible. Pete charged off to wait for the ambulance. I draped my shirt and jacket round his shoulders and advised him to remain seated until the ambulance arrived.

Fully dressed, blood still dripping from the jacket sleeve, I faced the reverend. 'Do I pass muster?'

He managed a thin smile. 'Apart from the blood and the cut sleeve you'll do. But is there anything else that I can do?'

'I'll manage thanks. You've told me what I need to know. Just sit there and wait for the ambulance.'

'I'll pray for you.'

I wasn't feeling charitable. 'Thank you for the sentiment, Reverend. But the man in there,' I pointed at the church, 'the man wearing the dog collar, has, since March 1945, raped and murdered thirteen women. One just fifteen years old. He's also murdered a Roman Catholic priest and his housekeeper. And today he's stabbed three clergymen, including you, and, kidnapped my wife and daughter at knife-point. Whilst you're praying please ask your God why he did nothing to prevent that happening.' I left him with that thought.

The church door opened without a sound. Claire was giving her lungs some real exercise. Sullivan was standing. Demanding that Lucy quieten Claire. Lucy's pleas for Sullivan to hand Claire over were falling on stony ground.

The light was good. No time to gaze. Drops of blood, like breadcrumbs, led to the font. I turned right towards the altar. Concentrating on what would be the fighting ground – between the pews and the Chancel rail. This was going to end as soon as possible. I had to control my breathing. Calm down. The sight of Lucy and Claire in these circumstances was not good. Lucy was sitting on the right-hand side of the steps five feet away from Sullivan. She'd been crying.

Sullivan, five eleven, thick set with broad shoulders, a spreading waistline looked strangely out of place in spite of his clerical shirt and dog collar. Claire in the crook of his left arm. A bloodstained chef's knife in his right hand. Back to the altar. He looked a mess. Face drawn. Jaw clamped tight. Born in August 1922 he was forty-three. Looked seventy.

The sight of him standing there made my blood run cold. Of everything that I'd experienced in my short career this is the only thing that truly frightened me. I had to slow my breathing. Remain calm and think. How could I separate Claire from Sullivan and get her and her mother away from that knife?

I was half way to the chancel steps when I stubbed my toe against an uneven flagstone. He turned thrusting the knife towards me. I opened my arms wide to show that I was unarmed and carried on walking. Lucy looked up, a thin smile replacing the look of astonishment when she recognised me. In hindsight she was probably looking at the jacket I was wearing. I didn't have a dark grey jacket never mind one with a gash in the right sleeve and large fresh blood stains.

He jabbed the knife towards me. 'Do you want some more? I told you, don't come back or else.'

This was good. He thought I was the Reverend Pomphrey returning. I kept walking towards him, smiled and reached across with my left hand and pulled the right sleeve back to the elbow. 'How would you like to be called,' I said, 'Iago or James?' I pulled the sleeve down.

'I cut you,' he looked puzzled. 'I can see the gash in your sleeve.'

I ignored him and smiled. 'You didn't say how you want to be called. Iago or James?'

'Iago,' his voice wavered. If he was concentrating on where the cut had gone he wasn't thinking of other things. I was trying to work out whether to kick or use a stranglehold: the stranglehold would disable him faster but with Lucy and Claire so close it had a high risk factor. So kick it was. I would have preferred to use a roundhouse kick - a *mawashi geri* – that was all encompassing not as pointed a 'gesture', but again the knife. So a *yoko geri* – a sideways kick, more power but a smaller, perhaps moving target. Then Claire really let rip. No wonder. He wasn't holding her. He was squeezing her. This was bloody difficult. Momentarily, mentally, I felt Sullivan's cervical vertebrae dislocate. Cut it out, Get serious. 'If you want Claire, that's her name by the way, to stop crying hand her back to her mother. You're hurting her. Or are you simply a coward, hiding behind an infant? ... Don't you think this is the time to bring this to an end. All these deaths. I was there when the police recovered the body of Isabel Bell the girl Cuthbert buried in Greenhead Park in Huddersfield. You know she was only fifteen?' now he was confused. 'Why don't you just put the knife down. I'm unarmed. I won't hurt you.' Sullivan didn't move. 'Well, Iago. What's it to be?

He relaxed his grip on Claire, which made no difference. 'How do you know my name?'

'How do you think? The same way that I know that your twin's name was Magnus. Your father's Jakob, and your mother, Magda. Now, are you going to hand Claire back to her mother? You've still got the knife. She's not going to do anything rash, is she?'

I couldn't do anything until Claire was safe. It was a question of what would he do next? I just had to be ready.

He looked at me for a lifetime. 'I'm not turning my back on you,' he said, inclining his head towards Lucy. 'If you want your baby come and get it.' I took the opportunity to flick my eyes twice to the right, hoping Lucy would understand.

She smiled and nodded slightly as she stood. 'Thank you,' she said. She walked gingerly in front of Sullivan and turned to face him. I could see the right side of Sullivan's head. I was using my right foot. It could have been better. But you have to work with what you've got. As Lucy was feeding her hands beneath Claire I noticed Sullivan

JON MASON

simultaneously relax, turn his head to look at Claire and lower the knife.

Whilst Sullivan was distracted, I took a half-pace diagonally to the left, opening up my target, drew my right knee into my abdomen and delivered the kick. The outer edge of my leather soled and heeled shoe leading. It sounds a long time but in total less than a second from start to finish. My foot flashed over Lucy's shoulder connecting with Sullivan's face, the zygomatic arch, with a truly cathartic crack. Followed by an equally cathartic scream from the recipient. Lucy was moving before I could shout, 'Run.' The floor of the chancel was a foot higher than the floor of the nave with the communion rail knee height, set back twelve inches. Sullivan piled backwards across the rail. In two strides I had hold of his right wrist with my left hand. I ripped the knife from his grasp and tossed it onto the chancel floor. Grabbing hold of his lapels with both hands I pulled him back into the nave and slammed him onto the flagstones. He'd have quite a lump on the back of his head. I knelt astride him and took a couple of seconds to assess what damage I'd done to his face. There was a distinct line below his right eye. It was beginning to swell and ooze blood. He took the same opportunity to lunge with both hands towards my throat. Not going to happen. Never in a million years.

I grabbed hold of his wrists and locked eyes. I began to force his hands apart. No rush. I wanted him to know the feeling. The look on Sullivan's face turned from fury to fear in a second. I smiled at him. 'Tch, tch. Naughty, naughty. You're not fighting a helpless female now. You should have put the knife down when I gave you the opportunity. How does it feel?'

He didn't answer or have the strength to mount an effective resistance.

Keeping his right wrist stationary I eased his left wrist towards the floor. He tried to lock his elbow but there is a handy little nerve point on the second metatarsal that broke his concentration. Whilst his mind was elsewhere I made him bend his elbow. The back of his left hand on the flagstones at shoulder level, I knelt on his wrist, my weight pressing directly on the radioulnar joint, in particular the styloid process of the ulnar. That would hurt. Quite a lot. 'You're going nowhere,' I smiled. 'Get used to it.' Left arm secured I used his right wrist as a lever. Rotating it inwards until he was on his side. I leaned forwards. 'Remember Alberto,' I said, 'Alberto de Mateo? Of course you do, he's your stepfather. He's got his own cell. Your mother's in custody as well. Isn't that nice? By the way my name is Blake, Brian Blake, I'm a police officer. That mean anything to you? My father was a detective sergeant.'

'He got what he deserved.'

That was a silly thing to say. I lifted my left knee off the floor. All my weight now on his left wrist joint which drew a yelp from Sullivan. 'Sorry,' I said and smiled. 'Did that hurt?'

Swapping hands and applying a wrist lock on Sullivan with my right hand I encouraged him to bend the arm. Then with my left hand cupped I drove it as hard as I could under his elbow forcing him onto his face. There was a howl of pain. I picked out the word - bastard. I suppose that if I were using this as an interrogative technique it might be described as torture. It wasn't, but it was satisfying. Sullivan had abducted Lucy and Claire at knifepoint. This was my method of explaining there were consequences. Was I tempted to do more serious damage? Fleetingly. In his present situation he wasn't worth it. His right arm in an arm-lock I hoisted him to his feet. I informed him that he was under arrest for the abduction of Lucy and Claire, the wounding with intent of the Reverend Martin Pomphrey and, on the suspicion of the rape and murder of Sally Dunster. His reply was pure Anglo-Saxon invective.

Claire was fast asleep. Lucy and I exchanged smiles. We both needed a hug. Yes they were safe but I needed physical contact. 'Is she all right?' I said, and smiled again as I passed Claire's rattle.

'Fine,' she smiled. 'She fell asleep almost straight away. You enjoyed that didn't you?'

I had to smile. 'Yep. Cathartic. How are you? He didn't touch you did he?'

'Just grabbed me by the arm to begin with. Once he had hold of Claire I didn't argue.'

'That was a neat trick flooding the engine like that,' I said. But before she could reply the church door opened and the 7th Cavalry arrived. Acting ACC Mithering, the DCI, DS Nicholson and Penny from the West Riding and seven other officers, mostly plain clothes, which I took to be York City.

'Superintendent Patrickson,' announced the first plain clothes officer. 'You're DC Blake?'

'Yes, sir. And this is my wife Lucy and daughter, Claire.'

He nodded. 'And you're both all right?'

'Yes, we are Mr Patrickson,' said Lucy. 'We're all, all right. Unlike him,' she gestured towards Sullivan.

Superintendent Patrickson put his hand under Sullivan's chin and lifted. The impression left by the edge of my shoe was a vivid red; blood running down his cheek and a growing livid bruise. The tissue below Sullivan's cheekbone was swelling nicely. He looked at me, his eyes questioning.

'Yes, sir. I did that. But before anyone jumps to the wrong conclusion I'd like to say that I am a martial arts instructor.'

'This was with a karate kick?'

'Yes, sir. Over Lucy's shoulder.'

There were several laughs. 'I remember that you've done this before, Brian,' said Penny. 'You gave a demo with DC Jackson and his lunchbox.'

I smiled. 'That was a long time ago, Penny, but, yes, I did.'

'We can discuss this at the station. Do you have the knife?'

'I took it off him and tossed it into the chancel, sir.'

The Superintendent turned his head. 'Sergeant.'

A plain clothes officer detached himself from the group and retrieved the knife. He held it up by the back of the blade, raising a few whistles. A pair of cuffs appeared and Sullivan departed under escort. The knife and the vicar's jacket went into evidence bags.

Outside the church the Reverend Pomphrey was long gone. I surrendered the vicar's shirt and dog collar and re-claimed my own. Another ambulance on standby. The ambulancemen waiting for Lucy to board. There was a small logistical problem. Lucy was holding Claire. Penny provided the solution. 'Lucy, let me hold her. I'll wait here.' Lucy gave her a watery smile as Penny took hold of the most precious thing in our lives. We clung to each other like limpets. This time the tears were of relief. I'd like to think that I didn't shed any but the sun was in my eyes.

'Will you stop running off with dangerous men,' I said at last. 'Especially those with knives.'

Lucy sniffed and wiped the tears away with the back of her hand. 'Are you mad at me?'

'Mad at you? I'm not mad at you. I'm as proud as hell at the way you handled it,' I glanced at Penny. 'Penny's getting broody, much longer and she'll want to keep Claire. I can see it in her eyes.' We got a little smile from Penny. Claire got a hug. 'Come on, it won't be long. I'll see you at the police station.'

Mr Johnston had calmed down once he was informed that Lucy had been abducted. The damage to both vehicles, purely cosmetic. Ten minutes later I cadged a lift with Penny and followed Mr Valentine into York. The last person I'd spoken to before I left was Pete Wilberforce. I thanked him for his assistance without which we would probably be still in the dark. He had been given a bit of a chewing off for carrying me as a pillion. I would probably get mine later.

It was organised chaos. This was probably the highest profile prisoner to be held in York since Dick Turpin was executed on the Knavesmire in April 1739 – a project of mine at the New College. The first thing was to get permission to call Lucy's mother. I hoped she didn't get too excited. I managed to satisfy her that Lucy and Claire weren't injured and were going to hospital for a check-up. I rang the Stadium and spoke with Neil. He arranged transport complete with an escort of Spartans.

I managed to catch Joe at work and had the same conversation. Bearing in mind that Claire was Mum's first grandchild and Joe was as caring as any grandfather could be I anticipated a similar reaction. I promised to keep them updated.

The two clerics were in serious condition awaiting surgery. There were more policemen on duty at the hospital keeping the unwanted out of the side-wards than enough. Statements had been obtained from Bishop Ridgeway and his colleague. I wanted to type mine, but first I had to give my story to Superintendent Patrickson, DI Kenton and a multitude of others, including Acting ACC Mithering and the DCI.

From thread to needle, everything as it happened. From leaving Lucy to buy the ice-creams to the arrival of the cavalry.

'Tell me, why did you not wait for back up? Why go in on your own bearing in mind the injuries inflicted on Reverend Pomphrey.'

'The original intention had been to ascertain exactly where Sullivan was with Lucy and Claire. Reverend Pomphrey clarified that as far as he knew when he left the church. But whilst Pc Wilberforce and I were bandaging the Reverend Pomphrey I was thinking about the best way to approach. If I'd gone into the church in my civvies, as Lucy's husband, it would have given Sullivan an added advantage. Whereas borrowing the Reverend's clothes ...'

The superintendent nodded. 'You were part of the furniture. Who else would you expect in a church but a cleric?'

'Exactly sir.'

'But why the jacket? Why not just put your own jacket on over the clerical shirt.'

'It was because of the blood, sir. He and I were the same height, more or less the same weight. Although completely dissimilar facially. But when Sullivan made reference to the jacket and the blood I pulled the sleeve up, that confused him, there was no wound. I tried to create a dichotomy. He asked me how I knew his first name, Iago. I told him the same way I knew all the family first names. That I was present when the police recovered the body of Isabel Bell, his first victim and her age, fifteen. The more he concentrated on things that couldn't be possible for a vicar from Bishopthorpe to know, the more confused he appeared to be and the less he thought about Lucy and Claire'

'That was good thinking, well done.'

'Thank you, sir. I told him Lucy wouldn't do anything rash whilst he had the knife. When Sullivan looked down to tell Lucy to collect Claire I indicated that she should move to her left by flicking my eyes to my right.'

'She understood?'

'I wasn't sure until she stood, said thank you and smiled. Then she stood directly in front of Sullivan. That was either very brave or foolhardy. As Lucy put her arms round Claire to take hold of her, Sullivan looked down and lowered the knife. Up to that point I had three principal options. Two I ruled out because Lucy was in the way and because he lowered the knife. But I couldn't do anything whilst he was holding Claire. The only option I considered viable was the kick I delivered.'

'Now then Blake. This kick you claim to have delivered. There has been a suggestion that you were, how can I put it, disingenuous in your description.' I had a quick glance at the assembled officers present. One Inspector was looking less than comfortable.

'That I lied? I stamped on Sullivan's face?'

'Not to put too fine a point on it, yes. Can you demonstrate what you did?'

'Certainly, sir. But I'll require a volunteer, about five eleven.'

Superintendent Patrickson didn't look round. 'Inspector Flake, you're about the correct height, perhaps you would care to assist DC Blake in his demonstration?' No-one moved. 'Inspector?'

The aforementioned guilty-looking Inspector stepped forwards. 'Thank you, Inspector. It won't hurt, I promise,' I said and smiled. 'Just as long as you keep absolutely still.' I stood him against the door and asked him to bend his left arm as though he were holding a baby. *I had no trouble in embarrassing him.* I turned to my audience. 'Right, the Inspector in his shoes is near enough six feet. My wife in her heels, is five six. She is standing here masking three quarters of Sullivan's body and face. Sullivan leaned forwards slightly as Lucy began to take hold of Claire. He had the knife in his right hand which he lowered. I didn't want to have to do anything until Lucy had control of Claire and is ready to move quickly. My target is what you can see. Not much. Just the edge of his right cheek bone, right cheek and ear. I was kicking over Lucy's left shoulder.'

I turned to the inspector. 'Sir, As if you were stopping traffic. Would you hold your right hand out at shoulder level, elbow slightly bent.' He looked reticent. 'It won't hurt, I promise.' He did as requested. I took a diagonal half pace to the left and delivered the kick in slow motion. There were a couple of comments from the York City officers about the height of the kick. Inspector Flake dropped his hand and began to walk away. 'If you'll just bear with me, sir, I'll demonstrate at full speed.' With some reluctance he took up his position once more. There was an almost stunned silence followed by a couple of, "bloody hells", as my kick hit the palm of his hand driving his elbow into the door.' A sullen Inspector Flake returned to his place.

'Well DC Blake, I think that answers that question. Thank you. Is there anything else that you feel is relevant?'

I could feel Mr Mithering's and the DCI's eyes burning into my head. 'Yes, sir,' I replied. 'Had either Mr Mithering or Mr Valentine been aware of what was happening or, what I was planning, I wouldn't have been allowed within half a mile of the church.'

Superintendent Patrickson frowned and looked at them both. 'Really?'

'Yes sir,' replied the DCI, although there was the semblance of a smile creeping round his lips. 'As you may know Sullivan's birth name was Iago Yarney. It was his younger twin Magnus who murdered DC Blake's father, DS Douglas Blake, whilst effecting the release of two hostages. Magnus Yarney had surrendered to DS Blake after he murdered Christine Jones twelve months earlier. Because of that relationship, DC Blake is theoretically shackled to DS Nicholson when involved on enquiries and out of the station. And, we have orders to keep DC Blake out of possible confrontational situations.' He paused waiting for the laughter to subside. 'However, in view of the circumstances in rescuing his wife and daughter I don't think any further action is required. In fact I might just buy him a pint,' he turned to the ACC. 'What do you think, sir?'

'I agree. And, if you're in the chair, I'll have one as well.'

My interrogation over I secured the use of a typewriter. Afterwards I met Lucy, Claire and Liz in the foyer for a reunion. The Spartans, barring Neil, returned to Tadcaster. I took Liz and Neil to the police canteen where they looked after Claire. Lucy I took downstairs to the C.I.D. office.

All statements concluded we were about to leave the police station when Mr Mithering collared me with a trio of pleasant surprises. I would be paid in full for today. Given an additional day off to compensate and, I had been granted seven days compassionate leave with the hope that I would stay out of trouble. I promised to try.

Mr Valentine had spoken with Bishop Ridgeway and secured his assistance in speaking with Wainwright in trying to unscramble his brain with regards to the threats made by Sullivan. I could only hope.

Well, that was it for now. I suppose that it was only to be expected but there were some pretty lurid headlines in the Press the following morning: For example:

Hero Pc Rescues Wife and Daughter from Knife Wielding Maniac

Except for the 'Hero' bit, factually I suppose it was correct but to Lucy and me it just looked odd, too American. We had a week's break in western Scotland. The weather held and no-one recognised us. It was perfect.

We set off for home after breakfast, driving east to Blair Athol and calling at the distillery for a few presents. We arrived home about six pm on the Monday to a houseful. It was good to see everybody although a little more crowded than Inveraray – we spent two nights there; the scenery was beautiful and Inveraray castle was magnificent. I think we left much of our stress on the bed of Loch Fyne. We had mail. Ninety seven pieces of mail. Who from we had no idea. It could wait.

Seventy

I went in for nine on Tuesday, not knowing what to expect. I needn't have worried. My day had been planned in advance. There were a few good natured cracks about me being a jammy bastard, even when I pointed out the level of skill required to be in the right place at the right time. I still got called a jammy bastard.

DS Nicholson informed me that Sullivan would be transferred to Hecton later today.

Before anyone else could comment the DCI walked in. 'Ah, Blake. Good holiday?'

'Excellent, sir. Just what we needed.'

'Good. Bishop Ridgeway is expected here in around twenty minutes. When he arrives take him to the canteen and get him a tea or coffee. Wait with him. I'll join you in due course.'

This was a novel experience. Until the Bishop arrived I had time to kill. I wandered into Inspector Meadowcroft's office. He indicated a vacant chair. 'This is not like you Brian, idle and disorderly,' he said and smiled.

I smiled in return and sat down. 'Just waiting for Bishop Ridgeway, sir, he's due in fifteen minutes or so.'

'He's the one who initially informed you of Lucy's abduction?'

I nodded. 'Yes sir, the DCI wants a word.'

'I couldn't begin to imagine what you both must have gone through.'

A black memory flashed through my mind. 'Neither of us want to go through that again, sir. We've never been as frightened in our lives.'

'I'm not surprised.' We spent the next fifteen minutes just chatting about York and the case in general. A knock at the door announcing the Bishop's arrival put an end to that.

The Bishop, looking happy and far more relaxed than he had been the last time I saw him, was standing by the counter. 'Good morning, Your Grace,' I said as we shook hands.

'I recognise you,' he said and laughed. 'You're Brian. Do you mind if I call you Brian?' There seemed no point in being pernickety so I agreed.

I introduced him to Inspector Meadowcroft then took him to the canteen and bought him a coffee. 'Your first time in a police station, Your Grace?' I asked. He was gazing about as if he'd never seen policemen and women before. Mind you the sight of an Anglican Bishop in a police canteen was also attracting some attention. The fact that he and I were sharing a table felt odd.

'Not quite, Brian,' he chuckled. 'I once had to report losing my driving licence. Other than that, yes, it is.'

'We're quite pleasant really,' I smiled. 'Unless of course there is some reason why you don't want us anywhere near you.'

'Such as James Sullivan in York last week?'

I agreed. He enquired after Lucy and Claire. Had they recovered after their ordeal. There were lots of questions about the case in general but more specifically about the events of the preceding Monday. It was not so bad talking about the case with members of the public, it was talking shop with bobbies that I tried to avoid. One of the things that concerned him was the fact that Sullivan was dressed as a cleric. That really disturbed him. As he put it. 'Had I read of such a plot in a novel I wouldn't have believed it.'

'Well, Your Grace,' I answered. 'They say that truth is stranger than fiction.'

'They do indeed. But I was speaking with Mr Valentine after you and your wife had departed from the police station. He tells me that you wish to speak with this man with regard to the killing of several young women.'

'I can confirm what the Chief Inspector said but can't elaborate, I'm sorry.'

'No, I understand. But to do so and to masquerade as a man of God in the process is beyond belief.'

I was saved from further comment as the door opened and the Chief walked in, spotted me and walked across. I stood. 'Congratulations, Blake,' he said and shook my hand. 'Are you both recovered after your ordeal?'

'I think so, sir. We drove up to the west coast of Scotland. Stayed in B&B's. A couple of nights in Inveraray. It was very peaceful.'

'I haven't been there in a long time. But, yes I agree.' Then he asked. 'Have you seen Mr Valentine?'

'I'm waiting for him, sir. Sir, this gentleman,' I indicated the Bishop, 'is Bishop Ridgeway. It was he who informed me of Lucy's and Claire's abduction. Your Grace, this is our Chief Constable, Mr Barton.'

Pleasantries exchanged we all sat down. The numbers in the canteen rapidly reduced.

The Chief smiled at the elderly churchman. 'Are you fully recovered from your exertions, Your Grace?'

'Yes, I am thank you, Mr Barton,' he replied.

DCI Valentine joined us, looked round at the empty tables, brought an extra chair and sat down. He pushed a ten shilling note across the table to me and asked me to get five coffees. When I returned he motioned for me to sit. 'Thank you for coming, Bishop Ridgeway. It is appreciated.'

'Not at all, Chief Inspector, I found your request intriguing even if a little short on detail. So, please tell me how may I be of assistance?'

There was a slight hiatus whilst the coffee was delivered. You could tell the Chief was here. We had a milk jug, sugar bowl and, a spoon each. We were joined by Penny. Introductions completed he began.

'We have a man in custody, Your Grace, Cuthbert Wainwright. You may have read of him in the newspapers.'

'I'm sorry. I don't believe that I have.'

'No matter,' said the DCI. 'It isn't necessary that I tell you exactly why he is in custody at this precise moment, however, the information that he has is vital to our case. And, he is literally terrified of what he believes will be the consequences if he speaks openly.'

'And he is connected to this James Sullivan?'

'Yes, Your Grace. We know that they have known each other since their teenage years, and are both deeply pious.'

'Sullivan is the dominant one?'

'Very much so. In his youth he was a bit of a firebrand. He formed some breakaway Roman Catholic evangelical group. Preached Old Testament values. He thought that the New Testament gospels were too soft, and, by all accounts built up a reasonable following.'

The Bishop smiled. 'The old-time religion. Hellfire. Brimstone. Damnation. Go directly to Hell!'

The DCI leaned forwards resting his forearms on the table. 'That's it in a nutshell, Your Grace.'

The bishop furrowed his brow and looked puzzled. 'Really?' he said. 'Could you perhaps give me a context?'

The DCI nodded to Penny. 'It was just one in a series of questions, Your Grace,' she said. 'Wainwright's answer to the last question that I had asked was, "You have no idea of his power. He will destroy me if I say." I asked if he meant that he would be killed.

Wainwright replied that it would be "far worse. He will strip my soul and I will go straight to Hell"."

A shocked Bishop Ridgeway sat back on his chair. 'And he obviously believes this nonsense.'

'He does, Your Grace.'

'But the poor man must be in torment,' he became quite animated. 'Sullivan is claiming to have the powers of the Almighty. Have you made enquiries to find out whether Sullivan is a minister of religion, Chief Inspector? Although I cannot believe that he is C of E.'

'We have made enquiries Your Grace. He is not. But since his arrest Sullivan hasn't uttered a single word.'

Bishop Ridgeway smiled inwardly. 'What exactly would you want of me, Chief Inspector?'

'Wainwright has been very forthcoming in some regards, but, because of his state of fear will only go so far. But for all that I genuinely feel sure that he would wish to clear his conscience.'

'I see,' he replied. 'You wish me to counsel him?'

'I suppose that's as good a word as any, Your Grace. But shall we go downstairs and I can show you the scale of this investigation.'

The chatter ceased as the Chief opened the door, stepping back to allow Bishop Ridgeway to enter. It wasn't every day that a Church of England Bishop became involved in a murder investigation. Introductions concluded the DCI asked whether Bishop Ridgeway would like to sit down. He declined. 'I think I shall be all right,' he said, and smiled.

'If you would care to turn round, Your Grace.'

He stared at the wall in disbelief. 'Dear God, Chief Inspector. All these you believe are Sullivan's victims?'

'With one slight exception, we do indeed, Your Grace.'

'And this man, Wainwright, he is involved in all of them?'

'He has admitted as much.'

You could have heard a pin drop as the Bishop studied the wall. 'I was a young army chaplain at Passchendaele during the Great War,' he mused. 'I accompanied the troops in North Africa during Operation Torch... I saw some terrible things. It was bad enough that they were soldiers in wartime. These appear to be young women ...'

The DCI caught my eye and nodded. 'They are Your Grace,' I said.

'The Chief Inspector mentioned one *slight* exception, Brian,' he said, the use of my first name causing a few smiles.

'Number three, Christine Jones, Your Grace. She was an eighteen year old prostitute. That was the younger twin. In those days the family name was Yarney. After the murder their father Jakob changed the family name to Sullivan, and Iago's first name to James.'

'The English translation of Iago,' said the Bishop.

'Indeed,' I said. 'However, according to Wainwright, apart from himself, Magnus and Iago Yarney one other adult male was present and involved,' I glanced up at the DCI who nodded. 'We now have that man in custody.'

The Bishop was silent for several seconds. 'Yes, I remember. Magnus Yarney? Wasn't he the identical twin referred to in the Yorkshire Post?'

'Yes, he was.'

He turned to the DCI. 'Didn't you tell me Chief Inspector that Magnus Yarney was the person who stabbed Brian's father?'

'Yes, I did.'

He stood there silent and immobile for a full twenty seconds then turned to me and frowned. 'There was a name mentioned in the newspaper, Sally?

'Sally Dunster, number thirteen,' I pointed to the right hand file.

'She is the most recent?'

'Yes, she is,' I pointed to the Isabel Bell's file. 'They are in chronological order. That is Isabel Bell. She was just fifteen years of age when she disappeared in March 1945.'

He suddenly looked ten years older. He turned to me. 'If that offer of a chair still stands?' He thanked us and sat down. 'Chief Inspector,' he said without taking his eyes from the wall. 'Would it be safe to surmise that these women, or girls, had been raped?'

'We know for certain that two had. As for the others, like you we can only surmise at the moment. However, it would follow a pattern, but we are awaiting information from our forensic scientists.'

'Yes,' he mused. 'We do like our patterns. In the church we call them rituals. It provides structure, makes people feel comfortable. I believe the police call it a *modus operandi*?'

'Yes, we do,' he said with a smile.

The Bishop nodded. There was a ripple of laughter with his next comment. He turned to the DCI and smiled. 'This is not going to be a ten minute chat over a cup of tea, is it?'

The DCI smiled in return. 'No, Your Grace,' he replied. 'I think not.'

He sat for a few seconds then once again turned to the DCI. 'Chief Inspector, is it safe to assume from the photographs, that the families have been notified?'

'Yes, Your Grace. All the families have been contacted. Three of the victims were married with families; at least one surviving spouse has re-married.'

'Do you know how many children lost their mothers?'

The DCI caught my eye. 'I believe eight, sir.'

He stood and turned to face the DCI. 'Mr Valentine, in essence, I have no hesitation in agreeing to help you, however, there will be stipulations. But first tell me what you see as your priorities.'

'Sullivan hasn't spoken a word since arriving at the police station in York. Seems to spend a lot of time on his knees. In view of that he

JON MASON

will be transferred to this station later today,' he looked at me. 'DC Blake, you will form part of the escort.'

'Yes sir,' I replied. I couldn't think of a better way to spend an afternoon, although how did that sit with the decision that I be kept out of confrontational situations?

The DCI continued. 'My priority is to get across to Wainwright that Sullivan is in custody and is now not a danger to him or anyone else or, ever has been. At least in relation to his claims of omnipotence. To that end DC's Farthing and Blake should be there with you. He has met them both before and, Pc Blake is Sullivan's arresting officer.'

'And neither is a senior officer. Therefore, should be seen as less of a threat.'

'Quite. And your stipulations?'

'I understand what you said a few moments ago, Chief Inspector. However as far as my contact with Cuthbert Wainwright is concerned and in order to gain his trust there must be no police officers present.' He noticed the sudden exchange of looks amongst the rest of us. 'If there is no trust, ladies and gentlemen, then he will not develop the confidence to speak openly. He has admitted his involvement and no doubt you will require a statement from both of us, and you will want him to give evidence?'

'Indeed, yes.'

The bishop took a step back and spoke to everyone present. 'In view of the way that people will view Cuthbert Wainwright it will take a great deal of courage on his part to make that admission in the glare of the Assize. Also to give evidence against Sullivan.'

'Very well, Your Grace,' the DCI replied. 'I accept. Wainwright is not a physical risk. Nevertheless, there will be a police officer outside the door, at all times. Call it a form of insurance if you like. The first thing that I want to do when Sullivan is returned to this police station is for Wainwright to see him in custody. It won't be face to face, but through the cell hatch. There will be no risk to him.'

Seventy-One

It was cathartic. Since Sullivan's arrest his aggression had gone. Dressed in a pair of Army and Navy Stores underpants, oversized boiler suit and a pair of plimsolls without laces. His clothing bagged separately. Handcuffed behind his back. All documents signed. Custody transferred from the City of York Police to the West Riding Police. DS Nicholson took possession of the documents. We said goodbye to our hosts and escorted a silent Sullivan from his cell and into the back of the van. Like the van used to transport Sullivan to York police station this one was fitted with a bench seat either side. DS Nicholson rode in front. The DCI had decided that two uniformed officers from Hecton would accompany us to bolster the escort, or perhaps just because I was there, prevent any possible confrontation even though Sullivan was handcuffed. I might have been tempted a while back, but now all three were in custody? I'm not naturally aggressive and I'd dealt with him firmly enough when he was arrested. Now it was almost over I felt different. I had a sense of relief in that I didn't need to avenge my father any more. As for the escort, Jim Baxter was a bit of a thug as was Chris Wilson. Both taller and heavier than I was. They were well known for meting out punishment as they saw fit.

We had two double-manned West Riding traffic cars as head and tail, led by a York City police motorcyclist. York City officers were manning the road junctions to speed our progress on our way back to the A64. If nothing else it looked impressive.

All was well until we were passing the race course. Jim Baxter, who was sitting opposite Sullivan, pulled a pair of black leather

346

gloves from his tunic pocket and put them on. In appearance police issue. I'd seen something like these before. These were *not* police issue gloves. They had lead shot sown into the backs of the fingers. With a clenched fist it would be like hitting someone with an iron bar at the same time protecting the assailant – in a fist-fight those involved usually had bruising to the knuckles. Not whilst wearing boxing gloves with sewn-in panels of lead shot.

'Jim, what the hell do you think you're playing at?' I said, aghast.

'It's what we agreed Brian, don't you remember?' The answer accompanied by a grim smile.

'Don't talk stupid, Jim,' I replied. This was getting dangerous. 'We've never discussed anything of the sort and you know it. In any case the answer's no!'

'It's two against one, Brian,' Chris Wilson's said. I glanced to my left as he put a pair of similar gloves on. 'Our word against yours. If we go down, we all go down together.'

They weren't joking, but which one would go first? 'Bollocks. If you want to beat the crap out of your prisoners that's up to you. You're not laying a finger on mine. So back off.'

'It's no good shouting to John Nicholson.' Jim Baxter laughed as I glanced to the front of the van. 'He knows the score. This bastard deserves everything he gets. You're too soft you young'uns are. In any case you should be pleased,. He murdered your father, didn't he?'

'No, he bloody well didn't, that was his brother and he's dead.' Glancing through the side windows we were now travelling about forty. No room for manoeuvre. Fortunately I had both hands free. Handling these two when they decided to act could be problematic, especially if they both went together. It would be like taking them both on in an arena the size of a dodgem car at speed.

I turned a tad to my right to give me a little more room. 'I'm warning you two, back off!'

Sullivan was acutely aware of what could be about to happen and cowered as several things happened in quick succession. Jim Baxter lunged forward with his right hand drawn back in an attempt to punch Sullivan. I blocked his punch as mine connected. His nose broke misting the air with blood. That felt quite satisfying. I shouted 'Sarge!' and thumped on the partition. Chris Wilson made a grab at me and overbalanced as the driver stood on the brakes. Wilson missed and fell across my back pinning me down. Crashed headlong into the bulkhead and knocked himself out. Jim Baxter sat back holding his nose and wailing. A steady stream of blood ran down his hands and forearms.

I'd just about extricated myself from under Wilson's body as the rear door was wrenched open by DS Nicholson, three Pc's at his back. 'What the hell's happened,' He demanded.' Are you all right, Brian? And whose is the blood?'

'I'm fine, Sarge,' I replied as I pulled myself clear. Not having me to lean against Chris Wilson slumped to the floor and wasn't moving. 'The blood's Jim Baxter's. Take a look at his gloves.' I told him briefly what had happened.

'Weighted gloves? You silly bastard, Baxter. What did you think you were playing at?'

'He snotted me. The bastard snotted me,' he wailed in return.

'Then you're very lucky he only hit you once, aren't you. Give me those gloves then get out and stand still. Make sure he doesn't wander off,' he called to the waiting Pc's.

Jim Baxter pulled the gloves off with his teeth, changing hands as he did so, the other hand holding his nose as the blood continued to drip onto his uniform.

'Are you sure you're all right?'

'I'm fine, Sarge. Are you all right?' I asked Sullivan, but he just sat there not speaking, head down. 'Sullivan's still breathing.'

'That's good, now what about Wilson?' DS Nicholson climbed into the back of the van. Together we leaned forwards as Chris Wilson groaned and began to move. 'More weighted gloves? What do these silly bastards think they're up to?' He said rhetorically. 'Come on, you,' he grabbed hold of Wilson's tunic by the collar and pulled, 'Up. Get up.' he snapped and yanked on Wilson's collar again. 'And get those bloody gloves off.'

A couple of minutes later, all bar Sullivan were standing behind the van attracting the attention of passing motorists when DI Kenton pushed his way through the assembly accompanied by a young WPC. 'DC Blake, are you all right?' His tone was urgent.

'Fine sir, thank you,' I replied, but what did he know?

'Manners,' he turned to the WPC. 'Can you see who it was? Are they here?'

'Yes, sir. That one over there,' she said pointing to Chris Wilson. 'He was one of them. But the one who showed me the gloves is the one holding his nose.' A couple of minutes before we left, Baxter and Wilson had been bragging to WPC Manners about what they intended in the mistaken belief that she wouldn't tell anyone, or that no-one would care. As we left she had gone to talk with DI Kenton.

'WPC Manners, are these what he showed you?' DS Nicholson said holding out both pairs of gloves.'

'Yes sir, I don't know which pair but they were just like them.'

DS Nicholson held up one pair. 'If it was Baxter these are his gloves, with the blood on.'

That settled it, at least in my mind. 'What do you think, Sarge, conspiracy to cause GBH with intent?' Whatever the outcome the facts fitted the definition. They had stepped on a landmine of their own making.

'Can't argue with that. Sir?'

'I agree.'

'Now, sir,' said DS Nicholson. 'We're still in the York City area. Would you like to deal or shall we clear up our own mess?'

'I think it would be better kept in-house, thank you Sergeant,' he replied. 'I'll arrange for the necessary statements to be taken and forwarded. In the meantime I'll call DCI Valentine and fill in the details.'

'Thanks, that saves having to pass awkward messages over the air,' he said turning to Baxter and Wilson. 'Right, Wilson get yourself into the traffic car behind. Keep your mouth shut. You stay put until such time as either I or the DCI say you can get out. Baxter, front car and the same applies to you. Don't bleed on their seats. Now, both of you, move. We're running late.' DS Nicholson spent the remainder of the journey with me, keeping Sullivan company.

We picked up a couple of speed-twins at the A64 – A1 intersection. They delivered us to the back door at Hecton. Members of the Press and public had been pushed back keeping the road clear. Chief Inspector Sampson took one look at Baxter's face and sent the traffic car to Dewsbury General accompanied by DS Cartwright.

Seventy-Two

Sullivan was booked in. Shortly afterwards Wilson was placed in an interview room. Derek Myers on the door to prevent any interference from his uniform colleagues. The atmosphere was sour. Probably because he and Baxter had sailed very close to the wind on numerous occasions and had gotten away with it they were quite popular with a certain mentality. And, I had spoiled what some saw as normal and justifiable practice. It didn't go down well.

DS Nicholson and I found ourselves in Chief Inspector Sampson's office explaining what had happened, to what appeared to be half the senior officers in the Division plus Detective Superintendent Creighton. DS Nicholson took up the story after I'd brayed on the partition.

There were numerous questions to both of us, principally me, after which I was interviewed under caution by Mr Creighton – well I had assaulted a police officer, even if he was a pillock.

Interview concluded I went to the office and was peppered with questions about the journey. Mr Creighton summoned Penny to be second officer during Wilson's interview. Concluded, he was arrested by Mr Creighton for conspiracy to cause GBH with intent. Booked in and then immediately bailed to return to the police station in twenty eight days. He was suspended from duty and surrendered his warrant card.

I'd just grabbed a swift coffee in the canteen. I was confronted by Zac Johnson and Eric Gould. They were a couple of Pc's from the same shift as Baxter. They didn't look happy. 'Blake,' said Johnson. 'Is it true what we've heard?'

'Depends what you've heard,' I replied, trying not to sound too defensive.

'That you've smacked Jim Baxter.'

This was annoying but I suppose I should have expected something of the sort. 'The prisoner we were transporting was cuffed behind his back. Baxter and Wilson using those weighted gloves of theirs decided they were going to knock seven kinds of shit out of him. Yes, I hit him once. What would you do if it was your prisoner? Stand back and let them?'

'Oh, we hadn't heard that,' Johnson muttered.

'No? Well that's what happened. Anything else?'

'You know Chris Wilson's been suspended?' He sounded surprised.

'Yes, I know.' They'd got enough information. I wasn't going to volunteer anything else.

'Arrested and bailed,' said Gould, from his expression he couldn't understand why.

'So I understand,' I replied. I didn't need this conversation. 'Right, I've got some work to do.' I left them at the top of the stairs and went back to the office. The Chief Super arrived from a meeting at HQ and wanted a report. I ended up in the Chief Inspector's office once more. Only this time DS Nicholson and I found out what Chris Wilson had said. They'd only intended to frighten Sullivan, not to assault him. Their threats to take me down with them were made in jest. Really? Mr Creighton didn't believe him either.

There was still no trace of DS Cartwright or Baxter when I went home. This afternoon's incident had left me with a sour taste in my mouth. I didn't like falling out with other coppers. We were all supposed to be on the same side. But there was no way I was going to sit back and let it happen. Plus, it was Jim Baxter and Chris Wilson who accused me of brown-nosing the chief super because I hadn't been kicked out on medical grounds after the explosion. Bob

Carlson, from the same shift as Baxter, had put me in the picture when we had a brief chat about the day's events. I felt better after that.

I was home earlier than expected and did my best to put work behind me. Fat chance. Lucy could detect stress like a magnet could metal. I managed to brush it off by describing it as just a disagreement. I don't think she believed me for a moment. Hopefully nothing had reached the ears of the press. If so it would be kept purely an internal matter. I spent five minutes rolling round on the floor with Claire, always a cure for the blues. Then it was bath-time, meal time and promotion exam question time. I could now get my answers completed in the twenty minute time slot. I just had to make sure that I knew the answers.

Apparently my defence of Sullivan had been too forceful. I had done more damage to Baxter's nose than intended. Not that I was worried about that. If he hadn't intended to do serious damage to Sullivan it would never have happened. But it had, and the doctor in casualty had given him an initial sick note for two weeks. On this occasion it was arrest prior to interview and not the other way round as it had been with Wilson. DS Cartwright arrested him as they left hospital. Much to the chagrin of some of those on duty at Hecton, he was booked in and immediately interviewed by Mr Creighton and Penny. He surrendered his warrant card and bailed to re-attend at the nick in twenty eight days.

Seventy-Three

Inspector Rawson from Discipline and Complaints Department attended at their homes serving them both with the relevant notices advising them of the restrictions: Not to wear police uniform. No access to any police station except at the public counter and no contact with the other. I suspect the last restriction wouldn't last long.

Aileen Wilson picked up the notice and read it again. 'Conspiracy to commit grievous bodily harm with intent, it says here,' she said, tears in her eyes. 'Chris, what the hell have you done? If you get the push we've no money and this is a police house, then what?'

Three doors further down the street Margery Baxter picked up the two suitcases. 'You stupid sod,' she said and turned to her two children. 'Say goodbye to your dad. We're going to spend some time with Grandma and Grandpa.'

Me? I was in the DCC's office alongside DS Nicholson. The DCC put the statement on his desk and looked at me, eyes narrowed, 'And you only hit him once, Blake?'

'Yes sir,' I replied. 'I didn't need a second.'

There was the merest semblance of a smile on the DCC's lips. 'Then as the driver hit the brakes Wilson lost his balance and fell across your back colliding with the bulkhead, knocking himself out in the process and pinning you.'

'Yes, sir.'

'And you concur, Sergeant?'

'Yes, sir. I heard Blake shout followed by the thump on the bulkhead. When I got the door open that's what I saw. Baxter holding his nose and Blake easing himself out from under Wilson.'

'Silly bugger,' the DCC turned to the Acting ACC and DS Creighton. 'Have you anything?'

'No, sir,' said Mr Mithering.

'The statements from York arrived this morning,' said Mr Creighton. 'In spite of Wilson's wriggling, it's watertight. I'll interview the other officers later today, get it all wrapped up.'

'As soon as possible, Mr Creighton. And you'd better have a look at these.' He passed him two manilla folders. 'Their divisional discipline files.' He turned to us. 'Thank you gentlemen that will be all.'

'What a bloody mess,' I heard as I closed the door.

'What do you think, Sarge?' I asked as we drove back.

'No,' he laughed. 'What do you think?'

'Great,' I said. The next ten minutes taken up by a discussion of the options open to the chief. What would his decision be?

A week after the event we found out. Baxter was dismissed from the service. Wilson was required to resign.

At 3pm the same day Chief Constable Ray Barton attended an extraordinary meeting of the Police Committee. There was one subject on the agenda: Albert Weatherspoon, currently Assistant Chief Constable Crime. Appraised of the full circumstances the vote to dismiss him was unanimous, as was a second vote to strip Weatherspoon of his pension rights. Mr Mithering was confirmed as the new ACC Crime. A report was submitted to the Home Secretary and confirmed.

The work begun before my compassionate leave in trying to ascertain what, if any, pattern existed in telephone calls surrounding the date of disappearance of Sullivan's victims had been completed.

Working with a team of Post Office investigators it had been ascertained that Sullivan always, with the exception of the first three victims, made a call to Weatherspoon seven to nine days prior to the event. Four days prior to the event Weatherspoon called Sullivan. Three days prior to the event Sullivan contacted Wainwright. One or two days after the event Sullivan contacted Weatherspoon.

Once the pattern had been identified it stuck out like a sore thumb. The first three victims did not fit the entire pattern. It proved impossible to find appropriate telephone records for victims one and two. However we had Wainwright's testimony, list and the human remains. For victim number three, Christine Jones, that was a random pick-up in the street. In addition, Wainwright's written testimony and hopefully his evidence at a future trial. The photographs having appeared in the press we received hundreds of calls identifying Sullivan. Several women who had broken off their friendship after he had suggested extra-marital sex when he claimed to be leaving the area, also called. The approximate dates they provided identified: (6) Geraldine Vasey, (7) Christine Griffiths, (8) Anne Clarke, (10) Elaine Walton as the replacement victims. There was no doubt in our minds that their decision not to indulge him had saved their lives. Unfortunately had cost others theirs. Whether Sullivan's drive was for sex or simply to kill is really academic. He had set his plans in motion and should there be a problem he sought a fresh victim, snatching them from the street. To that list we added Isabel Bell.

Whatever the reason, at some time in the future, psychiatrists or journalists would no doubt churn out numerous tomes filled with their theories.

Seventy Four

York Assize for the trial of Marsden (Murder) and Widdowson (Accessory after the fact). Not as grandiose as the Old Bailey but I don't suppose many court rooms were. The Judge? Who else but Lord Justice Nevison. Sir Justin Perry QC for the Prosecution and Sir Martin Greaves QC for the defence.

I bumped into John Bradbury and together we made ourselves know. DI Henderson withdrew to the police cafeteria. There was quite a surprise in store. The prosecution had accepted a guilty plea to the lesser charge of manslaughter. There would be no trial. It was all over within thirty minutes. Marsden was sentenced to eight years imprisonment and Widdowson to three.

DI Henderson re-appeared in company with Chief Inspector Reynolds, still deputy commandant at Pannal.

'Congratulations Blake,' he said. 'I understand from DI Henderson your attendance at the Assize is getting to be a habit. There is another one in the offing with your arrest of Sullivan.'

''Fraid so, sir.'

'Well, it's not a bad habit to develop.'

Seventy Five

It was wrapping up time. A dinner to celebrate our success had been organised for all of those involved in the investigation, both police and civilians plus wives and husbands at the Swiss Cottage, Wentbridge. Mr Mithering and his wife were invited. It was a great evening. Lucy wearing her best outshone them all. She was delighted with the bouquet of flowers presented by Mrs Valentine. I was embarrassed by the engraved Montblanc fountain pen. That was an expensive gift. Jacko pointed out the overtime payments received meant it was free. No chance. It was a good night.

Back at work there was really nothing for me to do. A week later I was returned to normality, if it would ever be that again. The story might have been over for now but there was a trial in the offing. However the mills of the law grind exceeding slow. A trial at the Assize likely to be twelve months ahead.

It took time, however the Press found something else to play with. The memories lost their rawness. So, we fed the chickens, collected the eggs and gardened together. I returned to the routine of uniform foot patrol and studying for my promotion exams. We had a family holiday in Liz's villa on Capri. All twelve of us. Norman and Jen springing the surprise of their engagement. Norman putting the ring on her finger in the *funiculare* between *La Marina Grande* and *La Piazzetta*. No-one noticed for over thirty minutes. That was a wonderful holiday. Claire finding a whole new family to make a fuss of her. Maria, who could now speak a little more English, as well as Carla and Chris, fascinated by the girls. They had never seen triplets before.

The last evening on Capri we booked a meal for us all at D'Agostinis where we refreshed our acquaintance with a very pregnant Angelina, proudly displaying a wedding ring. She was now Mrs Bruni. Antonio had plied her with flowers and love letters. The traditional way after it had been explained to him the length of the prison sentence for kidnapping. A case of *all's well the ends well.*

Whilst we were in Capri and prior to the paperwork resulting from Weatherspoon's malicious report of *my malfeasance* being filed, with the blessing of the Deputy Chief, DCI Valentine and DS Nicholson interviewed the BBC news editor, Bill Swanson, who had initially leaked the story of Wainwright's arrest. With a little persuasion he admitted that it was Weatherspoon who had been his informant, providing a statement to that effect. Clearing up these nasty little bits was important. The discipline papers were sealed. The envelope endorsed: *Only to be opened by the Deputy Chief Constable.* Signed R. Barton Chief Constable, and filed.

Three weeks after our return from Capri my appointment as a police officer was confirmed.

Two days prior to the sergeant's promotion exam my appendix ruptured. You only got one shot at the Special Course: Have proved you are suitable material for rapid advancement, pass your exams at the *first opportunity* with a sufficiently high mark to be put forward by the Force. Be selected for the Extended Interview. If you were lucky The Special Course and temporary rank of sergeant. A further twelve months as an operational sergeant and promotion to the rank of Inspector without having to sit the Inspectors' exam.

It wasn't that my studying over the past two years had been wasted. It hadn't. Far from it. I was simply disappointed that I had missed the opportunity. There was only one word to sum it all up.

Bollocks!

Epilogue

There was plenty of commiseration at my misfortune, much of it humourous. Still, I had to accept my lot. I was in hospital for ten days followed by my recuperation. Four weeks sick leave followed by light duties for a month. We were never short of visitors including the now Superintendent Valentine. The shortly to be Detective Chief Inspector Henderson; transferring to Derby. Inspector Nicholson and Detective Inspector Cartwright, plus Detective Sergeant Jackson. All thanked me for their promotions. Cheers.

A month after returning to work I was appointed detective constable and attended Bishopgarth for the Junior C.I.D. Course. My course instructor? DI Moore, he had been my tutor whilst studying for the Special Course – who else? In the final week of the course I received my court warning for the trial at the next York Assize.

The Court was packed. The Press shoehorned in. Every seat occupied including Liz, Lucy and the girls. Anne and Neil expecting their first in six months. Joe and Norman standing at the rear next to the Exit. Mum, my Mum, was babysitting; the memories dredged up over the last months were too raw. Wainwright pleaded guilty to all charges. His chats with Bishop Ridgeway had borne fruit. The charges: accessory after the fact relating to Christine Jones' rape and murder. Accessory before the fact and conspiracy to prevent thirteen lawful burials. He looked far happier than I had ever seen him. He even thanked the Judge when sentenced to ten years on each charge, to run concurrently. Taking into account his pre-trial incarceration, if he kept his nose clean he would be out in six years, maybe five.

Sullivan refused to speak and was held *mute of malice*. A not guilty plea was entered on each charge. The initial charges of conspiring to prevent lawful burial were left to lie on file. Weatherspoon pleaded not guilty to all charges. Sullivan and Weatherspoon were taken back to the cells.

Along with many others I'd stayed in Court for Wainwright's trial and sentencing, but now we, including Lucy, had to leave. She was giving evidence with regard to the stabbing of the two clerics in Rowntree Park and the Reverend Pomphrey, plus the kidnapping. Sullivan and Weatherspoon were produced. First to be called was Wainwright. He was giving evidence against the two men who had terrified him. Sullivan refused to make eye-contact and simply looked at the floor. Wainwright looked Weatherspoon in the eye as he took the oath, then pointed at him. 'You don't frighten me anymore,' he said. 'You pleaded not guilty. That's a lie, and, I'm on oath.' The Court dissolved in laughter as the Judge sought to regain control. A severely chastened Wainwright promised not to do it again.

Five weeks had been set aside for the trial. I didn't get into the witness box for over two weeks. My evidence-in-chief lasting for another five days. It took a half day to explain my light bulb moment with the Survey Grid. A full-sized one had been borrowed from the university. It was huge. The judge had it removed once I'd finished with it. How to find a map reference and how the eight digits in each number of Wainwright's list were broken down and used. Then work my way through the list to explain how I had calculated each location.

Evidence-in-chief finished I had three further days of cross examination. Eventually the Prosecution case concluded and the defence began. Weatherspoon gave evidence denying everything. That the telephone patterns that we had found were merely chance. He did have a little trouble explaining his relationship with Sullivan and Yarney especially after his marriage to their mother. But, that was his choice. Sullivan's Counsel was struggling from the off.

Other than Weatherspoon, Sullivan had no witnesses. That was left to his brief.

What we had was untold hours of blood and sweat from a dedicated team. Wainwright's list in his own hand, his testimony and the bodies. Plus the forensic.

Eventually all the closing speeches were made and the summing up by the Judge completed. The Jury retired to consider their verdicts.

Sullivan was sentenced to life imprisonment on all fifteen murders. Twelve years imprisonment on the woundings with intent of the two clerics in Rowntree Park. Ten for the wounding with intent of the Reverend Pomphrey at Bishopthorpe. Finally, fifteen years for the kidnap of Lucy and Claire. He would never see the outside of a prison again.

Because of who he was and the not guilty plea, Weatherspoon got the same. Life for the rape and murder of Christine Jones and for each charge of Conspiracy to Murder. Ten years for each Perverting the Course of Justice. If he ever got out he would be very old. His biggest problem was that he was a former Assistant Chief Constable and was now to be locked in a high-security prison with hard-men who had axes to grind.

17th June. It would have been Dad's birthday when we gathered by his graveside. The weather was glorious. Wall-to-wall sunshine. Not a breath of air. It hadn't been broadcast but nineteen turned up. There was no ceremony, just former colleagues plus Mum, me and the family. A one minute of silence. We placed our bouquets by the headstone. Others left theirs. Last of all Lucy put Claire on the grass.

Ivan Spencer, now in a wheelchair, handed her a single thornless red rose. 'Here you are, sweetheart,' he said and smiled.

Lucy nodded to him and crouched by her side, 'Put your flower on top, Claire,' she said and pointed. Claire, under the smiling faces walked uncertainly past the sea of legs and turned.

'That's right, Claire,' I said. 'Right at the top.' She reached out and dropped the rose, then laughed as she ran back to Lucy.

THE END

Wainwright's Tally

1. Isabel Bell. 15 years of age b. Grange Moor 10.07.1929 – 29.03.1945, shop worker. 5'2", auburn hair, green eyes, medium build. Disappeared whilst walking home from friend's house in Deighton. – Buried in Greenhead Park, Huddersfield.

2. Anne Baron. 20 years of age b. Darton 26.03.1927 – 10.05.1947, WRAF 5'4", dark brown hair, brown eyes, slim build. On leave. Last seen giving directions to driver of black saloon car 100 yards from home in Batley. Buried in Cawthorne Park, Cawthorne, Barnsley.

3. Christine Jones. 18 years of age b. Thorpe 31.03.31 – date murdered 01.04.1949, working prostitute. 5'3". Blonde hair, blue eyes, slim build, found murdered, Littletown, West Riding.

4. Sandra Thompson b 28.11.30 – 10.10.1949, 5'6", fair hair, proportionate build. Midgely – Buried in Denby Dale, West Riding.

5. Velma Davis b. 06.07.29 – 10.08.51, 5'1" blonde, brown eyes, plump. Disappeared from train returning to Barnsley from Sheffield – Buried in Newmillerdam, Wakefield.

6. Geraldine Vasey b. 02.03.1923 – 09.09.1953, 5'4", dark hair, brown eyes, slim build. MFH York – Buried in grounds of Temple Newsam House, Leeds.

7. Christine Griffiths b. 19.12.1927 – 11.07.1955, 5'1", black hair, brown eyes, proportionate build. MFH Shipley – Buried in Park Wood, Tong, Bradford.

8. Ann Clarke b. 01.01.1937 – 15.09.57, 5'4", fair hair, green eyes, slim build MFH Honley – Buried in Yateholme, Holmfirth, West Riding.

9. Anne Bellamy b. Holmfirth 03.11.1937- 04.06.1959, auburn hair, green eyes, slim build, MFH Kexborough – Buried near to Flouch crossroads, West Riding

10. Elaine Walton b. Denshaw 01.10.1937 – 17.09.60, 5'5", blonde hair, blue eyes, slim build MFH Hebden Bridge – Buried on Cupwith Hill, Huddersfield.

11. Sandra Chase 17years of age b. Eggborough 06.05.1946 – 16.05.63 Student. MFH Doncaster after row with father over boyfriend. Last seen York railway station. Buried at Farnley Bank, Farnley Tyas, Huddersfield.

12. Vivienne McKeen 25 years of age b. Sowerby Bridge 23.04.1938 – 19.09.1964. Married with 4 year old daughter. School teacher, car with front offside puncture found abandoned Palais car park Wakefield. Buried in Cold Hiendley Wood, Wakefield.

13. Sally Dunster b. 19.06.1944 – 05.03.1965 20 years of age, 5'3", brown hair and eyes – Buried at Westleigh

Don't miss out!

Visit the website below and you can sign up to receive emails whenever Jon Mason publishes a new book. There's no charge and no obligation.

https://books2read.com/r/B-A-ZRTW-HFVKC

BOOKS 2 READ

Connecting independent readers to independent writers.

Also by Jon Mason

Blake Detective Series
The Blooding of Brian Blake
Nemesis
Counting The Dead

Watch for more at www.jonmasonbooks.com.

About the Author

JON was born into post WW2 Yorkshire in England. His brother Stuart was born in 1938. His father, demobbed from the RAF where he had been a Dispatch Rider, returned to the tailoring industry. His mother had spent the war years x-raying wheels for battle tanks.

They lived in a small, inner two-bedroomed terrace house. There was no damp-proof course, double glazing, central heating or hot water on tap. The tin bath hung from a nail under the stairs and the lavatory was across the back yard..

Leaving school in 1962 he joined the West Riding Constabulary as a Cadet and as a Constable in 1965. His initial training carried out at No3 District Police Training Centre, Pannal Ash, Harrogate, in the then North Riding of Yorkshire.

Over the next three decades he gained experience across much of what the police service has to offer. 1965-70 on uniform beat patrol. From 1970-75 in the Road Traffic Division as an advanced driver and also where he was firearms trained. From 1975-77 Force Control where he learned his radio and computer skills before being promoted to the Western Area Control Room in January of 1977, Twelve months later he was seconded to the fledgling Computer

Development Unit working with Ferranti International in the development of Stage 4 of a resource handling and incident recording system known as Command and Control (Not big Brother) and the setting up of the Communications Training Wing at the West Yorkshire Police training school. December 1983 saw him transferred to an inner city sub-division where he spent the last 10 years of his service as uniform patrol sergeant where he also worked closely with the Air Support Unit, Custody Officer and the last four years as the Station Sergeant.

In May of 1967 Jon and his fiancee married. A marriage which so far has lasted for over 56 years. They had two children, tragically Andrew, the elder, died of a heart attack in January 2018 - he was 48. Their daughter is still going strong.

Prior to retirement Jon qualified as a fitness instructor and subsequently head-hunted to work in a new community based cardiac rehab programme where he had the opportunity to study cardiology at Leeds University Medical School and exercise physiology at Carnegie. He also studied bio-mechanics.

All that knowledge and experience Jon brings to his books.

Read more at www.jonmasonbooks.com.

Milton Keynes UK
Ingram Content Group UK Ltd.
UKHW040701050124
435493UK00001B/124

9 781916 757073